PASSION'S PROMISE

In a ravaged Southland, Travis Coltrane, soldier of the conquering army, and Kitty, the Southern belle who had conquered his heart, find union in marriage.

BITTER LOSS

But the man who marched with General Sherman soon grows restless with the quiet Southern life and longs for adventure. Left alone with their young son, Kitty falls victim to another man's violence—and Travis returns home to find her gone.

LASTING LOVE

Travis learns too late that the love he thought was his forever could be taken from him, and he suffers the torment of a man loved by many women, but unable to love any but Kitty.

Other Avon Books by
Patricia Hagan

GOLDEN ROSES
LOVE AND WAR
PASSION'S FURY
THE RAGING HEARTS
SOULS AFLAME
THIS SAVAGE HEART

AVON
PUBLISHERS OF BARD, CAMELOT, DISCUS AND FLARE BOOKS

LOVE AND GLORY is an original publication of Avon Books
This work has never before appeared in book form.

AVON BOOKS
A division of
The Hearst Corporation
1790 Broadway
New York, New York 10019

Published by arrangement with the author
Library of Congress Catalog Card Number: 81-52390
ISBN: 0-380-79665-1

First Avon Printing, April, 1982

Printed in the U.S.A.

WFH 10 9 8 7 6 5

Dedicated to the *real* Travis Coltrane,
whoever he may be. . . .

"Of all affections which attend human life,
the love of glory is the most ardent."

Sir Richard Steele
(1672–1729)

Chapter One

HE was tall and built well, firm, corded muscles glistening as the merciless sun beat against his bare back. Hard, lean thighs strained against tight denim pants as he doggedly followed the plow. The plodding mule struggled, pulling the plow through the dry, parched earth. Insects flitted annoyingly around man and beast. No breeze stirred, and the oppressive heat hung like a shroud.

Damn, it was hot. Travis Coltrane could feel his bare skin tingling, knew that already the sun was searing his flesh. But he would not burn. Before long, his skin would be the color of leather. Travis was a French creole, and naturally dark-skinned. He would only become darker. Sweat trailed down his forehead and into his gray eyes, stinging. He wiped the salty moisture away with one hand, ignoring the burning in the open blisters of his fingers and palms. Some were already bleeding from the rough, splintered wooden plow handles. It was this way every spring when he first began the plowing, but soon the blisters would close and become hard.

Suddenly the plow lurched sharply, hitting a mound of earth, and even as Travis saw the swarming wasps and realized he had hit an underground nest, the angry horde was upon him. He quickly dropped the worn reins, letting the mule trot away and escape. Travis stumbled backward, swinging his arms at the attacking wasps. Just as he felt a sharp sting on his shoulder, he ran across the field toward the bordering woods.

Reaching safety beneath the gnarled limbs of a great oak, he stared at the quickly rising welt, grateful to have been stung only once.

He leaned back against the rough bark of the trunk and breathed deeply, closing his eyes. Lord, how he hated this. He hated what he had been doing for the past two years and he dreaded what lay before him.

Two years. He shook his head, wiping at the sweat on his face. Had it really been only two years? Jesus, it seemed more like twenty. It was becoming harder and harder for Travis to remember any life other than the drudgery of the farm.

If this is all there is, he asked himself miserably, if this is what my life is all about, then why didn't I just die in the damned war?

Gettysburg. Antietam. Bull Run. He had been in all of them, by damn. One of the best officers and riders in the whole goddamn Union cavalry. That's what others had said about Captain Travis Coltrane, leader of the infamous Coltrane's Raiders, feared by the Rebels and respected and admired by the Union Army.

Sitting there, in the still, hot spring day, Travis could almost smell the sulfur and smoke once more, hear the shouts and cries of his men as they charged into battle, the clanging and clashing of sabers. And he had *led* those men, by God. They had looked up to him and—

Bullshit.

The steely gray eyes darkened as bitterness and self-loathing washed through him. Was he on his way to becoming just like the old men who spent their days sitting in front of the courthouse in Goldsboro, telling and retelling their battle stories, each tale becoming more glorified as it was repeated? Some still wore their tattered Confederate uniforms, even four years after the war had ended.

People, he told himself, particularly old soldiers, chose to forget what was painful. And Lord, there had been so much pain in that infernal war. Now that it was safely in the past, it was all glory.

Was he becoming just like them, sitting here beneath a tree and staring at the empty fields and hating his life so much?

Would he waste the rest of his life longing for remembered glories?

He lifted his gaze to the heavens as though there might be an answer somewhere up there. Why did it have to be this way? Year after year of coddling that goddamn ground, planting tobacco and corn and praying for rain, praying the insects would not come, praying for a good harvest in the fall so there would be money to get through the long winter and feed for the livestock he had managed to acquire. Was this all there was? Travis asked the sky.

He snorted with contempt. Pray! Hell, he never prayed. He just cursed life when things didn't go the way he wanted them to. Farmers prayed over their crops. Travis did not consider himself a farmer and he never would.

He looked across the field at the little cabin he had built with his bare hands from the smoldering ruin it had been. The neighbors had burned down the original house, for the good Southern patriots of Wayne County had not taken kindly to old John Wright marching off to fight for the North.

Now there were two rooms. It wasn't much, but Travis still felt pride over what he'd managed to do with the ruins. He had done it all alone, with sweat and grit. He had cut the oak trees, sawed them into planks, then smoothed the surfaces that would be on the inside. The results had been worth his hard work, for the interior walls shone brilliantly with the natural beauty of the blond oak wood.

He had done the same with the floors, not wanting Kitty or John to risk stepping on a rough, splintery surface.

A room for sleeping and loving. A room for cooking and living. And a little porch off the back, covered in twisting morning-glory vines, where they could sit and watch the sun go down . . . while holding hands and dreaming of what they hoped the future would hold for them.

For now, that's all there was, but by God, when there was enough money, he was going to make it bigger and better, because John and Kitty deserved so much more than a two-room cabin.

John.

He grinned, thinking of the little boy who looked so much like him that Travis sometimes thought he was looking at himself age three. But, he thought, John wasn't himself. He had Kitty's spirit, but seemed not to have inherited either of his parents' horrible temper. He was a serene child, a little too adult, perhaps, for his age. But he was accustomed to amusing himself, playing games in the corner of the kitchen. There were few children John's age in Goldsboro, and since the neighbors had never forgiven John Wright, for whom the boy was named, it was just as well that the child had been kept apart from those neighbors and their hatred.

His face softened as his thoughts turned to Kitty. She was still the most beautiful woman he had ever laid eyes on. Just thinking about her, he felt the familiar stirring in his loins. How good it was to hold her, be inside that tender, always eager, woman-flesh.

Kitty. His woman. His wife. The mother of his son.

They had been through hell, separately and together, but they shied away from discussing the past.

Neither liked to talk of the sadness and awful pain, but now the memories were washing over Travis.

Nathan Wright. He had been Kitty's first beau but turned out to be a cowardly bastard who wound up shooting Kitty's father in the back. Travis had killed Nathan by stomping the life from his wretched body. The citizens of Wayne County would never forget that Travis Coltrane, Union officer, had killed their hero.

Kitty, stubborn and high-spirited, would not be driven from the land her father had loved. She held her head high, determined that they would live here and raise their son on his grandfather's land.

Corey McRae. Another memory stung Travis.

When he rode away with General Sherman, Travis had not known that he was leaving Kitty carrying his child. And he had not known that McRae's hellish scheme to make Kitty his wife had included intercepting Travis' letters to Kitty. Travis had been filled with bitterness because, after pledging her undying love, there had been no word from Kitty.

When he returned to Goldsboro, Travis believed the gossip that Kitty had married Corey, a rich, powerful carpetbagger, to keep from losing her precious land. He also believed that she had presented her husband with a son. He'd had no idea that the baby was *his*.

Travis had returned to Goldsboro as a federal marshal with his lifelong friend, Sam Bucher. Having been through the war together, they were assigned to seek peace between people like

McRae and Jerome Danton, who were embroiled in a land war. Danton was another bastard, who, Travis discovered, was also the leader of the local Ku Klux Klan.

Danton and McRae's feud had finally erupted, Danton killing McRae on the same night Travis learned that he was the father of Kitty's son. He had taken the boy and fled to the peace of his beloved home in the Louisiana bayou, but Kitty had come after their son, taken him, and run through the swamps. Travis had followed but fell into deadly quicksand. Kitty saved his life, even knowing that he might once again take their son from her. Her saving him had shown Travis at long last that Kitty truly loved him.

They had returned to North Carolina to make a new life.

Damn! It had all seemed so simple at the time. They had their son and they had their love.

Now he was living this life for Kitty. This was what she wanted, to farm her father's land, *her* land, to live here despite the hatred of their neighbors.

But God damn it to hell, he swore to himself, grimacing, this wasn't what *he* wanted. Lord knew he had tried. No one could say he had not tried his damnedest. But he wasn't a farmer and never would be, and no matter how much he loved Kitty and little John and wanted them to be happy, he knew there was nothing before him in their life but misery. He had tried farming for two years, and blast hell and Satan, he didn't think he could stand one more day of it.

With a long weary sigh, he got to his feet and dusted the seat of his pants. He might not be able to stand one more day of it, but he had to. He must never let Kitty and John know how he felt. How would Kitty react if she knew of his misery? Would she be willing to give up all this, or would she tell him to go his own way without her, without their son?

He squinted in the bright sun as he stepped out from the shade and gazed up to the hilltop. She was there, beneath the pecan and peach trees on the west side of the field. He could see her clearly, bent over, plucking the weeds from around her father's grave, just as she did every day. He watched as she laid a tiny white bouquet beside the wooden cross. He could not see the flowers but surmised they were dogwood, for the trees within the forest were dotted with the gentle white blossoms, as though bits of clouds had floated down from the heavens.

She straightened and smoothed her worn yellow muslin dress. Her hair, the color of ripe strawberries, sparkled with threads of gold in the sunlight. Picking up a woven straw basket beside her feet, she turned, waving as she caught sight of him standing there watching her. The bodice of her dress stretched tightly across her bosom as she waved, and his heart quickened. Lord, he thought dizzily, did You ever create a more glorious creature?

She picked her way carefully across the rutted brown field. Spotting the mule standing idle at the farthest end of the field, she called out worriedly, "Travis, what's wrong? Why did you turn him loose like that?" She quickened her step until she was almost running, stumbling through the deep ruts.

"Travis, why won't you answer me? What's wrong?" Her eyes widened as she saw the angry red welt on his shoulder. She ran the short distance to him, tripping in her haste. His quickly moving arms reached out to stop her fall. "Something bit you."

"Plow turned over a wasp nest," he said absently, taking the basket from her and setting it down. Then all of a sudden he was holding her tightly, crushing her against him. Their lips held for long moments.

It was she who finally struggled to pull away, laughing. "Of all times . . ." Her voice trailed away and her face flushed. The kiss had aroused her.

Picking up the basket, she moved toward the shade he had just left. "I brought your lunch. John is asleep. He's been a real little devil this morning, and I thought I'd never get him quiet. I brought fried chicken, and there are sweet-potato cakes, and I made some lemonade."

"It's not food I'm hungry for Kitty."

She tilted her head to one side, lavender eyes sparkling as she smiled. "Travis Coltrane! Are you telling me that you want to make love right here?"

"Can't think of a better place," he murmured huskily.

Taking her hand, he led her deeper into the woods until he found what he was looking for, a soft bed of pine needles. He unbuttoned her dress, fondling her breasts possessively as they spilled forth. He paused to kiss each nipple to tautness before kneeling on the ground and pulling her down to lie beside him.

When she lay completely naked beneath him, he removed his own clothes, then straddled her. She could feel his throbbing organ lying on her belly, feel his pulsating strength.

"Travis, is it always going to be this way for us?" she asked dreamily as he stared down at her, his eyes glazed with lust. "Is it always going to be so wonderful every time?"

He did not speak. Travis had never liked to talk while making love. He let his body speak for him. He moved her legs upward until they were wrapped around his neck. It was best this way, for he could penetrate deeply and hold her down at the same time so that she could not give way completely to the undulations of her own body. That would take him to his release sooner than he liked. He liked to savor each moment, wanting to prolong the final ecstasy as long as possible. But it was never easy, for once he entered the soft velvet recesses of Kitty's body, he needed all the control he could muster to refrain from exploding in passion.

He kissed her again, loving the feel of her tongue against his. He could feel her wanting to move, to wriggle delightedly beneath him. He thrust deep within her, then harder. Soon, despite himself, he could hold back no longer. With hard, driving movements, he filled her with all he had to give, gasping aloud as he felt his very soul leave his body to enter hers briefly.

Her nails raked his back, moving up to squeeze his strong shoulders, her body quivering. He held her tighter, rocking to and fro till she returned from her journey to the peak of joy that made her tremble.

A little later, moving to one side, he lay quietly for a moment, trailing a fingertip down her smooth cheek. Then he murmured, "Yes, Princess. It's always going to be this good for us."

She burrowed her head against the dark hair of his chest, and he held her to him tightly. "You belong to me," he whispered harshly. "I'd kill a man who tried to take you away. You'll always be mine."

"Travis, you're hurting me!"

When she cried out he realized how tightly he had been holding her. He loosened his hold, smiling. "I guess I got carried away."

She pressed her fingers against his lips for a kiss. "It is always good for us, Travis. I always feel so . . . so possessed by you."

"You are," he grinned. "I own you. Just like that contrary

old mule out there. You're all mine. Don't ever forget it!"

She tousled his dark hair playfully, then sat up and began to put on her clothes. "Now that we've satisfied one of your hungers, it's time to satisfy another. Go down to the creek and wash up and I'll get your lunch ready."

When he returned, he found a cloth spread on the ground and food laid out on it. Sitting down, he picked up a chicken leg and began to eat.

Kitty stared at him thoughtfully for a moment, then said hesitantly, "You haven't gotten much plowing done this morning, Travis. When you've finished lunch, how about letting me help? I could plow and you could start the planting."

"No, goddamn it!" He tossed the chicken bone aside and glared at her.

Tears stung her eyes. If there was one thing Kitty feared, it was Travis' temper. He had never harmed her, but there was something frightening about him when those gray eyes flashed like lightning. She lowered her head, folding her hands in her lap, not wanting him to see her tears or her fright.

He was instantly contrite. He reached to squeeze her hand, then cupped her chin and forced her to look up at him as he murmured, "I'm sorry, baby, but you know how I feel about you working in the fields. I won't have it. It tears me apart to see you working as hard as you do. But I'll be damned to hell if I'll see you behind a plow like a common field hand."

"I don't mind hard work."

"We both know that. But you won't work the fields, not while you're my wife—and that's going to be always, so let's don't talk about it anymore."

She jerked her chin away, tilting it higher in the stubborn way that signaled anger. "Every other woman around here on a dirt farm works in the fields. Some people say that I don't because I think I'm too good. They call me uppity. They say I still try to behave as though I'm married to the richest man in Wayne County."

The gray eyes flashed again, this time reflecting tiny red dots. Travis was close to exploding. He growled, "Corey McRae was not the richest man in Wayne County, Kitty, not when he stole every damn thing he ever had. And I can't picture you being uppity. When are you going to learn not to care what your ignorant neighbors say about us? *I* say what goes on around here, and that's all you should care about."

"You aren't my master!" she cried furiously, but she knew it was futile to attempt reason just then. "Well, we'll just be late planting, and we'll be late harvesting, and it will probably be a terrible crop anyway." She got to her feet, lips set tightly. "I'm going back to the house."

"You aren't going anywhere." He reached out and grabbed her wrist and jerked her back to the ground. "Eat your lunch or sit there and pout."

She sat primly, skirt folded beneath her, chin tilted defiantly. She did not speak.

Finally, he motioned to the remaining food and asked if she were going to eat. When she shook her head, he laughed, "Suit yourself. I can sure see where John gets his stubbornness. I swear, I've never seen a woman—"

His voice trailed off at the sound of approaching hoofbeats. Someone was coming through the field. Travis got to his feet quickly, motioning for Kitty to remain where she was. Swiftly he brought out the knife from his boot. Even after two years, he trusted no one and was never without his knife.

He peered through the woods, eyes narrowed. Then suddenly a grin spread across his face. He hastily put his knife away and then waved his arms over his head. "Sam! Over here!

"What brings you to these parts?" he called as Sam Bucher reined his horse in and slid from the saddle. He made his way quickly through the brush, pausing to kiss Kitty's upturned cheek before taking Travis' hand in a hearty grasp.

"How come I always find you two in the bushes?" Sam laughed, brown eyes warm. "During the war, it seemed like every time I turned around, you two were honeyed up somewhere."

"Sam, that's not true," Kitty gasped. "Why, the last time you came by, we were inside eating."

"I know, I know, girl," Sam nodded, laughing. "But I do love to tease you, honey. I love the way them pink cheeks of yours get even pinker."

Kitty laughed, despite her embarrassment. Sam knew just about everything there was to know about them. He had been a part of her life as long as Travis had, and the three of them had all seen more sadness than joy. Sam had been there when Travis killed Nathan after Nathan had murdered Kitty's father. Sam had even helped to dig John Wright's grave. He had murmured the final prayers as her father was laid to his rest.

She looked at Sam closely. He had not changed much except for some white in the brown hair and the full brown beard. Bushy eyebrows framed the warm, sensitive eyes. He had added a few pounds around the middle but otherwise, well, he was still Sam. She often teased him about the extra pounds, though.

"How's the boy?" Sam asked her, stroking his beard.

"Asleep. I never knew a three-year-old could be so active. And he can be just as stubborn as his father, I'm afraid," she added with a meaningful glance in Travis' direction.

"You're both stubborn, girl," Sam grinned. "I reckon you two are about the oneriest two folks I ever knew, so little John gets it honest."

"Speaking of being stubborn," Travis smiled with a smugness that infuriated Kitty, "sit down and have some lunch. Kitty fixed enough for both of us, but she's pouting and won't eat. As hard as food is to come by these days, let's not waste any."

Sam sat down, smacking his lips hungrily. "Never could say no to Kitty's cooking." Glancing at her, he whispered, "What you poutin' about, honey? If he ain't treating you right, you can always ride off with me."

"Kitty thinks she can do a man's work," Travis snapped.

"Well, she always *did* a man's work," Sam raised an eyebrow in surprise. "She did things in them hospital tents during the war that made grown men faint."

"That was different. That was war. Now she thinks she can get behind a plow. No wife of mine is working in the fields."

Kitty spread her hands in a pleading gesture. "Sam, you tell me what is wrong with a wife helping her husband. How many farmers' wives don't work in the fields?"

"It's bad enough the way she's always riding off in the middle of the night to deliver a baby," Travis continued, not giving Sam a chance to speak. "I'm surprised she doesn't want to leave the boy with me and go to Goldsboro and work in the hospital all the time."

"Travis, that's not fair!" Kitty blinked furiously, determined to hold back the tears.

Sam patted her shoulder, sensing how upset she was becoming. "Now, honey, don't you fret. You're too pretty to be out in the sun, anyway. Besides, you know as well as I do that once this man of yours sets his mind to something, there just ain't no point in arguing."

Kitty looked at Travis and returned his steely glare. Sam was right. Travis was every bit as iron-willed as she, but being a man, he usually won, something she had never been able to accept. She never would accept that, despite loving him so fiercely.

"If I let her, she'd be doctoring everyone around here." Travis turned to Sam once more. "It doesn't matter that these people hate her and always will."

"They don't all hate me," she retorted. "There are fine people, like the widow Mattie Glass and her boys."

"But you aren't a doctor, you're my wife."

Sam interrupted, "Kitty always was good at doctoring folks, Travis, and—"

"What brings you out here, Sam?" Travis asked rudely. Then his voice softened. "How have things been going?"

"Things in town are quiet," Sam replied tonelessly. "Maybe too quiet. I'm getting restless."

Kitty looked from Sam's face to the shining star on his broad chest, searching for the real reason for this visit. "Do you still like being a marshal?" she asked.

"Yeah, I reckon. I wasn't about to stay in Louisiana after Travis left to come up here to live. He's about the closest thing to a brother I'll ever have. Or maybe I should say a son. I'm a mite older'n him, you know."

He paused to pour himself a cup of lemonade. "But you can't tie yourself down because you're close to somebody. Man has to live his own life. Right now I got an offer for a better job for a while, and though it'll take me away from here—even out of the country—can't see passing it up."

"You're leaving?" Travis cried. "Sam, you're the only person around here other than Kitty and the boy that I give a damn about."

"I won't be gone all that long, really," Sam said smoothly. "See, I've got a chance to go to Haiti and Santo Domingo for the government, and I want to see some of the world."

Travis' eyes widened. "Haiti and Santo Domingo? Why?"

"Hey, don't you keep up with what's going on in the world?" Sam teased. "You've been stuck out here on this farm too long, Travis."

Kitty watched Travis' eyes light up as Sam explained that the Civil War had brought to the attention of Navy officers that there was a need for American island bases in the Caribbean. Secretary of State Seward had, more or less, taken it on himself to press the matter.

"There was a big debate about it in the House of Representatives this past January," Sam explained. Seward had persuaded President Johnson to suggest to Congress that the United States incorporate Santo Domingo and Haiti, but Congress had turned the idea down. "Now Grant's been elected and he's going to push the issue. He's sending a committee over there to look around."

"And you're going?" Travis prodded.

Sam grinned proudly. "General William Tecumseh Sherman himself recommended me. Grant has appointed him General Commander of the Army, you know."

"Yes, and I'm proud. I've the utmost respect for General Sherman."

Kitty wrinkled her nose. "That butcher! When I think of what he did to the South . . ."

Travis reached to cover her hands with one of his. "That was necessary, Kitty," he said tenderly, and she knew he was no longer angry with her. "General Sherman is a fine man."

"Yeah, he thinks a lot of you, too," Sam said to Travis. Then he glanced at Kitty nervously before continuing. "See, the way it was explained to me, there are two leaders in the Dominican Republic, one named Pedro Santana and the other named Buenaventura Baez. They've swapped the presidency back and forth for a while now. Santana is from Spain, and you may have heard how he had himself named governor general during the time we was fighting the war over here."

Travis nodded and Kitty watched him, aching to see his intent expression. He was completely entranced by everything Sam was saying. His nostrils flared and his eyes shone, and she knew he was thinking of what a wonderful adventure this was all going to be.

"There was a series of battles and Spain finally withdrew its troops," Sam continued. "Baez came to our government with a plan, wanting protection. I don't know all the details, but I do know President Grant favors annexation, and that's the reason for sending a committee over there."

He spread his hands in a gesture of simple finality. "Sherman recommended me and I was asked. That's about it."

Travis was silent for a moment as he stared beyond at the brown fields. Finally, he asked quietly, "How long will you be gone, Sam?"

"Six months, more or less. No way of telling. There's a new marshal coming in here next week, and I'll head up to Washington to get all the details. I reckon the committee will leave within the month." He looked at each of them, saw the very different expressions on their faces, and decided he had sounded too excited over his trip. Shrugging as though it really did not matter, he said, "Heck, maybe I'm a crazy old coot to go over there. They got weird stuff in Haiti, I think they call them zombies. You know, people die, and witch doctors bring 'em back to life somehow. Could be dangerous in a place like that. Maybe I shouldn't even go."

"You would be crazy to pass up a chance like this, Sam." Travis gazed toward the field, speaking as though he were far, far away from this place. "And when you return, you will probably have a good offer to do something else for the government. Why molder away here? You have no family ties."

"I got you folks," Sam said defensively. Then, quickly deciding it best to change the subject, he turned to Kitty. "Where's that little one? Taking a nap? Let's go see if he's awake, 'cause I've got to be heading back to town and I'd like to see him before I go."

"Stay for supper," Travis said quietly, almost sadly. "It's been a while since we've had a real visit, and from the sound of things, it will be an even longer time before we see each other again."

Sam shook his head. "Thanks, but I've got to get back to town. Can't have my replacement coming in here and saying I did a lousy job. I've got plenty of work to do before he gets in."

"Well, try to see us again before you go." Travis walked away, still staring ahead thoughtfully, in a trance. Kitty reached out to touch Sam's arm, nodding toward Travis.

"He wants to go with you," she whispered. "You can see it. It's tearing him up, Sam. He loves me, and he loves little John, but he hates his life here."

"He's never said that to me," Sam responded uneasily. He

didn't like being in the middle of this but it could not be helped. "He'd be miserable if he wasn't with you and his boy, and you know it. Now let's gather up this stuff and get to the house, all right?"

Kitty stayed where she was, watching Travis trudge along, shoulders stooped toward the waiting mule like an old man. "He keeps it inside him, you know that. He never talks about his misery because he doesn't want me to know. But I do know. And so do you, Sam."

Sam gazed at her closely. What was the point in pretending? "Yeah, I guess I do. But he's trying, girl. You can't say he isn't trying. And he'll never leave you—though I reckon he'll always have the wanderlust. It's just his way."

Tears welled in her eyes. "I've known all along. I kept hoping things would change. I prayed this would all be enough for him, but it isn't and it never will be. He's slow on the spring planting right now because he doesn't really care, even though he's trying so hard to care. And it's killing him, Sam." She began to cry. "I can't stand seeing him so miserable."

Sam gathered her in his big arms and held her against his chest as she sobbed. "He won't leave you," he said gruffly. "You know you ain't got that to worry about, so just keep trying to make him happy. He loves you, Kitty."

She pulled away abruptly, wiping furiously at her tears. Kitty hated herself when she gave way to the weakness of crying. "I know he loves me, damn it, and I love him. I love him too much to see him so miserable.

"I want . . ." She took a deep breath, held it, then let it out in a rush. "I want him to go with you, Sam. To Haiti."

Sam stared down at her, astonished. "You don't mean that, girl."

She lifted her chin once more in the defiant way that Sam, like Travis, knew so well. "Yes, I do mean it. It won't be for too long. You said six months or so. It will be good for him to get away. Maybe General Sherman could even arrange a job for him when he returns, a job that would give him some of the adventure he needs. I'll still be here waiting, with our son. Lots of men move around and return to their women. I'm willing to live that way if it means making my husband happy."

Sam took her small hands in his burly ones and squeezed tightly. "Listen to me. I hated even to come over here and tell him about my plans, because I was afraid he'd take it just like he did. I know he wants to go, but he won't because of you. But I couldn't just ride off without saying good-bye. The truth is, Kitty, General Sherman picked me *and* Travis, and Travis' name was first. I wasn't going to tell him that. I didn't want to put him in the position of having to turn down that offer."

"General Sherman chose Travis, too?" she asked, awed. "Oh, Sam, he'll be so honored."

"I'm not going to tell him. And neither are you. It'd just hurt him worse to turn it down."

They fell silent, both turning to watch as Travis walked up to the mule and looped the worn leather reins around his neck. Then he began to plod doggedly through the field once more, head bent.

"His spirit is as broken as that mule's," Kitty whispered tremulously. "I can't stand seeing him like that, Sam. I never let myself realize it fully until this minute. I've got to let him go."

"Let's don't talk about it anymore because he won't go. Come along to the house, Kitty."

He gave her a gentle nudge, but she continued to watch Travis move under the blazing sun. The man did not belong behind a mule, she thought, heart pounding. He was a leader. A fighter. An adventurer. And she had him in a harness the same as that worn-old mule.

"You send a telegram to General Sherman," she said slowly, evenly. "Tell him that Travis Coltrane will be on that committee and will be leaving when you do."

"Kitty, dang it all!" He yanked off his felt hat and threw it to the ground in angry disgust. "This is nonsense and a waste of time. I done told you. He ain't gonna leave you."

She raised lavender eyes that flashed with determination. "He will leave, Sam. I can make him. But he will return, and when he does he'll love me all the more for setting him free."

"You're crazy. I won't be a party to any scheme. Travis would have my head."

"You will be a party to it, because you know I'm right, Sam Bucher. Now you do as I ask, please, and don't you dare say a word to Travis about this. Leave everything to me, and I promise that he will be leaving when you do."

Quickly she stuffed everything into the picnic basket and, with a determined stride, left the woods and began to make her way across the rutted field.

Sam hung back momentarily, and then began to follow. He knew from experience that Kitty would make good her promise and that there was nothing he could do to stop her, not when she had her mind made up. That was Kitty. He only hoped she knew what she was doing, and that Travis, once set free, would return to her.

But that, Sam reflected, was the chance you took when you unharnessed an animal and left the barn door open. Sometimes he wandered away and then came back.

Sometimes he just kept on going.

Chapter Two

THE past two weeks had been extremely difficult for Kitty. It was not easy to make Travis want to leave her, not when she loved him so much she ached with it. But she had to set him free. Her love would not allow her to keep him a prisoner in a place that made him so miserable.

Would he return? She could only pray that he would, that once he realized she would always be waiting for him, that he could follow his wanderlust and not be shackled, Travis would love her all the more.

She stared at her reflection in the mirror, smiling bitterly. It seemed ludicrous to be standing here in the beautiful gown, for this was not a house for fancy dress. One day, perhaps, they would have a nice home, but returning what Corey McRae had stolen and swindled had left them almost penniless.

She looked down at the dark green silk, the deep folds of material cut down from the shoulders in swaths to shape her ample décolletage. Travis was not going to like seeing her breasts so exposed, but then he didn't like anything about this evening. She was sure this would be the final step to his losing his temper, and she hated the thought.

She loathed the evening ahead almost as much as she loathed the dress she wore, however beautiful it might be, for it held so many painful memories. Nina Rivenbark, Goldsboro's foremost dress designer, had made the gown according to Corey McRae's instructions and Kitty had worn it the night of the ball he had given in honor of their wedding.

She shook herself quickly, wanting to exorcise all those memories. She should have thrown the dress away, but she had stored all those fine clothes in trunks out in the barn, thinking that one day there might be a need for them.

Her golden-red hair was piled on her head in poufs and dips, clusters of curls twisting down to her shoulders. She had entwined dogwood blossoms in her tresses, and as she patted her coiffure, she wondered if it had perhaps gone out of style. Was the dress also out of date? What could she know of fashion, out here on the farm?

Her hand went to her bare throat. Once there had been emeralds, and her violet eyes had somehow caught their luster. Those precious stones, like the rest of her fine jewelry, had been sold to pay Corey's debts. Corey had bought them for her with blood money and she was relieved to see the jewels go. Like everything else he had given her, the jewels reminded her of Corey's evil. Now she wished she had also gotten rid of the gowns he had bought her.

Closing her eyes, she thought back to happier times, wearing old muslin dresses, baggy pants, or nothing at all, as she and Travis frolicked in the barn hayloft like children, laughing and loving. They had answered the need of their never-ending hunger for each other, and nothing else had mattered. They had their love, their passion, and she had foolishly believed that nothing else would ever matter to either of them.

"Miss Kitty? It's me, Lottie."

She turned at the sound of the soft, hesitant voice, smiling at the old Negro woman's dear face peering through the door.

"Lordy, you is still as beautiful as ever, Miss Kitty," Lottie gasped as her eyes swept over her. "You ain't changed none. You look just the same, just like you did when you was mistress of. . . ." Her voice trailed away.

Kitty crossed the room to embrace her, murmuring gratefully, "Whatever would I do without you, Lottie? I'm so glad you agreed to come to stay with John tonight. Mattie is going to the party tonight, too, and couldn't stay."

Lottie laughed. "Ain't no trouble for me, missy. I love that youngun like he was my own, and you know it. Besides, I'm always glad to do something for you."

"I can't pay you with money," Kitty sighed apologetically, "but I can give you a nice fat hen for a stew."

"Didn't plan on taking anything from you. I'm getting along just fine. Besides, with me and my boys working the crops and sharing with you this summer, there'll be enough to see us through the winter."

Kitty pressed her finger to her lips quickly. Travis mustn't overhear. "Don't talk of that now, Lottie. Travis knows nothing of my plans, yet. I'm going to break it all to him tonight, all at once. It must be done that way."

"Miss Kitty, are you sure you wants to do this?" Lottie frowned, chocolate eyes shaded with doubt. "That man worships you and you is forcin' him to leave you. Why, he might be so hurt he won't never come back. You want that?"

"You know I don't," the words tore from Kitty's throat in anguish. "But it has to be this way. Travis was never meant to be a farmer and I was a fool to think he could be. He'll come back to me, Lottie. Who knows? Maybe he'll make a new life for us somewhere else."

Lottie stared, and her look was almost accusing. "Would you go? Would you sell your daddy's land and go traipsin' off somewheres else 'cause Travis wants to? You told me yourself you promised your daddy."

"I know, I know. I won't ever sell it, Lottie. I'll keep it for John. One day it will be his to farm if he chooses. Right now, I have to prove to Travis that he means more to me than this land. He's given me two years of his life, doing what he thought I wanted him to do, and now the time has come for me to prove to him that his happiness comes first. Poppa would understand, I know he would.

"And I will go anywhere Travis wants to take me. When he returns from Haiti with Sam, I'll tell him the whole story of why everything happened as it did, but not until then. He would never leave me if he knew this was all a scheme."

"Naw, he wouldn't. I ain't so certain he's gonna go anyway. Just because you think he's gonna get mad when he finds out what you're planning to do, that don't mean he's gonna pack his things and leave."

Kitty nodded firmly. "He will leave. Things haven't been

pleasant around here lately, Lottie. I've turned into a shrew in two weeks. I've made myself nag him about the plowing, the chores—everything I could think of just to needle him. I've even thrown up Jerome Danton to him, telling him that Jerome is such a success while we're so poor. I said every mean thing I could think of." She blinked back angry tears. "You don't know how I hate myself. There were times when he would just stare at me with so much hurt in those beautiful gray eyes that I would want desperately to tell him the truth. Oh, Lottie, it's been so hard! And I had to keep on doing it, driving us further and further apart."

Lottie shook her head, sighing. "I hope you knows what you is doin', girl. A man like that, lovin' you the way he does, if you drive him away and he never comes back, you gonna hate yourself for the rest of your life."

"I just have to keep telling myself that in the end, we will all be happier, Lottie. That's what keeps me going. I live for the day when I can tell him it was all an act, that I never meant the things I said to him."

"Like I said," the old Negro sighed once more, "I just hope you knows what you is doin'."

You could not hope that any more than I do, Kitty thought. It had been sheer, living hell. Once it began, it got worse every day. She and Travis snapped at each other constantly. Nights found them not daring to touch in bed. How long since he had held her tightly and made her body sing with the joy of his passion? Not since that day in the woods, that day when she had finally seen how miserable she had made his life.

"How'd you get him to agree to go to that party tonight?" Lottie wanted to know. "Mastah Travis hates parties and balls."

"No, that's not true," Kitty said, turning back to the mirror. "During the war, Travis went to military balls when his presence as an officer was required. It's just that here he's all too aware of how people in Wayne County feel about him."

"I know. That hussy, Nancy Danton, ain't never let nobody forget that Mastah Travis killed Mastah Nathan. But he deserved to die, just like Mastah McRae. She'll be at that party tonight, makin' trouble just like always."

Kitty nodded, then asked, "Did she ever mention Travis or me when you worked for her, Lottie?"

Lottie snorted. "I didn't work for her long. She can't keep help, though the good Lord knows my people need work. She and Mastah Danton about the only folks around here what can afford to hire help, but even so, nobody can stand them. But yes'm, she did mention you. Lots. She knowed I worked for you when you was married to Mastah McRae. She was all the time sayin' ugly things, like she was gonna see you run out of town. That woman's crazy. Don't nobody like her."

"I can believe that, but, unfortunately, her husband is quite wealthy and powerful, and Nancy can get away with a lot. She's the social queen of Goldsboro, and if she blacklists anyone, they can find themselves dropped from everyone's invitation list. People cater to Nancy. I wonder," she added thoughtfully, "if she even knows I will be at the hospital charity ball tonight."

"Hmph," Lottie snorted again, louder this time. "That busybody knows ever'thing. She knows you're gonna be there, and she's probably got them claws of hers real sharp, just for you.

"What me and my people ain't never understood," Lottie went on, reaching to smooth the folds of Kitty's dress, "is why she keeps on a'hatin' you. Everybody knows Mastah Nathan never loved her and wouldn't have married her, nohow. Then she went after Mastah McRae like the hussy she is, and she even went after Mastah Travis."

"Let's not talk about that." Kitty turned away, a familiar stab making her quiver. She would never be able to forget the night she found Nancy naked in Travis' arms in a Goldsboro hotel room. Kitty had been married to Corey at the time. Travis despised her and refused to believe she had married Corey only because she was destitute and left with a baby, Travis' baby. It was a scene that was carved in her heart forever, Travis' strong, sensuous body, naked and glistening as he held Nancy in his arms. She shuddered.

"I see you're ready and anxiously waiting."

Travis' voice was like ice.

Kitty turned to face him, and Lottie scurried back into the kitchen, where John was playing at eating supper. Travis was dirty, sweaty, and his face showed the deep fatigue of long hours toiling in the sun.

Her heart went out to him, but she forced herself to stand stiffly away from him. She spoke crisply. "Yes, I am ready, Travis. It's been a long time since I was able to dress nicely and go to a ball and enjoy myself."

His lips twisted. "And wearing a dress your late husband

bought for you, I imagine. I certainly haven't been able to buy you anything like that."

She twirled, hating herself as she preened. "You used to tell me I was beautiful, Travis. Don't you like the gown? Won't you be proud to have me by your side tonight?"

A shadow crossed his face as he whispered painfully, "I would rather have you naked in the hayloft tonight, Kitty, than show you off to those hypocrites. Why do you insist that we go?"

"It was by special invitation of Dr. Sims," she answered, not meeting his gaze, not able to bear the hurt she knew was there. "It's the annual charity ball for the hospital, and he especially requested that I be there."

She hated lying. Actually, she had asked Dr. Sims to invite her. That had been no problem, for he was quite pleased. When she told him of her scheme, Dr. Sims tried to talk her out of it, but he knew from experience that once Kitty's mind was made up, she could be amazingly stubborn. So he had given in to her plan, though reluctantly.

"You know I don't want to go." Travis was coldly angry.

"If you don't take me, I will go alone."

The sound of his fist smashing against the wall made her jump. She saw the flashing red dots in his eyes and she flinched. "Kitty, goddamn it, girl, what's come over you lately? I swear, I've never seen a person change so quickly. You seemed happy before, and now . . . God knows, I've tried." He shook his head, looked at the reddening bruises on his fist, and said, "Hell, I have to go with you. You're just contrary enough to take off by yourself in that old wagon, and a woman has no business on these roads at night by herself. But we won't stay long, understand? And if there's any trouble from that bitch Nancy Danton or her bastard husband, we're leaving, understand? And if you don't go when I say go, you can get home any way you know how."

He took a step closer, speaking between tightly clenched teeth. "Do you understand, Kitty? I can take just so much."

She gave her hair a nervous pat. "Of course, Travis. But it will be a lovely evening, you'll see. I don't know what you're worried about. Now please hurry. It's getting late, and you have to take a bath and get dressed."

"And what in hell am I supposed to wear?"

"I told you I would take care of that, and I did." She made

her voice bright as she hurried across the room to where she had hung the suit on a nail. She held it up for him. "See? Isn't it nice? Mattie Glass persuaded the owner of the shop where she sometimes works to let us borrow it just for tonight. Be very careful and don't spill anything on it."

He reached her in two giant steps and snatched the clothes from her. The pants were fawn-colored, and the coat was of bright green velvet with a satin lapel. The shirt was white and ruffled, and there was even a short, satiny top hat. It was an elegant outfit, but not one that Travis would ever have picked for himself.

"Hell, what difference does it make?" he muttered, turning away, shoulders slumped.

She was glad when he left the room, for she was having great difficulty holding back the tears. How she longed to throw herself in his arms and confess the whole wretched scheme! But she could not do that, for he would never leave her if she told him. He would stay here, shackled like a wild animal, slowly withering until he was but a shadow of the real Travis Coltrane.

Travis did not speak a word on the ride into town, sitting stiffly beside Kitty on the rough wooden wagon seat, staring straight ahead.

Occasionally, the wagon wheels would hit a hole in the road, and they would lurch against each other. Travis would stiffen. Kitty would pull away. God, she thought miserably, it has never been like this between us before.

When they reached Goldsboro, Kitty took a deep breath, mustering every bit of nerve within her, and spoke in her newly cultivated reproachful tone. "Tie the wagon well away from the hotel, Travis. There are so many fine carriages here. I hate for anyone to see us in this old wagon."

He gave the reins a sudden jerk and turned to her. "Kitty, you've never been ashamed of this wagon before. You've always said these folks in their fine carriages might have money but not love." Eyes averted, he muttered, "You've changed, woman. You're not the same Kitty."

Kitty steeled herself and continued in her high-pitched whine, "If you behave yourself tonight, Travis, everything will be all right. Just watch how much you drink. You know what a nasty mouth you have when you're drinking."

"Will you shut up?"

She looked up at him, stunned by the fury in his voice.

"I mean it," he glowered. "God damn it, Kitty, I can't take anymore."

As they walked toward the hotel from where Travis had tied the wagon, memories flooded back, memories of how they had loved and fought passionately throughout the war and after. No matter how angry they had ever been, there was always the love, smoldering, waiting to be ignited by a look or a touch, flaming into passion. Theirs was a special love that would never die. Never. She had to keep believing that. Hope was all she had left.

They reached the front door of the marshal's office, a block from the hotel. A light was burning inside, and Travis slowed. "I should stop in and speak to Sam. He'll be leaving soon."

Kitty held her breath. Would Sam keep his promise? He had reluctantly given his word to do as she asked. He assured her the telegrams had been sent to General Sherman and to President Grant and both had responded with enthusiasm to Travis being on the government committee.

"Well?" Travis barked.

Kitty tried to recall what he'd been saying.

"I asked if you want to go on and let me catch up with you," he repeated stiffly. "I want to speak to Sam."

"I . . . I suppose," she began, then breathed a sigh of relief as the door swung open.

Sam stood there looking quite uncomfortable in a dull-colored cotton suit which did not fit him well. His brown hair was slicked down flat against his head, the gray more prominent somehow. His usually scruffy beard had been trimmed. He did not look at Kitty at all but greeted Travis jovially. "Well! I'm surprised to see you two all spiffed up. Are you headed for the hospital ball, too?"

Travis was stunned. "You mean *you're* going? Sam, I've never known you to go to a ball."

"Well, I don't reckon I look too bad for an old coot, now do I?"

Kitty hoped Travis did not notice how forced Sam's gaiety sounded, but evidently Travis was too surprised to see through Sam's act.

"Sure I'm going." Sam stepped out of his office and locked the door behind him. "Seems Dr. Sims and some of the good folks around here want to say good-bye to me formally. They're using the ball as the occasion. Ain't that somethin'? I figured they'd be glad to see one less Yankee around here. Maybe that's the reason they're wanting me to stop by," he chuckled. "They want to tell me how glad they are I'm leaving."

He fell into step beside them but still did not speak to Kitty.

"When are you going, Sam?" Travis asked sadly.

"Tomorrow, as a matter of fact. First thing in the morning. The new marshal got here three days ago and I got him broke in already. I'm taking the train up to Richmond and on to Washington. Won't know till I get there just when the committee will be sailing. We've got some meetings up there for indoc—" he stumbled on the word.

"Indoctrination," Kitty aided him.

"Yeah, that's right." He nodded. "They want to tell us what we're to do. There's plenty of important folks goin', I hear. Senators and all. I guess they want some of us rowdies along on the trip in case of trouble."

They walked in silence, then, with Travis staring down at the boardwalk. Kitty reached behind him and punched Sam sharply in his back, cueing him.

"Uh," Sam cleared his throat nervously. "You all caught up on the plowing, boy? When I get back this fall, I want to see a good crop. Can't have you goin' lazy on me."

"He's already gone lazy," Kitty whined. "We may have to give up the farm. He's doing so poorly and showing such little interest that I've spoken to the widow Glass about her sons taking over. Some of the Negroes are willing to help, and it can all be done on a sharecropping basis."

Travis stopped dead still and turned slowly around to stare at her, a glassy expression in his eyes. "What in hell are you talking about? This is the first I've heard of this. Who's running the farm, you or me?"

"It's *my* land." She tilted her chin defiantly. She could feel Sam's eyes burning into her and she rushed on. "You aren't a farmer, Travis, and you never will be. If you'd worked like you should, we could have made a fine place, but your heart wasn't in it and you know it."

"And you're just stupid enough to think we could get enough to live on from our share with someone else farming that land? Have you lost your mind?"

"We'll talk later," she said crisply, walking on. "I'm sure Sam isn't interested in our personal problems."

Travis stood there a moment, staring after her, but Sam gave him a nudge and whispered, "Come on, boy. You know how women are. She's probably just runnin' off at the mouth. Let's go to the party and have a good time. Might be a while before we can get together again."

"Yeah," Travis snarled, then began to walk so fast that Sam had to hurry to keep up. "I feel like having a good party with you, old friend." He walked right by Kitty, but she made no attempt to catch up.

Sam looked over his shoulder at her in sympathy, his eyes sending the silent message. *It's not too late.*

Yes, it is, she sent the mute reply. *It's been too late far too long, Sam.*

The first person Kitty saw as she entered the hotel lobby was Nancy Warren. Actually, she was Nancy Danton, but Kitty would always see her as the childhood adversary who had grown up to inflict more cruelty on Kitty than she would have believed possible. And all because of Nathan Collins, who had never cared for the haughty Nancy in the first place, though Nancy had never accepted that fact. She never would.

Kitty spoke with several other people, then found herself being moved along toward Nancy, who was smiling arrogantly, her eyes glittering. "Why, I do declare, if it isn't Mrs. Travis Coltrane," she cooed with wildly overdone sweetness. She held out her hand. "To what do we owe this pleasure, dear? I don't think I've seen you off that little farm of yours in months. But then, I can imagine it keeps you busy, what with your not having *any* hired help and *all.*"

Holding Kitty's hand, Nancy looked past her to where Travis stood with Sam, exchanging pleasantries with guests but looking quite miserable. Leaning forward so no one could overhear, she whispered with mock sympathy, "That gorgeous husband of yours is a waste on a farm, darlin'. He's good for so many *other* things," she added.

Kitty tried furiously to pull her hand away. Nancy's smile was almost a snarl, ruby-painted lips curling back over her little pointed teeth. She held fast to Kitty's hand, still leaning forward, but there was no longer any pretense. "What are you doing here, you bitch?" she hissed. "You don't belong here. Do you want me to make a scene? I won't have you here."

Kitty jerked her hand back so quickly that Nancy pitched forward slightly. She righted herself, letting go of Kitty's hand as she did. "I don't think you want a scene, Nancy," Kitty said quietly. "If memory serves me well, it was upstairs in this very hotel that I found you frolicking in bed with my husband. Of course, he wasn't married at the time—but *you* were. Now, would you like me to become hysterical and shout that to everyone here?"

"You wouldn't dare!" Nancy paled, and the huge splotches of rouge on her cheeks appeared even brighter, giving her a clownish look.

"I would dare and you know I would. I seem to remember another time, at another party, when I dumped a pitcher of water on your head because you were saying unkind things about my father. That was back when you were chasing after Nathan, remember, Nancy?" Kitty gave her a wink and grinned. "You should have learned by now that I push only so far, Nancy. So let's make the best of having to be in the same room together, and don't you start anything I will be forced to finish."

Nancy's eyes widened. She was standing there, mouth agape, as Kitty felt hard fingers tightening around her bare arm. She looked up quickly to see Travis' cold gray eyes looking threateningly from her to Nancy. "I'm not going to put up with any sniping between you two tonight," he said in a low voice. "Is that clear?"

Nancy dismissed them both with a toss of her head and turned to another guest coming through the reception line, her voice sounding high and unnatural as she spoke. Travis steered Kitty to a corner where no one could hear them and lashed out, "Damn it, I'm not putting up with this, Kitty. Now go ahead and do whatever it is you came to do. I want to leave here just as quick as we can."

"It won't hurt you to be sociable once in a while," she snapped back. "Don't you think I get tired of being stuck on that farm all the time? We should make friends."

"Oh, to hell with it!" He turned away, heading for a far corner where the men were gathered, drinking. Sam was there. He threw her a sympathetic look, and she turned away. She was tired of this, tired of the strain. She just wanted it over with.

The orchestra began to play as the ballroom filled with people. Kitty moved through the crowd, speaking to people she thought would speak back to her. There were a few cold shoulders, mostly distant relatives of Nathan's who would never forget, others who would forever condemn her for marrying a Yankee.

Maybe, she thought dizzily, maybe it *had* been a mistake to come back here. There had been such tranquillity and beauty in the Louisiana bayou, and sometimes she longed to get away from here and return to that magical place. She remembered that almost frightening moment when the air turned delicate pale blue and everything was bathed in glorious azure. Blue Bayou. Travis had loved the bayou and had known peace there. Perhaps, she thought fearfully, perhaps they ought to have stayed.

A chill passed over her despite the warmth of the crowded room, and she was suddenly aware that the orchestra had stopped playing and that Dr. Sims had moved to the stage. All eyes were on him. A hush swept the room.

He began to speak, acknowledging the special guests, members of the hospital board, the benefactors, thanking everyone for making the charity ball a success. Then he gave a short speech of regret over Marshal Sam Bucher's leaving and presented him with a gift from the citizens of Goldsboro. Sam was visibly touched by the gold pocket watch. With tears in her eyes, Kitty applauded her old friend. Dear, crusty, comfortable old Sam had made even these people love him.

"Now I have a very special announcement to make," Dr. Sims' jovial voice boomed out across the room and Kitty froze. The moment was at hand. Curious murmurings rippled through the air, but the doctor waved his arms for silence. When all attention was on the stocky man once more, he smiled broadly and said, "We here in Goldsboro and Wayne County are very fortunate to have the talents of a brilliant and kindhearted young woman, a woman who served the sick so well during the terrible war.

"Not only did she tend the wounded of the Confederacy," he went on after a brief pause, "but she tended the soldiers of the Union as well, often performing tasks that made others faint. I am told that she was often more skilled than some of our doctors. There were times on the battlefield when she was called upon to do surgical tasks, such as amputations."

A gasp went through the listening crowd, and women clutched their throats in horror. To think that one of their genteel breed could cut into a man's flesh!

"This young woman," he continued, "never had formal training in our medical profession, but perhaps she had better schooling, in a way, than we did. Most of you here remember Dr. Musgrave. Why, I imagine he brought many of you or your children into this world. This woman followed Dr. Musgrave in his rounds almost from the time she was old enough to walk, learning all he had to teach her, and matching his deep compassion for his fellow man.

"Unfortunately," he paused, clearing his throat, "Dr. Musgrave tragically died in the early part of the war."

He did not die! Kitty screamed silently. *He was murdered. Murdered by that bastard Luke Tate, who I hope is burning in hell this very minute.*

"I am speaking of Mrs. Kitty Wright Coltrane." Dr. Sims smiled at her, his green eyes bright, but she could see the strain on his face, feel it in his gaze. "Mrs. Coltrane has graciously offered to return to work at our hospital as head nurse, to share with other young women her vast knowledge of medicine. We, the doctors and staff of Goldsboro Hospital, want to take this opportunity tonight to welcome her, and to thank her for coming forward to help us once again."

There was applause, but Kitty did not really know whether it was enthusiastic or simply polite. A few people standing near her murmured appreciation. The orchestra began to play, but no sound could drown out the great roaring that had begun in her ears.

"Here he comes," Mattie Glass whispered, reaching Kitty's side as the applause died. "Oh, dear God, he's got the wrath of the demons in his eyes. He's pushing people aside. Oh, dear, dear—"

Kitty placed her hand on top of Mattie's, squeezing hard. "Don't leave me now, Mattie, please. I can't handle this alone."

"No, no, I won't, I promised you. Oh, dear, dear." She rolled her eyes skyward, trembling.

Kitty gasped as Travis' fingers dug into her shoulder. He spun her around to face him, oblivious to others watching. "What the hell is going on?" he growled. "What was Sims talking about? If you think you're going off and leaving John to work at that hospital, you're crazy."

"Travis, this isn't the time," Mattie interrupted weakly. "Don't you think—?"

"I think you should mind your own business," he lashed out, withering her to silence with a quick piercing look from those flashing gray eyes.

Mattie retreated quickly, throwing an apologetic glance at Kitty. She had tried, but dear Lord, she was not able to fight Travis Coltrane. Surely Kitty would understand that.

"Answer me, woman!" He gave her a rough shake. She could smell the liquor on his breath, knew he was drunk or close to it. "Is this why you brought me here tonight?"

"Hold it, Travis."

Kitty looked up gratefully into Sam Bucher's worried face. Sam lifted Travis' hand from her shoulder and began to guide both of them through the ballroom, toward the French doors leading to a terrace—and privacy.

The cooling night air was welcome. Maybe it would sober Travis.

"Now talk, damn it," Travis thundered.

Sam stepped between them. "Now listen, Travis, Kitty talked to me about this, and I think it's a nice idea. She doesn't like being stuck out there on that farm, and she told me how the Widow Glass has agreed to look after little John so you won't have to worry with him while you're out in the fields."

"You think that's all that matters?" Travis stared down at her incredulously. "Having someone look after John? What about me? You don't like being stuck out there on that farm? Hell, woman, do you think I like it? You think I like stumbling through those everlasting fields behind that stinking mule till I start wondering which one of us is the animal? Hell, no, I don't like it, but I've done it for *you*. Always for you."

It took all Kitty had not to confess her scheme then and there. "It's different for a man." She forced herself to sound cool. "A man farms the land, but you won't let me do anything but tend to John and the house. I get so bored."

She glanced away, unable to face him with lies. She had never, never been bored caring for him and their son. Except for the times she grieved over his misery, her life had been fine.

"You get bored!" He spat out the words. "Jesus Christ, how could one woman change so much and me not realize it for so goddamned long? You've made a fool of me!"

He shook her so roughly that Sam pulled him away. "Just calm down, boy. You've had too much to drink. I've been watching you tonight, and you've been tossin' that stuff down like it was water. Tomorrow you'll feel better. You and Kitty can talk then."

Kitty took a deep breath, lifted her chin in what she hoped seemed utter defiance. "We can talk," she said coolly, smoothing the front of her green dress, "but my mind is made up. I start work at the hospital Monday. I have a right to live a part of my life just for me."

Travis stared at her for long, painful moments, during which Kitty and Sam did not look at each other. They knew they were about to hear the very words she had schemed to make him say.

"So have I, Kitty," Travis said coldly. "For too long I've given all my life to you, and now I realize it never meant a damn thing to you."

He turned to Sam. "I'm going with you. I don't know if they'll even let me be on that committee or not, but I'll go with you if I have to be a stowaway. I've got to get away from here."

"Sure, Travis, sure." Sam put his big arm across his friend's shoulders and led him away. He chanced a backward glance at Kitty, pity in his eyes, and saw that she was biting her lower lip hard, trying to hold back the tears. She couldn't give in now. "I'll fix it so you can go along," Sam was saying. "Maybe you two need to be apart for a little while to think things out. Then, when you come back, everything will be different. You'll see."

They reached the door leading back into the ballroom and Travis stopped suddenly. Without turning around to look at her, he muttered, "Sam will take you home. I'm staying in town tonight."

Sam led Travis back inside and she could hold back the tears no longer. Sinking to her knees on the terrace, she covered her face with her hands and began to sob.

Love something, set it free, she cried to herself. *Please, God, let me have done the right thing, for it's too late to turn back now.*

Chapter Three

ORANGE and pink streaked across the eastern horizon.

Kitty stood at the window, eyes burning from the sleepless night just past and from squinting into the darkness, praying for a sight of Travis. How many nights, she wondered wearily, and how many days would she spend in front of this very window, staring down that long, lonely road? She could only hope he would come home and say good-bye, if not to her, then surely to his son.

"I brought you some coffee, Miss Kitty," Lottie whispered, so as not to wake the little boy sleeping across the room.

Kitty murmured thanks. When Sam had brought her home, he had offered to take Lottie to her place but she declined, sensing something was very wrong.

Sam had returned to town, promising to find Travis and try to sober him up. "I think you should just tell him the truth," he had said angrily. "This has gone too far."

"He would never leave," she sighed wearily. "There's no need to keep discussing it, Sam. It's done. I am going to farm the land out on shares, and I will go back to work at the hospital to keep busy and make some money. Mattie will love taking care of John. I'm sorry Travis got so upset, but that's the way he is, headstrong and bullish."

"You knew all that when you married him," he reminded her, then added with a teasing grin, "That's probably one of the reasons you fell in love with him, girl. He's the only man you ever met that you couldn't charm right around your little finger."

He frowned and scratched his beard. "I could've told you he'd blow all the way to the moon, but I didn't figure he'd be so cockeyed drunk by then. Golly damn, I don't even know if I'll be able to run him down. No tellin' where he's gone."

She clutched the front of his ill-fitting coat and pleaded, "You've got to find him, Sam. I want him to go with you, but I can't just let him go this way, so blind angry that he won't even say good-bye to me or to our son."

"I know, I know." He touched his lips to her forehead and pushed her away with a gentle shake.

"Must be close to seven," Lottie interrupted in a worried voice. "I heard the marshal say his train left at ten. It's a good hour's ride into town, maybe more. He ain't rightly got time to get out here and back if'n he ain't left town yet."

Kitty gulped down the hot coffee. Lottie rambled on, but she did not hear. Her mind was whirling and in a moment she knew what she had to do. "Get John dressed for me, will you, please?"

Kitty roughly jerked the gown over her head, heedlessly. She would never wear that emerald gown again, ever. She should not have worn it last night. The damn thing was probably cursed because it had been paid for by Corey McRae. She found an old faded pair of cotton trousers that had once belonged to one of Mattie's sons.

John was fussing, not wanting to eat the corn mush Lottie had prepared for him. "You wanna see yo' daddy, don't you?" She hovered over him, urging him to spoon the food through his puckered lips. "If you don't eat, you ain't gonna go."

Tears welled in his eyes. Kitty saw and rushed over to kiss his forehead. Giving Lottie a warning look, she told him, "Mommy is in a hurry, darling, but I won't leave you, I promise."

Lottie gave her a cold stare, broadcasting a message that *she* was not the one sending the boy's daddy away, so there was no cause to look at *her* like that.

Finally, after what seemed an eternity, they were in the wagon. Lottie insisted on going along to hold John in her lap, and Kitty was grateful. She had always hated the ride into Goldsboro, for the scenery brought back so many unpleasant memories. Oh, there had been happy trips before the war, riding with her father, riding with Doc Musgrave, but such misery later on. She thought of the day she had ridden in with Travis, sitting on the back of his horse as the Yankees moved into Goldsboro. She had been furious when the Yankees sang, "Battle Hymn of the Republic," their song, so she had begun to sing "Dixie" as loudly as she could. The soldiers had fallen silent, glaring at her. Travis had tried to stop her, but she kept right on singing. Then General Sherman himself came galloping back through the line to see what was causing the disturbance. Kitty smiled tearfully, thinking of it.

Lottie leaned over to place her dark hand on Kitty's arm and give her a gentle shake. "You know it ain't too late, missy," she said quietly. "You could tell him the truth."

Kitty did not reply. Was she just possibly sending Travis away so she could follow her own dream and return to nursing? Was *she*, too, tired of grubbing on the little dirt farm? No! She gripped the leather reins tightly, squeezing her fingers against the worn thongs. She loved the farm and she loved Travis, and she would never send him away except for his own terrible needs.

She looked over at John, sleeping contentedly with his head against Lottie's big bosom. His home was being torn apart because his parents could not settle down and make a life for him. One had the wanderlust, and the other was not content without doing a man's work. Selfish, John's parents were selfish. It wasn't fair. But Kitty knew they could not help being what they were.

The clouds that had been gathering since they had left home now began to unleash a steady downpour. Kitty twisted around to retrieve the tarpaulin kept in the wagon bed, and Lottie spread it on top of her and John, but Kitty pushed it away when part of it was offered to her. Perhaps the cool rain would soothe a little of the pain, she thought.

By the time they reached the train station, Kitty was soaking wet.

"You gonna catch a cold," Lottie fussed with agitation. "You gonna take the fever and die. Just you wait and see."

"It's not a very cold rain, Lottie," Kitty said quietly, glancing around at the few people waiting for the train.

She got down out of the wagon and tied the mule's reins to a hitching post. "Take John and go wait under the shelter," she told Lottie. "I'm going to look for Sam and Travis."

Everyone under the shelter turned to stare at the young woman with golden-red hair stringing down her back, wearing wet and clinging men's trousers. Her shirt also stuck to her, revealing her firm, rounded breasts, the nipples protruding. But Kitty was oblivious to the stares or the picture she was presenting. There was one thought in her mind, to find Travis and Sam.

She glanced at the large clock hanging just above the door to the station ticket office. Nine forty-five. There was little time left, and even as she had the thought, the distant, mournful wail of a whistle sounded. She looked down the lonely stretch of crossties and railings to see puffs of grayish smoke drifting upward. At any moment, the big engine would chug into view. Where is Travis? Where is Sam?

She pushed her way through the crowd on the platform. With her heart pounding, Kitty suddenly spied a familiar face. Of all people, she sighed. She started to push on by, not about to waste precious moments dickering with the little snit.

"If you're looking for that no-good husband of yours, I might be able to tell you where you can find him."

Kitty froze, then turned slowly to look at the smug smile on Nancy Danton's haughty face.

"I said I *might* be able to tell you," Nancy said in a syrupy voice. "I didn't say I *would*, now did I?"

Kitty could hear the train. There was no time to waste. "Nancy, if you know where Travis is, please tell me," she cried, unable to keep the desperation from her voice. Let the vixen enjoy her moment of gloating, Kitty could stand that.

Nancy, wearing a bright yellow dress trimmed in lace and ruffles, twirled her matching parasol, which pointed at her neat kid boots.

"Please," Kitty said through gritted teeth, "tell me where I can find Travis."

With a shrill laugh that grated against what was left of Kitty's nerves, Nancy pointed a white-gloved finger toward the station. "The dirty old drunk is in there, passed out in a corner. That nasty Marshal Bucher is in there trying to get him on his feet and on the train. I assume the two are leaving town. That will be *such* an improvement. Why don't you go with them and take Corey McRae's brat with you? Wayne County would be such a better place without the likes of you all." Nancy's shrill voice got higher and higher as Kitty turned away.

Without sparing time to retort, Kitty pushed her way to the door, jerked it open, and stepped inside just as the engine screeched to a halt. Travis was slumped in a corner, with Sam standing next to him.

"If you're going, boy, you gotta get up," Sam was saying desperately. "The train's here. I gotta be on it. If I have to leave you behind, I will."

"Don't leave me." Travis took the hand Sam extended, stumbling and weaving as he allowed himself to be raised. "I gotta go, gotta leave this goddamn place. Never should'a come back. Kitty never loved me."

"I do love you," Kitty stepped forward and spoke quietly, tears streaming down her cheeks.

Travis looked at her with red-rimmed eyes. Sam stepped back, leaving Travis to struggle with his own huge, weaving body.

"Well, look at you." Travis hiccuped. "You get me outta the way, and then you can traipse around and do as you damn please."

He almost fell but grabbed a nearby bench to steady himself. Sam picked up his worn bag and moved toward the door.

"You wait for me," Travis yelled. "Don't you leave me, Bucher."

To Kitty he said in a heavily slurred voice, "I tell you one thing, woman, I'll be back to get my boy. I don't have any money now. I sank it all in your stinking farm. But I'll get paid for this trip, and when I come back, I'm coming for my boy. You can do whatever the hell you want to do."

Suddenly, Kitty could stand it no longer. "Travis, I love you," she cried, moving to put her arms about him, but he gave her a shove that sent her reeling.

"Leave him alone, girl," Sam called to her gruffly. "He's dog-ass drunk and has been all night. I'll talk to him after we get on our way, but there ain't no point tryin' to explain to him now."

She shook her head from side to side wildly, wet hair flying through the air as she sobbed, "I can't let him go like this, Sam. I want to tell him the truth."

Travis hiccuped again. "The truth is we never should have

got married. I'm not the marrying kind, and you're not the kind a man should marry, either."

"That's enough of that!" Sam stepped forward and grabbed Travis by his shirt and gave him a jerk. He knew he was no match for the man's strength, but anger was blinding him. "I ain't goin' to stand here and let you talk to her that way. Now let's just go get on that train, and when you sober up, we'll talk. I'll tell you what she's trying to tell you. You're too drunk to listen now. You can take a train back from Washington after I explain, if you want to, but this fussin' ain't doin' nothin' but hurtin' both of you."

"Come back?" Travis laughed, lurching sideways. "Are you crazy, Sam? I'm not coming back here till I've got the money to take my son away from this woman."

"He's outside," Kitty said quickly, hoping the thoughts of seeing John would sober him. "I brought him so you could say good-bye to him, Travis. Lottie has him outside, under the shelter. Be angry with me if you want, but don't take it out on John. Please. I told him he was coming to see his daddy."

Travis threw back his head and laughed. "I'll just bet you did. It would really give you pleasure for my son to see me like this, wouldn't it?"

Dear God, why hadn't she listened to Sam and everyone else? They could have talked. Perhaps Travis would have admitted his craving for adventure. Not this way. Lord, no, not this way. He must not leave hating her.

"Travis, at least say good-bye to John," she pleaded, moving toward him again. Sam pulled her away.

"All right," Travis slurred, eyes squinting down at her with such loathing that her heart constricted. "I'll see him. I'll tell him I'll be coming back. But you stay away from me, Kitty."

He stumbled to the door. Kitty clung to Sam, crying, heart breaking as she watched Travis stumble away.

"He's pretty upset, Kitty," Sam sighed. "Not just over what happened last night. It's the way things have been goin' the past months. I guess it's just finally caught up with him."

"It's caught up with me, too."

He cupped her chin in his hand, forced her to meet his probing gaze. "You been doing some soul-searchin', too, haven't you, girl? You've missed your work, haven't you? Now you feel like hell, because you're thinkin' how maybe this is all for the best, you two goin' your separate ways. But

I can tell you this. It won't stay this way. I've known you two kids too long. You love each other. You'll get back together. I just feel it in these old bones of mine. Maybe this is what you both need, being apart for a while. It might just do you some good."

Kitty moved to the window to stare out at the people milling about on the platform. There was Lottie, eyes wide with shock over Travis' drunk and disheveled appearance. And there was Travis, holding John tightly in his arms, his head bowed over the little boy's head.

"But don't you fret." Sam came to stand beside her. "Once we're on our way and he's sobered up, I'll tell him the whole story, how you had it planned all along. Once he understands, he won't be mad no more. He'll come runnin' back here when our business is done. You'll see."

She turned to look at Sam as hope fluttered within for the first time since the nightmare had begun. "Do you really think it will be like that?"

"Well, I think you better do some thinkin' yourself while he's gone," he answered uncomfortably, clearing his throat and glancing away, not wanting to meet her anxious gaze. "I think maybe you better think about how you just might be lookin' forward to goin' back to work at that hospital. Maybe Travis wasn't the only one gettin' itchy britches on that farm. Maybe you were just as miserable as he was."

Kitty felt a rush of love for the grizzled old man as she stood on tiptoe to kiss his cheek. "You always could see right inside me, Sam. I never could hide anything from you."

"That's right," he grinned proudly, giving her a squeeze. "I told you you was in love with Travis before you'd even admit it to yourself. And I have to admit there was a time when even I got to thinkin' you two would never get together, 'cause you're both so goldang stubborn."

Suddenly the cry of "All aboard!" wailed through the air and the train gave three short whistle blasts.

Sam took her hand and led her outside. They walked to where Travis stood, holding John against him. Lottie looked at them and shook her head from side to side in dismay. John looked up, saw Kitty, and began to cry, "Mommy!"

Travis jerked his head up, eyes narrowing as he saw her. "I'll be back," he said evenly, menacingly, as he held John out to her waiting arms. "You can be sure of that, Kitty."

"I'll be waiting for you." She began to sob. "We'll talk then."

"There won't be a damn thing to talk about except me taking my son, Kitty. You and I have nothing left to discuss."

She realized that he was sobering, for the slur was almost absent from his tone. He must have realized it, too, because he nodded to Lottie. "Take the boy and go wait somewhere." To Sam he said, "I'll see you on the train."

Alone with Kitty, he growled, "I've worked my guts out for you." He squeezed down on her wrists and she winced, but if he noticed, he gave no sign. "All because of your goddamn land. I lived my life to please you, and what did it get me?"

"Travis, let me explain. It isn't like you think."

"You always were the most beautiful damn woman I ever laid eyes on," he went on as though she had not interrupted. "I was never with a woman who could make me feel like you could, like I'd climbed the highest mountain in the world and could just keep right on climbing as long as I had you."

His lips curled and his eyes were hard. "Now I see it was just what you kept telling me it was during the war, when you hated me. It was lust, Kitty. Plain and simple animal lust. But I was fool enough to think it was love."

"Travis, it *was* love," she cried. He clutched her wrists tighter and pushed her back against the wooden wall of the station house. "You have to believe me," she cried. "It *was* love, and it *is* love, and I'll never stop loving you, not ever!"

"You hitched me to a goddamn plow like a mule, when all you really wanted was someone to tend your daddy's precious land. Well, Kitty, it's time you learned that I have to dream. I'm going to follow my dreams now, but heed me well—I'll be back for my son. You won't keep John from me."

He released her and turned to walk rapidly and then run toward the train, which was already beginning to chug slowly down the tracks. Kitty stood watching for a split second, and then she took off, running behind him, pleading for him to stop. Leaping for the train, Travis caught a railing and swung himself up, disappearing inside the train without looking back.

With every turn of the chugging wheels, Kitty felt her life being pulled from her. Suddenly she realized she could not let Travis leave this way, hating her. She began to run, desperate to keep up with the train, arms outstretched. The train was all she had left of Travis, and when it outdistanced her, he would be gone. She ran faster . . . then suddenly felt herself being clutched around the waist and swung around, away from the tracks. "Let me go!" She screamed, struggling against the hands that held her.

The train pulled away from the station, and when the caboose rattled by, Kitty slumped defeatedly into the arms that held her. Travis was gone. It was too late now.

"Kitty, what were you trying to do? Get yourself killed?"

That soft Virginia accent! She stiffened, turning slowly to face the hazel eyes of Jerome Danton, his lips twitching smugly beneath his neatly trimmed moustache. Hands clenched tightly at her sides, she spat, "You take your filthy hands off of me, you damn carpetbagger!"

"Kitty, Kitty, Kitty," he laughed softly, releasing her. "When are you ever going to stop calling me that? And when are you going to realize that I just want to be your friend?"

"Friend!" She scoffed. "Every time you tried to be my friend, you had an ugly motive. You scalawag! I will never forget how you and your hooded friends killed helpless Negroes before Travis put a stop to it, or your pretending to be my friend when you accompanied me to New Orleans to get my son back, then trying to rape me."

"Make love to you, my dear," he said softly, shaking his head. "I never pretended I did not want to make love to you. As for killing helpless Negroes, well, someone had to bring order to these parts when the worthless animals were running wild after the war, stealing. Let's don't talk of nonsense."

"I will thank you to stay out of my life, Jerome, and if you don't let go of my arm, I'm going to rake my nails right down your face. How will you explain that to your wife? Nancy would not like to know you were here now, grabbing at me."

"Now, Kitty, what makes you think Jerome has to explain anything to me?"

They both whirled around to see Nancy standing a few feet away, twirling her parasol over her head, lips twisted in a triumphant smile. Jerome hastily removed his hand from Kitty's arm.

"I've always known you had designs on my husband," Nancy cocked her head to one side, appraising Kitty carefully. "But really, now, if you're going to go man-chasing the very minute your husband gets the good sense to leave you, I should think you would wear some decent clothes."

Jerome moved to slip his arm around his wife's shoulders. "Now, darling, it isn't what you think. Kitty was a bit hysterical. She was getting too close to the train, and—"

Nancy silenced him with a frosty look. "I saw and heard the whole thing, you ninny. Don't lie to me. Travis left her, and I say good riddance to him. What happens to her now is her concern, not yours."

His eyes narrowed. He had always hated for Nancy to make him look like a fool in public, and in front of Kitty it was even worse. "Don't tell me what to do, woman. Kitty is a friend of mine and always will be. So you take Cousin Leroy to the carriage, and ask him if he collected all his luggage. I will see that Kitty gets to hers. She's upset."

"You're coming with me!" Nancy stomped her foot, swinging her parasol at Kitty in a menacing gesture. "I'll not have you escorting this trollop for the whole town to see and laugh at me."

"Nancy, I won't have you calling her names, and I won't have you ordering me about. I am your husband, and *you* will do as *I* say."

Kitty had had enough of the two pompous idiots. She turned and hurried toward the wagon where Lottie was waiting with John.

Jerome called after her, but she kept on going. He started to follow, but Nancy reached out and clutched his sleeve, hissing, "Damn you, don't you dare go running after her and make me look like a fool."

"You've already done a good job of that all by yourself, Nancy," he snapped, shoving her and hurrying away. Kitty had already untied the mule and was climbing into the wagon beside Lottie and John.

Nancy watched her husband go, eyes narrowed, fury making her body quiver. She could not hear what was being said between the two, but Jerome's expression told her that he was pleading, and Kitty looked angry. No matter, Nancy thought with a swish of her skirts, turning away. This was all an act, anyway. Now that Travis was gone, Kitty would do what she had always done when she was without a man. She would go after Nancy's man. Only this time, she would not get him.

She had wooed Nathan away with her filthy hayloft tricks that drove him wild, Nancy thought for the hundredth time, with hatred burning through her. She had done the same thing with Corey McRae. Why, before Kitty Wright came back to town, Corey was on the verge of asking Nancy to marry him. But whatever it was that Kitty did to men—and it was probably something no respectable woman would ever think of doing—she had done to Corey, for he was quickly smitten with her.

So, now that Travis had left, Nancy fumed, Kitty would try to take Jerome away from her. As much as she hated to admit it, Kitty had almost succeeded once before, but had thrown Jerome over for Travis. Nancy sighed. She couldn't really blame Kitty. Jerome might be her husband, but he wasn't a tenth of the man Travis Coltrane was. A smile touched her lips and a warm flush crept through her body as she remembered the night Kitty had walked into the hotel room and found Nancy and Travis naked in bed. God, she would never forget what had taken place during those wild, passionate moments. No man had ever possessed her like that. No man had ever made her feel thundering emotions that left her shaking. Nancy had never known the wonder of it all with any other man.

Oh, damn Kitty, she cursed, bosom heaving with emotion. Damn her to hell! Jerome still wanted Kitty, Nancy knew it. What was it about her that drove men wild? She was beautiful, yes, with golden-red hair and violet eyes and a perfectly sculptured body, but that wasn't all. No, there had to be something else, something secret. Perhaps she was a witch. Nancy laughed, thinking that she might just have discovered Kitty's secret after all these years.

"You little fool!" Jerome snapped, squeezing her shoulder. "We come here to meet my cousin Leroy, and you have to make a spectacle of yourself."

"You've been making a spectacle of yourself over that trollop for years, you bastard!" Nancy snapped, jerking away. "And don't you touch me like that again or I *will* make a scene."

The carriage was farther away, and Jerome continued to limp toward it. Nancy fell into step beside him. "I won't have you running after that bitch," she said harshly. "I mean it, Jerome. I won't have it. Good heavens, she shot you and gave you that limp!"

"Just shut up," he snarled, trying to move away from her. "Whatever differences Kitty and I might have had are in the past. She's alone now. Her husband has obviously left her. She has a small child and a farm to look after, and she's going to need friends. I intend to be one, and you are going to keep your mouth shut about it."

Nancy slowed, allowing him to move ahead as she thought, lips pursed together tightly, frowning.

Some way, she vowed silently, somehow, this time Kitty Wright would not get her man. She had been in Nancy's craw far too long. It would take some planning, but this time, Nancy promised herself, this time *she* would come out on top.

Chapter Four

KITTY was curious and also annoyed. Dr. Sims had sent word that he wanted her to go to his office when she was through for the day. As always, she was anxious to get home. She had traded in the wagon and mule for a mare, for it was faster to travel on horseback. The ride to Mattie's to pick up John usually took a little over a half hour if she cantered the mare at a leisurely pace, and then it was another fifteen-minute ride home.

As she walked down the long hallway to Dr. Sims' office, she glanced out a window and saw that another spring storm was gathering in the west. The prospect of riding in the rain did nothing to lift her spirits.

All in all, the day had been extremely trying. Twelve young women had signed up to work under her at the hospital, and after two weeks, seven had remained. Now there were six, and one of them had fainted that day while watching an operation. Kitty knew that was the end of the young lady's nursing career.

Perhaps, Kitty thought with a sigh, the whole program had been foolish. Goldsboro was a small town, with a small hospital. If women were genuinely interested in nursing, it would probably be best for them to go to a city like Raleigh or Wilmington, where there were better facilities and they could learn modern techniques.

She paused outside Dr. Sims' closed door. There had been a time when she did not care for the man, when he was lazy and often drunk, given to defeatism like so many other Southerners right after the war. Then when the Yankees had gradually moved back north, the responsibilities of running things had fallen on Dr. Sims. Despite his age, he had answered the call valiantly and had earned renewed respect, not only from Kitty but from the townsfolk as well.

Standing there brought back other memories—painful memories. Kitty had only to close her eyes and envision that fateful, painful day when she had been banished from the hospital, cast into the streets with nowhere to go, carrying Travis' child.

The Yankee doctor in charge, Dr. Malpass, had summoned her to this very same office to discuss the pregnancy she had tried to hide. Incensed, she had told him bluntly that she was not ashamed to be carrying Captain Coltrane's child, and that they were going to be married as soon as he returned from whatever mission General Sherman had sent him on. She had asked to be excused from the embarrassing discussion, reminding him there were patients to be ministered to.

She could recall so vividly the way he had leaped to his feet angrily and agreed that yes, there were patients out there, and then he had yelled, "Patients who should not be exposed to a woman of questionable morals."

Then he had told her to leave the hospital, not only for the sake of the patients but also for the relationship between the federal government and the townspeople. She shuddered at the memory, for that had been the beginning of the nightmare with Corey, and that nightmare would haunt her forever.

Chiding herself for letting the past come back to hurt, Kitty knocked on the door. Dr. Sims called out immediately and she walked into the room. He was already up and moving around his desk to greet her with an extended hand.

"Sit down, sit down," he smiled broadly. "Kitty, my girl, it's so seldom we get a chance to chat. I've been wanting to tell you what a splendid job you are doing here, not only with the nurses but with the patients as well. You are a very special person. If anyone was born to minister to the sick, it was you, dear."

She returned his smile stiffly and reluctantly took the chair he offered. Praise was nice, but she was so tired and still had the ride home facing her. Staring down at her blood-stained smock, she said bluntly, "I thank you for your compliments, Doctor, but I really need to be on my way. It is a long ride to my home."

"I know it's a long ride," he interrupted, clamping his hand on her shoulder in a gesture of understanding. "And that is precisely why I asked you to come to my office today. Mrs. Sims and I have been worrying about you having to make that ride every day."

He perched on the edge of his desk, folding his arms across his vested chest. She stared at him quizzically, and he went on to say that now, while the days were getting longer, there was probably enough daylight for her to make the trip home without having to ride in darkness. "But take this evening, for instance," he waved toward the window and the gathering twilight beyond. "See how late you have stayed again? Your students left hours ago."

"There was a very sick patient," she explained quickly. "He asked me to sit with him, and I couldn't refuse."

"Ahh, but you do so much of that, don't you?" He wagged his finger at her. "You go beyond the call of duty, Kitty, which is admirable, but not when you have such a long way to ride at the end of the day. And let's be realistic. It is not that safe for a lady to be out on the country roads alone."

"Then you want me to leave the hospital earlier," she shrugged. "All right, I will try. Now if I may bid you good evening, I'll just get started on that long ride."

She had started to rise, but he motioned for her to remain seated as he rushed on. "No, that is not why I called you here. Mrs. Sims and I have discussed it, and we would like to offer you room and board in our home, so that you can remain in Goldsboro and not have to make that trip every night and every morning. There will be no charge. It's our way of expressing our appreciation for all the fine work you do here, because we both realize that you don't get paid nearly enough for your services, and—"

"Wait a minute, Doctor." Kitty held up her hands in a halting gesture. "It is wonderful for you and your wife to make the offer, and I really appreciate your kindness, but please remember that I have a son, and it's hard enough not being with him during the day. I certainly can't give up what little time I have with him at night."

He nodded. "I know, Kitty. I understand how you feel, but I'm sure Mrs. Glass would be glad to keep him overnight, and you will still have the weekends."

"No. Absolutely not." She got to her feet this time. "I won't leave my son with Mattie all week. Perhaps I should not have taken this job, but my husband is away for a spell, and I have no choice but to work and make whatever I can to keep John and me fed and clothed. It's hard, but when Travis returns, we can get our lives back in order."

She saw the sympathetic look in his eyes and knew that he, like so many others, did not believe Travis would come back.

"I thank you for your kind offer and your concern, Dr. Sims." She nodded and then backed toward the door. "And please tell Mrs. Sims of my appreciation. But I can't accept. I'll just try to leave earlier each day. Now if you will excuse me, I'll be on my way."

She fled the room, closing the door behind her and leaning back against it to take a deep breath, letting it out slowly. There was no way she was going to leave John all day and all night, too. It was ridiculous even to think of such a thing. Besides, she was not afraid of the ride, even after dark.

She was almost out the front doorway when one of the nurses called out to her. "Mrs. Coltrane, may I speak with you, please?"

Kitty sighed and turned to face the anxious-looking woman.

"Mr. Wallace, the one they operated on this morning, he's not doing so well," she said, out of breath. "I was afraid I would miss you. He's asking for you. I know it's late, but if you could just speak to him, maybe calm him down. The other nurses have tried, but we just can't handle him."

Kitty did not hesitate. Following the woman up the stairs, all the way to the third floor, she rationalized that it was no wonder the nurses could not handle Frank Wallace. Probably not a single one of them had ever witnessed an amputation, much less helped to care for someone after such an operation. None of them had worked during the war. They were to be commended for wanting to help the sick, but they were going to have to learn to stomach all kinds of repulsive situations.

Frank Wallace lay on his back, moaning. His eyes were open and glassy with pain. The white sheet covering the stump of his left leg was splotched with blood.

"Dr. Batson just checked him and gave him some morphine, so there's nothing we can do," the woman clucked nervously.

"You can change his dressing," Kitty snapped, hating herself for sounding so waspish but unable to stop herself.

The woman stiffened. "We did that, too. Not a half hour ago."

"Then do it again, please." Kitty moved to the side of the bed. Reaching out, she touched the man's forehead with her fingertips. "Frank? It's Kitty. Have you been asking for me?" she whispered.

With surprising strength, he lifted his hand to wrap clammy fingers about her wrist. "Kitty, thank God you came." His voice was weak, barely audible. "I always feel better when you're here."

"Well, I'm going to sit with you till you fall asleep, Frank." She pulled her hand back, placing his across his chest, then tucked the sheet up under his chin. Some of the glassiness had left his eyes, and he looked up at her gratefully. Picking up a nearby chair, she set it down next to his bed.

"Will you be here when I wake up?" he asked hopefully.

She leaned over so he could see what she hoped was a reassuring smile. "Frank, you are going to feel so much better after a good night's sleep that it won't matter whether I'm here or not. And you know I have a little boy. He'll be wondering where his mommy is. So you just lie there and try to go to sleep."

". . . took my leg off," he choked out the words, tears spilling from the corners of his eyes. ". . . said I'd rather die than let 'em cut it off, and I would. Ain't no man now."

Kitty's tone was stern. "Frank, if you are going to talk nonsense, I won't stay here with you. Now, you aren't the first soldier to lose a leg so long after the war, and you won't be the last. There are a lot of wounded soldiers with bullets in them that will sooner or later fester and give them trouble. Don't you talk about wanting to die, and don't let me hear you say again that you aren't a man. You are very much a man, and I'm proud of you."

She stopped talking, leaned forward once more, then sighed with relief to see that he had already fallen asleep. The morphine, combined with a few words of comfort from a friend, had done the job.

The nurse was awed. "You have such a way with the patients, Mrs. Coltrane. It's a touch the rest of us just don't have, I'm afraid."

Kitty wearily got to her feet. "It isn't a touch. It's simply a matter of letting them know that someone else cares." With a gesture to the soiled sheet, she said, "Please change that. It won't help him any to wake up and see all that blood."

By the time she left the building and went to the shed in back where the mare was kept, darkness had descended. Slipping on the mare's bridle and saddle, she mounted and moved out toward the street.

Riding through town was not too bad. There were street lamps to show the way, and, as always, passing the stores and houses conjured up memories, some good, some bad. Danton's Dry Goods Store made Kitty frown. She passed the darkened windows. Jerome Danton owned half of Goldsboro and most of the land surrounding, but Kitty felt no envy. She only wished she never had to see him or his shrewish wife ever again.

There was no moon, for the storm clouds had gathered in the night sky to make the world seem even darker. Now and then a zigzag flash of lightning would streak across the sky, showing the road ahead only briefly as the mare moved into the countryside. A warm wind blew briskly, rattling the leaves overhead, creating an eerie sound. Kitty gave the mare her lead, allowing her to set her own pace lest she stumble and fall in haste, though Lord, she wanted to get home.

Kitty's head began to nod. How wonderful it would be to climb into bed right then. She admonished herself for being so late. John would be asleep by the time she reached Mattie's, and Mattie would insist that he stay overnight, pointing out the foolishness of taking him home only to return early the next morning. But Kitty had to be with him, if only for a short while.

Travis. How she missed him, and prayed he missed her just as much. If only things had turned out differently.

A drop of rain splashed her nose, and that was the only warning before the sky opened, unleashing a downpour. In only moments she was drenched to the skin, and there was no shelter in sight. The rain, the increasing bolts of lightning, and the rolls of thunder were all making the mare skittish.

The sky exploded with a yellow-white flash, and suddenly

the bridge was visible. Soon the sound of the mare's hooves striking the wooden planks was barely audible above the sound of the angry, rushing waters of the Neuse River. They moved into the deep, swampy area on the other side of the bridge. Kitty's nerves were taut. She knew the mare could be mired in water in this lowland at any time.

Then lightning lit the sky once more, and she saw what she had been looking for, the old log cabin that had once belonged to the Orville Shaw family. It had never been much of a place, rotting even when it was lived in. Now, abandoned, it was all but falling apart, but it would give them shelter.

"This way, girl." Kitty reined the mare to the right slowly, hoping the horse could make her way around the decaying stumps littering the yard without much trouble. "We'll be out of all this in just a few more minutes. I'm going to take you right inside with me, and we'll wait this out if it takes all night."

The mare reached the porch and Kitty dismounted, leading her inside slowly, fearful that the roof might come crashing down around them at any moment. The storm made what was left of the cabin tremble and quake, but mercifully, the inside was dry.

Finding a nail in the wall, Kitty looped the reins around it, then sank down gratefully on the rough wood floor.

Being there brought back memories of Andy Shaw. Of all Ruth and Orville's children, Andy had been her favorite. His hair was a fiery red, and despite the family's poverty and his father's drunkenness, Andy's freckled face was always smiling.

Pain stabbed her as it all came flooding back again. Andy had gone off to fight for the South, but had eventually pledged his allegiance to the North, more because of his fierce devotion to Travis than anything else, or so Kitty suspected. And it was in Travis' arms that Andy had died after being wounded at the Battle of Lookout Mountain. Sam had been there, and Poppa, too. Andy had died bravely, Travis told her, like a man, even though he had really been only a boy.

She winced, thinking of his father, Orville. A meaner man than Orville Shaw had never lived, unless it was Luke Tate. Luke, once overseer for Nathan's family, had been fired for attacking Kitty. In revenge, he had taken Kitty away with him and his vicious band of men. Orville Shaw had been part of that band. They had gone to the mountains of North Carolina, in the dead of winter, Luke feeling safe along that western Virginia–North Carolina border. That region of both states was against the war and it was open country. Luke and his men plundered, dressing as Confederates when they wanted to steal from Union sympathizers, and as Yankees when they wanted to steal from Southerners. Luke seemed at ease where loyalties divided people.

It was on one of their plundering raids that Orville Shaw had been shot. Luke had brought him back to the cabin and ordered her to treat the injury. The bones of his elbow had been splintered, and she knew from all Doc Musgrave had taught her that there was nothing to do but amputate. She had never done an amputation before, and had never seen one done without anesthesia. But she remembered everything Doc had told her, and she performed the surgery, calling on her memory and God to help her.

Later she went outside for water and just kept right on going, even at the risk of freezing to death, for she wanted only to escape Luke and his evil. But he had come after her, had been about to ravish her right there in the snow, when suddenly the Yankees arrived.

A smile lit her face as she remembered looking up into the coldest eyes she had ever seen. They were the color of steel, not blue or black, but a gray luster in between. The man's hair was shining black, the color of a raven's wing, and despite the anger on his face, he was quite handsome.

She had thrown herself on his chest in desperation, beating at him with her fists as she told him she had to go back home to care for her mother, to help her people.

He had ignored her pleas, staring down at her with those damn shining eyes. Then he had whispered, "You're beautiful. I can see why a man would hold you his prisoner if he couldn't keep you in his bed any other way."

She had exploded with anger, furious over the way his eyes raked over her body. He knew she wanted him to kiss her. "I demand you take me home," she had screamed at him.

And he had quietly whispered, "Miss Wright, I don't think you understand. You see, I'm Captain Coltrane of the *Union* Army, and you are now *my* prisoner."

Kitty laughed softly, sitting there in the decaying cabin. That was how she had met Travis. At the time, she felt it was only the continuation of her nightmare. But while there had been anger and rage, there had also been sweetness and passion. Fire and passion. Man and woman. Desire and love mixed with hatred. No, she would never tell John of this private world she had shared with his father. She only prayed that one day she would know the same joy, the same all-consuming love.

Lost in reverie, she screamed as a man's shadow appeared in the doorway.

"Don't be frightened," called a familiar Virginia accent. "It's me, Kitty. I was worried about you and I followed you."

"Jerome!" She scrambled to her feet, furious. "How did you know I was here?" she demanded.

His voice was closer now, as he made his way across the room. "I saw you pass my store as I was closing up. I could see there was a bad storm brewing, so I decided to follow you in my carriage and offer to take you home. I had some problems with my horse's harness, though, and you got ahead of me. This was the first shelter, and I assumed you would be here."

"And you assumed I would want to ride with you," she snapped. "Jerome, how many times do I have to tell you that I just don't want your help? We can never be friends. Please leave. I'll be on my way as soon as the rain lets up."

"It isn't going to let up. Not tonight. I've seen too many of these spring storms. You will be here till daylight, and it isn't safe for you to continue on your way alone, anyway, not the way these lowlands flood after a rain like this."

"I would rather take my chances with the lowlands than be alone with you, Jerome Danton." She placed her hands on her hips. Her eyes flashed in the darkness. "I'm warning you. Get out of here and just leave me alone."

"Or what?" He laughed. "What can you do, Kitty? We're all alone in the midst of a raging storm. But the storm is no wilder than the one in me, the one that has been tossing around inside me since the first time I laid eyes on that beautiful body of yours."

He lunged at her, hands groping for her breasts, squeezing roughly as his lips mashed hers.

"Now I will have you, my dear," he whispered harshly, maneuvering his leg behind her knees to knock her off balance, lowering her quickly to the floor, and then falling on top of her.

He silenced her screams with his mouth, and when she bit

his lip, he jerked the bodice of her dress down, pinching her left nipple brutally. "Try that again, you little spitfire, and I'll pinch it off."

He squeezed harder, and she moaned with pain.

"You bastard!" A woman's shriek split the stillness. "You goddamn, sneaking bastard! And you, you slutty bitch! I suspected all along you'd go after my husband the first chance you got!"

There was a sudden flash, a split-second spark, and then a lantern was lit.

"Nancy, no!" Jerome was on his knees, staggering to his feet, arms spread in a pleading gesture. "She lured me here. I had no idea what she had in mind. She—"

"Just shut your lying mouth!" Nancy cried, holding the lantern higher. "I can see well enough what was going on here. Did you think I wasn't watching you? I followed you here, gave you just enough time so I would catch you in the act."

"It isn't like you think," he repeated, beginning to recover his dignity. "You know what a conniving little hussy she is. She needs money. She tricked me. She pretended to be in trouble."

"And you fell for it," Nancy sneered. "Like all the other men she has charmed with her evil ways. I know her well, my husband. She has caused me pain for many years. But no more."

Kitty had reached for the shreds of her bodice and jerked it across her. Sitting up, she faced Nancy angrily and cried, "You conceited fool! How dare you believe that I want your husband? Jerome followed me here and tried to rape me. You may rest assured I am going straight to the marshal. I will even show him the bruises on my breasts if I have to. Neither of you are going to get away with blaming me for this." She stood up, holding the bodice across herself with her right arm.

"I am sick of you, Nancy!" Kitty's voice cracked. Her knees were wobbling. "How many times have you hurt me? I've lost count. But no more."

"Stay right where you are!"

Jerome gasped, "My God, Nancy, put that gun away!"

"I won't use it unless she makes me," Nancy said menacingly. "But believe me, I will use it, and I won't have a moment's regret."

Kitty blinked. "You . . . you are *mad!*" she whispered, shaking her head.

Nancy smiled, lips curling back. Her teeth looked like fangs. "Perhaps I am mad, Kitty Wright. Having to worry about you stealing every man I ever wanted is enough to make any woman lose her mind. But I am getting rid of you once and for all. No more will you hurt me, Kitty."

Jerome took a step forward, but Nancy waved the gun at him and screamed, "I will use this if you make me, Jerome. Now I want you to get out of here. Get out of here and get in your carriage and go back to town. I'll handle this."

He looked from her to Kitty uncertainly, then returned his gaze to Nancy. "I can't leave you here like this. I can't leave you just to shoot her, Nancy. Now put the gun away, and we can talk."

"Talk, indeed!" Nancy laughed shrilly. "Just go home, my loving husband. I will follow you later. And don't worry. I won't shoot the scheming little bitch unless she forces me to."

"But what are you going to do?" he stammered.

Nancy held the lantern high with her left hand, while her right held the gun unwaveringly pointed at Kitty. Turning her head slightly so that he could see the contemptuous look she was giving him, she said evenly, "I am losing my patience, Jerome. Get out of here. I will deal with you when I return."

He shook his head adamantly. "No. I am not going to leave you here to do something crazy. You are my wife, and you will do as I say."

She raised an eyebrow, eyes glittering with amusement. "Oh, so now it's *you* giving orders, is it? Do not make me any angrier than I already am, Jerome. The only reason I haven't shot you is that I know Kitty and the spell she casts over men. I realize you can't help yourself. But you would be wise not to interfere. After all, you should know that I am aware of your shady dealings through the years, and if I tell what I know about your crooked business methods you will wind up behind bars for the rest of your worthless life."

He gasped in outrage, working his lips silently before exploding, "You don't know what the hell you're talking about. I won't listen to such threats."

"You yellow-bellied bastard!" Nancy's screams raged above the storm. "If you don't get out of here, I'll shoot both of you and be done with it."

"Go ahead! Shoot her! Hang for it! They hang women, you know."

While he was speaking, he was limping slowly backward toward the door.

"I don't give a damn what you do, woman. You're crazy. You've always been crazy. I was a fool to marry you."

Reaching the door, he turned and lurched through it, disappearing into the howling wind and wild, driving rain.

Drenched to the skin, he reached his carriage and pulled himself up. Lost in thought, Jerome Danton did not see the figure of a man sitting atop his horse. The man watched, water dripping steadily from the brim of the hat pulled down tightly around his face. He was soaked to his bones, but he did not mind.

The man gazed steadily at the cabin, trying to make out the figures inside.

His waiting was almost over.

Chapter Five

NANCY'S smile flickered. "My, my, Kitty, I do have to admit you have some nerve. Here I stand, pointing a gun right at your heart, and you don't appear the least bit nervous. Maybe you really are a witch, and you've cast a spell over yourself to make you strong and brave so you won't give me the satisfaction of seeing you squirm."

Kitty stared directly into her eyes without flinching. "If I could cast spells, I would have turned you into the snake you are long, long ago, Nancy."

Nancy's upper lip curled back over her teeth. "I don't plan to kill you, you know. I never did. But you can talk me into it with your vicious tongue."

"Now," Kitty said calmly. "May we talk about this? Nancy? I am not after your husband, as you seem to think. I happen to love Travis very much. Jerome tried to rape me, and I'm glad you came along to stop him. I hope this will teach him a lesson. Now I would really like to be on my way."

Nancy kept the gun pointed steadily at her. "Do you think I'm going to worry constantly about my husband just because you can't hang onto Travis?"

Without giving Kitty a chance to reply, she rushed on, gloating, "I knew you would never be woman enough for a man like Travis. He only married you because you got yourself pregnant. He had to do the honorable thing. I'm not surprised he left you." Like a coiled spring, Nancy continued, "You are not getting Jerome. He may not be the handsomest man in the world, nor the greatest lover, but he happens to be quite rich, and that is all that interests me. He belongs to me, and I'm going to keep him."

"Do so. With my blessings." Kitty was weary and getting angry. "Dear Lord, Nancy, I want nothing to do with Jerome. Just put that gun away and let me go home. My little boy is waiting, and I'm sure Mattie is worried sick by now."

Nancy giggled mischievously. "Mattie is going to be even sicker, and your little boy is going to wait forever for his mommy to come home, because you aren't going home, Kitty. Not tonight. Not tomorrow. Not ever. Once and for all, I am getting you out of my life."

Kitty had had enough. "Then you're going to have to use that gun, damn it, because I'm not standing around here listening to your ravings any longer."

She walked across the cabin to where the mare was tied, unfastened the reins from the nail, and moved toward the door, leading her horse. She knew the gun might fire at any moment, but that was the chance she had to take.

Kitty and the mare moved through the door into the storm and rain outside. Suddenly Kitty froze, shock paralyzing her.

"It can't be. . . ." The words were torn from the depths of her soul.

The man stood a few feet away, legs spread, hands on his hips. Water still ran from his hat brim in a steady rain and his black poncho ran with water. His yellowed, chipped teeth gleamed as his lips spread in a triumphant grin.

"It *is* me, Kitty," he chuckled. "I've been waitin' a long time for this."

"No!" She backed into the doorway again, dropping the mare's reins. "Not you! Oh, God, not you. You're dead. You were killed."

"By them Injuns?" He hooted. "Naw, it'd take more than a bunch of crazy Injuns to kill me off, woman. I been around, and I figured one day we'd meet up again if you didn't get yourself killed in the war. Now I see you're as alive as ever and lookin' mighty fine."

He reached out to touch her, but she shrank away, still staring at him wildly. "Don't touch me, Luke Tate. I'd rather die than have you touch me."

Luke looked beyond her to where Nancy was standing, and the two exchanged grins over Kitty's terrified state. Then Nancy walked over and handed the gun to Luke, then turned to smile at Kitty. "Luke and I are old friends, you know. He is one of the few people who remembers how Nathan and I loved each other before *you* stepped in to interfere."

"That's right, Nancy." Luke nodded, his heavily hooded eyes never leaving Kitty's stricken face. He was enjoying her fright, her submission to the inevitable. "Them two loved each other, but you're evil. Why, hell, woman, look at all the *evil* things you made me do."

Luke's laugh was deep and guttural.

"I told Luke how you used to make eyes at Jerome," Nancy continued, "and I told him how, with Travis gone, I knew you'd be after him again. He agreed to help me out . . . for a price." She glanced at Luke sharply.

His response was quick and defensive. "Don't throw that money up to me, woman. You said you wanted me to get her far away from here, and I told you I was broke. Hell, I was lookin' to rob the bank when that fool, Bucher, got out of town, but this is a much better deal than havin' to kill that greenhorn marshal that took his place."

Some of the shock was subsiding, and Kitty's anger gave her the courage to find her voice. "This is insane. I don't know what you two devils have in mind, but you will never get away with it."

Luke's hand snaked out to wrap around her waist and pull her tightly against his chest. She reached up with her free hand to rake her nails down his face, screaming with rage, and he slapped her hard. Kitty sprawled to the floor as Nancy laughed shrilly.

"Oh, I'm enjoying all of this," Nancy cried, her face mirroring triumph. "I wish I could stay and watch the fun, but I really have to get back home."

Kitty was struggling to get up, but Luke placed his mud-caked boot on her stomach and held her on the floor. Above her screams, he called to Nancy, "Have you figured out a way to explain your pulling that much of your old man's money out of the bank?"

"Of course. I'm just going to tell him the truth."

Luke's eyebrows shot up. "Are you crazy? We agreed that nobody was supposed to know I've been in town."

"Well, how did I know Jerome would follow her out here tonight?" she snapped belligerently.

"I could have made up something about the money," she rushed on, staring up into Luke's narrowed, suspicious eyes, "but now he's going to ask all sorts of questions when it spreads around town that Kitty is missing. The fool might think I really did kill her and hid her body. So I'll just tell him the truth—that I paid someone to get her out of the way once and for all."

"And what if he decides to go to the law and tell them about it?"

"He won't," Nancy sounded happy and contented. "I know enough about him to put him in jail. He'll keep his mouth shut, believe me. You don't have a thing to worry about. Just take her and go." She looked down at Kitty with smug satisfaction, watching her squirming on the floor.

Luke chewed his lower lip thoughtfully for a moment, then said, "I reckon it's all right. I'll be so damn far away it won't matter nohow, and you say that sonofabitch Coltrane won't be back?"

"I told you about the scene at the train station," she snapped impatiently. "If he does come back, it will only be to get their brat."

"He will come back," Kitty shrieked, beating at the floor with her fists, "and he'll kill both of you."

"Oh, shut up, damn you. I'm sick of listening to your squawlin'." He reached down and twisted his fingers in her hair and yanked painfully. She continued to scream, and he yanked harder, warning, "I'll pull every bit of it out if you don't shut up, woman. There'll be plenty of time for you to yell later, and you can bet I'll give you somethin' to yell about!"

Kitty fell silent, and Luke released his grip. Reaching down, he jerked her to her feet. "Now we're leavin' here, girl, 'cause I want to put some distance between us and this town by daylight. If you make one sound, I'm gonna stop ridin' and beat the hell outta you. You understand?"

She nodded, head aching, face stinging yet from his slap. She stared at Nancy silently, conveying her hatred in a look that made Nancy step backward, startled. "I will get you for this, Nancy," Kitty said in a low, ominous whisper. "And if I don't, you can be sure you will answer in hell one day for all your evil."

She screamed sharply as Luke gave her hair another vicious

yank. "I told you to shut your mouth, and I mean it. Now let's get goin'." He gave her a quick shove in the direction of the mare. "Get on that nag and don't try nothin' funny, or I'll tie you across the saddle."

Kitty stumbled, throwing her arms around the mare's neck for support. Looking at each of them in turn, she could feel the heat of her own hatred emanating from her eyes. She knew she should feel terror, for the memories of past encounters with Luke Tate were branded on her soul. But for the moment, she was too enraptured with fury to be scared.

"I'm not afraid of you, Kitty," Nancy sneered. "I never was. You deserve everything you're getting. Maybe now, with you out of the way and Travis Coltrane out of the South, poor Nathan can rest in peace."

"You'd better be afraid of me, Nancy," Kitty retorted, forcing herself not to leap for that smug, spiteful face. "Your day will come."

"I told you to get on that goddamned horse." Luke took a menacing step forward and Kitty quickly mounted.

He began to lead her from the cabin, and Nancy hurried alongside. "I'll follow you back to town."

"No. Hell, we ain't goin' back through town. We're movin' in the other direction."

"But . . . but you said you'd see me back to town," Nancy stammered, whining, suddenly frightened. "It's a long ride, and it's nighttime and raining, and I'm all alone. It's not safe for a lady to be out alone."

Luke snorted his laughter. "Pity the man who happens upon you, Nancy. It'd be the best thing that ever happened to Jerome Danton if lightnin' struck and killed him on his way home tonight. Then he'd never have to put up with your misery again."

"That . . . that's a fine thing for you to say after I set you up with all that money," she sputtered. She slipped in the mud, almost falling, then righted herself quickly as she rushed on. "I set you up good, I did. And you got Kitty. You said yourself you'd always wanted her."

"Makes me feel even better to know I'm taking her away from that sonofabitch Yankee that killed all my men," Luke mused aloud.

"Listen to me," Nancy shrieked as the rain and wind snuffed out her lantern. "You can't just ride off and leave me here. I gave you the money to get all the way to Nevada."

"Damn right you did. You wanted her out of the way, and I'm obliging you. That money ain't gonna last forever, you know, and I want to go after silver. Folks are gettin' rich findin' silver in Nevada. But my main concern right now is gettin' the hell out of these parts as quick as I can before people start lookin' for her, and that won't be long."

Kitty listened to them argue as the rain pelted down. It no longer mattered that she was cold and wet and hungry. She could think only of John. What would he think when his mommy did not come home? What would Mattie tell him? How could she hope that anyone would search for her when no one but Nancy knew what had happened?

Think! She commanded her weary, angry brain. *Think! You've been in bad situations before, and you've survived. Four years in that damn war and you survived. You've got a son to think about now.*

Suddenly hope sprang all the way up from the depths of her tormented soul, and she cried out, "Have either of you thought about Travis? He'll move heaven and earth to find me. And he'll kill both of you."

"Keep talkin', woman, and I swear, I'm gonna gag you and tie you across that saddle," Luke cried. "You can forget about that bastard. He won't know where to start lookin'."

"I certainly won't tell him," Nancy spoke up in her high-pitched voice. Then she begged Luke once more, "Please ride with me back to town. You can't leave me out here."

They had struggled through the mud and reached the dark outline of a grove of trees just across the road. Luke found his horse tethered there and mounted. He stared down at Nancy and said evenly, "I'm not goin' back to town and that's final. Now if you're scared to go by yourself, the best thing for you to do is go back inside that cabin and wait till daylight. We're gettin' out of here."

Her shrieks and curses carried above the wailing of the storm as Luke headed in the direction opposite town, leading Kitty's mare by the reins.

They had not gone far when Kitty realized she had a chance to escape. Nancy was sure to have left a horse somewhere nearby. All she had to do was leap from the mare, run into the darkness and follow Nancy, then take the horse from her.

Gasping, Kitty threw her right leg over the back of the horse and jumped to the ground, miring ankle-deep in mud.

"Hey!" Luke cried, and as she ran she could hear him scrambling from his horse.

She ran through the muck as fast as she could, desperation driving her.

"You're gonna be sorry you did that!" Luke cried hoarsely, close behind. "I'm gonna fix you good, woman."

The sky turned a bright yellow for just an instant, but it was long enough for Kitty to spot Nancy about fifty feet down the road, struggling to get on her horse. Kitty moved faster through the quagmire, reaching Nancy, and did not hesitate to shove her aside, ignoring Nancy's cry of pain as she struck the ground. Then she grabbed the horse around the neck, swung herself up, and kicked him hard in the flanks.

"No, hell, you don't!"

She felt hands groping for her. The horse reared on his hind legs, hooves frantically thrashing the darkness above and around him. Then Luke got his fingers into the horse's mane. Yanking, pulling, he got the horse's front legs down and took hold of the reins.

"You won't give me no more trouble, you bitch."

Luke sprang upwards, hands closing about her throat as he yanked her from the horse. She felt his fist smash into the side of her head, and then her face struck the cold, muddy earth and she felt herself slip away into a deep, dark void. Just before she gave way to it, she saw John's little face floating before her.

Kitty felt a sharp, probing pain from the other side of that heavy drape that was keeping her from the real world. Her head hurt. She did not want to leave where she was and go to the other side of that drape. Something inside was telling her to stay here, here in this inky black world, but pain was pulling her, awakening her, forcing her to open her eyes.

She looked up and screamed, screamed until Luke Tate's hand closed around her throat.

"Now listen to me," he said in a reasonable tone. "If you'll notice, it's daylight. We're a good piece from back yonder, and we're deep enough in the woods so's I don't imagine nobody could hear you scream, but I'm tired, and I just plain don't feel like listening to you. So I want you just to shut up."

She made deep, rasping sounds as she struggled to breathe.

"You're chokin', Kitty, honey, and I don't want to kill you. I want to enjoy you for a long, long time. So I'm gonna let you breathe, but if you start screamin', then I may just have to go ahead and shut you up for good. Bad as I'd hate to kill a fine piece of woman-flesh like you, I'll do it. You understand me?"

He released her abruptly, and she gasped, clutching at her aching throat. He knelt over her, watching her with glittering eyes. She glanced around and saw that they were in a thicket. She could not see beyond it. Where they were, she had no idea.

"Now what we're gonna do, Kitty," he spoke as though she were a child, "is get somethin' from my saddlebags and you're gonna fix us some vittles. We're gonna eat and rest a spell. Maybe even take some time for some lovin'. You like it, and you know you do."

He looked down at her and chuckled, reaching to pinch her nipple and laughing out loud as she cringed.

"We've got a long way to go," he continued, watching her intently. "All the way to Nevada. I'll bet you don't even know where that is, do you?"

She did not answer, but lay still, staring up at him in mute terror. The anger had turned to fright. Fear, grasping as surely as his fingers had grasped her throat, was inching its way through her, taking control of her.

He talked on, fondling her breast gently, then moving his fingertips down to caress her belly. "Well, we go up through Tennessee and then head due west. We'll go through Missouri, Kansas, Colorado, and then Utah. It's pretty country, Kitty, real pretty. I've been there once, when I was on the run after that Injun raid. Decided I'd had my bellyful of war and all that went with it. So I know the way. Now I hear there's a silver boom goin' on, and I want in on it."

His fingers slid down to her thigh. His touch was possessive yet tender, and she continued to lie there motionlessly and stare at him blankly.

"I plan to get rich, Kitty. You'll live like a queen. I promise you that. You're gonna be my woman. For always and always."

He smiled at her fondly. She was bewildered. Luke Tate was evil, surely a spawn of the devil himself, and yet he was stroking her gently and speaking softly and smiling as though . . . he cared for her. He must know that she would plunge a knife into his heart if given a chance. What was wrong with Luke? Why was he acting this way?

He leaned over to brush his lips against her cheek before saying in a strained voice, "I gotta tell you somethin', Kitty, and I want you to know I'm tellin' the truth. All them times I was mean to you, I didn't like doin' it to you. I swear I didn't. You was always special to me."

He leaned back, an incredulous expression taking over his grizzled face. "I swear it. I know you think I'm mean and rough but you made me be that way 'cause you always fought me. I liked your spirit, sure, but not your fightin' me off. Just one time, I wanted to see you use that spunk to show me how much you enjoyed what I was doin' to you."

He trailed his fingertips down her face as though touching a delicate work of art. "Beautiful. I swear you are the most beautiful woman I ever saw. Back when I was overseer for them snooty Collinses, and that young buck, Nathan, was courtin' you, I'd watch the two of you and I'd want you so fierce I'd have to go find me a nigra gal and take my pleasure with her. All the time, it was your face I was seein' . . . your body I was touchin'."

He sat up, his brown eyes wide, gesturing in a plea for understanding. "Kitty, you just gotta believe me. What I'm tryin' to say is that despite the way I've treated you, I think underneath it all, I loved you. That's why I want you with me now. That's why I aim to keep you with me always, and I'll kill any sonofabitch that tries to take you away from me. Nobody ever will, Kitty. I promise."

He clamped his hands on her shoulders and pulled her up to a sitting position. "It's gonna be good times from now on, Kitty, darlin'. You'll see. Now, I know you'll miss that youngun o' yours, but we'll have kids of our own. I don't care so long as you don't get all fat and loose on me, you know?" he laughed shakily. "I love that body o' yours, and I don't want nothin' changin' it. We're gonna have the good life out in Nevada. You might not think so now, but if you'll just relax and believe in what's gonna be, then you can be happy."

He cocked his head to one side and stared at her, eyes squinted as he studied her face quizzically. "Hey." He gave her a little shake, and when she did not respond but continued to look back at him silently, blankly, he shook her harder. He kept on shaking her till her head bobbed like a cornshuck doll's.

"Hey!" he yelled finally. "What's wrong with you? Say somethin'. I been sittin' here pourin' out my guts to you, woman, and you're starin' at me like one o' them loonies. Answer me. You tell me what I been sayin' is just fine with you, that you understand that's the way it's gonna be, that you're gonna be my woman from now on, and you're gonna like it, 'cause you know I mean what I say, and if you let me, I'll be good to you."

Kitty felt herself somewhere far, far away, staring down at herself from someplace up above. The mute creature with that evil man was not she, but a living thing that was also dead. The spirit was gone. The body breathed on but the soul could no longer feel pain or dread or worry. It was as though all that was Kitty had gone away.

"Goddamn you, say something!" he screamed, slapping her so hard her head snapped back. Then he exploded, "See what you made me do, you bitch? Made me hurt you again! You like for me to hurt you? You like for me to beat you? Didn't you hear me just get through sayin' how I'd rather be good to you 'cause, damn it, I think I love you?"

He slapped her again, harder. "You speak to me or I'll kill you, Kitty Wright." He was nearing hysteria, furious with her and with himself. "You tell me you're gonna make the best of it, 'cause I swear to you I'll see you dead before you leave me again."

"I wish . . ." she spoke in a feathery voice so frail it was caught on the wind and swept away, "I wish I were dead."

He jerked away, stunned.

"I think . . ." she forced the words past numb lips, "I think I am already dead."

Her eyes closed, long, silky lashes sweeping against ivory-smooth cheeks. She went limp. Luke carefully lowered her body back to the ground.

She was breathing. He knew she was alive, but a cold chill passed through him as he saw that something in her *had* died. A part of her really was dead.

And as Luke stared down at her, he wondered whether Kitty would ever live again.

Chapter Six

TRAVIS did not have to open his eyes and look outside to see that it was raining. The rumble of the thunder matched the constant throbbing in his head. Another night spent soaking up too much rum, and the only thing that was going to ease his pain was to get up and start drinking again.

Damn the rain. It had poured every day and every night since he had arrived in Haiti. Someone had said there were two rainy seasons—April to June and August to October. That meant he could look forward to July. It was nice to have at least that much to anticipate, even if the blasted rains came again after one month.

He licked his dry lips. Blast it, did everything have to taste of rum? He felt disgusting, saturated by the sickly sweet drink, but at least it helped ease his emptiness for a little while. He fingered his recently grown beard and thought about opening his eyes but decided against it for the moment. He did not want to know just yet whether the girl was still lying beside him. Probably she was, for it was, after all, her hut. He remembered staggering down the road sometime during the night, with her helping him, the two of them entering the thatched-roof hut with its dirt floor. He vaguely recalled her undressing him, fondling him between his legs, and finally cursing him in that strange mixed language of French and Spanish that she used when she was angry. Which was often.

The straw in the mattress beneath him was starting to prickle his bare buttocks. Soon he would have to get up and get dressed and get the hell out of that place. There would be another day of drinking rum, staring out at the mountains, and wondering what the hell he was doing in Haiti.

Haiti, he had been told by one of the government officials on the voyage over, was an old Indian word meaning mountainous land. He could well believe it. The mountains were densely wooded with peaks that rose to great heights. The tallest, Pic la Selle, was almost nine thousand feet high.

At first, Travis had enjoyed exploring. It was something to do besides brooding, which he had begun doing when he'd found out that his only role here was to serve as a marshal, of sorts, should he be needed. He hadn't been needed so far, so there was much free time. Wandering around the coastline of cliffs, broken by indented coves and harbors, had been an adventure at first. In some places the mountains rose straight from the sea. He had enjoyed learning of the different kinds of fine woods found in these forests, mahogany, oak, pine, lignum vitae, cedar, satinwood, and rosewood. He had never seen some of them before and doubted he ever would again. In an arid area there had also been cacti and a tiny tree called a dwarfed thorn.

He had not minded the food so much, either. *Diri et djon-djon*, a concoction of rice and black fried mushrooms, served with a sauce of onions and herbs called *ti malice,* had been particularly tasty. There were ample tropical fruits growing wild, but the peasants mostly ate rice and beans.

So, he thought with eyes still closed and the straw still prickling his buttocks, he could get up and eat some beans or rice, and then go wander around the coves or into the forest and get soaking wet in the infernal rain. And a little later he could get soused on rum and wind up in bed again with Molina.

Molina. Lord, she was beautiful. Of course, he had not seen too many native girls who were not lovely. But there was just something special about Molina. Her skin was black and shiny, and her body molded into delicate curves that made a man's fingers itch to reach out and touch. Her coffee-colored eyes were fringed with thick, silky lashes, but good God, they could spit fire when she was in one of her rages.

Molina was, no doubt, a descendant of the slaves from Africa who had been imported to replace a race of people called

Arawaks, exterminated by the Spaniards in the 1600s. Masters intermingling with slaves through the years had produced a class of mulattoes, and Louis XIV had declared them free.

Molina, he figured, was part African, part French, part Spanish, with a little bit of English slipped in somewhere down the line. She was darker than most of the other people on the islands.

He let his breath out in a long sigh. Damn it, he had never meant to take up with another woman, but he had never been the kind of man to go without one for long. Besides, he had nothing else to do with his time besides drink and make love. If there had even been Sam around to talk to, but how in the hell was he supposed to know Sam would be sent with the other committee to Santo Domingo, for Christ's sake?

Travis did not remember much about the train trip to Washington. He was drunk when he got on the damn thing and drunk when he got off, and Sam kept pouring hot coffee down his throat and telling him if he didn't sober up he'd get left behind, but he didn't give a damn. He just wanted to stay in a stupor.

Somehow he wound up on the boat, and the second day one of the men on the committee came around and told him it was time he sobered up. Travis had agreed. He felt like hell by then and could not remember the last time he had eaten. With solid food in his stomach, a bath, and clean clothes, he had gone in search of Sam, and that's when he learned his friend was on another ship heading for another place.

He felt a stirring beside him, then the cool touch of fingers wrapping around his penis, gently squeezing. He felt himself rising.

"You make up for last night, no?" Molina's voice was as soft as her touch. "You make Molina feel like a real woman, for you are such a real man. See what I make you do? Oh, *mon,* but you are big. I never had a *mon* so big before."

"Molina, you never had a man before I came along, and you know it," Travis said wearily. Her virginity was a sore subject with him. Damn it, he never would have taken her if he had known she had never lain with a man, but she still continued to pretend to be grown up and sophisticated in the ways of womanhood. He still had not been able to get the truth out of her about her age. She damn well was not the twenty years old she swore she was.

"Not this morning," he said firmly, grasping her wrist and

pulling her hand from his swollen organ. "My head feels like one of those blasted drums that beat every night, and I think I might be sick."

"Too much rum again," she said petulantly. "Molina is getting tired of her man being such a drunk. You do not please me. I think I will go to the *mambo* and tell her how you treat me, and she will call on the *loa* to make you want me."

Travis' eyes flashed open and turned to stare down at her in fury and disgust. "Damn it, Molina, I have told you I will not listen to any of that voodoo nonsense. I don't believe in it, and I don't like it."

He swung his feet around and winced at the feel of the soggy mud floor. The rains had soaked the ground outside and seepage had moved into the cabin.

Glancing around, he spotted his boots far away and was obliged to walk through the squishy mire to retrieve them. His pants were tossed carelessly on the floor nearby, and as he pulled them on, he cursed because they, too, were damp.

"You should not make fun of things you do not understand." Molina's voice cut into the silence. "The *loa* will not like it. You could be punished. People have died. . . ."

Travis stood up. "Molina, I'm not listening to any more of this. I told you—I don't feel good. I'm going out to get something to eat. When I come back, I'll make it all up to you, I promise."

He swayed suddenly and realized he was still not rid of the alcohol he had consumed the night before. As he lowered himself slowly back to the bed, Molina hovered over him. "I see you are sick, Travis. Molina is sorry she is so mean to you. It is only that I want you so bad."

"Yeah, yeah, okay." Travis closed his eyes, threw his arm over his face. Damn. Bored or not, he was not going to drink any rum today. All he wanted was to get some food in his stomach and then sleep, if possible.

"You lie there, my beautiful *mon,* and Molina will prepare something that will make your insides feel not so sick."

He was too weak to protest, and soon she said, "Here. You eat."

He looked up to see Molina standing over him with a wooden bowl in her hands. She was smiling, her brown eyes warm.

"This will make you feel all better. The *mambo* said so."

Travis took the bowl and managed to keep from lashing out

at her about the *mambo*. There would be time, later, to talk to her about the fat old hag who ran the village where Molina lived. He was ravenous, and the hot, savory-smelling stew appeased his stomach quickly.

He had seen her only a few times, and there was something about her that made him want to take a stiff drink and hope she was only a nightmare. Old, fat, she wore some kind of white paint on her black face. Like most of the women around there, she wore only a cloth skirt wrapped about her hips and allowed her breasts to hang freely. Hang they did, all the way below her waist. Travis found the sight disgusting. He enjoyed viewing Molina's bare breasts, firm, with delectable nipples that resembled chocolate drops, just as he had liked seeing the naked breasts of the other island women. But the *mambo* was revolting.

Once he had asked Molina what those god-awful-looking things were that she wore hanging on a string around her neck. Molina had promptly told him not to ask questions about the *mambo,* but he had persisted, and after persuasion she had told him they were teeth. Human and animal.

"Strange jewelry," he had said sarcastically, figuring it was just a stupid native custom that only an old washed-up hog like the *mambo* would follow.

"Not jewelry," Molina had shrieked at him, eyes wild with fright. "You must not say such things. You do not understand *voodoo*."

She whispered the word with awe. Travis knew what voodoo was about. To the natives, like Molina, it was big magic. To Travis, it was bullshit. He had known about it before ever setting foot on Haiti. Many Negroes in the South, especially in his home state of Louisiana, as well as in Mississippi and Alabama, believed in voodoo. They also believed in zombies, bodies that voodoo rites supposedly brought back from the dead. He had talked to a Negro about it once, when they were both only boys and had fished in the bayou together on occasion.

The boy's name was Lemuel, and he had told Travis about the belief that a *bocor,* a sorcerer, possessed an evil power that enabled him to put a death spell on a victim. Then, after the victim was buried, the *bocor* would revive him and make him a slave.

Lemuel had said, trembling all the while, that a *bocor* could also resurrect a buried person who had died of natural causes. That was why, he explained, a dead person's family tried to have their relative's body buried in the part of the cemetery closest to a road, where there would be activity, so that the *bocor* would have difficulty digging up the corpse without being seen. Travis had considered the tale so much rubbish then, and he felt the same way now.

When he had finished eating the stew, he looked up at Molina and murmured his thanks, then his eyes fastened on her breasts, naked, inviting. He reached up to cup one, pulling her forward until he could fasten his lips about the nipple.

"You make me happy, yes?" she whispered eagerly, lowering herself on top of him, bracing her hands on either side of him to hold herself up. He continued to suckle. "You be big *mon* for Molina?"

The only woman Travis had ever liked to talk to while he was making love had been Kitty, and that was because he loved her and wanted to tell her so. In the beginning, it had been like the others—take what he wanted, but always make sure the woman was satisfied. That didn't take conversation.

But everything about Kitty had been different, he thought, a painful flash of memory going through him. Damn! He wanted to be with her, not with Molina, not with any other woman in the world. But she was not here, and Molina was, and he could only apologize for being a man, because already she was spreading her thighs to lower herself onto his shaft, undulating her hips to and fro but still leaning over him so that he could keep his lips on her taut nipple.

He closed his eyes, saw Kitty's face swimming before him, then opened them to see Molina, head thrown back, lips slightly parted as she moaned in unison with their steady rhythm. Cupping her buttocks, he pulled her tighter against him. She screamed out loud and he began to push upwards, plunging into her to meet her downward thrusts.

"So good . . ." she cried. "Oh, Travis, you are one big man, and you fill me up, and I must have you always."

Then she stopped talking and threw her head back farther. Her teeth sank into her lower lip, but she could not suppress the loud cry of joy as she climaxed against him. A few more quick thrusts, and he released himself, sighing contentedly, but still wishing foggily that it was Kitty he held.

"Again," Molina cried suddenly, pushing herself up and

down. "We do it again and again. I never get enough of you."

Travis swore under his breath as he gently lifted her up and off of him. "Not this day, lady. I've got to check in with the bosses and see if there's any word on when we'll be going home. There might even be work for me to do."

Seeing her eyes flash red, he playfully squeezed her breast and murmured appeasingly, "Tonight I won't let that devil, rum, get hold of me. I'll make it good for you all night long."

Suddenly she leaped from the bed, her hair flying wildly about her face. "You take me for a *jeunesse?* Or a *bousin?*" She screamed, stalking about the room and waving her arms. "I do not even have the reward of a *jeunesse* or a *bousin,* for you give me no money."

"You never asked for money." Travis felt his own ire rising, and he sat up to fasten his pants. She had deftly undone them in her eagerness. It was time, he figured, to leave, for he had seen her mad.

"I do not ask for money because I do not want money." She was shrieking. "I want to be your *placée.* Is that asking too much? At first I lie. I tell you I have been with men before, so you will think me smart in the ways of pleasing you, but you say yourself you know the truth, that I was virgin when you took me. You make me *placée!* You do not talk of leaving Haiti and returning to America!"

Travis tugged at his beard. *Placée.* What the hell was she talking about? Reaching for his boots, he decided not to hang around. "We'll talk later, Molina. I've got to be going."

She ran across the floor and threw herself at him, catching him off balance and knocking him backward across the bed. He stared up at her, stunned, as she shrieked, "No! We talk now. I already talk with *houngan.* I talk with *mambo.* Both say they talk with *hounsi,* and I become your *placée.* They say *wanga* power not working because you strong man. You not of our kind. You too strong. *Hounsi* will fix."

Travis had no idea what she was talking about, but there was something in her tone that made him realize he was in big trouble. Gently, he asked, "Molina, you know that I don't know what all those words you are using mean. Now calm down and explain." He tried to push her away, but she pressed down harder on his chest. He did not want to use force, so he just lay there and looked up at her in puzzled misery.

"You need *placée.* All men need *placée.* I deserve, because you were first man. I be good to you." She pushed back her black hair, which had tumbled across her forehead, and he saw the play of a smile on her lips. "You will like Molina. I give you many fine sons."

Travis muttered a quick "Uh-oh!" He caught her off guard, and shoved her quickly to one side. He leaped from the bed. "If you're talking about what I think you're talking about, you better understand something, Molina." He backed away, spreading his hands and hoping he sounded sympathetic. "Now, I never promised you anything except a good time in bed, and we had that. If that word *placée* means wife, I'm sorry you got the wrong idea, because I happen to have a wife at home that I love very much, and a son, and I'm going back there."

She had stopped listening at the word "wife." Eyes narrowed to slits, she moved on her hands and knees, crouching on the bed as though to spring at him like an angry panther. Her lips parted, and her teeth even looked like fangs, long and deadly. "You have *placée!*" She hissed accusingly. "You never tell Molina. You make fool of Molina."

Travis had had enough. He snatched his hat from a nail on the wall. "I never had to tell you a goddamn thing, Molina. You knew what you were doing. I never forced you."

He turned to leave, and that was when she sprang, leaping up from the bed to throw herself upon his back, arms going around him, hands and nails reaching for his face. He felt the flesh tear as he struggled to get her off of him, but she was digging in, clawing, screaming, and he turned around and around, trying to loosen her hold.

He felt a nail catch the corner of his eye and rip downward, and then he understood that it was time to forget she was a woman. Hell, he wasn't going to let her keep on till she blinded him. He threw himself backward against the wall, and the impact caused her to let go. She fell to the floor. Towering above her, blood streaming from his eye and mouth, he yelled, "Woman, are you crazy? If you were a man, I'd—"

"I am not man! I am woman!" Tears ran down her cheeks, but rage made her tremble as she lay looking up at him with a venomous glare. "You will not go home. You will stay here. Molina will be your *placée*. *Hounsi* will make it so. You will see."

"That's all I'm listening to, Molina, and it's over for us. I'm sorry if you got the wrong idea about things." He hurried from the hut into the torrential rain, heedless of the soaking he was getting. All he wanted was to escape from the sound of her shrieks.

He hurried down the muddy street, breaking into a run. He needed a drink, but he was damned if he would let whiskey or rum or anything else make him get involved with another woman. He would serve out his time on this infernal island and then he would head for home, where he would try to piece his life together, with or without Kitty. There was still John.

He finally reached the small hotel in Port-au-Prince that was serving as headquarters for the committee, and where he had a room. It wasn't much but it beat that hut of Molina's.

Suddenly Travis realized he did not like himself very much. Since arriving in Haiti, it seemed he had been steadily turning into a bum. It was time for a change. A bath, a shave, some decent food, and hot coffee, then to bed to sleep for the rest of the day and on into the night. Tomorrow he would feel like pulling himself together once again.

"Coltrane, you look like hell."

The voice came from a corner of the shadowy lobby. Travis turned quickly to see Eldon Harcourt rising from a chair to walk toward him, one eyebrow raised as his gaze raked Travis' appearance. "You look worse up close, man. Those are some nasty scratches. Better have them taken care of. Have you been messing with an island girl? I should have told you about them. They're dangerous."

Travis did not know Eldon very well, only that he was an aide to one of the politicians on the committee. Eldon had seemed friendly enough, but Travis had not been looking for friends.

"Eldon, how would you know so much about the women here?" Travis asked, not sarcastically but out of sheer curiosity. "This is your first trip here, isn't it? Yet you really do seem to know a lot about Haiti."

Eldon smiled. "I do. And you're right. It is my first trip here, but you see, my grandfather was involved in slave trading, and he lived here for many years. He brought my grandmother here from England, and my father was born here. They moved to America while my father was still a young boy. My grandmother was always frightened of voodoo, and I can remember Grandfather telling how she nagged him constantly to get her off of this evil island."

"Voodoo!" Travis shook his head in disgust. "Those infernal drums they beat at night. They are like children playing a game. I find it ridiculous."

Eldon frowned. "Don't make light of it, Coltrane. At least not while we are here."

"You believe in all that superstitious nonsense? Then I should introduce you to the native girl who damn near blinded me a short while ago. She was screaming names like *hounsi* and *houngan* and *wanga* power, and she did this to me because I wouldn't make her my *placée,* whatever the hell that is." He pointed to his face angrily. "The two of you might get along."

Travis did not miss the shift in Eldon's expression to one of sudden fright. "You *do* believe in that mumbo jumbo, don't you? And something I just said scared you. I'd like to know what."

Eldon glanced around, saw that no one else was in the lobby, and placed a hand on Travis' shoulder. He whispered, "Come with me to my room. I've some whiskey we can wash those scratches with, and you're going to need a drink when I finish telling you just what that girl was talking about." He sucked in his lower lip, face paling. "I hope it's not what I think it is."

Travis stood his ground. "Look, I appreciate your concern, but I just want to go to bed and forget the whole damn thing."

"No!"

He all be screamed the word, and Travis sobered. Eldon was no blabbering native. He was an American, by God, like himself, and something was frightening him.

Travis allowed himself to be led up the stairs and to Eldon's room. Eldon went to the rickety wooden dresser and grabbed the bottle of whiskey and a cloth. "Here, put this on your face and wash off that blood. I'll find some cups."

Travis winced as the alcohol touched his flesh. Looking in a cracked mirror, he cursed at the sight of his face. She had worked him over, all right, and he was lucky he still had his eyeball. He tilted the bottle to his lips and took a long, burning swallow.

"Sit down." Eldon motioned to the only chair in the room. He perched on the side of the sagging cot and sighed. "Tell me the whole story, everything she said. No, wait." His eyes widened. "First I want to know if you raped her."

"Raped her?" Travis hooted. "I've never raped a woman in my life!"

"All right, all right." Eldon waved his arms. "You did *do* it, though, didn't you?"

"If you mean did I take her to bed and make love to her, yes, I did. I was drunk, and she was all over me. Maybe I shouldn't have, but my whole damn life is a series of 'shouldn't haves.' I can't worry about every one." He took another long swallow from the bottle.

"Was she . . ." Eldon lowered his voice to a whisper. "Was she a virgin?"

Travis nodded, and Eldon cried, "Oh, God, no," and slapped his hands over his head, twisting his body from side to side.

Travis had had enough. "Goddamn it, man, will you get on with what you were so all-fired anxious to tell me? I'm getting a little tired."

Once more, Eldon held up his hands. "All right, but first tell me all the things she said to you about *houngans* and *wanga* power. Tell me all the words she used that you don't understand."

By the time Travis finished talking, Eldon looked about to faint. It was difficult to make out his words. "You . . . you are in big trouble, Coltrane. If I were you, I'd get out of Haiti as quickly as possible. Forget the committee, your job, everything. Just get *out* of here."

Travis calmly pulled a cheroot from his shirt pocket, saw that it was wet and soggy, then tossed it into a nearby spittoon. Spying one on Eldon's dresser, he got up and took it without asking. After lighting up and watching the smoke spiral, he faced the man and said in a low voice, "All right, I want to know exactly what you are talking about, Harcourt, and spit it out fast."

Eldon took a deep breath and then began talking in a great rush, as though if he did not get it all out quickly, he would not be able to tell it all. "You took a virgin. A young girl. She accused you of looking upon her as a *jeunesse*, what we call a mistress. You say she also accused you of not treating her as respectably as a *bousin*, a prostitute. So you were not paying her for the use of her body?"

"No, I wasn't," Travis drew on the cheroot, talking with his teeth clenched around it. "She never asked for money. She just wanted me to make love to her. I obliged. End of bargain."

"No," Eldon shook his head with dread finality. "The beginning of big trouble. She never wanted to be a *jeunesse* or a *bousin*. She wanted to be your *placée*, which is a common-law wife. She probably doesn't have a family, or she would have had them demand that you make her your lawful wife, called a *pas placée*.

"When she mentioned *houngan*, she was talking about a voodoo priest. A *mambo* is a voodoo priestess, a woman. They make things happen. They have the power. And speaking of power, when she said '*wanga* power,' she used a concoction to try to make you love her."

Travis' eyebrows shot up. "What kind of concoction?"

"Probably food with her nail and hair clippings mixed in, I imagine."

Travis fought the impulse to gag. Damn, what had he gotten himself into? He bit down hard on the cheroot. "Go on. What else has the wench done to me?"

"It's not what she *has* done," Eldon said, eyes wide. "It is what she is *going* to do to you. She spoke of *hounsi*. That is the spouse of the god. She has obviously been to the *houngan* and the *mambo* of her village, and they are going to use voodoo to make you want her, to make you stay here, in Haiti, and make a respectable woman of her since you took her virginity."

"Eldon, I don't know who's crazier, you or Molina. Now, maybe you believed your grandfather's fairy tales. That's nice. I can't remember having a grandfather and I've often wished I had. It must be nice to hear stories. But that is all they are. Stories."

"Then *listen* to my stories," Eldon sighed dismally. "Listen to me and then I think you will agree it best for you to leave Haiti at once."

He began by explaining how the voodoo rites had come from Africa to Haiti, and Travis interrupted to say that he had heard it was practiced in some parts of Louisiana. "That's where I was raised. In the bayou. I never believed in it then, either."

Eldon nodded, then went on to explain that in the early days of slavery in America, the voodoo priest carried on without attracting too much attention, but in time, the "possessions" or "seizures," as they were sometimes called, which occurred in the slave quarters, along with the sounds of the conical drums beating, attracted the attention of their masters. Afraid that it would make the slaves band together to rebel, the masters prohibited voodoo. It was decreed that anyone found possessing a voodoo symbol would be beaten and, sometimes to set an example, hanged.

Eldon explained how all of this cruelty merely made the slaves cling to their gods all the more tightly. "Voodoo did not die. It will never die."

"You still haven't told me anything to make me believe in it."

"I was trying to make you understand how *strong* it is." Eldon slammed his fist down on his knee. "Now I will tell you what it is really like."

Voodoo in Haiti, he described, was a systematic religion where the gods descended and possessed their worshipers, and the spirits of dead ancestors entered their living relatives to give them power.

Children, he said, were taught to be good for fear of punishment from the gods. They were taught not to allow their heads to get wet, particularly with dew, for it was believed that water was a magnet for spirits, and a spirit of a person lives in the head.

At night, bogies were about. Doors and windows were carefully closed to keep them out. Some, however, could get inside no matter what precautions were taken. These were the *loup-garous* who sucked children's blood. They could be seen whizzing through the night as bright lights.

The middle of the day was considered terribly dangerous, for that was the time when no man cast a shadow, and his soul was said to disappear. With soul and shadow together, a spirit flew around looking for a body to make a home in.

"Then there is the *tonton macoute,* a witch doctor of sorts," Eldon continued. "He carries such medicines as dead spiders and live centipedes, or the heart of a cat."

Eldon looked at Travis with deep sympathy. "What I am trying to tell you, Travis, is that you have made this girl very angry. You have scorned her. She has gone to a *houngan and* a *mambo,* and these are great priests. They got their position by going through an initiation that is too horrible to describe. My grandfather never saw one, but he said the rites lasted forty days or more. They ate spiders, bugs, and raw animals. They were put through all manner of misery and sickness. They even walked on fire—stones placed in saucers with hot rum poured over them and set aflame.

"These priests," Eldon said firmly, "come out of the initiation *as* priests, and they can call on the *loas,* the gods, to invoke their spells and do all kinds of evil. They can kill. They can raise the dead and make zombies of them. Don't you see? There is no telling what the girl is going to ask the *houngan* to do to you."

"Kill me? Raise me from the dead?" Travis scoffed. "Make a zombie out of me? Yes, I've heard of zombies." He recounted the story the little Negro boy had told him about why graves were placed near well-traveled places.

"That is true. That is true." Eldon nodded enthusiastically, as though he were finally getting through to the skeptical man before him. "A zombie has no soul and only goes through the motions of life. It's a slave, compelled to follow his master's bidding forever, doing the hardest labor possible, fed only a flat, unseasoned food called *bouillie*."

Eldon leaned forward, clasping and unclasping his perspiring hands. "My grandfather even told me how it happens. A sorcerer goes to someone's hut late at night with an empty corked bottle and a hollow bamboo rod. When he's sure his victim is sound asleep, for that is when the soul is completely unprotected by its owner, he whispers an incantation to Damballa, the god of the home, invoking Damballa to look the other way so he won't see what is being done."

He rushed on excitedly. "He puts the end of the bamboo rod against the slit under the door and sucks out the soul of the person inside. Then he spits it into the bottle and puts a cork on it. He goes home, sacrifices a hen to Damballa, recites an incantation of gratitude. Then he buries the soul, imprisoned in the bottle, along with the dead hen, under a big rock somewhere. All he has to do then is wait for his victim to die, which usually happens in around three days. The night he's buried, he goes to the graveyard, invokes the voodoo god Baron Samedi, the keeper of the dead, asking him to let him dig up the corpse without any interference. He digs up the body and sticks a freshly cut fern of a plant called *mouri leve* in its mouth. In just a few minutes, the corpse sits up."

He spread his hands in a gesture of finality and leaned back to await Travis' reaction.

Travis chuckled. "Now I'm actually glad I never knew my

grandfather. If he had told me wild tales like that, I think I would have broken his heart by calling him a senile old fool."

Eldon leaped to his feet. "Damn it, Coltrane, this is serious. You go to some of the government officials here and tell them what happened and see how fast they *help* you out of Haiti. From what you told me, this girl has already been to a *houngan*, and when she tells him about the episode today, you can believe that when you hear drums beating tonight, they will be beating at a rite calling on spirits to come down and help punish Travis Coltrane."

"Eldon, I'm so damn tired right now that by the time I have a few more drinks, I'm going to be so sound asleep they can use my *head* for a drum if they want to. I won't hear a thing."

Eldon began to pace the room nervously. "It's too late to apologize. The damage has been done. You took the girl's virginity. You refused to make her your *placée*. You rejected her and humiliated her. She was terribly angry or she would not have attacked you as she did. Right now she is probably with her *houngan* or *mambo*, making plans. No . . . it would do no good to go to her and apologize. You must leave at once."

"Look, Harcourt. I never meant to hurt Molina. She was lovely, and she offered herself to me, and I made love to her, and it was good for both of us. I never made her any promises, and I had no idea she was making plans. I tried to tell her that, but she wouldn't listen. She just went crazy. You're right, there's no need for me to go and see her and apologize, because it wouldn't do any good. I just hope to God I never see her again, anyway."

"So leave Haiti!" Eldon cried imploringly. "Lord, man, I heard this morning that we may be here for months yet. It seems that the committee has discovered some dirty dealings. Certain rich Americans have learned of President Grant's plan, and they're slipping in to buy up land on speculation, hoping to make a fortune. The committee is going to conduct a full investigation."

"I still have a job here. The pay is good, and you must admit the work is easy. You are summoned occasionally to take in brandy and cigars, and I wait around in case a marshal is needed for protection. It's an easy life, Eldon."

"If you don't get out of Haiti, the only life you will have is that of a zombie!" He yanked the empty whiskey bottle from

Travis' hand and threw it against the wall. Shards of glass scattered at his feet. "Listen to me, God damn you! Get out while you can."

"I think . . ." Travis yawned as he got to his feet and stretched, "that I'm going to get that bath and that food and those drinks I promised myself, and then I'm going to bed. When I wake up, I *will* leave Haiti."

Eldon breathed a sigh, sinking down on the cot in relief. He had finally gotten through to Travis. "Thank God! Oh, thank God, you're listening to reason."

"Yeah," Travis went on as though he had not spoken. "I think I'll take a few days off and find a boat to take me to Santo Domingo to look up Sam Bucher. By the time I get back, Molina will have a new lover, and everybody will be happy."

Eldon looked at him in weary disbelief. "You're coming back? After everything I've told you? You're coming back in only a few days?"

Travis smiled and walked to the door, pausing with his hand on the knob. "That's right, Eldon. You see, I've never been scared of a damn thing in my life."

With one final chuckle, Travis opened the door and walked out.

Eldon Harcourt sat on his cot for a long, long time, staring at the closed door. Travis Coltrane would not understand that he was a marked man. He was already dead, soon to walk the earth forever as the living dead, a zombie.

In the distance, the drums began to beat.

Chapter Seven

TRAVIS lay on his bed in the small, dingy hotel room and listened to the rhythmic falling of the never-ceasing rain. A hot bath, decent food, and a half bottle of rum could work miracles, he thought drowsily. Now he could get some much-needed sleep. When morning came, he would feel like setting out for Santo Domingo. Finding Sam had suddenly, for some reason he could not explain, become very important. He cursed himself for not going sooner. But why hadn't Sam come to him? Maybe the work Sam was doing was important, and he had not been relegated to sitting around, waiting.

Just lying there, peacefully waiting for slumber to take him, Travis could already think more clearly. He had not only discovered the urgent need to find Sam but now questioned the wisdom of having left home. Kitty had behaved strangely, but he had been too damned pigheaded to try to figure out that strange behavior. Something had been bothering her, just as he had been plagued with misery over the way they were living, but hell, why hadn't they talked it out? Why did it have to lead to this? And what, he asked again, had made Kitty act so strangely?

His eyelids grew heavier, closed, and sleep came, but only for an instant. Suddenly he was wide awake, staring toward the window. It was very dark. Hours must have passed. The rain was not quite so heavy but the roll of thunder was constant. Sleepily, he turned on his side and thought that a big storm was probably about to explode, but he was too tired to care. Let an ocean fall from the sky. He was going back to sleep. The thunder was getting louder. It was so rhythmic that it might have been drums beating, but he was too drowsy to listen.

A sharp rapping on the door brought him fully awake, and he sat up and yelled irritably into the darkness, "Who the hell is it?"

"Eldon Harcourt," the frightened voice called through the door. "Coltrane, I have to talk to you. Let me in."

His patience snapped. "Goddamn it, Harcourt, I'm not listening to any more of your superstitious drivel," he yelled. "Now go away and let me sleep or I'm really going to get mad."

"It's the drums. Can't you hear them?"

The man sounded almost hysterical, Travis realized.

"They're different tonight. I *know* what they mean. My grandfather had a drum like they use, and he beat out the different rhythms for me."

Travis wearily covered his face with his hands and asked tonelessly, "And what song are they playing tonight, Harcourt?" He really didn't care. He just wanted the man to go away. Eldon meant well, but damn it, he was making Travis mad.

"That's the beat they use for Baron Samedi. It's bad, Travis. Real bad. I told you about Baron Samedi. He's the king of the cemetery spirits. The drums have been beating like that for over an hour. If I remember everything Grandfather told me correctly, there is going to be a sacrifice tonight, Travis. *Sacrifice!*"

Travis got up and stomped across the room to unlock the door and fling it open. The man's voice had risen to an hysterical shriek, and as he stood there looking at him, Travis could see that he was scared out of his wits. Clamping his hand on Eldon's shoulder, he yanked him into the room.

Slamming the door behind him, Travis faced Eldon, pointing an angry, accusing finger. "Now listen to me, Harcourt. I wish to God I'd never told you a damn thing today, because it seems to have triggered some kind of insanity. I wish you could see yourself."

Eldon held out trembling arms. "Please, Coltrane, listen to me. You're in danger. Lock your doors and windows and make sure your guns are loaded. First thing in the morning, get out of here. They'll come for you tonight. I know they will. Listen!" His eyes widened, and he fell silent for a moment, then cried. "They're getting louder. Hear them? The drums are louder. They'll be coming soon."

Travis felt sorry for the man. Trying to make his voice gentle, Travis said, "Look. I only let you in here to try to calm you down before you woke everybody and they carried you away to wherever they put crazy people around here. Now believe me when I say I am not frightened, and while I appreciate your concern for my welfare, I wish you would just butt out of my business."

"Will you leave town in the morning?" Harcourt persisted, perspiration beading his forehead.

"I am going to Santo Domingo to look up an old friend of mine I think I told you about—Sam Bucher. He's with the committee there. I am not leaving because of any voodoo. Now will you just get out of here and let me get some sleep?"

Eldon sank down into a rickety chair, the only piece of furniture in the room other than the bed and the table beside it. His face was the color of snow, and he was shaking so hard Travis could hear his teeth clicking.

"Let me get you a drink. You're going to pass out on me, man," Travis murmured in disgust, going to the table where he had left the bottle of rum. Reaching for it, he thought that he must not have consumed as much as he remembered. The bottle was almost three-quarters full. Good. That meant he could indulge in one more drink, and Lord knew, after listening to this loony, he deserved another drink.

There were no cups or glasses, so he tilted the bottle, took a long gulp, then handed it to Eldon, who did likewise. "Now will you go to your room and get some sleep?" Travis asked gently.

Reluctantly, the man nodded but took one more drink before returning the bottle to Travis. "I tried, but you won't listen. I'm just going to have to save you from yourself."

Travis raised an eyebrow. "Now, what does *that* mean?"

"I'm going to my room and get my gun and sit outside your door until morning," he replied simply. "I know what is going on out there, what they have planned for you, and since you won't listen to reason, then I have to protect you."

Travis laughed, then instantly hated himself for it. The man was sincere, after all. "Why do you feel responsible for me?" he asked curiously.

"You're a fellow human being. You don't understand that you are in grave danger. I know voodoo. I believe in it. I would never forgive myself if I just walked away and left you to suffer the consequences of being so blasted stubborn. It could mean your *life.*"

Eldon had stopped trembling and was speaking calmly. The rum was doing its job, Travis thought. "Why don't you just go to the local police if you feel so strongly about this?" he asked suddenly. "I mean, if these natives really mean to do me harm, why not go to the marshal or whatever they call it around here?"

Eldon threw back his head and laughed sharply. "You're a fool, Coltrane. You think the law would interfere? They have already heard the drums. They hear them every time. Some of the authorities might even know who is marked, but they would never interfere. To do so would mean retribution from the *loas,* and you can be sure they do not want that. Why, the law would not even interfere to save one of their own family. When the *loas* wish to punish, when the souls of the dead are angry and demand to be appeased, no one gets in the way, Coltrane. *No one.*"

Travis had had it. The rum was suddenly making him very sleepy, as though he had never been to bed, and there was no point in listening to a drunk rattle on either. Harcourt was even more obnoxious when he *wasn't* hysterical. Travis went to the door, opened it, and made a waving gesture. "Out, Harcourt. Enough is enough. Go to bed or sit outside my door all night long if that is what you want to do. I don't care. The only thing I *do* care about is getting some sleep. I've heard enough of your nonsense for one night."

Eldon nodded. His eyes looked a little glassy. He must not be used to drinking, Travis reasoned. "I'll look out for you," Eldon mumbled as he passed. "Don't worry. I'd never forgive myself if I let anything happen to you."

Travis slammed the door. His head had suddenly begun to pound, and he was so damn sleepy he found himself weaving as he moved back to the bed. That devil, rum. That fool,

Harcourt. The two had combined to make his evening miserable, and he would probably awaken in the morning feeling as though he had never even slept. Damn!

The wind was howling, screaming, causing the windows to rattle in protest. And those drums, those goddamn drums were getting louder and louder, as though floating right inside his head to beat there. His brain began to spin, and there was a strange tightening in his throat. He tried to take a deep breath and couldn't. Alarmed, he tried to bring himself out of the stupor engulfing him. The lantern beside the bed still burned, but he could not see the flame through the grayish fog that had descended on him.

Something had to be done about those infernal drums. They *were* inside his head. His eyeballs were contracting, squeezing with each thud. It was becoming harder and harder to breathe. His hand went to his throat but he could not find it. Where was his throat? His hands flailed the air. Where was his body? Where was his head? His eyes were gone . . . gone with the drumbeat. He had no body. The fog had taken it away. All that remained was his soul, but the soul had nowhere to go and hung suspended in midair, seeking a home but finding none.

Movements. There was someone there with him. But who? Eldon? Eldon had come back. He tried to think, tried to make the words come to tell Eldon to get a doctor. He was sick. God, but he was sick. Too much rum. Never again. Whiskey had never done this, not that he could remember. It came to him then with frightening clarity that he could not remember anything anymore. What was his name? Why was he here? Those drums . . . inside him. He gasped, but how did he gasp? He had no mouth, no throat. No body at all. Only a soul, and then he felt that, too, slipping away.

Faces in the fog. Some were black. Some were brown. There were white stripes painted across noses, red circles around bulging eyes. Bones. Why were there stark, white bones rattling together? Blood. Where was the blood coming from? It trickled down on him, warm, thick, sticky. He wanted to wipe it away but had no hand.

A voice from out of the mist spoke angrily, accusingly, "This is the one?"

Travis felt nauseous at the sound, so cold and dreadful. But how could he feel anything? He had no body, only this soul that was not visible, lost, somewhere in the gray fog. Yet, he could smell. Even without a body, there was a horrible odor of something rotten . . . something decaying.

"Yes, oh, *houngan,* he is the one."

Molina. Yes it was Molina speaking, and she spoke with a venom strong enough to kill.

The man spoke again, loudly, nearly screaming above the thunderous drums which had begun to beat wildly. "The *loas* Ogoun and Erzulie will come this night to bring you peace."

Shouts of approval rang through the mist. From somewhere, chanting began, and hands clapped together. There was movement, and Travis' soul allowed him to see bodies dancing around and around in a frenzy, arms waving, bones rattling, and those infernal drums that never stopped.

"He will die," the *houngan* shouted. "The evil spirit will die. The soul of your long-dead grandfather will be appeased. Bring the sacrifice."

Part of what was being said was in the French creole dialect that Travis had learned in the Louisiana bayou. The fog was starting to lift, and he realized that it was from sheer willpower alone that he was bringing himself out of the drug-induced stupor. Slowly it was coming back to him. The rum. The goddamn rum bottle that he had thought half empty and surprisingly found almost full. Someone had slipped into his room and poured something into the bottle that had drugged him. He had taken only one swallow, but Eldon had taken two. That explained Eldon's change in behavior.

He dared not open his eyes all the way. Let them think he was still drugged, which was not altogether untrue, for there was still great difficulty in coordinating his thoughts. His thoughts were coming in slow motion, thickly, hard to grasp.

Through partially closed lids he could see the flames of many torches and weirdly dressed natives dancing. They were dressed in black and purple robes, but most of the women were covered only below the waist, their bare breasts bouncing in the glow of the fires.

"Guédé will come this night. Baron Samedi will demand it. *Jeunesse,* you will have your honor."

He could see that the one called *houngan* was a tall, skinny black man covered in feathers with white and yellow stripes painted on his face. He was shaking something over his head as he stood before Molina, who was kneeling, head bowed.

"You will have your honor to appease your grandfather,"

he cried, "and then Baron Samedi will decree that he shall be sacrificed." He ran toward Travis, who quickly closed his eyes. He lay still, listening to the frenzied rattling of that gourdlike thing over his face.

"No. No kill."

Travis could hear Molina crying out to the *houngan,* but Travis was having difficulty staying awake. The drug was trying to take him away again. That damn rattling above his head. Slowly it came back to him. The boy he had known down in the bayou had told him about the *asson,* a gourd filled with pebbles, snake bones, dirt from a graveyard. There would be the bony vertebrae of a snake around it. And it was this that a voodoo priest used to command the dead and master the living. Even now the drums were following the rhythm of the rattling gourd. The boy had wanted to show an *asson* to him . . . had said his father had one and he would sneak it out to show it off. Travis had not wanted to see it then, and he did not want to see it now. He only wished he had the strength to pull himself up and give these dancing idiots something to remember him by. He was heavily outnumbered, but by God, he would go down fighting.

Instinctively, he clenched his fists, then realized his wrists were bound. The *houngan* saw the movement and shrieked, "He awakens. We must sacrifice. We must call up Baron Samedi and let him be appeased."

"No, no! I want him only punished. I want him only to be mine, to do my bidding and remain by my side forever and never leave me. You cannot sacrifice him, O *houngan*. I never asked that he be sacrificed."

"Then we must have a sacrifice."

Travis felt the warm blood splashing on his face and his eyes flashed open to see the chicken being swung above him in front of a leering black face. The chicken's throat had been cut, and its life blood was pouring down on him.

"Dance the *banda,*" Molina was sobbing. "That will appease Baron Samedi. Please!

Banda. Travis did not know what that meant. But here, tied down on some kind of flat stone, stripped naked, nothing was going to save him from whatever these lunatics had in mind.

"You will dance the *banda,*" the *houngan* cried triumphantly, and Travis saw the tall, skinny man reach out and jerk away the black and purple cloth that covered Molina's lower body. Picking her up, he swung her about to the pleased cheers of the crowd. As she cried out in pain, he brought her down.

Travis strained at the ropes that bound him, watching as women were grabbed and thrown to the ground. Everyone began to copulate. Only the drummers did not stop. They kept up their crazed beating, and men assaulted women to the rhythm of the drums.

Where is everybody else? he thought wildly, while this insane orgy was going on amid bloody chicken feathers, and—good Lord—they were in the middle of a graveyard. Did nobody in Haiti care about anything except this insane party?

He stiffened as he felt a movement to his right, on the side away from the others. "Don't move. I'm going to get you out of here," a trembling whisper penetrated his whirling brain.

It was Eldon, crouched on his knees. Travis could see the glint of a knife. "How'd you find me?" he whispered back gratefully. "Hell, it doesn't matter. Just get me out of this place, fast, before they finish their party."

The rope holding down his right wrist was severed, but he did not move. Eldon's arm reached over his bare stomach to saw at the binding on his left wrist.

"Evidently the *houngan* did not have the power this night to call up Baron Samedi," Eldon said nervously as he moved to Travis' ankles. "That's why he went along with the *banda*. I've been hiding and watching. Believe me, you're lucky. If he had called him up, you'd be dead by now."

Travis felt his ankles freed. "What do we do now?"

"We run," Eldon sounded as though he were about to burst into tears. "We run as damn hard and as fast as we can. You follow me. I know the way out of here to a place where we can hide till morning. Just roll off the altar and crawl until I give a signal, and unless the drummers see us, we can get a good piece from here before we are spotted. They may not even miss us, from the looks of this rite."

Rite, Travis mused in amusement, was a strange name for mass intercourse, but it was not the time for musing. He rolled over to his right, fell from the stone slab, then began to crawl behind Eldon, who was moving faster on his hands and knees than Travis had ever seen him move on his feet.

When they were out of the graveyard, Eldon stood and gave the signal to run. There was no moonlight, but Travis could make out his figure and managed to keep up. Behind, there were still the sounds of ecstasy and screaming and the ever-beating drums.

They ran hard and fast through brambles and brush for a half hour or more before Eldon halted. "A cave. My grandfather told me about it being near the graveyard here. When I first got here, I went for a walk one day just to see if I could find it. I had to look a long time, because it was hidden by so much growth, but we can get inside, and they will never find us here. I could tell it hadn't been used in a long, long time."

Travis was beyond caring that the brambles were tearing his flesh. He was already bleeding from the run through the thickets and weeds. He was only too glad to follow Eldon inside the cave.

"All right, we can rest now."

Travis sank to the cold, hard ground. They had moved back inside the cave perhaps a hundred feet. He could not see Eldon but knew where he was from the sound of his harsh, labored breathing. "All right," Travis said finally, also gasping. "What do we do now?"

"We wait till almost daylight and then go back to the hotel and get our things and take the first boat out of here. They'll be busy the rest of the night swapping partners, and the *houngan* will pass out drugs to make their sexual appetite go on for hours. Eventually they will all sleep. Even if they find you missing, they probably won't come after you tonight. They figure they can get you any time they want you, and next time they'll kill you on the spot—wherever they find you."

Travis shrugged. "I plan to go to the politicians on that committee and tell them the whole story, and you can believe they will go to the local law and demand something be done to protect a citizen of the United States."

"You are crazy." Eldon sighed. "The law will say you brought it all on yourself. I wouldn't be a bit surprised if one of those painted-up devils out there tonight wasn't a constable, anyway, or some government big shot. The best thing for you to do is get out of this place, just as I plan to do, because they're going to be after me, too. They'll know it was I who helped you."

"How will they know that? And how did you know where to find me? I'm grateful, believe me, because those people are crazy, but you drank out of that same bottle, and once I came out of my stupor, it wasn't hard to figure out that I had been drugged. The only thing I can think of is that someone slipped in and put something into the rum."

"That's right. It was the rum. I realized it when I went back to my room to get my gun and found myself passing out. I made myself throw up, and I fought it like hell, but I still passed out. When I finally did struggle awake, I knew where to come, because I had done some checking on that girl, Molina, after we talked this afternoon, and I knew that her particular tribe holds their rites in that graveyard. Just be thankful Molina cared enough about you not to want you dead. She asked for the *banda* instead."

"And what in hell is the *banda?*" Travis demanded. "And who is this baron who never put in an appearance at my party?"

Eldon was deeply reproachful. "I think it's time you stopped making light of the situation, Coltrane. You almost died tonight."

Travis nodded acknowledgment of the possibility and urged him to go on.

Eldon told him that Baron Samedi was the king of the cemetery spirits. "If you will recall, I explained that earlier, but you did not listen. The baron is the first person to be buried in a churchyard, and he can and does appear at any ceremony. He's a greedy and tricky spirit and it is always his prerogative to devour all offerings made to any other *loa* before they get to them."

"The *houngan* said something about some people named Ogoun and Erzulie."

"They are what you call gods, who are always called on in marriage rites. You probably heard the name Guédé, too. Guédé is a collective title for all the cemetery spirits. It was obviously Molina's intention that the two of you be married, and the *houngan* wanted you sacrificed to appease one of her dead relatives who was angered because you violated her honor."

Travis nodded in the darkness. "Yeah, something was said about her grandfather. But what about the *banda?*"

"The dance of the *banda* combines sexual fascination with the scorn for pleasure and willful contempt of love, which is, in Molina's eyes and the *houngan*'s, the way you treated her. They use a stick as a mock penis. I saw some of them waving one around. That's when I dared to hope they would dance the *banda* and wind up having sex and forget about you long enough for me to get you out of there." He sighed loudly in relief. "We were lucky. I have an idea that when the sun came up, the *houngan* would have slit your throat like a chicken's anyway. There was no way he was going to see one of his tribe married to a foreigner, especially one who had turned the virtuous young lady aside after *robbing* her of her virtue."

"Well, I'm indebted to you, Eldon," Travis said with as much sincerity as he could muster over the chill going through his body and the headache that was exploding due to the drug. "I just wish we could head on back now and let me get some clothes and go to bed. What I would really like to do is go back and get my gun and then go to that cemetery and kill a few of those bastards, especially that *houngan*."

"No, we can't leave. You might as well try to sleep, Travis. They might be out looking for us. We'll have a better chance to make it in daylight, and they won't just come running up and murder you out in the open. They will wait till dark, but we'll both be gone by then."

Travis leaned his head back against the rocky wall behind him. What a night. If anyone had ever told him that he would wind up in such an infernal mess all because he got drunk and could not resist the temptations of a beautiful native girl, he would have told them to go to hell and probably rapped them in the mouth as well. When Sam heard of this escapade, Travis thought wearily, he would spend the next ten years reminding Travis what a damn fool he was.

The next thing he knew Eldon was shaking him awake, and he was blinking rebelliously at the intrusion. His neck was stiff and aching. In fact, he realized, he ached all over. There were rope burns on his wrists and ankles, and he wondered how he had ever slept in the damp, cold cave without any clothes on.

"Come on, Travis, we've got to get out of here," Eldon spoke in the pale light that filtered through the brush-hidden mouth of the cave. "We're going to run all the way to the village and get our stuff and go to the docks and take the first boat out, just as I said last night. To hell with the committee, our jobs, all of it. Our lives are at stake."

Travis looked at him long and hard. The man was scared to death. No doubt about it. His eyes were dark sockets, like someone dead and not yet buried. His skin was pasty white, and his lips had turned a funny blue color. He looked sick.

"You need some rest, Harcourt." Travis struggled to his feet and then stretched to try to get some of the stiffness from his bones. "I'm going to the committee and tell them about that bunch of lunatics, and then I'm going to Santo Domingo and track down Sam."

Eldon made a strange, strangling sound deep in his throat, and he reached out to place ice-cold hands on Travis' bare shoulders, shaking him as hard as his strength would allow. "You are wasting your time and risking your life going to the law. What is it going to take to make you realize that you must leave?"

Travis sucked in his breath and resisted the impulse to tell the man he thought he was just as crazy as those wild, dancing, painted-up natives. After all, Eldon had come to his aid when he needed it desperately, and there was no way of knowing how things would have turned out without Eldon.

Travis decided to try humor for the present and then try reasoning later, when he returned from Santo Domingo and Harcourt had had time to rest.

"Anything you say, my friend." Travis forced himself to sound jovial. "I'm not looking forward to running into the village naked, but I can't hide here in this cave forever. Let's go."

Harcourt looked relieved, so relieved, in fact, that Travis felt a momentary wave of remorse.

They walked to the entrance of the cave, peered out through the brush, and then, after deciding all was clear, made their way toward the village.

Eldon gave Travis his shirt, which kept him from walking down the street totally unclothed. Still, there were many stares. More than that, there was a smothering air about the village. Travis had the feeling that, though there were not many people out, eyes were watching from behind every window.

"They're here," Eldon whispered, terrified, eyes widening as his gaze darted from left to right. "They're watching us. I can feel it. We've got to move fast."

Travis threw what he hoped was a reassuring arm across his shoulders. "Don't worry so much, Eldon. You're just tired. We're both going to feel better after some rest and some food. I'd say we deserve a drink, too, even if it is so damn early, but this time we'll make sure it isn't rum and that it comes from a bottle that hasn't been opened." He laughed, but the sound fell flat against the shroud that had engulfed Eldon.

"No. You eat and rest if you want," was his barely audible comment. "I'm getting my things and heading for the harbor. I'm getting on the first boat I see. I don't even care where it's headed."

Travis was not about to let him do anything so foolish, but he did not tell him so. He steered Eldon on toward the hotel, arm still across his shoulders.

The desk clerk was nowhere to be seen. The silent, empty lobby was like a tomb. There was even a damp, decaying smell, and the odor reminded Travis of that smell of the night before. He bit down on his lower lip. Damned if he would admit it, but he did not like the situation. Something . . . something he could not put his finger on was just not right. Perhaps he was just letting Eldon's fright rub off on him. Travis stiffened. Hell, he had never been scared in four years of that goddamn war, and he was not going to let a bunch of rum-drunk natives make him wet himself now.

He gave Eldon a gentle push up the stairs.

"Stay with me, Travis," he was saying tremulously. "Go with me to my room. Get my gun. Don't like it. Something is funny. I just feel it—"

"It's going to be all right, my friend." Travis wished he would hurry up. When he got to his room, he would probably fall asleep, and that was the thing Eldon needed most now, rest. He would see George Carpenter, one of the congressmen's aides who roomed just down the hall, and tell him to keep an eye on Harcourt till Travis returned from Santo Domingo. By then he should have himself together. If not, Travis would just ask the committee to send the man back to America.

They reached the top of the stairs and turned to the left, Eldon shuffling along and Travis trying to hurry him without actually pushing him.

"Gun," Eldon babbled as he fumbled in his pocket for his key and shakily inserted it in the door. "Get the gun first."

The door swung open, and then Eldon fell backward, a scream lodged in his throat. He clutched at his face and fell to his knees, rocking to and fro, gasping for breath.

Travis stepped over him and into the room. "What in hell?" He took in the sight before him. Bones! Bones were scattered across Eldon's bed. They were human bones—a leg, an arm, and there was even a grinning skull sitting upright on the pillow, staring at them mockingly.

"Granddaddy," Eldon was moaning over and over, rhythmically pounding his head on the floor. "I'm a dead man . . . dead, dead, dead."

The moans changed to an ear-splitting scream, and Travis reached down to grasp Eldon's hair, yanking his head back. He smashed his fist into Eldon's face and knocked him out cold, both to put the wretched man out of his misery for a moment and to stop that insane shrieking.

Eldon Harcourt slumped all the way to the floor, unconscious. The sound of running footsteps in the hall made Travis whip around, fists clenched, expecting to see that wild-eyed, painted-up *houngan*.

It was George Carpenter, still in his nightshirt, heavy-lidded and sleepy as he rushed into the room. "What in blazes is going on here, Coltrane?" His voice trailed off as he looked from Eldon's unconscious body to the bones scattered over the bed. "Oh, my God."

Other doors opened, and soon several people were gathered around the doorway. Travis tried to explain without sounding like a madman himself, but he knew that no one was listening, for they all stood in silence staring in horror at those macabre, bleached white bones.

Suddenly the black desk clerk appeared. "Voodoo," he whispered hoarsely, horror in his voice. He backed away from the doorway. "There is a curse on Mr. Harcourt. He will die now."

"What do you mean, a curse?" one of the men scoffed. "I've heard about voodoo but paid it no mind. A bunch of dog bones means Eldon Harcourt will die because of some silly native superstition?" He chuckled, amused, and was joined by less convincing chuckles from the others.

The desk clerk retreated even farther, moving away from the gathering. "Not dog bones," he pointed, his whole arm trembling violently. "Those are the bones of Mr. Harcourt's grandfather. When the bones of a man's ancestor are removed from its grave, it means that man is cursed. He will die."

Travis knocked several people aside in his sudden lunge for the man. He pinned him against the wall. "Now you tell me how you know so goddamn much, you sonofabitch," he ground out the words. "How do you know those are the bones of Harcourt's grandfather?"

"He . . . he told me . . ." He choked out the words. "He told me . . . his grandfather was buried here . . . in Haiti. I heard of the curse."

"*How* did you hear of the curse?" he demanded, shaking him. "Talk, damn you."

"Drums. The drums tell the story. They stopped beating only a little while ago. Mr. Harcourt, he is dead man." His eyes raked over Travis reproachfully. "He interfered with the Baron Samedi," he said contemptuously. "He interfered for you. Now he will pay, for the Baron Samedi has cursed him. You they will deal with later."

Travis' hand cracked across his face. He would have hit him again if the others had not stepped forward to pull him away. The little bastard had probably been one of those painted-up lunatics out there dancing. Travis wanted to kill him and let the whole bunch of them know he was not scared.

"Calm down, Coltrane," George was saying. "We'll take care of Eldon. We'll take him to my room and get these bones cleaned out of here. You just get some rest. You look like you've had a rough night."

Travis gave the black one long, contemptuous look, then stalked to his room. Tucking his gun in his belt, he grabbed his rifle from the corner, then returned to the hall.

The crowd was still gathered in the hallway. To hell with them, Travis thought bitterly. He was going to Santo Domingo to find Sam, and, for a little while, be in sane company. Eldon Harcourt would sleep it off.

Travis turned to give the crowd one parting glare, then ran down the stairs.

Chapter Eight

THE old man at the stable spoke a mixture of French and creole, and Travis was able to understand that Santo Domingo was around a hundred and fifty miles away, and that it would be quicker to go by land than by sea. The trip would probably take four or five days on horseback, but it still would be quicker than taking a ship, which would stop at every port along the way.

Travis told the man to sell him his best horse and saddle and have everything ready within the hour. Then he left the stable and walked to the nearest store to buy supplies for the journey. He was looking at a blanket when the sound of heavy footsteps caused him to whip around, drawing his gun.

"You can put that away, Coltrane. We came to talk to you."

He recognized two of the aides on the committee—Walton Turner and Vinson Craley.

"Orville Babcock is in town. He came in from Santo Domingo a couple of days ago to check on the committee work here. He wants to see you," said Turner.

Travis put his gun away, squinting in thoughtful annoyance. "Yeah? And what would President Grant's private secretary be wanting to see me about?"

The two men exchanged uncomfortable glances. Finally,

after an awkward silence, Vinson Craley cleared his throat nervously. "Coltrane, what happened last night has spread all over. You know these natives talk, and it gets around." He looked to his companion helplessly, not wanting to continue.

Walton Turner spoke up. "The fact is, Coltrane, that Babcock has heard about it, and he wants to talk to you about the situation."

Travis' reply was crisp. "There is no situation. There is nothing to discuss."

"Babcock doesn't think so," Walton went on quickly.

Travis laughed. "What is this? Are you telling me Babcock believes in this voodoo nonsense?"

"Hell, it's not that simple," Walton snapped. He didn't want to make Coltrane angry, for he had been wary of him since they had first met. Not that Coltrane was unlikable. Walton admired the man greatly, had heard of his many heroic feats during the war. But there was just an air about Coltrane that made a man want to stay on his good side.

"President Grant wants to acquire the Dominican Republic for the United States." Walton spoke in a rush, wanting to get it all over with. "When Congress offered our protection to Haiti and the Dominican Republic, that didn't include approving annexation. That's why the President sent Babcock and the rest of the committee over here to try to arrange a treaty of annexation. Things aren't going well, and your having this trouble last night hasn't helped matters any."

Vinson interjected quickly, "That's why he wants to talk to you. There are a lot of people irritated. You've stirred up the locals."

Travis raised an eyebrow in amusement. "Are they stirred up because I don't choose to believe in voodoo or because I had a brief affair with a native girl?" He shook his head. "I dare say several of you have partaken of the fruits of the island."

The men exchanged glances once more, faces coloring slightly.

"That's not the point," Walton said. "Babcock sent us to get you. You're working for the United States government, and you should have the courtesy to answer the request of the President's own personal secretary, especially after the fuss you kicked up last night."

"*I* kicked up?" Travis threw back his head, laughing. "I

could have been killed, and if it hadn't been for Eldon Harcourt, there's no telling what might have happened."

Vinson sighed, holding out his hands in a pleading gesture. "Look, Coltrane, I know you're upset. We'd be, too, if it had happened to us. But now Harcourt is in some kind of a coma, the doctor says, and the natives are backing away from all of us like we've got the plague. Babcock doesn't like the situation, and he wants to talk to you about it. He's even got a priest waiting."

"A priest?" Travis echoed in disbelief.

"Yes, a priest. They want to explain some of the customs. Now come with us, all right?" Vinson forced a coaxing smile. "We heard you were planning on leaving for Santo Domingo, and that's fine, but you can at least take a few minutes and hear Babcock, okay? It might make things better for all of us."

"It might even help Harcourt," Walton murmured.

"Harcourt will come out of it," Travis said quickly. "He's exhausted. It was a rough night."

Vinson asked impatiently, "Are you coming, or do you want us to go back and tell Babcock you just don't give a damn?"

Travis agreed to go. He followed them from the store to the small wooden building that Orville Babcock was using for his headquarters while in Port-au-Prince. Two black guards stood outside, holding rifles, and their eyes darted suspiciously at Travis as he passed between them. Fleetingly, he wondered if they had been among those fools dressed in blue and purple, faces painted in macabre patterns. It would be good to get out of this place.

Vinson and Walton led him to the door of the inner office, then left. Travis knocked once, heard someone call out, then walked inside. He saw a somber-faced, dark-haired man seated behind a large desk, and a priest standing to the left of the desk. Travis nodded to the man behind the desk and bluntly asked, "What did you want to see me about, Babcock? I'm on my way to Santo Domingo to see Sam Bucher."

"Sam Bucher seems anxious to see you, too, Coltrane," Babcock remarked as he reached for his pipe and began to pack it with tobacco from a leather humidor. "He's been wanting to take time off to get over here, but I haven't been able to give him any time. Seems we've had more work to do there than you people have had here in Haiti. None of my men have gotten themselves into a . . . diplomatic situation with the natives," he added meaningfully.

Travis glanced around the sparsely furnished room, spotted a chair, turned it around backward, sat, and faced the two men. He said tightly, "You're insinuating that *I* have gotten myself in a 'diplomatic situation'? I don't think it's anything for the American government to worry about. The government here, if there is one," he smiled sarcastically, "should be concerned. An American citizen was almost killed last night by a bunch of crazed natives."

He propped his chin on his hands and stared straight at Babcock. "What do you intend to do about that?"

The priest, a tall, fat, balding man with condemning ice-blue eyes, spoke up. "Did you deflower a young native girl called Molina?"

Travis looked him over carefully, trying to decide whether or not to tell him to mind his own business. Never one to mince words, he snapped, "Yeah, if you want to call it that. She may have been a virgin, but she sure came on like a woman who's known plenty of men. I didn't force her. In fact, she offered herself in no uncertain terms. I'm only human."

"You are also married!" The priest hissed like a snake, face reddening.

Travis made his decision. "That is none of your damn business."

"Coltrane, this isn't getting us anywhere!" Babcock slammed his fist on the desk. "You deflowered a native girl. In the eyes of her people, you shamed her. The rites they performed last night, if I have heard the gossip correctly, were meant to punish you."

"They thought they were going to make me marry her. Oh, hell, I don't know what they thought. All I know is I was drugged and woke up naked and tied down to a rock in a graveyard with a dead chicken bleeding all over my face. If that's not enough to get pissed off over, I don't know what is." He pointed his finger at Babcock. "Did anyone try to take revenge on you like those bastards did with me last night? Sit there and tell me that if they had you wouldn't be pissed off about it and I'll call you a goddamn liar."

The priest puffed himself out like a toad. "Have you no respect?" he whispered hoarsely.

"I'm sorry," Travis said contritely. "I know you are a man

of the cloth, but tell me, what is your interest in all this? No one has told me yet what this meeting is about, and I would like to be on my way."

The priest sat down near Babcock's desk and folded his hands in his lap. "I have been told by Mr. Babcock and others that you are a strong-willed man, Mr. Coltrane, and that you have a very nasty temper. I can understand why you are upset, but if you will refrain from further outbursts and hear me out, I will attempt to tell you the reasons for this meeting."

"That sounds fair," Travis nodded. "But let's hurry up."

The priest closed his eyes for a moment, as though praying for the right words to come. When he opened them, he stared at Travis thoughtfully, then said, "Let me explain how it all came about, Mr. Coltrane."

He spoke in slow, even tones, clearly wanting Travis to understand everything. He told of how almost half a million slaves won their freedom in a struggle that ended with Haiti's independence back in 1804. He explained that most of the Africans brought to the island before the middle of the century came from the Dahomeyton town of Ouidah, in West Africa, and later from the Congo. There were mulattoes, who had some education, and a few Europeans, and since 1804 there had been many immigrants, mostly traders and mechanics, along with a few priests and teachers, who had come first from the British Isles, then from America, to form part of a repatriation movement.

"Nine years ago, a concordat with the Pope," he continued in the same slow tone, "gave Haiti an all-French clergy, which helped attract more French-speaking residents. Some came from France, others from Guadeloupe and Martinique."

Travis interrupted, "I'm sure the history of the settlement of Haiti is quite interesting, but what does all this mean now?"

The priest assumed the air of a man who is not accustomed to being questioned. "Mr. Coltrane, if you will listen, I am quite sure you will understand. Since Haiti was left without a regular clergy until nine years ago, a syncretic cult was formed in 1860. This is what is called voodoo. To explain as simply as possible, voodoo is a religion whereby the Catholic God rules over an African pantheon."

Travis viewed the priest skeptically. "Then you are trying to tell me that voodoo is, in fact, a religion? And that it has its roots in the Catholic Church? I find that hard to believe, and even harder to understand why the Catholics would admit it. Who would want to claim any association with a bunch of lunatics?"

"They believe in a single God and other elements borrowed from Roman Catholicism," the priest continued, ignoring Travis' criticism. "They believe in the saints, but this becomes confused with voodoo gods, which, to those who believe, are objects of all kinds of veneration. The power of performing evil and good comes with the permission of God, whom they call the Great Master. This is what I mean by 'syncretism,' which, basically, is an accurate description of the mixture of all elements in Haitian voodoo—the belief in a universal, sovereign, supreme God, but, at the same time, belief in secondary gods, whom they call *loas*.

"The most important *loa* is Legba, entrusted with guardianship of the temple," he went on. "Then there is Erzulie, goddess of love."

Travis sighed with disgust, stood, and slung his chair across the room. "I've heard about the *loas,*" he said in a clipped voice. "I have also heard you out. I still don't understand what all this has to do with us."

"What he is trying to tell you, Coltrane," Babcock said impatiently, "is that these people have deeply rooted beliefs. It's serious business to them. That is why the American government, in the process of trying to gain military and commercial privileges here and also in discussing annexation, cannot afford to have one of its emissaries involved in a scandal. Sherman himself recommended you for this committee, and—"

"Whoa, now!" Travis held up his hand in protest. "Sam Bucher got me on the committee, after I asked him to. I was having a few personal problems, and I wanted some time away. So don't go telling me I was *selected* for this job to try to make me feel like I've disgraced my country. I asked to come here."

Orville Babcock stared down at some papers on his desk and spoke without looking up. "I have your records right here. Your name was recommended by Sherman back in March when the committee was first being formed. You were selected on the basis of your illustrious service to the Union during the war. Sherman recommended you very highly and wrote a long letter to President Grant citing the reasons why you should be appointed."

"Let me see that, please." Travis held out his hand. Babcock shrugged and gave him the papers.

As Travis scanned the correspondence, his gray eyes narrowed. Why hadn't Sam told him about this? Why had he kept it from him? Slowly, an uneasy feeling began in the pit of his stomach. Something was not right, and whatever it was, he sensed that all of it had to do with Kitty's strange behavior. She had changed so suddenly. Was this why?

"Coltrane, we want you to go back to America," said Babcock.

Travis looked up, but not at Babcock. He turned to the priest and asked quietly, ominously, "Do *you* believe that the curse on Harcourt will cause him to die?"

The priest fidgeted nervously, glancing around, lips working silently. Babcock's fist suddenly slammed the desk. "Coltrane, I repeat, we want you to go back to America. Leave Haiti. Don't concern yourself with Harcourt."

"Don't concern myself with Harcourt?" Travis echoed in disbelief. "Are you crazy? The man may have saved my life. He's obviously been drugged—"

"Not drugged, Mr. Coltrane," the priest corrected quickly. "Cursed. Eldon Harcourt is cursed. There is nothing you or anyone else can do about it."

"We'll see about that." Travis stalked toward the door, whirled about to glare at both of them in turn, and say, "I have no intentions of letting them kill Harcourt."

The men had risen. Babcock's face reddened. "I cannot allow you to cause any more trouble in this country, Coltrane. If I have to have you placed under arrest and deported—"

Travis' hand moved to his gun, not quite touching the weapon but making the implication. "Just try it, Babcock. Just you or anybody else try it."

Travis walked out and slammed the door, standing outside for a few moments, breathing deeply to calm himself. This was going to call for rational thinking, and his temper must not be allowed to rule him. Not now.

Hurrying along, he passed the stable, head down, walking in a manner that made anyone in his way step aside.

He entered the little hotel and went straight to the desk. The clerk backed away, frightened.

"Go, please," he said quickly. "You bring curse."

Travis reached across the desk and grabbed the man by his

collar and jerked him close. "You can tell your friends I don't buy any goddamn curse unless it's me laying one on them. Now I'm going upstairs to sit with Eldon Harcourt till he wakes up from whatever they've given him, and if anybody comes around, they're going to wind up in the same place those bones came from. Understand?"

The clerk was having trouble breathing. It was only with great effort that he was able to nod, eyes bulging. Travis released him, and he stumbled backward, clutching his throat and coughing.

Travis took the steps three at a time. Reaching the second floor, he turned toward Harcourt's room and saw Vinson Craley and Walton Turner standing outside the door talking to a black man. As Travis approached, they fell silent.

Travis growled, "Who's he?"

"This is Dr. Lamedi," Vinson spoke as Walton looked on uneasily. "He was called in to check on Harcourt."

"And how is he?"

The doctor stared down at the worn floor and shook his head. "Nothing I can do. Nothing anyone can do."

"What are you talking about?" Travis' fists clenched at his sides. "I didn't hit him that hard, just hard enough to knock him out because he got hysterical when he saw those damn bones."

"He hasn't woke up yet, Coltrane," Vinson spoke as though he wished he did not have to. "He's still out cold. The doc here says it has nothing to do with your hitting him. He just won't wake up."

Travis pushed the three men aside, shoved the door open, and stepped inside the room. Eldon Harcourt lay on his bed, wearing only his trousers, his bare chest rising and falling slowly. His eyes were partially opened, but from where Travis stood, he knew there was no vision. Eldon was unconscious.

The three men followed Travis into the room.

"Voodoo curse," Walton said matter-of-factly. "I've heard Eldon's tales about his grandfather. He believes in all of it. If what we've heard about last night is true, some witch doctor has put a curse on him for helping you out."

"It is true," the doctor nodded nervously. "Curse of Baron Samedi. Nothing I can do."

"*Can't* do or *won't* do?" Travis snapped, clamping a powerful hand on the man's shoulder and feeling the trembling of his body. "You know what went on? Tell me about it."

"No, no, no," he shook his head back and forth frantically. "I hear things, yes. I hear of curse, yes. But I do not know anything else. I do not know this man. I do not know you. I come because I was called, but there is nothing I can do for this man."

"Who removed the bones from the room?"

Again, the doctor shook his head. "I know nothing. You must believe me. Let me go now, please."

Travis pressed harder. "Tell me what is wrong with him."

"I do not know. I swear to you. It is a curse. I do not know what kind of curse. There is nothing anyone can do but *houngan*. Maybe he can do nothing. Baron Samedi is all-powerful."

Travis nodded as though he understood. He wanted to get as much as possible out of the doctor, but he realized he was not accomplishing anything by scaring him. "All right," he made his voice gentle, "I understand that you do not have the power to remove the curse, but can you at least tell me what is wrong with him right now and why he won't wake up? Is he drugged?"

The doctor glanced around nervously as though he might be overheard by the *loas* themselves, then whispered, "He will awaken, but then he will sleep again. Then he will awaken, then sleep. This will go on until the *gros bon ange* is completely taken by the Baron Samedi. Then he will be dead."

Vinson and Walton looked at each other uncomfortably. The doctor continued in a great rush, "The soul is called *gros bon ange*. That is soul of shadow and breath. *'Ti bon ange* is spirit. Both in dead body. This man already dead. *Gros bon ange* and *'ti bon ange* become no longer together because of curse. Now *corps cadavre* there. Man you knew no longer lives."

"He's still breathing."

"I do not know how long he will breathe. As I say, he will awake, then sleep. Baron Samedi will take him when he chooses. No one can help."

Travis did not remove his gaze from the doctor's wide, bulging eyes. "Go downstairs and leave us alone, you two. I want to talk to the doctor alone."

"We aren't going to have any more trouble, Travis," Vinson said.

"There won't be any trouble," Travis answered. "I have some

more questions I want to ask the doctor, and I want to ask him alone. The only trouble there is going to be is if you don't get the hell out of here now."

"Please," Dr. Lamedi spoke quickly when they were alone. "I can tell you nothing. You put my life in danger. Let me go."

Travis guided him to a chair and pushed him into it. "You're right. I do put your life in danger." He reached for his pistol and pointed it straight at the man's forehead, pulling the hammer back with an ominous click. "Because, if you don't answer my questions, I'm going to kill you. I never point a gun unless I plan to use it, and I have every intention of blowing your brains out if you don't start talking."

The doctor licked his lips and panicked, squeezing his eyes shut as though anticipating the bullet. He felt himself urinating, and was humiliated as a puddle formed beneath him on the chair. "What . . . do you want to know?" He finally got the words past his throat.

"I want to know about this curse. I want to know what they did to him."

The doctor kept his eyes closed. "Believe me, please, when I tell you I do not know. You do not understand voodoo. Strange things happen that no one can explain. I only know that this man has angered the *loas*, the Baron Samedi. He is cursed. He will die. I have seen it happen before. My own father died of a curse."

Suddenly his voice broke, and he lowered his head, covering his face with his hands and sobbing uncontrollably. "They say my father serves the *loas* in the mountains. That he is zombie, the walking dead. I pray this is not so. I pray if it is so that I never see him. Never see his soul in torment as he walks in death."

He lifted his tear-streaked face to stare up at Travis in torment. "Kill me if you must, but there is nothing else I can tell you. I do not practice voodoo. I am afraid of voodoo. I want nothing to do with voodoo. There is nothing else I can say to you except that your friend will die."

He was telling the truth. A man, Travis had learned, will seldom lie with a gun pointed at his head.

"Is he drugged?" he asked quietly, replacing the gun.

The doctor sighed with relief, breathing deeply a few times. "I do not know. To be honest with you, I think he may be. I study medicine in Paris. Questions were asked about voodoo among my people, but the professors there laughed. They say a man can kill himself by being afraid. Your friend may be frightening himself to death. Or maybe he is drugged. I did not drug him," he added nervously.

"Or," he rushed on, "voodoo may be real, even though there are those who do not believe. As I say, my father died after he was cursed."

"And you think he may be one of those things they call a zombie?"

Fresh tears filled his eyes. "I have been told this."

"Have you ever thought about digging up his body to find out?" Travis was curious.

"No! I would never do that. Never! To do so would bring down the wrath of Baron Samedi. Then I, too, would be cursed."

"If I were you, I would leave Haiti," Travis said as he walked over to stand beside Eldon's bed and stare down at him. "You're an educated man. A doctor. Yet you talk like a fool. Now get out of here. You make me sick."

He heard the man run from the room, making little choking sounds as though he were about to be sick.

Travis touched Eldon's chest. He was breathing in a labored way but he was breathing. He pulled back Eldon's left eyelid and looked at the glassy gaze. He was drugged. Curse indeed. The man was drugged.

He looked around the room. No bottles. No cups or glasses. Quickly he examined Eldon's body. There were no marks of any kind. Frustrated, he slammed his fist into the wall, left a hole in it, brought his knuckles away bloody.

Eldon Harcourt did not stir.

Damn it, he couldn't just let him die. He reasoned that if he had been drugged, then more drugs would have to be administered to finish killing him. Or he might already have been given enough to kill him, but the drug was going to take a while. For the moment, Travis was sure of only one thing. If more drugs were required to finish him off, they were not going to get to him.

There was a soft knock on the door. Travis' hand went to his gun as he called out, "Come in."

He was surprised to see the priest.

"We were never introduced. I am Father Debinem. The two men who brought you to Mr. Babcock's office returned and told us of Mr. Harcourt's condition. I came to ask if I might be of assistance."

Travis looked him up and down and decided that he had put his superior airs aside. "That was kind of you," he said. "But according to the doctor who just left, there's nothing to be done. *I* think he's drugged."

Father Debinem walked over to the bed and stared down at Eldon, then reached out to wrap his fingers around his wrist. Releasing it, the wrist fell limply to the mattress. "Drugged or cursed?"

"If you believe in this voodoo nonsense, then he's cursed. I don't believe in it."

"I understand Mr. Harcourt does. He could be willing himself to die, you know, because he *believes* he *is* cursed. I imagine seeing the bones of your grandfather scattered about on your bed would be enough to frighten you to death all by itself."

The priest looked at Travis as he stepped away from the bed. "And what do you intend to do? Wait for him to die? If so, I shall wait with you."

Outside, the rain had begun to fall in torrents once again. The wind howled and whipped against the windows. Even the inside seemed gray and grim. A fitting place to wait for death, Travis thought.

"He isn't going to die," he said with finality.

"I will wait with you, and I will pray for him. By the way," the priest added, "Mr. Babcock inquired about having him admitted to a hospital, but there was not one who wished to accept him."

Travis snorted. "That's just as well. I'd do everything I could to keep him out of a hospital. I trust me and I trust you, but I damn well don't want him in a place where I can't trust anybody. They would probably finish him off there. We'll just take turns sitting with him and be ready if they try to come back and drug him some more."

Travis sat down on the floor, leaning back against the wall in a position from which he could keep an eye on both the door and the window.

"Then you do think he is drugged?" Father Debinem asked.

Travis nodded. "I sure as hell don't believe he's going to die from any curse. When whatever they've given him wears off enough that I can get through to him, I'm going to try to make him see that he's scaring himself to death."

"And what happens if they try to come back here?"

Travis grinned slowly. "Then I lay down some curses of my own."

Chapter Nine

TRAVIS staggered to his room and collapsed across his bed without even removing his boots. He was so tired that it was difficult to focus his eyes.

For three days and nights he and Father Debinem had taken turns sitting with Eldon Harcourt. Travis' shifts were longer, for the priest, due to his age, could not endure easily.

Eldon still lived. They force-fed him hot liquids, careful that he did not choke. Every so often he would open his eyes to stare about wildly, then succumb once more to whatever possessed him.

Travis slammed his fist into the knotted pillow. What had those sonsofbitches given him? What was keeping the man in that damn trance or coma or whatever the hell it was? Two other doctors had been called in and neither could, or would, say. Their only comment had been that they were helpless against voodoo.

He would see Babcock when he awoke, Travis vowed as he finally succumbed to sleep . . . see Babcock and insist that Eldon Harcourt be taken home. . . .

Suddenly someone was shaking him roughly and calling his name hysterically.

"Travis, get up. In the name of God, wake up."

He struggled awake, sitting up to see Father Debinem standing beside the bed, tears streaming down his cheeks. "God forgive me, but I never meant to fall asleep. I was just so tired."

Travis bounded to his feet, grabbing the man by his shoulders and shaking him. "You fell asleep?" he demanded. "You left Eldon alone?"

He pushed by the priest, bolting for the door, but the priest's solemn words stopped him cold.

"He's gone."

Travis turned slowly, blinking furiously, a cold dread moving through him. "What do you mean, he's gone?" he whispered raggedly.

The priest sank to the bed, covering his face with his hands, his hoarse voice barely audible through his fingers. "I fell asleep. God forgive me. I was so tired. I don't know how long I slept. When I awoke, he was gone."

Travis ran from his room and down the hall. When he reached Eldon's open door, his hands gripped each side of the frame. He stared at the empty bed. The blanket was pulled back, the sheets still rumpled.

Behind him, Father Debinem whispered brokenly, "I don't know how they got in. The door was locked. The window was locked and shuttered. I just don't understand. Lord forgive me."

"They have ways of getting in. Stop blaming yourself. You're a good deal older than I am, and I should have known you couldn't keep pushing yourself. If any of the others had helped us . . ." he shook his head, remembering how everyone had refused to cooperate.

His head drooped. They had Eldon. The bastards had him and never had Travis felt more helpless or alone. The man had helped him, probably saved his life, and Travis had failed to do the same for him.

He squeezed his eyes shut. Damn them, he thought furiously. Damn them to hell.

His eyes opened slowly. At first, he could not believe what he saw there on the floor, lying just outside the door, in the hallway. Moving very cautiously, as though a quick movement would make the object disappear. Travis knelt down and touched the long, slender, bamboo rod.

He touched it gingerly, then snatched it up with a roar.

"They've got him!" he screamed. "Goddamn them, they've got him."

Travis' gray eyes turned the color of melting iron, flashing red as fury consumed him. He would be damned if they would get away with making a zombie out of Eldon Harcourt!

He hurried back to his room to get his guns, thinking rapidly. According to the story Eldon had told him, the sorcerer sucked out the soul of his victim, and *then* the victim went into a coma and died in a few days. He had not said anything about death coming immediately.

Maybe Eldon was not dead. Maybe the *houngan* had gotten tired of waiting and realized that Travis and the priest were keeping Eldon alive. So he had taken matters into his own hands. Sure, he was probably somewhere slitting the throat of a chicken to sacrifice to their god. Then he would also bury the head and the bottle supposedly containing Eldon's soul.

He knew what would happen next. Eldon would have to be buried, and then the rest of the rite would take place.

There might still be time to save him.

"Do you want me to go and report what has happened to the authorities?" The priest was watching anxiously from the open doorway.

"Yeah," Travis responded quickly, thinking it best to get the man out of the way. He could be of no further help now.

A soft mist was falling outside, and from the gray darkness descending, Travis surmised it was close to eight o'clock. He had to move fast.

There was one person who might know what was going on, he reasoned as he buckled on his gun belt. One person.

He was running down the steps when the front door of the hotel opened and Orville Babcock and Father Debinem rushed in. "I found him coming down the street," the priest called excitedly. "I told him what happened."

Babcock was pale and shaken. "Now, Travis, I want you to calm down and let the authorities handle this," he said quickly, nervously, moving to block his path. "Evidently Harcourt died, and the natives wanted to bury him in their own way. Perhaps they were friends of his grandfather's. Who knows? We will have all the graveyards checked and I will personally see that his body is sent home."

"Do what you have to do," Travis said and shoved him aside, "just as I plan to do."

"Coltrane, the man is dead." Babcock followed him through the door and out into the street. "I can't have you running off half cocked, causing more trouble than you already have. You never should have gotten yourself involved with that girl."

"She got *her*self involved with *me,*" Travis snarled. "I never asked her for a damn thing."

Babcock stopped and screamed, "Coltrane, I order you to come back here. If you don't follow my orders, I will have you arrested."

Travis moved to the shadows. Babcock wasn't bluffing. He would be calling out his men to have him locked up. The private secretary to the President of the United States certainly did not want to stir up the locals.

Travis turned down a cobblestone path that wound between huts and small store buildings, moving with determination through the night, ignoring the soft rain that fell on him. He was not afraid. When the day came that he let a lot of mumbo-jumbo-shrieking natives scare him, then he hoped he would just lie down and die.

In the distance, the drums began to beat, slowly at first, then picking up in rhythm that seemed to stamp out his every footfall. Let them see him. Let them know he was coming. Reaching to touch the gun in his belt, he pitied any man who got in his way this night, for when the sun rose on another day in Port-au-Prince, Travis Coltrane was determined that he would have found Eldon Harcourt, dead or alive, as well as those responsible for his disappearance.

He could feel eyes watching him in the darkness. Let them look. Goddamn it, he thought, let them come out of the shadows and meet him face to face. He would love it.

Reaching Molina's hut, he sent the door crashing open against the inner wall.

Molina lay on her bed, naked, arms stretched above her head, her bronze skin glistening in the mellow glow of a nearby lantern.

"I thought perhaps you might come," she whispered, lips curling in a triumphant smile. "I hear *houngan* send sorcerer for your foolish friend."

Travis' eyes flicked over her, noting the luster of her skin, as though she had rubbed herself in oil. Despite his fury he felt a stirring in his loins and cursed himself.

He returned her smile arrogantly. "If you were expecting me, then you know why I have come, so let's not waste time, Molina."

"You have come too late to save your friend. He was a fool. He was wise to our ways. He knew the danger of interfering. He knew better. You shamed me, Travis Coltrane. You made me . . . a fallen woman." Her brown eyes snapped.

"I made you what you wanted to be," he snapped, "a *satisfied* woman." He moved close to the bed. "Where have those bastards taken Harcourt? And don't talk *houngans* and 'sorcerers' and 'zombies' to me, because I don't believe in that nonsense. He's still alive and you know it."

She sat up, stretching her long legs lazily as she raised her arms above her, lifting her small, firm breasts even higher. Tilting her head to one side, she whispered huskily, "He will always live, Travis Coltrane. He will be one of the living dead. It is the will of the *loas*, and Baron Samedi has given his approval. But why must we talk of things we cannot change?"

"You and your crazy friends aren't going to make a walking dummy out of him. This I swear to you," he replied tightly.

Raising an eyebrow, he asked her, "Why is Harcourt the target? I thought I was the one they were after. I don't see anyone looking for me."

Her eyes narrowed as she moved her fingertips to rub her nipples, arching her back in delight as she murmured, "I asked the *loas* to forgive you, Travis Coltrane, as I have forgiven you. You are right. You did make me a satisfied woman. For this I will forever be grateful."

She stood with the sensuous grace of a snake rising to hypnotize its prey before striking. Reaching out, she touched his crotch, squeezing gently and smiling at the response. "I can be more grateful. I can tell you where to find your friend."

"Why would you do that, Molina? You would anger your friends, wouldn't you?"

She did not look up but stared at his rising manhood, fascinated as it sprang to life beneath her gentle manipulations. "You give me pleasure. I tell you where to find this man you seek. I gave *houngan* pleasure, and now I can deal with him if he is angry . . . the way I deal with you when you are angry." She raised chocolate eyes fringed with thick lashes in a seductive invitation.

Travis still made no move to touch her. "We don't have much time, Molina. If they buried him alive, I've got to find him before he suffocates."

"If he is removed from his grave before the rites take place at the lowest hour, he will live. It is up to you to decide if this will happen."

With a questioning gaze, she fastened her eyes upon his eyes. All the while, her hands moved deftly to unfasten his trousers and release his swollen organ. She lifted her lips for his kiss, but he pushed her roughly back across the bed, falling on top of her.

"You want it, baby?" he murmured huskily as he spread her thighs. "You're going to get it. You're going to get it till you beg for me to stop, and then you're going to take me to find Harcourt yourself."

"No," she squirmed, suddenly frightened. "No! I cannot take you, only *tell* you."

"You'll do anything I want you to do, you little she-devil, because I'm going to make it so you'll think *I'm* your precious *loa!*"

He placed the tip of his throbbing penis between her legs, barely making entry as he thrust his hips to and fro teasingly. "Is this what you want?" he asked, tantalizing her as he stared down at her with mocking eyes. "Is this what you want me to give you, baby? Is this what it takes to make you do what I tell you?"

A moan escaped her lips as her neck arched backward, nails digging into the rock-hard flesh of his back. "Yes, oh, yes, my Travis. Anything. Anything. Just give it to me."

"When I'm good and damn ready," he snapped, lowering his lips to her breasts, circling her nipple with his tongue. "You want to play games, I'll oblige. But this is one game I always win."

"Travis," she pleaded, struggling to push him inside her eager body. Her hips moved up and down in hungry anticipation. "Now, please."

He ignored her whimpering pleas as he continued to devour her breasts. He ignored the frantic clawing of her sharp nails on his buttocks as she tried to pull him closer. Even in that moment of anger, Travis was not about to break his vow. He would not take a woman selfishly. She would get her pleasuring, and it would be a night she would remember forever, no matter how many men she bedded. Her punishment for the hell she had put him and Harcourt through, would be to remember this night, and never again to know such joy.

He took his time, moving strong, possessive hands over her twisting, writhing body. He moved probing fingers between her legs to make her scream and beg. All the while, he watched her.

Finally, and only when he could hold back no longer, Travis lifted her legs and encircled them around his neck. Drawing his hips back, he took a deep breath and shoved himself into her as deeply as possible.

She took all of him, sobbing out loud and clutching at him, moaning his name over and over, speaking in a mixture of Spanish and French. He did not understand, but it made no difference. It was the same in any language.

The woman was in the throes of ecstasy. He felt himself about to explode but held back to allow her one more crest. Then and only then did he afford himself the pleasure of release. He fell against her, exhausted, absently aware that she was lowering her weary legs from his shoulders.

They lay together, the silence broken only by gasps as they returned from the pinnacle of joy they had reached together. Long moments passed, and then Travis rolled to the side. Squeezing her face with one powerful hand, he harshly commanded, "All right. You got what you wanted. Now I'm getting my half of the bargain. Get your clothes on. We're going to move fast and find Harcourt. So help me, you try to double-cross me and I'll break your goddamn neck."

She had only to look into the steely gray eyes flashing red fire to know that he meant what he said. Nodding, trembling still from passion, she moved away. "Yes," she nodded obediently, subdued. "I will take you to find your friend. It will not be too late. But we must go fast."

She wrapped a bright cloth around her hips, not bothering to cover her breasts. Stepping toward the door, she motioned for him to follow. Dressed, making sure his gun was still in place, he moved behind her and ordered, "Lead the way, and remember what I told you, Molina."

She took a half step through the door, then turned suddenly and threw her arms around his neck, thrusting her face as close to his as she could reach by standing on tiptoes. With tears sparkling in her chocolate eyes, she asked, "Will you tell me you do not hate me, Travis Coltrane? Will you tell me that what we have is good for you, and that you will return?"

He sucked in his breath, then let it out slowly. "I never made you any promises, Molina, and I'm not going to now. Let's just move. We've wasted enough time."

"But you will think about it, no?" she persisted.

He pushed her forward. "Move," he growled. "Take me to where Harcourt is, Molina. I'm not fooling around anymore."

Her voice breaking as she stumbled along, she said, "You could at least give me something to hope for, Travis Coltrane. You could at least make me think that maybe this is not good-bye forever."

"God damn it, Molina, move!"

She mumbled to herself in that broken language again, but began to move forward. Travis would not let her slow her pace. Each time she faltered, he was right behind her to give her a quick push. The wind from the bay picked up, blowing wildly, causing them to struggle against it.

He felt a gut-gnawing urgency to hurry. Every moment counted. Damn, he never would have taken the time to make love to the wench, but had he not done so, she would not be cooperating.

At least the blasted drums were silent, he thought absently as they moved along, then tensed at the realization. He yelled to Molina above the wind, "Why have the drums stopped? What's going on? And don't lie to me."

"We must hurry," she replied, gasping. "The drums do not beat. I had not noticed. I do not like."

"What does it mean, Molina?" he gripped her bare shoulders and squeezed. "Why have they stopped?"

She began to cry, her words tumbling out so fast that it was difficult for him to make sense of what she was saying. And all the while the wind continued to beat at them relentlessly as the rains slashed their bodies. "Could mean . . . sorcerer is invoking . . . Baron Samedi. Sorcerer must . . . ask permission to dig up your friend from his grave . . . without interference of spirits in graveyard. Drums must be silent while Baron Samedi is called upon."

"Molina, listen to me and listen carefully." *God,* Travis thought frantically, furiously, *I've got to make this stupid, superstitious girl realize what's happening!* He kept his hands on her bare shoulders, felt her tremble beneath his touch. Her terrified eyes on his face surprised him. The depth of her superstition was awesome.

"I know you believe in all this," he yelled. "I know you don't know any different, because you were raised in all of this, but there is no way that anybody is going to raise Eldon Harcourt from the dead if he is, in fact, dead. But if they do get him out of that grave and drug him again, or if they've got him so damn scared he's lost his mind and became a lunatic, then he's just as good as dead. We've *got* to get him before they do, understand? You've got to help me save a man's life!"

"I try!"

He could barely make out her broken whimper.

"Travis Coltrane, I try!"

He gave her a careless hug. Then, taking her hand in his, he said, "Tell me the way. I can't let you lead anymore. You might get hurt. Just help me along."

"Straight ahead. The graveyard is straight ahead. We must be careful. Perhaps we arrive before the sorcerer. We may still be in time."

Holding onto her right arm tightly, Travis groped along. They had not moved far when she exclaimed suddenly, excitedly, "Here! Feel it? The fence! The graveyard fence. Follow me to the gate. I was here when they brought him. I know where he is buried."

Travis felt as though he had just been hurled into the depths of an icy ocean. "You were here?" he echoed hollowly. "You saw them bury him? Then he *is* dead."

"No. He is under spell. Come. Hurry. We may be in time to break spell before sorcerer comes to dig up man, make him living dead."

Defeat was not a familiar emotion to Travis, and he was having great difficulty accepting the overwhelming inevitability now. But logic pointed to the fact that, indeed, Eldon Harcourt was dead. And how would they ever find him in this damned darkness?

Molina tugged at his hand. "You hurry, please. Afraid of graveyard. Baron Samedi not like nonbelievers here. You are in danger."

Damn it to hell and back, how had he gotten himself into such a mess?

"Here!"

Molina's hand slipped from his and, for an instant, he panicked, thinking she had run away.

"Here!" she repeated urgently. "Down here. Help me, quickly."

Travis groped in the darkness, falling against her. "Help me dig. He can breathe. There is hole for air."

Travis began to claw with his hands at the muddy earth. "Damn it, Molina, why did you make me make love to you?" he cursed, digging frantically. "Why did you take so much time when you knew he was buried? If he's dead—"

"He will live," she said calmly. "And Molina only wanted you to love her once again. I have a terrible hunger for you, Travis Coltrane. I will never get enough of you."

You've gotten all you're getting, he swore silently, coldly.

His hands touched something rough, splintery, a plank. Molina felt it and warned, "Careful, now. The board lies on top of his body. Careful not to make dirt fall on him when it is lifted."

"Hang on, Harcourt," Travis muttered, more to himself than to the man he hoped was still living. "We've almost got you. Damn this rain. If only I could see what the hell I'm doing."

His fingers worked their way through the dirt clods till he found the end of the plank. With a strong, quick jerk he lifted it upward and flung it up and out into the night. He reached down and groped for Harcourt's body, lifting him up to a sitting position, found his nose, and placed fingertips beneath his nostrils. He was still breathing! But there was no time to lose.

Placing his hands beneath his shoulders, Travis lifted the limp body from the shallow grave and hoisted him up and over his left shoulder. "We've got to get him back to the village," he said brusquely. "Lead the way and hurry. If we reach a clearing, let me know so we can run."

Suddenly there was a flash of light, and Travis blinked against the flare of a torch, squinting to make out the face of the black man who held it. The face was painted in a distortion of weird designs in many colors, and his mouth was twisted with fury.

"Back off, you crazy bastard," Travis warned. He was not scared, only angry. He ordered himself not to do what he really wanted to do, and shoot the man where he stood. The important thing was to get Harcourt to a hospital. There would be time later for retribution.

The black man wore a headdress of wildly colored feathers, and only a scrap of cloth covered his genitals. In the lantern's glow, his eyes bulged, shining eerily. He held some sort of greenery in his left hand. Shrieking maniacally, he cried to Harcourt, "By Dambella, by Baron Samedi, by your *loa,* which I now possess, I order you to rise from the grave and be obedient to my every command henceforth!"

Travis took a step forward, wondering absently what had happened to Molina, for he could not see her in the halo of light. "I'm warning you, old man! Get out of my way!"

The sorcerer stood his ground. Travis had spotted the long, slender spear held in his left hand along with the greenery. Shaking the spear and the greenery, he spoke once more to Harcourt's body. "By Dambella, by Baron Samedi, by your *loa,*" he repeated his incantation, "which I now possess, I order you to rise!"

Travis gave him a rough shove with his free hand and sent him sprawling into the mud. The lantern fell to one side but did not go out.

"Your voodoo didn't work, you fool," Travis yelled as he moved by him. "Not this time." Travis called to Molina, "Get his lantern. It will help us move faster."

She stepped out of the darkness, trembling with fright. To obey him meant going against the sorcerer, the *houngan,* the *loas,* and everything else she had been taught to believe in from the day she was born.

Travis knew the turmoil churning within her, and he made his voice gentle. "Please, Molina. We have to get him back to a doctor. Do as I ask. They can't hurt you unless you let them."

Avoiding the sorcerer's blazing stare, Molina knelt slowly, reaching out with trembling fingers to clutch the lantern.

"Good girl." Travis nodded, but then, in a flash, he saw the movement as the black man lifted his arm, spear poised. Without hesitation, Travis whipped out his gun and fired before the deadly weapon could be flung through the air at Molina.

With a single garbled cry of rage, the sorcerer clutched his stomach and slumped back into the mud, face up, his body jerking convulsively. Then he lay still.

Molina stared down at the sorcerer. The golden lantern glow danced across the man's black skin, making it shine and sparkle as bright red blood ran from the gaping wound in his stomach.

"You . . . have . . . killed him," she choked.

"I had no choice. Let's move." Travis put his gun away and turned. He had killed men before, and while he did not like taking another man's life, he never hesitated if it meant saving a more worthy life.

Molina hung back.

"Move!" Travis cried, bringing her to life again. "He was going to put that spear in your back, woman. I saved your life. Now you help me save Harcourt's."

She led the way from the graveyard, and Travis glanced around apprehensively. Molina sensed what was bothering him. "You do not have to fear another," she cried above the wind. "The sorcerer must always come here alone to bring back the dead."

Travis said nothing. Shifting Harcourt carefully across his shoulder, he followed Molina out of the graveyard.

When they reached Port-au-Prince, Molina led him to the closest hospital. He was weary from carrying Harcourt so far, but determination would not let him give way to exhaustion. He started up the steps, washed with relief, then realized that Molina was no longer in front of him. Why was she hanging back? He turned to talk to her.

She was gone. She had disappeared into the night. He called to her, but there was no answer. Somehow, he had not expected there would be.

It was all over between Travis and Molina, of that he was sure.

Travis sat before Orville Babcock's desk, booted feet propped on the edge. Travis studied his fingernails, a slight smile touching his lips. He knew his obvious preoccupation was annoying the man.

"Damn it, Coltrane, you could have caused a big problem! This might have led to fighting here!" Babcock's fist hit the desk with a resounding thud.

Without raising his head, Travis looked at him out of the corners of his lowered eyes. "I don't like people to bang their fists at me, mister. It annoys me."

"You killed a man. You shot a citizen of this country." Babcock glared at him accusingly.

"He was going to kill the girl."

Babcock sighed. "Couldn't you have just wounded him? Did you have to kill him, for God's sake?"

Travis continued to pick at his fingernails. "I don't draw my gun unless I plan to use it, and I don't shoot unless I aim to kill."

Babcock emitted another sigh. "Well, thank heavens we were able to smooth things over, cover up the incident."

"I think a hell of a lot has been covered up." Travis lowered his feet to the floor with a loud thud. He sat up straight, facing the other man. "Doesn't it mean anything that those fools almost killed an American? That they drugged him? Buried him alive? If it hadn't been for that girl, they'd have him out staggering around in a field somewhere, drugged, and calling him a zombie!"

Travis' voice had risen and Babcock sank lower in his chair, uncomfortable. He attempted a smile. "Well, it's all over. That's why I called you in here, to tell you it's over."

"No, hell, you didn't!" Travis laughed shortly, then snarled, "You wanted to rap my knuckles like a bad little boy but it didn't work, because I don't feel a damn bit bad about any of it. *You* just better be glad they took Harcourt into the hospital that night and brought him around, because if he had died, you can bet your ass you would have had a lot more trouble on your hands because I would have gone after everyone responsible.

"Do we understand each other, Babcock?" Travis gazed, unrelenting into the man's eyes. Unable to meet his look, Babcock lowered his gaze. Travis smiled. It was not a nice smile.

"Uh, yes, of course." Babcock cleared his throat and sat up quickly.

"Is that all?"

"No," Babcock replied almost happily. "Sam Bucher is waiting for you down at the dock. There is a ship leaving for the States today. You are dismissed."

"Dismissed or fired?" Travis laughed. "You know, it makes no difference. I was leaving anyway."

Tipping his hat, flashing a grin, Travis Coltrane left the room, closing the door quietly behind him.

Orville Babcock sagged in his chair, feeling absolutely

drained. Lord, he was glad that man was leaving. It had been a terrible, exhausting experience.

He stared at the closed door thoughtfully. Yes, he was glad to see him go. But there was one thing he would never forget. Travis Coltrane was a man.

He wished he were more like him, and, though he would never dare admit it aloud, Babcock was proud of what that man had had the courage to do.

Chapter Ten

TRAVIS reacted to Sam's story with incredulous shock and with fury.

Kitty had deliberately plotted to get him out of North Carolina because she thought he was miserable. Plotted! Sam had kept from Travis the news about his having been chosen to be a part of the committee. Sam had not wanted to be a party to his leaving, but Kitty had convinced him it was for the best.

"God damn!" Travis had exploded. "Can't I make decisions for myself?"

"Travis, she did it because she loved you," Sam had told him, hoping he would understand. "And I didn't tell you about the committee invitation because I was afraid you would want to go, and she wouldn't want you to, and it would cause a problem. But when she asked me to get you on it, I went ahead and told her about the original invitation."

"Both of you were scheming behind my back! Did you ever stop to think that I am capable of making my own decisions?" He had stared at his lifelong friend with blazing eyes.

"Would you have left if she hadn't driven you away?" Sam asked carefully, "or would you have chained yourself to that plow and gone on being miserable?"

Travis had thrown up his hands in disgust. "How the hell

do I know? All I'm saying is that it should have been *my* damn decision, and I'm pretty well pissed off that you and Kitty treated me like a child!"

Sam apologized, repeating that he wished he had been able to keep his promise to Kitty to tell Travis the truth during the trip to Washington, D.C. Hearing that only made Travis feel worse. Had he known that Kitty had schemed for his benefit, would he have succumbed to Molina's charms? Hell, all he wanted now was to get home as fast as possible. Lord, did he ever have a few things to say to that woman.

By the time the ship reached Norfolk, Virginia, Travis had forgiven Sam. After all, Travis reasoned, Kitty could be very beguiling when she wanted her way, and he was well aware that Sam loved her like a daughter and could be wrapped around her little finger.

Kitty, herself, was another matter. While he missed her fiercely and longed to wrap his arms around her, he was furious at being reacquainted with her conniving ways. Damn, he had had his fill of that during the war!

During the sea voyage, Travis spent much time considering his life in North Carolina. He had to admit that he did hate it, that it could not continue. He and Kitty would sit down and discuss it, and, together, they would plan a new life. Thinking about it filled him with new zest.

But underlying the longing for Kitty, the desire to have the trip behind him, there was also a strange urgency to get home as quickly as possible.

"I just feel it," he confided to Sam their last night on board ship. "Like during the war, when I had this gut feeling that Rebs were all around us, about to attack. I just have this gnawing inside that says I need to get home fast."

Sam patted him on the back, hiding his own feelings of concern. "We'll be there soon enough, boy. Don't worry. Kitty will be waiting for you with open arms, them purple eyes of hers just a'shinin'. And think how much little John will have grown. Yeah, I imagine you are anxious to get back there."

"Five months and it seems more like five years," Travis muttered, his stomach churning with that mysterious need to get back to his wife and son as quickly as possible. Something was wrong. By damn, he'd had too many feelings like this in the past for it to be anything else except a premonition that he was needed.

Upon reaching Norfolk, Sam urged Travis to go with him to the capital in Washington. "We need to make reports, and we can also check on new jobs. There's bound to be openings for federal marshals somewhere, and you know you and Kitty will be wanting to leave North Carolina."

Travis refused. "I can worry about a job later. Right now, I just want to get back to Kitty."

Sam said he would catch up to him later. Travis went directly to the train station, bought a ticket, and spent several hours pacing up and down anxiously beside the tracks.

When he reached Goldsboro, Travis went directly to a livery stable to rent a horse. "And don't give me an old nag, either," he said impatiently to the old man who stared up at him curiously. "I'm in a hurry, and I want a horse that can run a full gallop for about ten miles."

The man continued to look up at him, eyes slowly widening. He made no move.

Travis sighed impatiently, forcing his temper to remain under control. "Did you hear me? I want a horse. I'm in a hurry."

The old man lifted a gnarled finger to point at him. He whispered, "You're Coltrane, ain't you?"

"Yes, yes, I'm Travis Coltrane," he answered hurriedly. "Now will you get the damn horse or do I have to get him myself?"

"You just now comin' home? Heard you was away."

"Yes, I just got off the train." Travis took a deep breath, looked down at the ground, then tossed his head to stare at the rafters, finally facing the old man again as he fought for control. "Get my horse, will you, please?" He spoke through gritted teeth.

He sighed with relief as the man turned and shuffled toward one of the stalls.

When he returned, leading a saddled gelding, Travis inspected the horse quickly and commented, "He looks strong. How much? I'll have him back tomorrow evening."

"Uh . . . two dollars," he stammered nervously. "You goin' home now? Out to your place?"

Travis handed him the money, eyeing him suspiciously. "Why are you acting so strangely?" he asked in his usual direct way. "What's wrong?"

"Nothing . . . nothing at all." The old man stuffed the money in the pocket of his bib overalls and backed away, doffing his straw hat slightly. Then he turned and fled to the shadows of the stable.

Travis stared after him, puzzled. Swinging up into the saddle, he guided the horse out into the street, nudging him to a trot until they reached the edge of town, then moving him to a full gallop.

Familiar sights were just barely visible in the moonlight. Stars shone overhead. It was a beautiful evening, and Travis welcomed the hours that lay before him. First he would have it all out with Kitty, her deceit and lies. Then, when John was asleep, they would make up in the way they always had. It was going to be one of the best nights of lovemaking they had ever shared.

Travis' heart was pounding furiously as he and the horse approached the last bend in the road. Around that curve, the little cabin would be in sight, windows aglow with lights. Kitty would be inside, and John.

He reined the horse to such an abrupt halt that the animal reared up on his back legs, forelegs wildly pawing the air.

The cabin was dark. He could make out the lines in the moonlight. Not only was it dark, but also there was something deserted about it.

Moving forward, he rode the horse onward, turning onto the dirt path to gallop across the yard and around to the back door. Reining to a stop, he swung down, taking all four of the porch steps in one great leap and shoving the back door open as he called out Kitty's name.

Only silence and a musty odor lay before him in the darkness. Stepping inside, he fumbled for a match and lit it. Glancing around in alarm, he saw layers of dust on the furniture. Where was Kitty?

The match burned his fingers and he swore and dropped it to the floor and stomped on it. Lighting another, he moved to the other room, the one they had used for sleeping and as a sitting room as well. The cobwebs and dirt and the stripped bed told him it had been quite a while since anyone had been there.

He took a deep breath and slowly let it out. There were all kinds of explanations, he knew, but that feeling in his gut was eating at him again. He supposed there was nothing to do but return to town and look for her. Someone at the hospital could surely tell him where she was. He mounted the horse again and began to make his way back to the road, pausing to take in the air of neglect over the entire farm. Kitty had said some of the Negroes were going to work the land as sharecroppers, but in the silver glow of the moon, Travis could see that nothing was growing in the fields except weeds. What the hell was going on?

Suddenly he remembered that the Widow Mattie Glass was to keep John for her while she worked at the hospital. She lived only a few miles up the road. He turned the horse south and put him to a full gallop.

A lantern still burned in the window of Mattie's small cottage. Travis called out to her as he rode into the yard, not having forgotten the unwritten code of country folk—don't go around anyone's house after dark without yelling out your presence, not unless you want to get your head blown off.

When Mattie did not appear right away, Travis slid from the horse and walked to the steps. "Mrs. Glass? It's me, Travis Coltrane. I'd like to speak to you, please."

The door squeaked open, and Mattie Glass peered out, holding her robe clutched at her throat with one hand. Her other hand held up a lantern. She squinted in the faint light, brows furrowed tightly as she strained to see. Suddenly she recognized him, and flung the door all the way open. She ran to him, sobbing wildly.

Travis was stunned but opened his arms to her, taking the lantern from her quickly as she flung herself against him.

"Mrs. Glass, what's wrong?" he asked. "If I came at a bad time, I'm sorry. It's just that I can't find Kitty."

She began to sob hysterically, and his puzzlement grew. Shaking her gently, he urged her to tell him what was wrong but she continued to cry.

Suddenly, a small figure appeared in the doorway. It was a little boy wearing pajamas, thumb stuck in his mouth as he stared at the two of them, eyes wide with fright. John!

Travis pushed Mattie gently away from him and set the lantern down on the ground. He ran up onto the porch and gathered his son in his arms, holding him close. Turning, he saw Mattie watching, misery etched in every line of her face. "For the love of God, woman," he whispered, hurting and not knowing why, "what is wrong? Where is Kitty? Why is John here with you at this time of night?"

She lifted the bottom of her long robe and hurried by him

to the inside of the cabin. Travis followed, holding John. "Now, I don't want to frighten the boy," he said sternly. "I can see he's already upset, but damn it, I've got to know what's going on. The house looks as though nobody has been in it in months, and you break down and cry at the sight of me. I want to know what the hell is going on, and I want to know where my wife is!"

His voice had risen angrily, and John whimpered and squirmed in his arms. Mattie held her finger in front of her lips in a plea to Travis to be quiet. Tears still streaming down her cheeks, she padded across the room to take John from him. "I'll put him to bed. He was asleep but woke up when you yelled. Then we can talk." Her voice cracked as she disappeared through a doorway to the side of the parlor.

Travis paced impatiently. Soon he heard the door close and she entered the little parlor again. She began to cry again, and suddenly Travis could stand no more. "Mattie Glass, will you stop that infernal blubbering and tell me what is going on around here before I lose my mind? Enough is enough!"

"I don't know where Kitty is," she said in a squeaky voice as she sank down on the faded black horsehair sofa.

Travis blinked. "What do you mean?"

Her tone rose, and her crying stopped as she stared up at him, lips quivering. "I have not seen Kitty for almost five months and neither has anyone else. Lord forgive me for being the one to tell you this, but no one knows what happened to her. She just disappeared."

Travis stood rigid, fighting the weakness that had suddenly taken over his body. "Mattie," he said slowly, evenly, "you better explain all this to me and tell me everything you know."

She shrugged helplessly, tilting her head to one side. "I just did, Travis. That's all I know . . . all anybody knows. The marshal did what he could about searching, but she just disappeared without a trace. The last anybody saw of her was when she left the hospital that night, and it was storming something fierce. When she didn't come for John that night, I assumed she had stayed in town because of the storm. But when she didn't show up the next evening either, I got one of my boys to ride into town. He was told at the hospital that she hadn't shown up that morning, so he went to the marshall. The marshall got a bunch together to search for her. But they couldn't find a trace. She just disappeared, Travis."

It couldn't be happening, but it was. Kitty was gone. The words whirled around in his head until he became dizzy and struggled to lower himself onto the sofa beside Mattie.

"Oh, Travis, I'm sorry. I know this is terrible for you. I've got some homemade wine." She hurried from the room and returned with a bottle and a glass, but Travis pushed the glass aside and snatched the bottle, tilting it. He took a long gulp.

"I'll find her," he said in a tight, strained voice, staring straight ahead. "So help me God, I'll find her."

Suddenly he leaped to his feet and whirled around to stare at her. "Why in hell wasn't I notified? Why wasn't a message sent to me in Haiti?"

She lowered her eyes, unable to face him. "We talked about it. Me and the parson and the marshal and the doctors at the hospital. There was nothing you could do, Travis. Believe me when I say that everything possible was done to try to find her. There was simply nothing left to do. So we decided that since John was loved and well cared for with me, there was no sense in sending for you and getting you all upset." She added in a bare whisper, "As you are now."

He gave her an incredulous glare, then ran his fingers through his hair and began to pace the room. "*I'll* find her. I swear to God, I'll find her." He felt hot tears of fury burning his eyes.

There was silence for a moment, and then Mattie cleared her throat. She stood up and touched his shoulder gently. "Travis, I hate to put my thoughts and everyone else's into words, but Kitty may be . . . dead."

He gazed straight through her. "Dead? Oh, no. Not dead." He shook his head. "I need time to think. No, I need to get to town and find the marshal."

"You need to rest," she interrupted. "You need something to eat. Nothing can be done tonight."

Travis protested that he could eat nothing, but Mattie went to the little kitchen that was connected to the house by a porch running along the outside.

Alone, he slumped to the sofa once more, covering his face with his hands. Kitty could not be dead. No. Something had happened. Something terrible. He could feel it in his bones. But she was not dead.

He reached for the bottle of wine once more. Hell, yes, he would find her. Someone, somewhere knew something. He just had to find that someone.

When Mattie returned with a plate of cold chicken and collards, she found him slumped over, the empty wine bottle propped between his legs. She laid the plate of food aside and took the knitted afghan from the back of the sofa and spread it across him. Then she tiptoed from the room, blowing out the lanterns as she went.

Total darkness consumed the house, just as it had so quickly consumed Travis Coltrane's life.

He awoke to the smell of hot, fresh coffee, and for a moment stared groggily around the room, wondering where he was. Then it all came flooding back, and he sat up rigidly, reaching for the coffee Mattie was offering.

"Travis, do you feel any better? It was such a terrible shock last night."

The morning sun streamed in through the windows, dancing across the polished hardwood floor. It should be raining, he thought wearily, head aching. Raining, with thunder and lightning and wind and hail. How could the sun be shining? Birds even dared to sing and he cursed them.

"Daddy."

John toddled into the room, grinning widely, and hurried to his arms. Travis pulled him up on his lap and held him close. "He seems well," he said to Mattie by way of thanks.

"Yes, he's doing fine," she said quickly. "For a while, he cried a lot, but then he settled down. Children have such a marvelous way of adjusting. Much better than we grown-ups do. He certainly hasn't forgotten you."

"He hasn't forgotten her, either, and neither have I. I'll find her. I swear it."

She managed a wan smile. "I've fixed you some breakfast and don't argue with me about it. I know you need to eat. Then you can ride into town and do whatever it is you feel you must do. And don't worry about John. You know he's fine right here, and I'll take care of him as long as you want me to."

"Thank you, Mattie," he said sincerely, also managing a smile. "At least I won't have to worry about my son." He gave him a fierce hug.

John touched his face with a soft, chubby hand, and Travis looked down into his eyes. They were gray, like his own, but there was also a touch of lavender, so like his mother's.

"I'm going to find her, boy," he said gruffly, resting his chin on the little head gently. "For you and for me, I'm going to find her. And God help anybody who stands in my way."

The little boy looked up at his father with rounded eyes. There was a feeling of fear, but as he continued to stare at the man who held him, the fear went away and was replaced by a different emotion. He knew only that he had no need to be afraid as long as these strong arms held him.

The child had no way of knowing that his mother knew that emotion well, could have explained it to him, knew that no one need fear anything or anyone as long as Travis Coltrane held them dear.

Travis rode into town and returned the horse to the livery stable. The old man was there, still watching him in that strange way. Travis snapped, "You knew, didn't you? That's why you acted so strange last night. You knew about my wife, didn't you?"

The old man ducked his head, staring at the straw-littered floor. "Yeah, I knew, and I didn't want to be the one to tell you. I'm sorry."

"Not half as sorry as the sonofabitch responsible for this is going to be."

The old man jerked his head up to stare at him in wonder. "You think somebody did away with her? Is that what you think? The marshal, he said she probably drowned. We had a bad storm that night. Everybody remembers it. The creeks swoll up, and we near 'bout had a flood. The marshal said she and her horse probably stumbled and fell in a creek and got swept away."

"Kitty was a damn good rider," Travis said. "She would not have taken any chances if the creeks were flooded. She would have known what she was doing."

"But they never found her body."

Travis withered him with a look and then walked on out. He headed toward the marshal's office, walking purposefully, eyes straight head.

"Well, I do declare!"

Travis glanced to his right. Nancy Danton stood in the open doorway of her husband's office. He noticed her surreptitious smile and glittering eyes. She looked—what? Triumphant? Of course, she would be happy that anything bad had happened to either him or Kitty, but especially Kitty.

"Travis Coltrane," she cooed. "You just keep on getting handsomer."

He tipped his hat, begrudging her even that, and started on by, but she called out, "Are you lonely since your wife left you, Travis? Would you like to come have dinner with my husband and me some night?"

He stopped. "What?"

"I said," she giggled softly, "that you could come and have dinner with me and—"

"No." He gestured. "Before that. About my wife."

She twirled the blue parasol above her head, eyes dancing with glee. "I asked if you were lonely since your wife left you."

"What makes you think she left me, Nancy?"

"Well, she's *gone,* isn't she?" came the haughty reply. "She sure didn't hang around long after you left."

"Kitty has disappeared," he said tightly. "I have no reason to think she left of her own free will, particularly since our son remains with Mrs. Glass. So watch that sharp tongue. You've done enough to hurt Kitty in the past. Stay out of this."

She snapped her parasol shut in an angry gesture. Placing her hands on her hips, she stared up at him and sputtered, "Just who do you think you are talking to? Plenty of people think your wife ran away. Heaven knows, the little trollop was always chasing after men. First it was my Nathan. Then even you, a despicable Yankee.

"Did you really think she would sit by and wait for you? And as for your little boy, did you really think she would give him a second thought if she had herself set on running away with some man?"

"If you were a man," Travis growled, "I would beat the hell out of you, Nancy. You lying little slut! You dare talk about Kitty that way, when you are one of the filthiest, most conniving little whores I've ever known?"

Enraged, Nancy raised the parasol to strike him across his face, but Travis saw the movement and grabbed her wrist, squeezing so tightly that she screamed in pain, dropping her weapon.

Her cries brought Jerome Danton running from his office. He looked from his screaming wife to the agitated expression on Travis' face. "What's going on here? Coltrane, unhand my wife."

Travis slung her toward Jerome and the two collided and stumbled. "Take her," he dusted his hands on his shirt sleeves. "Damned if I want her."

"Do something, Jerome." Nancy righted herself and turned to her husband. "He was assaulting me. Are you going to let him get away with it?"

Travis smiled at Jerome. "Well, *are* you going to let me get away with it, Danton? Have you anything to settle with me?"

"No, no," Jerome shook his head nervously, then gave Nancy a push toward the open door. "Go inside. I'll discuss this with him and see what's wrong."

Nancy jerked away from him. "I'll tell you what is wrong! I'm not going anywhere! He assaulted me because I told him how everyone is talking about that trashy wife of his running off with another man. He had the nerve to call me a horrid name." She looked from him to Travis as she stamped her foot. "Don't you let him get away with this, Jerome! He has disgraced my good name."

"You never had a good name," Travis laughed. "And your husband knows that well enough. Just keep your mouth shut about Kitty, or you will answer to me, Nancy."

She shrieked again, whirling about to beat at Jerome with her fists. "Don't you let him get away with this, damn you. He's threatening me!"

Jerome's eyes locked with Travis' as Jerome grabbed Nancy's wrists and wrestled her into the office. He despised the man and always had, but he knew that Nancy deserved the insults.

With one last look at Travis, he kicked the door shut and flung Nancy into a nearby chair. "Don't you get up!" He pointed his finger, towering over her. "What are you trying to do, you crazy woman? Get me killed? That man has the reputation of being as deadly with his fists as he is with his gun. Why did you have to goad him?"

Her upper lip turned back in a snarl as she hissed the words, "Because I hate him! Because I want to hurt him as he hurt me!" Her gaze moved up and down his body, mirroring the disgust that was rippling through her. "You call yourself a man! You're nothing but a sniveling coward. The idea of you letting that bastard stand there and say such things about me!"

Jerome limped back to his desk, not wanting the scene to continue. He knew from years of agonizing experience that when she was having one of her tantrums it was best just to ignore her, for there was no reasoning with Nancy.

"Look at you!" she cried shrilly, pointing to his leg. "You limp because of Kitty Wright! She put a bullet in your leg and made a cripple of you, yet you defend her and let her husband stand in the street and insult *me*, your wife."

"You deserved it." He sat down behind his desk and began to resume working on the weekly payroll for his lumber mill.

"I deserved it?" She snatched up a sheaf of papers and flung them in his face. "How dare you say such a thing to me! How dare you!"

He got to his feet, clutching the edge of the desk as he fought to keep from slamming his fist into her twisted, shrieking face. "Hell, yes, you deserved it, you shrew! You are wicked, Nancy. *I* know what happened to Kitty. Remember? I was there. I know a lot of other things, too, how you went to bed with Travis Coltrane once, and he scorned you, and you've hated him ever since."

"That's . . . not true," she stammered, stepping back, her hand fluttering to her throat. "I never . . ."

"Oh, hell, yes, you did!" He ground out the words as he began to straighten the papers. "I knew all about it, but I didn't give a damn. I still don't. You can bed any man you choose. You can go to hell, for all I care. Just get out of here and give me some peace."

"You . . . you can't speak to me that way."

"The hell I can't. And don't threaten me, the way you did the night you found me with Kitty. If I go to jail, what would happen to you? No other man would have you, and you like the life I have provided for you."

She tilted her head to one side, lips twisted in a gloating smirk. "Then why didn't you say so that night? Why did you turn tail and run? You really are a coward, Jerome."

"Maybe I am," he sighed wearily. "If being tired of fighting makes me a coward, then I am a coward."

"You let me deal with Kitty. She couldn't have meant so much to you."

He looked up at her, eyes unwavering. "She meant a great deal to me. I loved her more than any woman I have ever known. But she made it plain too many times that she did not want me. Perhaps I let you deal with her that night because I was angry, angry with her for her continuous rejection of me, and angry with myself for being so foolish as to keep chasing her. Perhaps I felt it was just a relief to have her out of my life."

They had never before discussed that night, and just then, suddenly, she had to know his thoughts. Quietly she asked, "Do you think I killed her? Do you think I shot her after you left, and hid her body?"

"I don't think about it, Nancy. Now will you get out of here and let me get back to work? It takes a great deal of money to support you."

She clutched the edge of the desk and threw her head back to laugh, then smiled down at him as she whispered, "Yes, I suppose it does, you bastard, just as it takes a great deal of money to support your mistress in Raleigh. Did you think I didn't know about her? I know a lot of things about you."

To her surprise, he laughed. "Yes, yes, I imagine you do, and I know much about you, too, darling. So we each realize that the other is totally without scruples and a wretched person."

She whirled around and left quietly. Jerome leaned back in his chair, chewing on the tip of a pencil. No, he didn't think Nancy had killed Kitty. He *knew* she hadn't. He had slipped back that night and listened and watched. He knew all about Luke Tate taking Kitty away, paid to do so by Nancy.

Jerome thought of Travis Coltrane. He despised the man. And he thought of Kitty, of how much he loved her. What had happened to her these past months? From what he knew of Luke Tate, the man had probably turned Kitty's life into a hell.

Suddenly Jerome Danton did not like himself very much. In fact, he realized as he got up from his chair and limped to the window, he did not like himself at all.

But what could he do? he asked himself. Nothing at all, nothing to make up for all the terrible things he had done.

Except, his eyes widened at the thought, he could do something for Kitty. Perhaps a good deed, for the first time in his life, would ease some of the misery he was feeling. If he told Travis what he knew, perhaps he could track down Luke and Kitty.

But did he dare?

Chapter Eleven

NANCY Danton sat before the oval gilt-edged mirror in her boudoir, staring pensively at her reflection.

She was not, she thought with a satisfied smile, unattractive. Her chestnut-brown hair glimmered with golden highlights and looked quite appealing brushed down around her shoulders. She also liked her eyes, the color of ginger and edged with thick lashes that she knew how to lower and flutter seductively.

Expensive oils and creams kept her skin smooth.

She wore a yellow silk dressing gown and reached to tug at the ribbon which held it together, allowing it to fall open and expose her breasts. Cupping them in her hands, she stared down. They were not quite as large and voluptuous as she would have liked, but they were, she mused, satisfactory.

She pulled her gown together once more, gloating in the fact that her entire body was still firm and flawless. She had no marks from childbearing, thanks to the skilled, however unethical doctor in Raleigh who had on three occasions rid her of babies she refused to have. Her nose wrinkled in disdain. The *last* thing she wanted was a whining, groping child nuzzling at her breast.

She met the mischievous reflection of her eyes, saw the warm lust there. She wanted Travis Coltrane at her breast.

She wanted Travis. Oh, yes, she wanted him with desperation. No matter that he had scorned her publicly, though no one else had heard his angry taunts. No matter that he had not come near her since marrying that damned Kitty. He was the one man she wanted to take her, possess her, ravish her.

And she was going to have him.

With fierce determination igniting her, Nancy arose from the velvet bench and strode quickly to her closet, flinging open the doors. The closet was filled with elegant gowns of every imaginable design and color. Perhaps marriage to Jerome was suffocatingly boring, she thought, but at least he was rich and able to give her anything she wanted, and she wanted a lot.

She chose a green watered silk with a deeply plunging neckline. A matching fringed shawl would cover her until she wanted to expose her cleavage, but the main reason she chose this costume was the skirt. It was a latest creation from Paris and required no bulky hoop. Several lace petticoats would provide the necessary fullness.

As she dressed, she recalled the gossip she had heard about Travis since his return. Of course, she dared ask no questions, feigning disgust whenever his name was mentioned. But the women in Goldsboro were quite taken with his feral good looks, and he was the object of much curiosity and speculation. All Nancy had to do was listen, and she was able to keep up with his every move.

He was, they were saying, ensconced in a hotel room drowning his grief in whiskey. She also knew that that scruffy Sam Bucher had returned and was trying to sober him up.

Soon, she figured, he would move on at the urgings of Sam. A man like Travis Coltrane was not about to hang around a place he made no secret of despising. That was fine. Let him leave. It was too disturbing to have him around and not be able to have him anytime she pleased. But, and a new wave of longing washed over her, she would have him one more time.

She made her way through the elegantly furnished house and down the winding stairway to the foyer. The servants had retired for the night, following her instructions. She left by the back door, keeping to the shadows so as not to be seen. The hotel was five blocks away, but she was able to cover the distance without encountering anyone.

She paused outside the rear of the building, listening to the raucous sounds from the saloon in front. It had cost her a small sum to seal the lips of the man she had instructed to learn Travis' room number, so after glancing around one last time to make sure no one was watching, she was able to go inside and move directly up the back stairs, knowing exactly where she was going.

The hallway smelled of urine and whiskey, and she wrinkled her nose in distaste. There was little light from the kerosene lantern that hung from the ceiling. All was quiet, and she tiptoed across the faded carpet to stand outside Room 14, pressing her ear against the door. Hearing no sounds, she smiled to herself. If he was in there, he was alone.

She lifted her hand and knocked softly. There was no answer, and she frowned and knocked louder, glancing around anxiously.

"Yeah, who is?" came the annoyed voice.

She knocked again.

He boomed out, "Who the hell is it?"

She knocked in soft, insistent little raps.

Finally she heard, "Oh, hell, wait a minute." There were sounds of movement within, footsteps clumping across the floor, the lock turning.

The door swung open, and she caught sight of his raised eyebrows as she scurried inside, slamming the door herself and leaning back against it to smile up at him. "Hello, Travis," she whispered huskily. "I thought you might be lonely."

"Not for you."

He tried to reach around her to open the door, but she stepped forward and threw her arms around his neck, letting her shawl fall from her shoulders, pressing her bosom hard against his bare chest. "It was good for us, Travis," she said quickly. "You know it was always good. I'm just what you need."

"Nancy, you're the last person I need." He reached for her arms and yanked them down. "Now just get out of here before you get us both in trouble."

She stepped back, eyes moving over his body. He wore only tight denim pants, and her fingers ached to dance through the thick mat of hair on his chest that tapered down to what she wanted the most. Boldly, she reached out and clutched him between his legs and caressed him gently, feeling the instant arousal. "See?" she teased. "I know you want me."

"Nancy, stop."

She stepped back once more and, with deft fingers unfastened her dress and let it fall to her ankles.

"What the hell do you think you're doing?" He weaved slightly as he watched her. He had been drinking, but he didn't seem drunk.

Quickly, she was naked. With a little curtsey, she ran to the bed and threw herself upon it. Lying on her back, she spread her legs and held out her arms to him. "Now then, can you ask me to leave, Travis Coltrane? Or would you like to come over here and do what you do best?"

Cursing himself, he moved toward the bed. Hell, he might as well go ahead and take what she was offering so freely. There was no getting around the fact that she was pretty good in bed, and it had been a long time, and damn it, he was, after all, only a man.

When he stood beside the bed, she reached out and pulled him down. Their lips met and held, and then he raised back to stare down at her and murmur, "You know I think you're a bitch, Nancy. So why do you come here and offer yourself to me this way?"

She tilted her head to one side and laughed. "I think you're a bastard, Travis, but you're still the best man I've ever had. We don't have to be friends to be lovers, do we?"

"No," he laughed, shaking his head in wonder at her candor. "I don't guess we do. But you're still a bitch."

"And you're still a bastard. Now come here and love me." She grasped his swollen organ and gently tugged. "God, you're built like a bull."

It was going to be quick, he decided. Animal desire was all he felt for her, and the sooner he got his pleasure, the better. He did not want to kiss her again, only to get it over with and have her out of there as soon as possible. He positioned her legs and plunged right in, feeling her nails raking down his back, her moans or pleasure hot against her ear. "Travis, oh, God, Travis, you feel so good . . . so damn good. Harder . . . harder!"

He moved in and out, thrusting hard and quick. He felt himself about to explode but held back long enough to feel her quivering against him, knew that she was rising to her own crest. Only then did he allow his release.

Afterward, he fell to the side of her, lying on his back and staring up at the ceiling, wishing he had not been so damn weak. At least, he consoled himself, he had not taken her selfishly.

He shuddered involuntarily as Nancy rolled on her side and tucked her head on his shoulder, fingertips moving through the hair on his chest. "That was so wonderful," she cooed. "It always is. Oh, Travis, why do we have to fight? We could be so good together."

"I'm sure your husband would love that," he bit out the words. "Not to mention my wife."

"You don't have a wife right now," she pointed out.

He stiffened. "If I did, this wouldn't have happened. You can believe that. So don't start seeing things that don't exist. You came up here and took your clothes off and offered yourself to me. I was just hungry enough not to turn you down."

"But it doesn't have to be this way. I mean, we could see each other, Travis. We could make arrangements. You'd learn not to hate me. You might even learn to love me."

"Nancy, I've never given you reason to think so. Now suppose you get on out of here. You got what you came for."

He started to sit up, but she placed her hand between his legs and pressed down. "Don't move," she commanded, "or I might hurt you."

"You do, and I'll kill you," he said fiercely. "Now what the hell do you want?"

"I want you to take me again," she said petulantly. "You might leave town, and I might never see you again. I want this to be a very special night, one we'll both always remember."

"Get out of my bed, Nancy. Get your clothes on and leave." He almost snarled the words, suddenly hating himself for having been so weak as to empty himself inside her.

"Can I come back tomorrow night?" she persisted. "You know you want me, Travis. Look at you. My touch made you want me again. If you weren't so stubborn, we'd have time for seconds tonight."

He pointed to the door. "Out!"

Angry, she got up and began dressing. Once was never enough with a man like Travis Coltrane, and she knew he was quite capable of a repeat performance, even several.

"How long will you be in town?" she asked, fumbling with her chemise, planning ahead.

He still lay on the bed, arms folded behind his head, his magnificent body naked and exposed, enticing her more. "That's none of your business," he replied quietly.

"Do you still believe Kitty didn't run off with another man?" She decided to goad him, getting even for his refusal to offer seconds. "Everyone else is not so foolish as you. They know her for what she is."

To her chagrin, he chuckled softly. "You know, Mrs. Danton, if anyone else said that, I might be upset. But I know you only speak the words of a scorned woman. You aren't fit for Kitty to wipe her feet on, and you know it."

She faced him, eyes blazing, fury boiling. "You pompous, arrogant sonofabitch! Kitty Wright is a slut, and you're too damn blind to see it. She left town with another man . . . left you and that little brat of yours. Everyone is laughing at you behind your back!"

He was off the bed in a streak of lightning-quick anger, wrapping his hand around her throat to cut off her taunts. "I could kill you, Nancy," he hissed between clenched teeth. "I could wring your goddamn neck. Don't you ever speak of Kitty or my son in such a way ever again. Say what you will about me, but never them. Do you understand? And if I hear that you've said these things to other people, I'll come after you."

Her eyes were bulging and her cheeks were turning blue. She could not breathe. She clawed out wildly, catching his cheek and tearing the flesh, and he flung her away. Stumbling, she fell backward on the bed and began to scream, not in terror, but in fury.

"Will you shut up?" he yelled, moving forward. "You want to bring the whole goddman town in here?"

The door was flung open and Jerome Danton stood there, his face contorted with anger. "Yes, Coltrane, she does want to bring the whole town in here!" He kicked the door shut as Travis moved quickly to where his pistol lay. "You won't need that," Jerome said quickly. "I've no quarrel with you."

Travis picked up the gun, not about to take any chances with an irate husband. He knew it was a pretty nasty scene, him naked and Nancy on the bed wearing only her chemise.

He held the gun down to his side and faced Danton. "She came here," he said quietly. "I didn't invite her."

"No, I don't imagine you did." The man's eyes narrowed

as he looked down on his wife in scorn. "You get yourself dressed and get out of here. I've been watching you ever since he came back to town. I'm no fool, Nancy. I know how you've lusted after him, and I knew you wouldn't be able to stay away."

She was slowly regaining her composure. Propping herself up on her elbows, she crossed her long, slender legs and began to bounce one foot up and down playfully as she smiled. "You seem to forget, darling, that you don't order me around. There are certain things *I* know about you, remember?"

He moved quickly, wrapping his fingers in her hair and yanking her up and off the bed. He pushed her down on her knees before him. "You won't threaten me, woman. Not ever again. I find you in another man's hotel room half naked, and you dare to be insolent? Go home at once and prepare yourself for the thrashing of your life. Then pray I don't throw you out in the streets just as you are now and shout to the whole goddamn world what a slut you are!"

She looked to Travis. Surely he would not allow Jerome to bully her this way, not after what they had just shared.

She gasped. Travis had turned his back and was stepping into his trousers, reaching for his shirt, ignoring her. "Travis, please," she begged.

Jerome slapped her, knocking her backward to crouch in terror on the floor. "Do as I say, Nancy, or I'll kill you here and now."

"I think he means it," Travis murmured quietly, "and I hate all this going on in my room. Would you just go, Nancy?"

She scrambled to her feet, jerking on her dress in rapid movements, glancing wildly from one man to the other. She wanted to explode but Jerome was angrier than she had ever seen him. Later, when he had calmed down, she could wheedle her way around him, or resort to threats once more. But for the moment, there was nothing to do but get out quickly.

Dressed, she ran to the door and opened it, but humiliation got the better of her. Turning, she threw a hating glare at Travis and hissed, "I hope he kills you! You should know better than to seduce a married woman, you . . . you white trash!" She slammed the door behind her.

Travis slowly took a bottle of brandy from the bedside table and poured himself a drink. Gesturing to Danton, he casually offered, "Have one?"

Danton licked his lips nervously. "Yes, I will." He waited for the drink to be poured, then downed it quickly and held out the empty glass for another.

Travis raised an eyebrow. "Do you need a drink to muster the courage to kill me?" he asked quietly. "You have every right, you know. Who would condemn you for killing me after walking in here and finding your wife? By the way, the door was locked. You had a key."

"I did. I have connections. And I haven't drawn my gun, have I?" He laughed, an empty, hollow sound. "Besides, you wouldn't just stand there and let me kill you without a fight, would you?"

"Probably not." Travis eyed him over his upturned glass as he took a swallow, then said, "It's likely you would wind up being the one who got killed. So"—he set the glass down and folded his arms across his broad chest—"what do we do now?"

"I'm not here to quarrel with you, Coltrane. And I'm not defending Nancy's honor. She has none. I found out quickly enough after we were married just what she is. But my marital problems are not your concern." He took a deep breath and started for another drink, then decided against it. The two he had already consumed were making him woozy. He forced his eyes to meet Travis'. "I think it's time you were told the truth about Kitty's disappearance. After you hear it, *you* may want to kill *me*."

Travis tensed, every muscle in his body taut. He fought the impulse to grab the man. "Start talking," he growled. "And you better talk fast, Danton."

Jerome glanced about, spotted a rickety chair, then lowered himself into it, knees weak. Travis continued to stand, eyes narrowed. He looked like a wild animal, crouched and ready to strike.

Jerome began to talk, admitting that he had followed Kitty that night with the intention of seducing her. Travis' eyes glittered but he maintained his stony silence.

Then he told of Nancy's bursting into the deserted cabin, brandishing a gun.

"I don't give a goddamn about Nancy, Danton," Travis said tightly, the muscles in his jaw twitching ominously. "Just tell me what happened to Kitty. Nancy didn't kill her. You've got more sense than to come here and tell me that. So talk, damn you."

Danton licked his lips once more, swallowing hard. He began to speak quickly, words running together. He told Travis everything he knew, and what he had pieced together later.

"The man," Travis said hoarsely. "Who was the man?"

"Tate," Danton whispered. "Luke Tate."

The roar that came from the depths of Travis Coltrane's soul was like the death roar of a gored bull. The anguish, the fury, the overwhelming horror all exploded. Danton rose from the chair slowly, eyes wide with fear as he backed away toward the door. Just as he had touched the doorknob, the cry faded, and Travis whirled on him with wild eyes. "Get out of here, Danton!" he screamed. "Get out of here before I crush you with my bare hands! Get out! Now!"

Danton opened the door and charged out, straight into Sam Bucher, bouncing back as Sam stood rigid, gazing from him to Travis.

"What in hell is going on here?" Sam asked. "Damn, Travis, everybody in town could hear you yelling."

Travis' chest was heaving. He pointed at Danton but spoke to Sam. "Let him go. Let him get out of here or I'm going to kill him."

Sam stepped back and Jerome scurried by, stumbling to his knees, righting himself, and pushing by the curious onlookers who had gathered in the hall.

Sam watched him, then gestured to the crowd. "Get out of here. All of you," he commanded. "This ain't none of your concern. Go on. Git!"

Mumbling among themselves, they began moving back down the stairs. Sam stepped inside the room and closed the door.

As soon as the door closed, Travis said, "He told me about Kitty."

Travis turned wretched eyes on his lifelong friend and forced the anguished words through his lips: "Luke Tate's got her, Sam."

"Luke Tate!" Sam whispered, echoing the dreaded name. "No!"

"Oh, yes." Travis began to pace up and down, slamming his fists together. He told Sam everything as quickly as he could.

"You should've killed Danton," Sam said.

"No. He didn't have to tell me," Travis pointed out. "Besides, he's worse off alive, having to live with that bitch and with himself."

Both were silent for a few moments, and then they faced each other, eyes locking, thoughts melding. Finally Travis spoke. "We leave tomorrow."

Nothing else needed saying.

Chapter Twelve

TRAVIS awoke with a shiver as a frigid mountain breeze whipped his blanket from his body. He lifted his head from his saddle, which was his pillow, and stared out at the great green span of valley below. A whispering mist danced just above the ground as the first light of morning reached out to claim the earth from darkness.

Wrapping his worn blanket around his body, Travis rolled over on his side, gaze hungry for the world around him. He loved this wilderness, the untouched beauty, the excitement of knowing that so much was yet to be discovered here.

He and Sam had started out intending to travel along the same route to Nevada that Luke Tate had probably taken. However, it quickly became obvious that it was foolhardy to try to track a man through seven states, especially through a vast wilderness. The thing to do, they decided, was to reach Nevada as quickly as possible, then search for Tate and Kitty, who had certainly arrived by then.

Until the Comstock Lode had been discovered, Nevada was like every other territory between the East and West coasts, merely a rough spot for gold seekers to pass through on their way to California.

Travis looked over at his friend, who slept soundly. It had

been a long journey. This was the day they would, at last, reach Virginia City. It was none too soon, for the first winter snows had dusted them as they saw the Sierra Nevadas rising majestically on the southwestern horizon.

Sam had pointed out, "What can we expect but snow? That's how Nevada got its name. It's Spanish, meaning 'snow-clad,' so I reckon we're due to see a lot of it."

Travis thought how easy it would be to call this place home. There was a special kind of peace and beauty here. The lower desert areas were rife with mesquite, creosote, greasewood, and yucca. Cacti of all varieties abounded, and as they moved into higher elevations, they were surrounded by sagebrush and Joshua trees, as well as pines, firs, spruce, juniper, and mountain mahogany.

There were rugged mountains here and flat valleys with buttes and mesas and sandy desert regions all around. Travis marveled that, at one point, they would seem to be at the bottom of the earth, surrounded by sand and moving ever lower, only to be faced suddenly with a mountain peak reaching to heaven.

During the long, plodding ride, they had amused themselves by trying to identify the wildlife they encountered. They had seen most before, like deer and coyote and bobcats, but it took an old prospector to name the bighorn sheep and the pronghorn antelope.

Rabbits, horned toads, tortoises, there were plenty of those, and they came across more sidewinder rattlesnakes than they had ever seen before in their entire lives.

Sage grouse, pheasants, and quails were killed and roasted over campfires for their supper, and when they tired of those, they paused along the rivers and lakes for bass, trout, crappy, and catfish.

Travis smiled wryly as he recalled how Sam had cursed as they had moved through the Alkali Desert, heading into the Toiyabe Range. "I can't believe they made this godforsaken wilderness our thirty-sixth state. And all because Lincoln figured its mineral wealth would help the Union."

"What difference does it make?" Travis had asked, anxious to discuss anything that could take his mind off the worries he harbored over Kitty. "Lincoln also got something else he wanted—a Northern state to support his proposed antislavery amendments to the Constitution. Nevada Territory didn't even have a fifth of the number of people needed for statehood, but Congress voted them into the Union in '64."

"But the Comstock Lode will change this wilderness," Sam pointed out quickly. "You wait and see. There are more folks looking for silver in Nevada than there are looking for gold in California.

"And," he had continued, casting a worried look in Travis' direction, "if Tate told Nancy he was going to Nevada to find silver, you can bet he'll be headed for Virginia City. It's the biggest mining camp in the West."

Travis stared out across the misty green world once more. The haze was clearing. Soon, he told himself, he would find Kitty and they would make a new life. Perhaps they would come back here one day after they went home to get their son. There was so much to be discovered here. In this place of awesome beauty, the past lay behind forever.

He looked over at Sam sleeping so peacefully. The old bear of a man would probably want to come too, and that was fine. Sam didn't much care for North Carolina or the South anymore, either. Sam might even find a woman here and settle down himself, and then the four of them could . . .

A loud, anguished scream pierced the air and Travis sprang to his feet, grabbing his gun from beneath his saddle so fast he hardly knew what he was doing.

Sam awoke, instantly alert, glancing anxiously over at Travis. "What the hell was that?"

"It was no animal," Travis called to him, "and it came from over there." He nodded toward a distant butte, tugging on his boots, gun ready. Sam quickly joined him and they began to move stealthily toward the butte.

There was a second long, loud, agonized scream and the two men exchanged looks.

"Indians?" Travis offered.

Sam shook his head. "Don't think so. I talked to that fellow at the last outpost, and he said they hadn't had no trouble near here."

"We'd better be careful. We might be next." Travis held his rifle in his left hand, his pistol in his right. He could shoot with both at the same time, a talent acquired on horseback during the war.

They darted from one clump of sagebrush to another, ever alert. Twice more they heard the scream that raised the hair on the back of their necks. When they were near the sound, Travis motioned to Sam to move to his right, where thick clumps of cacti and juniper made a cover. "I'm going in," Travis whispered.

Sam knew better than to argue. Travis always followed his own instincts. If something told him to be covert, he could move with the stealth of an Indian scout. But if his gut feeling was to charge right in, he would do so without hesitation. So far, he had never been wrong, but Sam knew there might be a first time . . . which could also be his last. Sam moved into position and waited. When Travis fired, Sam would run forward.

Travis crouched down behind a clump of sage and waited. He could hear the murmur of men talking, the sounds of someone whimpering in pain. When the next scream erupted, Travis sprang forward, blasting his guns. Taken by surprise, the men froze.

"Hold it!" Travis cried. Sam moved in from his right. The three men in the clearing glanced around wildly. One reached for his gun, but Travis fired, killing him instantly. "If you want to follow your buddy," he warned the other two, "just move."

He quickly took in the situation. One dead, two glaring at him, one holding a smoking poker near a small campfire. A fourth man lay naked, spread-eagled on the ground, hands and feet tied to stakes. Travis shuddered at the sight of the man's burned flesh.

"Help me," he whispered, struggling to lift his head, tears streaming down his cheeks. "They're burning me alive. Please help me. . . ."

"Drop it," Travis motioned to the shorter man, the one holding the poker.

The man did, snarling, "Who the hell you think you are, busting in on what ain't none of your business?"

Travis said calmly, "Who the hell do you think you are, burning a man?"

"He's gonna tell us something," the taller man spoke up quickly. "You just get back outta the way and let us finish, and we'll give you a share."

Travis sized them up. They were both coarse and rough in appearance, their faces reflecting the renegade lives they had led. There was probably no crime these two had not committed. A man, Travis had long ago learned, cannot mask his true character if you look deep into his eyes, and these two revealed themselves as rogues of the worst kind. He nodded to Sam to go to the suffering man's aid.

"What was he going to tell you?" Travis asked quietly, holding both weapons unwaveringly, while Sam untied the victim.

"He found a silver lode," the taller one volunteered. He was older, his eyes partially hidden by thick, flashy lids. A small black spot was centered on his left cheek. A bullet scar, Travis surmised.

"We saw him in Virginia City at the claims office," he rushed on, sensing Travis' immediate interest and mistaking it for his own greed. "We followed him around for two weeks, thinkin' he'd go to his find, but he was onto us and leadin' us on a wild goose chase. So we jumped him and decided to make him talk. We want that silver, and if you help us get it outta him, then we'll split with you and your partner."

"It's bound to be a good lode," the shorter man spoke up, a note of hope in his gravelly voice. "There'll be enough for all of us. Look, my name is Frank Bailey and my partner is Josh Warren. The man you kilt was Abe Fordham, but he won't worth a shit, nohow. We don't care if you kilt him, do we, Josh? We ain't mad."

Josh shook his head, a nervous smile touching his lips. "No, we don't care. We'll gladly give you his share and part of ours. You look like a smart man. Maybe you can get it outta this bastard without havin' to kill him."

"No," the victim choked. Sam was holding a canteen for him to sip water, but he pushed it away, turning beseeching eyes on Travis. "No. I won't tell. Go on and kill me. My stake is claimed. It'll go to my wife and my boy if I die. I've worked too hard to give up anything to you sonsofbitches."

"Aw, shit, you fool," Frank Bailey snapped. "You go on and tell us where it is, and we'll all work together. There's enough for all of us. Why do you want to be so damn selfish?" His voice ended in a whine.

"Why don't you get out and find your own strike?" he cried, then turned to Travis once more. "My name's Wiley Odom. I come from Louisiana. Help me, and I'll share with you."

"A fuckin' Reb," Josh spat on the ground. "Mighta known."

"Shut up!" Travis snapped. To Sam, he said, "Keep an eye on them."

He moved to Wiley Odom's side and knelt down beside him. "I'm Travis Coltrane, and I hail from Louisiana, too. You've nothing to fear from me. I'm not after your silver. Now we're going to see what we can do about taking care of your burns, and then we'll take these two into Virginia City and turn them over to the marshal there. You can come with us if you want to see a doctor, or you can go your way."

He blinked in suspicious confusion. "You don't want my silver?" he asked, incredulous.

Frank Bailey screamed in a rage, "If you don't want a part of it, you're a goddamn fool."

Josh Warren sputtered, "He's willing to share with you two but not with us? That ain't fair. We're the ones who tracked him down, and it cost Fordham his life. I say you make the bastard talk, and then we'll all share. That's fair!"

Travis stared at first one and then the other in silence. "There will be no sharing of this man's strike. He found it and staked a claim and it's his." He nodded to Sam. "Tie them up."

"No you don't." Frank moved for his gun with incredible speed, managing to clear his holster but not to aim before an explosion sounded and he toppled forward to the ground.

Josh Warren had seen the movement and followed, but his gun never cleared before Travis fired and sent him after his partner into death.

Wiley Odom stared wide-eyed, then licked his lips nervously. "Lord, now you're gonna torture me, ain't you? But there ain't no need. I said I'd share with you."

"Relax, Odom." Travis got to his feet and walked over to the two bodies. "We're not interested in your silver. I told you that."

"Then why . . . why did you help me?" he asked in wonder. "Everybody is after silver."

Travis knelt and searched the men's pockets. There was nothing of value to be turned over to the marshal in Virginia City. He pondered whether to bury them. Digging three graves was going to take a while, and he had hoped to make it to the mining town that day.

"Why did you help me?" Odom turned to Sam when Travis ignored him. "How come you ain't after my silver?"

"He's looking for his wife," Sam explained. "Besides, we don't want anything we don't work for. We never have. As for helping you, well, you're a fellow human being, and Travis

Coltrane has never turned his back on anyone in need. I've tried to do likewise, but I'm not as good at it as my friend is. I lose patience, and I ain't one to stick my neck out. He manages to stick it out for me, though," he added with a soft chuckle. Travis couldn't quite suppress his own grin.

Sam spotted Wiley Odom's clothes and retrieved them for him. "Wait and let me get some salve from my saddlebag. It's good for everything, including burns. We'll rip up something for a bandage." He turned to Travis, who was still kneeling over the bodies. "You want to bury them?"

"No," came his quiet response. "I want to get to Virginia City. Before the sun rises on another day, I want to find Luke Tate."

"I heard of him."

Travis was on his feet in a flash, rushing to Wiley Odom's side so quickly that the man shrank back in fear. "What did you say? You know Luke Tate?"

"I . . . I said I heard of him," Wiley stammered, fright making him tremble. "I don't know him."

Travis realized he was terrifying the man. He forced himself to speak calmly. "Please. It's very important to me. Luke Tate kidnaped my wife back in North Carolina and brought her out here. *Anything* you can tell me will be helpful. Just try to remember all you've heard about him." Please, God, Travis prayed, let him say Tate is still in Virginia City and he's seen Kitty and she's all right. Please, God, I've waited so long.

Wiley winced with pain as Sam began to rub the black salve into his burned flesh. Then, swallowing hard, he said, "I ain't never met him, and from what I've heard I don't want to. He's real trouble. Shot five men that I know of and the law don't touch him. If he's made a strike, I ain't heard about it. He don't seem to do nothing but hang around and make trouble.

"The reason I heard so much about him," he continued, "is 'cause everybody in Virginia City stays clear of him if they got any sense."

He paused, looking up at Travis as he whispered, "You say he's got your wife? You poor man."

"Save your pity for Tate," Travis snapped. "He's going to need it when I find him." He took a deep breath and rushed on hopefully, "Did you ever see him with a woman? A beautiful woman with red hair and violet eyes?" Wiley Odom shook his head sorrowfully.

When I was in Virginia City last week, I was there for five days. I saw Tate around in saloons and out in the street, but I never saw him with a woman." Seeing the look on Travis' face, he hastened to add, "Now, that ain't to say he ain't got your wife stashed away somewheres. He wouldn't be a'bringin' her into no saloon, anyhow."

"Yes, he would," Travis murmured sadly. "He'd take her everywhere with him."

Sam spoke loudly, forcing heartiness. "Hey, that ain't necessarily so, boy. He might keep her hid out somewheres. Hell, how did he know Nancy Dalton would keep her mouth shut? He can't be too careful, knowing the law might be after him."

"I should have wired the marshal and had him picked up. But damn it, I wanted him myself. Wanted the pleasure of killing him. And I didn't want to take any chances with a marshal I don't know. Now it may be too late," Travis finished in a whisper.

"No, it's not too late." Sam said gruffly. "Let's get going. We can make Virginia City by midafternoon if we ride hard."

To Odom, Travis offered, "We'll be glad to take you in with us and have a doctor see to those burns."

"I'm going to be just fine." He struggled to his feet, his wounds hurting but gratitude overcoming pain. He held out his hand first to Travis, then to Sam. "I'll never forget what you did. Never. I hope you find your wife. I'll be praying for you."

They reached the outskirts of Virginia City, Nevada, as the sun sank low in the west. Pausing atop a ridge, they immediately felt the boom-town excitement that hovered then over the mining city. Now and then a shrill laugh danced on the wind. A gunshot rang out, then another. Shouts. Sounds of revelry.

"It looks busy," Travis said, fighting his teeming emotions.

"It is," Sam responded. "Now we got to remember that if Tate sees us first, we're in trouble. He'll crawl in a hole and stay there."

"I'm not so sure he would recognize me. It's been several years, and there was only that brief encounter the day we followed his band of outlaws, the day I found Kitty." His voice trailed off painfully.

Suddenly a realization flashed through Sam's mind.

"Travis! Did you ever stop to think we won't recognize Luke Tate? Hell, I just realized I don't really know what I'm looking for."

"Kitty described him to me very clearly," said Travis. "I keep a picture in my head, a picture that wouldn't go away even if I wanted it to." Travis described Luke Tate for Sam, who listened carefully, nodding.

They rode the rest of the way in silence, and when they reached the teeming camp town, with its one main street fronted by saloons and gambling houses, miners' supply stores and claim offices, they were easily swallowed up by the crowd.

"We start at one end of the street and go all the way down," Travis instructed as they dismounted and tied their horses beside a watering trough. "Then we go up the other side. We stay at it all night long . . . as long as it takes to find Tate."

Sam nodded agreement. "If he's here, we'll find him, and I'd bet my last drink of whiskey he's here somewhere. And so is Kitty."

Travis sucked in his breath quickly, his heart skipping. *Kitty*. He had to find her, had to. "Let's go," he said gruffly with a quick look at Sam, stepping up onto the boardwalk with determination.

It didn't take long to find out that each saloon was like another. Prospectors were either celebrating their good fortune or drowning their sorrows in drink. Fights broke out frequently, and in the third saloon they visited, they ducked behind an overturned table as shots whizzed across the room.

Sam said very little during their search. He knew Travis was lost in his own world of misery and self-condemnation and he let his friend be. Like Travis, Sam prayed they were not too late for Kitty.

Piano music drifted through the open doorway of a saloon. They paused before entering it, eyes scanning the crowd of drunken revelers.

"Maybe we should just go to the marshal," Sam said, frustrated after many hours of searching.

Travis shook his head. "I don't want the marshal in on this. Even if this is a boom town, I don't imagine there are many secrets. If Tate gets wind we're around, he'll run and take Kitty with him. No. We've got to take him by surprise, all by ourselves, and we've got to find him *tonight*."

He walked into the smokey saloon and Sam followed, knowing Travis was right. Neither of them would rest until Kitty was found.

Travis took a table in a corner, his back to the wall, where he could see everything. Sam sat at his right. A girl dressed in a scanty costume of tight red satin and dyed ostrich feathers breezed over. Her eyes flicked over Travis, and her bored expression quickly livened. "Well, hello there, handsome," she cooed, leaning over to give him a better view of her cleavage. "Ain't seen you around here before. You come to find your fortune like everybody else? My name's Sally, and I'll be glad to show you around."

Travis was scanning the room, ignoring her obvious play. "Just bring us a bottle of your best whiskey," he said quietly, "and two glasses."

"You ain't so friendly, are you?" She sniffed, straightening.

She started to move away, but he reached out to clamp his hand on her wrist and pull her back. She sat down on his lap, pretending to struggle, but her eyes were shining. Her painted mouth turned up in a wide grin. "Hey, what do you think you're doing? I got a job to do, you know."

"Worry about your job later," he murmured, his breath warm on her ear. "Right now I need a little information."

Sam glanced at him sharply. Travis had said he did not want anyone to know they were looking for Tate. Sam started to say something, then decided against it. Travis always knew what he was doing.

"Sure, honey," Sally was cooing again. "I'm always glad to oblige when I can. You're lookin' for somebody, ain't you? Well, just so you don't tell anybody I run my mouth off, and as long as you don't do no shootin' in here."

"No shooting." Travis slipped both arms around her and smiled. "You see, sweetheart, I'm looking for my sister. She ran away from home a while back. My folks are all upset, and they sent me to look for her. I thought she might head out here to find work. You'd know her if you saw her, because she's a real pretty thing. Not as pretty as you, of course," he winked and grinned, "but still pretty. She's tall, and she's got golden-red hair and her eyes are an unusual color, sort of purple."

She knew whom he was talking about. The smile faded, and she stiffened. "Yeah, I remember her," she said quickly, too quickly, he thought. "She ain't around no more, and I'm glad. Menfolks drooled over her, they did. But she's gone now. It's just as well."

Travis struggled to keep himself calm. "Did she work here?" he asked quietly.

She shook her head. "Naw, Luke wouldn't let her work. He just wanted to parade her around so's the guys would see her and think how pretty she was, and how he was somethin' special to have a filly like her around. It was plain she hated him, though. For a while, anyhow."

Travis felt his heart quicken. Without realizing it, he held her tighter as he ground out the words, "What do you mean, 'for a while'? What happened? Did he take her away?"

"Hey, you're hurting me," she protested, squirming, and he loosened his grip. "That's better. No, she just went away. Like I said, it was plain she hated him, but she acted funny, following him around like she was tetched or something. One day she just wasn't around no more."

She threw back her head and laughed, then leaned to kiss the tip of his nose. "She isn't your sister, now is she? She was your sweetheart? Well, she's gone. So that means you ain't got nobody but me."

Travis stared straight ahead, eyes narrowed ominously. Leaning forward, Sam asked Sally, "Where did Luke go, honey? Maybe he can tell us something."

"Luke?" she snorted derisively. "That old drunk sonofabitch? He's right where he always is—over there at the bar sousing liquor."

She jerked her head to her right, and Sam and Travis jerked around to follow her gaze.

They hadn't recognized him because his back was to them. Sitting on a stool at the end of the bar, shoulders hunched, beefy hands clamped around a mug of beer, he looked like part of the bar itself. His clothes were rumpled and soiled. When he glanced over toward the door, they saw that his face wore the lines of a man who has seen too much. Puffy eyes stared out toward the door. Someone near the doorway called out to him and he laughed, displaying yellow, chipped teeth. His chin was stubbled, and as he lifted the mug to drink, bits of foam caught, giving him the look of a mad dog.

Travis started to rise, and the girl gasped as she felt herself falling. Sam moved to pull her to her feet. "Travis," he hissed, "hold on, now. Don't do nothing foolish."

But Travis Coltrane was already walking across the room, shoving people aside, kicking chairs out of his way.

People were scrambling right and left, alarmed by the maniacal expression on his face. There were angry mumblings and gasps, but no one tried to stop him.

Luke Tate heard the commotion and glanced around. Recognition was instant. He slipped from the stool, right hand going for his gun, but Travis was faster. Leaping forward, he knocked Luke off his feet, falling on top of him. The two crashed to the floor.

Sam was right there. He saw Travis' hands go for Luke's throat, knew that he would choke the life from him before realizing what he was doing. He had seen him enraged before but never like this. He fell on top of the thrashing bodies and grabbed Travis' hands. "You kill him, boy, and you'll never find out where Kitty is."

It registered. Travis released his hold on Tate's throat but clutched his shirt, dragging him up. "Now, you goddamn sonofabitch"—Travis slammed Luke against the bar—"you're going to tell me what you've done with my wife."

Luke Tate's eyes bulged with terror and he held up his hands in a pleading gesture. "Don't kill me, Coltrane. I didn't do nothing to Kitty, I swear it."

"Do you know where she is?" Travis banged Luke's head on the bar as hard as he could, nearly knocking him out. Tate struggled to remain conscious. "Is she here? In Virginia City?" Travis screamed.

"Yes, yes," Tate choked out the words. "I'll take you to her, tell you what happened, if you promise to let me go."

"I'll let you go all right," Travis said as he jerked him up and flung him toward the door. "Start walking," he roared, stalking after him. "And if you try anything, you're a dead man."

The three men, the bedraggled dirty one in front and the two taller grim-faced men behind him, walked through the stone-silent saloon and out the swinging doors into the night.

"I knowed you'd come one day . . ." Luke was saying as he turned and walked backward in front of Travis down the middle of the dark street, stumbling. "I knowed you'd come after her and blame me. I never shoulda took her, I know that. But Nancy paid me to take her off, said she was after her husband.

I needed the money bad. That's the only reason I did it. I shoulda knowed she was too delicate for this life. I knowed you'd come, but you remember what you said . . . if I showed you where she was, you'd let me go."

"Just take me to her, Tate," Travis said thickly.

"I am. I am. We need a lantern. I ain't got one."

"I'll get one," said Sam. They were passing a hotel, the lobby well lit. He darted inside and grabbed a lantern hanging from a hook just inside the wall and rushed back out, ignoring the shouts of the desk clerk.

After a few minutes of silent walking, they reached the edge of town and Tate led them off onto a dirt path which wound around cactus and sagebrush. "It ain't much farther," he said, beginning to get back some of his nerve. "Now, you just remember what you promised. It's like I said. She just sort of give up. Acted like she was tetched."

He paused to take a breath and pointed to the graveyard, wooden crosses illuminated by the half moon. "She just laid down and died," he said raggedly.

Travis' scream tore through the night. "You lie! She's not dead! She can't be!" The scream tapered to a sob.

Sam stepped up to Tate. "Tate, if you're lying, so help me . . ." he said menacingly.

"I ain't lying!" Tate shrieked. "It's right here. Look." He ran forward and pointed down toward a mound of dirt in front of a crudely carved wooden cross. "See? Right there."

Sam followed, holding up the lantern, and read the scrawling words carved into the wood: "*Kitty Wright. Died September 1, 1869. Rest in Peace.*" Falling to his knees with a wrenching sob, Sam moaned, "God, no. Not Kitty. Oh, God, no, no!" He dropped the lantern, covering his face with his hands.

Travis stepped forward quietly, like a sleepwalker, staring at the grave.

"Now, don't you get mad," Luke Tate faced him, forcing his voice to sound brave. "I never shoulda took her off. I know that. But it's like I said. Nancy paid me to do it. She always hated Kitty. And I ain't denyin' I always had a yen for her. But I didn't have *nothin'* to do with her dyin'. Ain't no need in you hangin' for killin' me. It ain't gonna bring Kitty back."

Travis' right hand shot out to strike him across his face, sending him sprawling across the dirt mound.

Luke held up his arms. "Now, you wait a minute, Coltrane. You promised if I showed you where she was, you'd let me go."

"I always keep my word, Tate." Travis kicked him backward, mashing his booted foot against his throat to hold him, helpless, on top of the grave. "I'm going to let you go. I'm going to let you go straight to hell."

Travis began to allow a little of his fury out, then a little more, pressing harder and harder on Luke Tate's throat with his booted foot. Tate's agonized scream grew thinner and thinner until it became a mere squeak. His life ebbed away with every gush of air Travis pressed from his throat.

Sam Bucher gazed unflinchingly at the scene, eerie in the yellow lantern light. He recalled a similar scene from years before, when Travis had killed Nathan Collins for shooting John Wright, Kitty's father. Sam had pulled Travis away then, but too late. Now he had no wish to stop him, could only wish that it were he taking life from the worthless bastard.

Astonished, he felt tears rolling down his cheeks. He who had never shed a tear in his life. He looked up at Travis, at the gray eyes shooting red sparks.

"Die, damn you," Travis whispered, pressing his foot harder. "Die like the scum you are."

Sam looked away. No, he was not going to pull his friend away. He waited, staring toward the lights of the town in the distance. Finally, the sounds of Luke Tate's death agony faded, and Travis' curses stopped as well.

Silence hung about them like a shroud. It was an eternity before Travis finally muttered, "He's dead. He's dead and Kitty's dead. We didn't make it in time, Sam."

Sam nodded, still staring straight ahead. "It's over. We can go home."

"Home?" Travis sat down beside him, folding his arms around his knees and laughed sharply, painfully. "Where is home, Sam? My home is buried here, with Kitty."

"You've got your son, yours and Kitty's," Sam said sharply. "You can't go off the deep end, boy. She wouldn't want you to."

Travis was silent for a long time and Sam did not interfere. At last, Travis took a deep breath and lifted his face to the sky. "I always loved her. I always will. I just wish . . ." His voice broke and he dropped his head to his knees, shoulders heaving.

Sam stole silently away and began walking back to town. No, he had never seen Travis cry, and he never would. He was not going to hang around and watch.

The man was in his own private hell and he would have to endure it alone for the time being. Only God Himself, knew just how long that time was going to last.

Chapter Thirteen

THE voice was coming from beyond a thick haze.

Travis lifted his head, squinting. He hiccuped, shoulders jerking. He could not see beyond the mist, but the voice seemed familiar. Who? He could not think.

"Travis, damn you, you've got to come out of this. You're killing yourself!"

The voice was angry. Travis forced his lips to turn upward in a smile to show that he was not angry. But as he opened his eyes an image appeared, the one that drove him crazy whenever he saw it, the image that danced across his brain so often it almost drove him mad. Kitty was there, laughing with those sensuous lips, violet eyes sparkling as she danced before him with arms outstretched.

"No," he moaned. "Devil's tryin' to drive me insane." His words were ragged and he stared off into space, eyes riveted on something in the air, shaking his head wildly from side to side. His hands groped blindly outward, and he grasped the cool whiskey bottle.

"Travis, no!" The bottle was knocked away, falling to shatter upon the floor.

He tried to stand, legs wobbling. Someone was going to die. Someone had broken his bottle, and now the floating vision of Kitty would not go away. Whoever had taken his bottle was going to die.

He groped to his right side with both hands, feeling for his gun. The holster was empty.

"I put that up a long time ago, Travis."

The voice was sad, edged with pity. Pity?

Feeling weak, Travis sank back into his chair. A hand pushed a mug under his bowed head, and the steam touched his nostrils. "Drink this," the voice commanded from out of the fog. "You're going to feel better. I've got some food ordered, and you're going to eat. You've been on a drunk for weeks, Travis, and it's time you came out of it."

Disgust... pity... anger... all these were in that voice. Why? What had he done?

"You are going to drink the coffee."

The mug was held to his lips and, reluctantly, he sipped. It felt good going down. In a flash, some of the queasiness left him, and he took a full swallow.

"That's it," the voice said warmly. "I got a whole pot ready, and you're going to drink every drop. Then you're going to eat."

The mention of food made his stomach lurch and he quickly downed the coffee. When a second mug was gone, Travis lifted his eyes wearily and saw that the mist was clearing. "Sam," he whispered gratefully. "Sam."

"It's me," Sam grinned crookedly, reaching to fill the mug. "It's about time you came out of it. You know how long you been sousing, boy? Weeks. You're gonna kill yourself if you don't sober up and get some food in your belly.

"Look at you," he went on, allowing a little harshness into his voice. "Skin and bones. God knows, I can understand your grief, but life has to go on. Kitty wouldn't want you to be like this, and you've got little John to think of. We got to be heading back to North Carolina as soon as you get yourself in shape."

North Carolina seemed a world away, and the recent past began to return to Travis.

"I imagine the law's looking for me. I'll face that. I won't run."

"You don't have to. I talked to the marshal and told him the whole story. As far as he's concerned, a no-good scoundrel was found dead in the graveyard, and nobody knows who done it. Tate was buried on Boot Hill with the rest of the unknowns and outlaws. The marshal don't want to hear no more about it."

Travis was not surprised. The town was bursting and the law couldn't keep up with everything. One more dead made little difference, especially when it was someone like Luke Tate.

A bowl of delicious-smelling beef stew from the saloon kitchen was placed before Travis.

While Travis ate, Sam said, "Maybe we can leave for home in a day or two."

"What's your hurry?" Travis eyed Sam curiously over another helping of the stew, ignoring the smiling waitress who brought it.

"I figured you'd want to get back to little John."

"I do, but I need time. What can I offer my son? A broken man for a father? A little boy needs a mother. I can't give him one. I can't give him anything right now. He's better off with Mattie Glass. Kitty's land will one day be his, I'll see to that. She'd want it that way and so would John Wright. What I need to do is get my life in order. But there's no need in your hanging around waiting for me to do that, Sam. You've been a good friend. You've stood by me. I can't ask for more than that. You've got your own life to live."

"Sure," Sam laughed shortly. "I'm just an old trail rat who ain't happy unless I'm on the go. I'll ride back with you when you go, but I don't imagine I'll hang around North Carolina for long."

He leaned back in his chair, folding his arms across his stomach. "You know something, Travis?" he said in a thoughtful tone, going on without waiting for a reply. "In these past weeks, I've had a lot of time to look around here and I like what I've seen. I like the West. It's new, fresh territory. It's exciting just to think about being a part of all this." He waved a hand in a wide gesture.

He leaned forward suddenly in his enthusiasm, the front chair legs hitting the floor with a thud as he propped his elbows on the table and rested his chin in his hands. His brown eyes were glowing. "Did you know that there are nearly two hundred silver mines within four square miles? This country is alive, Travis. *Alive!*" His fist pounded the table. "And to think the whole thing happened almost by accident. When the gold rush of '49 in California petered out, the miners moved into Nevada and Colorado to look for more gold, but they found silver instead. Like the strike I told you about at the Ophir mine here. It's booming. This is the place to be."

Travis pushed the empty bowl aside and this time poured his own coffee. He was starting to feel human. "You're saying you want to try prospecting, Sam?" he asked, suppressing his amusement. "You've got the silver fever like the rest of these lunatics."

"Hell, no, not the fever," Sam guffawed. "It's the territory, boy. The West is where the excitement is. It's like discovering a new world. Hell, it *is* a new world. I know now why the pioneers have such spirit. It's a feeling that gets in the blood, and you can't get it out. Why, to think of living back in North Carolina or even the Louisiana bayou just makes me feel smothered."

"I can't blame you," Travis said sincerely. "If I didn't have a son to care for, I'd probably stay." He fell silent. "Trouble is, I'm just not ready to go back and face him yet.

"And there's another reason," he took a deep breath. "Kitty's death is too fresh, Sam. I need time. If I go back there now, I'll kill Nancy for causing it, and then I'll kill Danton for waiting so long to tell me what he knew." He shook his head slowly. "No, I can't go back now."

He licked his lips, thinking that a stiff drink would taste very good. But suddenly, all in a rush, he had sense enough to know that the time had come to stop hiding in the depths of a bottle.

Sam kept quiet, letting his friend do battle with his demons. After several minutes Travis said, "I'll send a letter to Mattie and explain things, thank her again for watching John. I gave her most of my pay from the Haiti job before we came out here, so my son isn't costing her anything and she's got some extra money for herself. Still, I will always owe Mattie Glass a debt of gratitude. Quite a debt. What would I have done without her?"

A little later he sighed, "Maybe I'll get myself a pick and head for the hills." He tried to smile but didn't quite make it.

Sam looked him square in the eye and said, "You can go with me to Kentucky."

"Kentucky?" Travis echoed, raising an eyebrow. "What are you talking about? You just got through talking about staying in Nevada."

Sam leaned forward, glancing right and left to make sure no one could overhear. The saloon was nearly empty anyway. He told of having been in touch with Washington about a job as a federal marshal. The job had been promised Sam as part of the Dominican Republic deal. "I was told that plenty of marshals are needed in Kentucky because of the situation with the Negroes there. They're being hurt something terrible. There's a lot of violence—homes, schools, churches set on fire, whole families run out of their homes by white mobs. There's even reports of lynch mobs hanging Negroes.

"It's happening, I'm told," he continued after a deep sigh of pity, "because white Southern extremists in them parts don't see any other alternative to the Reconstruction program that's been imposed on the South by the radical Republicans in the North. Now I don't care nothing about politicians or politics, either, you know that. But I don't like the idea of Negroes being killed and burned out of their homes and mobs taking over." Sam shook his head emphatically.

Travis smiled. "So you sent a wire back to Washington saying you would be most happy to accept the assignment in Kentucky as a federal marshal."

Sam nodded firmly. "Damn right. I'm going to do my part, and also save what money I can. Then I'm coming back out here and make me a home in the new world. He paused, a worried expression wrinkling his face. "I'm an old man, Travis. It's time I thought about settling down. I could find peace out here when I need it and excitement when I want it. But first, there's a job to be done in Kentucky."

Travis signaled to the waitress. "Bring us a bottle of wine," he ordered, "and two glasses."

"Are you going to start drinking again, Travis?" Sam asked incredulously.

"Relax," Travis said and waved his hand. "I ordered wine for celebration. I want to propose a toast to your new adventure . . . yours and mine."

"You're going *with* me? Hot damn!" Sam leaped to his feet and danced a jig around the table before slamming his large body down once more. "We'll clean out the state of Kentucky, and then we'll go to North Carolina and get little John and head West. We'll work hard, and we'll save our money, and—"

"Sam, don't."

He fell silent and stared at Travis, puzzled.

"I'm taking things slowly, Sam," Travis explained quietly, sadly. "I'm not thinking beyond that. What money I make, I'll send home to Mattie for John. That's the only plan I have at the moment, so don't start making any for me, all right?"

"All right," Sam nodded, suddenly subdued. "I guess you do have to move slow. I'm just glad you're moving at all."

The wine was brought and Sam tensed, looking away from Travis, wondering what the bottle would do to him. Sam gripped his hands together in his lap, deliberately keeping his face a blank, and watched as Travis uncorked the bottle and poured out two glasses of the red wine. Travis put the cork back in the bottle, giving it a final tap, and then picked up his glass.

"To Kentucky!" he said, and took a sip. Sam picked up his own glass reluctantly and sipped at it, trying not to watch Travis too closely. When his friend set his glass aside with a determined shove, Sam almost collapsed with relief. His friend was not going to drink any more. The one ceremonial sip had been all he would take.

Sam was proud, but knew better than to say so. Travis had been to hell and back, and the agonizing grief had not left him. Maybe it never would. But he wasn't going to drown himself in booze. Travis Coltrane was no coward.

Chapter Fourteen

TRAVIS sat at his large wooden desk, gazing at the scuff marks on it and speculating about the men who'd sat there before him. What kind of men had they been? He knew they hadn't been brave enough to stand up to the Klan. And that, he reflected wryly, was really all he needed to know.

It was ironic that Travis was there at all. He no longer needed the job, any job. A series of things had happened to Travis that he'd learned about only a few days before. Wiley Odom had died. A combination of things had killed him—his injuries, weakness, not enough decent food, and maybe even despair. Knowing he was dying, Odom had willed his silver mine to Travis Coltrane and Sam Bucher (to whom he referred only as Travis' friend), in gratitude for saving his life—and saving the mine from the thieves. Odom's wife and son had gotten another, smaller mine. Odom, perhaps, had worried about all the hard things that went with wealth, the envy and the danger, and hadn't wanted his family to inherit something they might not be able to handle. But he knew Travis and Sam could handle danger, and knew they'd make something of the strike that had taken so much out of him. Odom's family would be well off with the smaller mine.

Sam had given his share to Travis, brooking no argument.

"I don't have a son, and you do. Besides, if I own half a mine now it'll kill my appetite for going back out there and making a strike of my own. No, Travis, it's better for me if you take the whole damn thing. If you don't want it, save it for your son." And Travis had had to accept full ownership. Sam, when he chose, could be as stubborn as . . . well, as stubborn as Travis.

So, Travis considered as he sat staring at his desk, he was a wealthy man. And what good was it to him? If he'd had money before, then maybe he and Kitty wouldn't have fought so hard over the farm and maybe . . . He shook his head. He couldn't allow himself to think that way. With a silent prayer of thanks to Wiley Odom for the wealth Travis could now give his son, he turned to the reports in front of him. Since arriving, he and Sam had done little except investigate crimes. As Travis swept through the reports, he seethed. So many cruelties inflicted upon the Negroes. Beatings. Lynchings. Homes and churches burned. But not one single incident had resulted in anyone being charged with anything.

"Can you believe this?" he cried, waving a sheaf of papers in Sam's direction. "You'd think someone would talk. You'd think the people in this county would raise hell about all this."

"I know. I know." Sam nodded from behind his own desk. "But everyone just looks the other way. Even the nigras themselves refuse to tell when they know who's responsible. We've been here nearly a week, though, and so far nothing's happened. Maybe it's going to quiet down."

Travis snorted. "You don't believe that any more than I do. The goddamn Klan is just sitting back and watching to see what we plan to do. They're not scared of us. They're just trying to decide if we are a threat. They're asking themselves if we're sympathetic to the Negroes and plan to uphold the law, or if we'll turn our heads. Well, I've got news for the sonsofbitches. We will never leave Kentucky till we find out who's responsible for this." He slapped the sheaf of papers down on top of the other reports.

"It ain't going to be easy," Sam growled. "Hell, nobody will talk to us. It's like we got the pox or something. Even the nigras cross to the other side of the street when they see us coming. They're scared to death to be seen talking to us."

"I know. That's why I had our office moved back in this

alley. I hoped that by working here and sleeping in the back room, that if anyone did want to talk to us, they'd figure on not being seen as easily slipping in and out here as they would if we were in the old marshal's office out on Main Street. So far, nobody's been around."

"Well," Sam sighed and leaned back from his desk, "we have to give it time. Right now, the Klan aren't the only ones watching us. I imagine the nigras are checking us out, too. They don't know if we can be trusted."

"Time." Travis stared through the glass pane in the door leading to the alley, seeing only the brick wall of the building opposite. "That's one thing I seem to have plenty of these days."

Sam scratched his beard thoughtfully, wondering whether to speak his mind. Finally, he could hold back no longer. "Damn it, Travis, you need to take some time off and go home and see little John. You're not being fair to him or yourself, and he's going to forget he's even got a daddy."

Travis continued to stare at the brick wall through the door glass. "That's the chance I have to take," he responded quietly. "As long as I know I'll kill Nancy and Jerome Danton on sight, I don't want to go back to Goldsboro."

He looked back to the paperwork on his desk, anxious to pull away from the pain. "I suppose we need to put these in some sort of order," he said, signaling that the subject was changed. "Let's put each crime in a separate pile—beatings, hangings, burnings, shootings. Then we'll go over each and question survivors or witnesses. Maybe we can establish a pattern or find some small clue."

Sam agreed, knowing it was futile to continue to press him about seeing John. Travis would cope in his own way.

"It's surprising," Travis reflected out loud, "that Kentucky turned so pro-South once the war was over, because when the war started, the state was divided. About ninety thousand fought for the Union, and about forty thousand for the South. Yet, when the fighting was over, you'd have thought the whole state had been a united part of the Confederacy. It's a mystery to me."

"Yeah," Sam agreed, shuffling papers into separate piles. "But I can understand a little of it. When they passed that law in '33 that said slaves couldn't be brought in for sale, Kentucky was already a quarter black, so the proslavery folks kept an iron fist on things and wouldn't let the law change nothing. But the war took care of all that, and there's some diehards who won't accept it."

"Right," Travis agreed, jaws set grimly. "And they're the ones we've got to get our hands on, because they're either responsible for all the crimes or they know who is."

Sam waved a paper in the air, the cheeks above his brown and gray beard splotching red. He yelled angrily, "Have you read this report? A fifteen-year-old boy was found dead, a rope still around his neck, and a sign pinned to his shirt that said, 'one less vote.' A *fifteen*-year-old, Travis!"

"There are two more over here just like it," Travis said. "One was fifteen, the other, fourteen. But think how many may have gone unreported, for fear of reprisals. I think we've got quite a job ahead of us, Sam, quite an ugly job.

"I also think," he continued, giving his companion a wry grin, "that you and I had best keep our backs to the wall. I've a feeling we aren't going to be well liked around here."

"I know, I know." Sam got up and walked over to stare out the door glass into the empty alley. "I keep telling myself that not every white Kentuckian is responsible for this. They aren't all bad, for God's sake. Just a few rotten eggs. Just a few we've got to make stop."

"Be patient, Sam," Travis said, forcing a lightness to his tone. "We've got to . . ." he stopped talking to stare at Sam, who was looking through the glass, eyes narrowed, alert and tense. Travis got up and hurried to the door to stand beside him.

"There." Sam moved away so he could see. "Behind that trash barrel. See him?"

Travis looked just in time to see the top of a straw hat disappear from view.

"It's a nigra." Sam said. "I saw him slipping along the side of the wall, looking behind him like he was afraid he was being followed. Then he ducked behind that barrel."

Travis opened the door, looked around to make sure no one was watching, then called out softly, "It's okay. You haven't been seen. Get on in here fast."

Very slowly the hat rose into view once again. Soon they saw the wide-eyed, frightened face of an old Negro man. Trembling, he looked fearfully at Travis, but he made no move.

"Come on inside here," Travis called. "Get on in here. We won't hurt you."

When the old Negro didn't budge, Travis went out and grabbed his arm and pulled at him gently. The black said in a quavering whisper, "I's gonna get kilt if anybody sees me, Marshal. Just let me go. I shouldn't have come here."

"Nonsense." Travis pulled him firmly into the office, closed the door behind them, and locked it. "We're your friends. We came to Kentucky to help your people. You obviously have something to tell us." He nodded to Sam. "This is Marshal Bucher, and I'm Marshal Coltrane. Now suppose you tell us why you came."

The Negro glanced around the room, removing his hat to twist it round and round in his gnarled, veined hands. He wore a shabby, tattered cloth coat over faded green trousers that were far too large for his bony frame. They were tied at the waist by a length of frayed rope. The top of his head was a shining glimmer of baldness set in a frame of snow-white fuzz. His eyes, milky chocolate, were red-veined, the vessels strained by age.

"You can talk to us," Travis urged him, helping him to a chair and seating him gently. Then he and Sam leaned against the back of the desk with arms folded across their badged chests, looking down at him. They hoped their expressions conveyed solace and safety.

"It's my boy," he spoke finally. "Munroe. I'm afraid he's gonna get hisself *kilt*. . . ." His eyes bulged as he spoke the terrifying word.

"Now, what makes you think Munroe is going to be killed?" Travis urged. "Tell us, and we'll do what we can to help."

The words poured from the old man's trembling lips. He seemed to gather strength as he talked. "He's been shootin' his mouth off. I told him he couldn't do that, not with so many ears around. He's been sayin' that if our people gets together, we can fight back. He's talkin' about buyin' guns and goin' after them that is killin' and whippin' our people. He's talkin' 'bout takin' the law in his own hands 'cause he says the law is on *their* side."

"Whose side?" Travis prodded. "Who are you talking about?"

The old man swallowed hard. "Them what wears the white hoods and rides at night," he whispered tremulously. "Night riders. They is the ones what will come and kill him. They has ears ever'where, and they'll hear what he's sayin' and kill him. They will."

"And that is why you came to us," Travis said, exchanging an anxious glance with Sam. This was what they had been waiting for, someone with the courage to come forward with something . . . anything. "Now tell us your name and where you live."

He looked at the door nervously, then said, "Israel. My name's Israel. Can't never say my last name. Man what owns me give it to me. His family done own me all my life."

"No one owns you any longer, Israel," Sam said firmly. "The war has been over almost five years now. You're a free man."

"I don't worry about that none," he said with surprising candor. "Mastah Mason, he say I'm too old to beat anymo', that I gonna die any time now, anyhow, so he lets me stay on his place if'n I does what I can, like clean the chicken pen and looks after the chickens. I can still wring their necks, and as long as I can do a lil' sumpin', he won't run me off.

"But if he finds out I is here," he lowered his voice and gripped the arms of the chair, "he gonna run me off, and I won't have nowheres to go. My wife, she died last year, and my chil'run, they all run off 'cause they was scairt of the night riders. All 'ceptin' Munroe. He's so crazy mad, he ain't scairt o' nothin', and that's why you gotta talk some sense into him and make him see he's gonna get hisself kilt."

His bony arms snaked out and pencil-thin fingers pushed against Travis' chest. "You gotta save my boy, Marshal. He's all I got left, and you can't let him get kilt. Make him see he ain't doin' no good. Can't nobody do nothin' with him."

Sam opened his desk drawer and brought out a bottle of whiskey. The old man gratefully took the glass offered him.

"Now, I disagree with you, Israel, when you say no one can do anything," Sam said. "That's why we are here. Marshal Coltrane and I are here to enforce the law, and I want you to tell your son that. Tell the other Negroes that we can be trusted, and if they have a problem, they can come to us. We'll do everything we can to protect them. That is the only way that all this is going to stop.

"It's admirable that your son is so courageous as to stay here rather than run away," Travis said. "But he cannot take the law into his own hands. I can understand why any of you might want to, but it will only cause more trouble. It's going to take people like you, people willing to give us information, if we're going to be able to do anything about all this."

Israel swallowed hard and said, "You don't understand, Marshal. I won't have me no home if'n Mastah Mason finds out I been here. He might even beat me, too, he be so mad." He gripped the chair to lift himself up, but Travis gently pushed him back down. With a whimper from deep within, he whispered, "Please, Marshal. Just let me go on outta heah. I nevah shoulda come. You do what you can fo' my boy, but please just let me go and fo'gets you evah saw me in heah."

"I won't say anything about you coming in here, Israel. You can trust me." Travis gave him what he hoped was a reassuring pat on his shoulder. "But now that you are here, at least go ahead and tell me what you do know."

"That's right," Sam said quickly. "We're strangers here, and nobody has talked to us. If someone like you can tell us anything, anything at all, then we've got a start."

Israel shook his head, clasping and unclasping his hands in his lap. "Don't know nothin'. Can't tell you nothin'. Just find my boy and talk to him. Try to get him to just shut his mouth."

Travis bluntly asked, "Is this man Mason you speak of one of the night riders?"

Israel's body suddenly jerked upward as though he had been shot. "I don't know nothin' about them riders," he cried hoarsely. "They wears white hoods, with slits cut in so's they can see, and slits so's they can talk. But don't nobody see their faces."

"But surely there is talk among your people, Israel," Travis coaxed. "Surely you must have some idea who wears those hoods."

Israel lifted tear-filled eyes to plead. "Marshal, jus' let me go. I can't be found heah. Please."

Travis and Sam exchanged looks and sighs, and then Travis nodded. "All right. You can go. But if you don't give us some idea where to locate your son, then we can't talk to him, can we?"

Israel stood, legs trembling. "He's hidin' out in the mountains with some o' his friends. I don't know 'zactly where. I heard up on Blue Bird. Can't say fo' sho. Can I go now?"

"Yes, you can go. But please tell your people that if any

of them want to talk to us, that they can trust us. We're here to stop all this, Israel, and you've been a big help in getting us started." Travis went to the door first and peered into the alley before nodding to the old man.

Israel shuffled as quickly to the door as his feeble legs would allow. After looking the alley over carefully, he placed a gnarled hand on the knob. Turning slowly to give them one last, frightened look, he bolted, disappearing down the alley.

"He never would have come in here if you hadn't dragged him," mused Sam. "And we ain't got that much to go on now that's he's been here."

Travis was silent for a moment as he stood in the doorway and stared down the empty alley. Then he spoke over his shoulder, "Let's take a walk around town. We've got to find out about this Blue Bird Mountain, and we also need to ask some questions about Mason."

Sam got up to go with him. Even if they did not learn anything, he reasoned, anything was better than going over those depressing reports again.

Outside in the cool, midmorning air, they stepped onto the main street of the town. They said nothing, silently noting how the Negroes moved to cross away from them as they approached, and how the townspeople eyed them suspiciously, condemningly, as they passed by.

"We've made the rounds of the saloons, and we won't find out anything there," Travis pointed out as they approached the town's only hotel. "Let's go in here. There's a tearoom, and we should run into a different class."

Sam laughed. "You trying to tell me that the higher-ups might give us information? I'm betting they're the ones who pay the ruffians to do their dirty work."

"Not everyone in this town condones what's happening, Sam. There might be a few who're willing to help us once they know which side we're on."

"Don't count on anybody talking to us. Whites are probably just as scared as old Israel," Sam replied.

"Sometimes it isn't what people say," Travis said as he pushed open the doors to the hotel. "It's what they *don't* say."

They entered the shadowed, musty lobby, glancing briefly at the desk clerk, who eyed them suspiciously from behind his counter. They moved across the faded rose-patterned rug in the direction of the tearoom. Frosted panes of glass painted with golden scrolls surrounded the entrance.

Stepping inside, they sensed every eye upon them. Travis led the way and they sat down at a table draped in spotless white. A waiter, attired in a short black coat, approached them with suspicious eyes. "Yes, what can I get for you, Marshals?" he asked quickly.

"Coffee," Travis ordered for them both, and as the waiter hurried back toward the kitchen, turned to glance around the room.

Four tables were occupied, and the occupants all looked away as Travis' eyes raked them over. There was one exception, a young woman sitting alone near the window facing the street.

She met Travis' gaze with quiet amusement, emerald eyes sparkling beneath long, dusty lashes. Leaning forward to lift her china cup to perfectly formed lips painted pale pink, she offered a teasing view of the small, perfectly formed breasts swelling above her white velvet morning dress.

He suddenly realized that, besides Kitty, this young woman was the most beautiful he had ever seen. The green eyes were of a deep shade and brilliantly clear. The light brown hair was lustrous and touched with gold.

With a haughty yet playful lift of her chin, she looked away, through the window to the street beyond. Her profile was flawless.

Just then the waiter returned with two fragile-looking floral cups filled with steaming coffee. As he began to move away, Travis gestured to him. "That young woman," he nodded in her direction. "Might I ask who she is?"

The waiter hesitated briefly, then shrugged as though telling himself there was no harm in answering. "That is Miss Alaina Barbeau, Marshal." Then, with a laugh, he added, "Sure can tell you haven't been around here long if you don't know the Barbeau family. Jordan Barbeau is the richest man in these parts and maybe the most powerful in the whole state of Kentucky."

Travis had heard of Jordan Barbeau but knew from experience that the best way to get information was to feign ignorance. People felt superior when they thought they knew more than you did, and were delighted to tell all they knew.

With a blank expression, he looked up at the waiter and said humbly, "I didn't know that. I must admit I have never heard of the Barbeaus."

A smug expression crept over the waiter's face as he moved to brush imaginary crumbs from the white linen tablecloth. "Well, don't go around admitting that, Marshal," he spoke quietly, "or folks will think you're just plain dumb. Jordan Barbeau owns most all of this county. He's got hundreds of acres of tobacco, not to mention corn, hay, and big herds of cattle. He also breeds Thoroughbred saddle horses and race-horses. He's even got interest in two big manufacturing plants over in Louisville."

"Is that right?" Travis pretended awe. "Then I guess I do seem awfully ignorant."

His informant smiled obligingly, "I'm glad to be able to help you out."

He nodded and walked away. Travis turned to look at Alaina Barbeau, marveling once again at her breathtaking beauty. She had been watching him but glanced quickly away when he turned toward her.

Sam snorted, "She looks like a rich little snob. I know the type."

Travis did not respond. Something told him he had not yet met the likes of Alaina Barbeau. Beneath the cool appearance, he could sense, even from across the room, something intriguing, something he could not name.

He caught her looking at him from the corner of his eye and jerked around so quickly that they were facing each other. She remained unruffled. Their eyes met and held. Suddenly she pushed back her chair, stood, and walked over to Travis.

"What's she coming over here for?" Sam growled under his breath. "That's all we need—some woman chasing after you when we got more trouble than we can handle already."

"Who says she's chasing me, Sam?" Travis chuckled in quiet amusement.

She approached, a smile on her lips, looking Travis up and down. In a voice so soft he could feel the hairs rising along the backs of his arms, she said, "I assume, sir, from that badge, that you are the new marshal."

Travis politely stood and Sam reluctantly followed suit. "Yes, ma'am. I'm Marshal Coltrane. This is Marshal Bucher. I must confess to having taken the liberty to inquire about you,

Miss Barbeau." He pulled out the chair next to him. "Would you care to join us?"

"I shouldn't," she said thoughtfully, glancing toward the window. "I'm waiting for someone. Oh, very well. I might as well take the opportunity to welcome you all to Kentucky."

Travis watched her bright green eyes sparkle with what he decided was sheer mischief. She took her seat and coyly smiled, "I must confess to having taken the liberty to inquire about you as well, Marshal, but my sources gave me much more information, I'm sure, than the waiter gave you about me."

He laughed. "What makes you think I asked the waiter?"

"Come now." She placed her hand against her throat. "Do give me credit for knowing when a man asks about me."

Sam had not sat down again. He cleared his throat pointedly, and Travis looked up. "If you two will excuse me, I think I'll go make some inquiries of my own. For *business* reasons," he added stonily.

Travis murmured absently, "See you back at the office," and turned his full attention to Alaina. "Let me also give you credit for knowing when a man finds you quite lovely, Miss Barbeau, as I obviously do."

With candor he found refreshing, she told him, "Yes, I must admit I do have that perception. Oh, and please call me Alaina. I intend to call you Travis. It's much less formal." She leaned forward to prop her chin on folded, white-gloved hands. "Now that we have the social proprieties out of the way, we can chat. I hear you came all the way from Nevada just to help the poor Negroes."

"To *try* to help," he corrected her.

"I also hear you had quite an impressive record as a cavalry officer for the Union during the war. My father was loyal to the South. Since you will be meeting him in the future, you might bear that in mind."

"The war is over, Miss Barbeau . . . Alaina," he said pointedly. "It doesn't matter to me on which side your father placed his loyalties."

She laughed, a soft, silvery sound that was pleasing to his ear. "If you knew my father, you would know that it matters very much." Nodding her head she said brightly, "We will just have to see that you do meet Daddy. Would you like to come to our home this Friday night? It's my birthday, and Daddy is giving me a party. I'd love for you to come."

She reached out and covered his large hand with her tiny gloved one and squeezed. Instinct told him to be wary. Her touch alone caused gentle quivers of emotion to move through him. Damn, she was beautiful, but it was not merely her loveliness that he found so appealing. There was a freshness, a delightful candor, as well.

"Come now, Travis"—she squeezed his hand once more—"I don't take you for the shy kind. I imagine you love going to parties and meeting people. And you'll love my home. It's a big house with a sprawling yard at the base of a mountain. If you come early enough, we can go riding, and I'll see that you have one of Daddy's prize Thoroughbreds. He's terribly proud of his horses."

Travis raised an eyebrow. "Your daddy might not want me riding one of his prize horses, Alaina."

She pretended to pout. "Daddy will do whatever I want him to do, especially on my birthday." Then she laughed happily. "Oh, do say you will come, Travis. Already the young ladies here are talking about what a handsome devil you are, and I will be the envy of all of them if you come to my birthday party."

He did not blush. It was not one of his weaknesses. "All right, then. I'll be happy to come, Alaina."

"More than that," she lowered her lashes over the twinkling emerald eyes, instantly changing from ebullient child to seductive lady. "I think I should like to have you as my weekend guest. Come prepared to stay until Sunday. Then I will have a chance to really show you around. We can have a picnic on Saturday. Just the two of us."

"I don't think I can take the time off from my work, Alaina. Not now."

"But if you're needed, Marshal Bucher can ride out to get you. Besides, I hear you sleep in the back of that horrid little office you insisted on moving to, and it will do you a world of good to have a change. Do say you will come," she coaxed.

Travis did not have to ask himself if he wanted to accept her invitation. He damn well knew he did. Alaina was looking at him in a way that said she wanted him, and it had been a long time since he had known a woman's body. Still, something was telling him to stay away.

"I'm afraid I will have to decline, Alaina. Perhaps I can

visit later, when I've got a better hold on things here."

"Oh, you're terrible!" She stomped her foot beneath the table. "At least say you will come to the party."

He was about to tell her that he was not even sure that was a good idea, when a tall, muscular man appeared in the doorway. His eyes fastened on Alaina, swept over Travis, then narrowed. The man strode purposefully toward the table.

"I think the friend you were waiting for has arrived." Travis inclined his head slightly in the direction of the man approaching.

Alaina looked around and flashed an innocent grin. "Stewart! Where have you been, darling? You're late."

"I see you found a way to occupy yourself," he said tightly, looking down at her, ignoring Travis.

Travis sized him up quickly. Big. Probably wealthy, judging by his clothes. Not bad looking but a bit rough around the edges. Probably fell into his fortune rather than being born into it. He was probably quick to anger. This, coupled with his size, no doubt made him bullish.

"Of course I occupied myself," Alaina said quickly, obviously not intimidated. "This is our new marshal, Travis Coltrane. He's a very nice man, and we've been getting acquainted."

The man glanced at Travis coldly, then looked back to Alaina. "We need to be on our way. I have business to discuss with your father."

She dismissed him with a wave of her hand. "Poor Stewart. He's always so busy. He's Daddy's foreman, you see. He looks after everything and sees that everything gets done. Daddy looks after business matters."

"Alaina, we must be going," he persisted.

She sighed, reaching for her small beaded white bag. "Oh, for goodness' sake, Stewart, all right. Really, sometimes you can be so trying. I think I liked you better before Daddy made you his foreman. You weren't so stodgy." He moved to pull her chair back as she rose.

"At least," she said, clearly irritated, "allow me to introduce you to the marshal."

Travis had stood as Alaina did, and he obligingly held out his hand to the glowering stranger. It was taken reluctantly and released at once.

"This is Stewart Mason, Travis," Alaina was saying. "He isn't always like this, believe me, or I could not put up with him."

Travis hid his reaction to the name. "I believe I have you mixed up with someone else," he said, on guard then. "I had heard of a gentleman named Mason, but he was a landowner, not an overseer."

Mason stiffened. Clearly a sore spot had been touched. "I do own land. Any law that says a man can't own land and work another man's land as well?"

Travis stifled the impulse to smirk. "Of course not. It appears I have offended you. I'm sorry."

Alaina laughed. "He's not offended. He's just jealous because we were sitting here talking, so he's trying to see how nasty he can be. Pay no attention."

"Alaina, you do go on," Mason snapped. "Let's be on our way."

She held out her hand to Travis, and he lifted it to his lips for a gentle kiss, silently pleased with the angry look this provoked from Mason. "I will see you Friday," he murmured, giving Alaina a warm smile.

"What about Friday?" Mason quickly reacted. "Friday is your birthday, Alaina."

"Well, I know that," she said with feigned exasperation. "I have invited the marshal to my party. I invited him to come stay with us for the whole weekend, as my guest, but he declined."

"On second thought," Travis spoke up quickly, "I have thought it over a bit more carefully and I will be able to accept your gracious invitation after all, Alaina. I'll be delighted."

"Oh, that's marvelous!" She squeezed his arm in her enthusiasm. "I'll be expecting you around four. You'll have a wonderful time. I promise."

Mason looked him straight in the eye then for the first time, and Travis met him full force, not glancing away. They were of equal height and nearly equal build. The glare Stewart gave Travis plainly mirrored not only his malice but also his intention to do something about it.

"I am sure I will see you there, Mason," Travis said evenly.

"Yes," was the clipped response. "You can be sure of that, Marshal."

Stewart Mason took Alaina's arm and they walked toward

the door, but just before disappearing through it, Alaina turned ever so slightly to give Travis a very special smile.

He knew the meaning behind that smile. Women had given him that smile before. Most he had ignored. Others he had not ignored.

This was one he would not ignore.

Chapter Fifteen

TRAVIS rode his horse up onto a knoll just off the main road in order to survey the land around him without being observed by others on their way to Alaina's birthday party.

He shook his head as he stared at Jordan Barbeau's mansion. Of gray fieldstone, it stood four stories high, a turret at all four corners. The windows were long, narrow, and arched at the tops, each composed of many small panes of glass. A low wall wrapped around the edge of the roof, probably a walkway.

The front doors were large and arched like the windows. A winding terrace joined the house to a narrow stairway rising from the cobblestone driveway. Neatly trimmed shrubs hugged the base of the stone house.

There were six separate gardens, laid out in various patterns. Regal oaks and maples stretched to the sky, bordering the property for as far as he could see.

It was all too showy for Travis' tastes. Barbeau, he surmised, wanted everyone to be aware of his vast wealth and had no hesitancy about being ostentatious if that was what it took. He was powerful, no doubt about that. Travis' inquiries over the past few days had revealed that in this part of the state, whatever Barbeau did not own, he managed to control.

Local gossips had also provided the information that Stewart Mason and Alaina Barbeau were unofficially engaged, and that it was Alaina who refused to make definite plans for marriage.

What about Mason? Israel had spoken his name in terror. People questioned about him seemed reluctant, almost afraid, to talk about him. But why? He was not rich. He owned land, true, but it had not taken long to find out that his property was heavily mortgaged . . . by Jordan Barbeau. Maybe Sam was right in his theory that the rich hired ruffians to do their dirty work. It just might be, Travis thought with ever-growing suspicion, that Mason was behind much, if not all, of what was happening to the Negroes around there, and that Barbeau was paying the bills and giving the orders.

Twilight turned the sky to a dusty purple blush against the hazy green mountains. The first twinkling stars appeared as a gentle night wind blew down across the valley. Nudging his horse back to the road, Travis headed for the Gothic mansion, noting the large number of carriages in the driveway.

In his saddlebags was a fresh change of clothing. Sam had told him he was crazy to be spending the weekend in the home of the man who just might be in charge of all the Klan's activities.

"All the more reason to stay there," Travis had grinned.

To which Sam had replied, "That ain't the reason you're going, and you know it. It's that girl." He hastened to add, "Don't get me wrong. I'm not condemning you for having a yen. You're only human. But hell, man, look at who she is. You don't want to go getting mixed up with that family. If what we suspect is true, it could be dangerous."

Travis did not like to admit that Sam spoke the truth. But life had to go on. Travis thought Fate had decreed whatever would happen between him and Alaina Barbeau.

He gave his horse over to the Negro groom who stood waiting at the foot of the stairs, elegantly dressed in a bright red coat and short black velvet pants. Then he made his way up the stairs toward the open doors where another Negro, resplendent in a white silk coat and black trousers, waited to announce his arrival.

Stepping into the huge, round entrance foyer, Travis was immediately struck by the opulence of the place. The largest crystal chandelier he had ever seen hung from the high, domed ceiling, sparkling with lights. The walls were covered in a rich paper embossed with huge red velvet roses and intertwining bright green vines. Polished cherrywood frames held oil portraits of austere ancestors. Beneath his feet lay an expensive handwoven Oriental rug trimmed in thick gold-braided fringe. On both sides of the foyer rose oak stairways covered in bright red carpet, curving up to the second-floor landing.

Rich. Very rich. There was no doubt about Jordan Barbeau's wealth.

"I will announce your arrival, Marshal Coltrane," the Negro butler pronounced in his very excellent English.

"No need." Travis brushed him aside, handing over his hat but deciding to keep his gun holster. He was not dressed formally but had worn a new leather dress coat, starched white shirt, and black corded tie. His trousers were also new, dark blue, neatly pressed, and he had spit-shined his black riding boots. Thinking it over during the past couple of days he had seen no advantage in pretending to be anything other than what he was, a federal district marshal.

The butler nervously cleared his throat as he hurried after Travis. "Sir," he called softly, anxiously, "please, sir, allow me to announce you. It is customary, and—"

"It's quite all right, Willis. *I* will announce the marshal." The soft, feminine voice floated down from the staircase.

Alaina Barbeau stood on the staircase looking down at them in quiet amusement. Travis' eyes swept over her appreciatively. She wore a dark green ball gown of watered silk, its shimmering highlights reflecting her sultry emerald eyes. Stones to match sparkled brilliantly at her throat and in her hair, where jewels held her golden-brown tresses in ringlets and waves.

Her small but firm bosom rose provocatively above the daring décolletage, and he watched as she trailed lace-gloved hands to touch the stones at her throat. She smiled with moist, coral lips. "Marshal Coltrane," she spoke in a husky whisper, "would you do me the honor of escorting me into the ballroom?"

The butler stepped back, aghast at the flaunting of protocol as Alaina made her way down the stairs. She seemed to float, her dainty green-satin slippers barely brushing the red carpet. Travis met her burning gaze, the challenge there for him and him alone.

Reaching the foyer, she tucked her hand in the crook of his

arm and looked up at him with a teasing smile. "I can't tell you how pleased I am that you decided to accept my invitation, Travis. I suppose I will have to show you . . . later." She gave him a mischievous wink.

Travis held his expression, suppressing the instinct to raise his eyebrows in surprise. A very bold lady, indeed, he thought with amusement. Either that or she was a first-class tease. He had his own way of dealing with coquettish females who carried their ploy too far. He enjoyed no game better, for he had yet to lose.

"Alaina," he responded quietly, evenly, eyes moving to her delightful bosom, then returning to her amused expression, "you have offered me hospitality, and that is quite sufficient."

She tilted her head to one side. "I have much more to offer, Marshal. Will you be spending the weekend?"

"I had planned to. It does get lonely in that small room back in town."

"You won't be lonely here. I can promise you that. Now, shall we enter?"

He nodded, and they stepped through the doorway into the ballroom. All eyes turned to them as if on signal. The music trailed away, and a surprised murmuring skipped through the throng. It had, Travis decided at once, been in poor taste to escort Alaina into her own party. He was, after all, a stranger who had not even been announced.

A man emerged from the crowd, and Travis knew at once that this was Jordan Barbeau. He was of average height, but his sturdy build and powerful shoulders made him seem taller. His dark hair was short, silvered at the temples, and curled close to his head in tight ringlets. Clean-shaven, a blue shadow lingered along his square jaw. The same green eyes that sparkled so for Alaina were narrowed and angry in Jordan Barbeau.

He was the host and could not afford to voice his anger at the breach of protocol, so Jordan kissed his daughter's cheek before turning to Travis and extending a stiff hand. "Marshal," he murmured politely, "nice of you to come to my daughter's party."

"Nice of her to invite me," Travis offered, noting the pleased expression on Alaina's face. She seemed to be signaling that he was not to worry, for she could handle her father.

Stewart Mason was another matter, Travis realized as he saw him push through the crowd. Removing Alaina's hand from Travis' arm and tucking it beneath his own, Stewart glared at Travis.

Travis found himself shut out as the trio—Jordan, Alaina, and Stewart—faced their guests. "My daughter," Jordan heralded proudly. "On the occasion of her eighteenth birthday, I present her to you."

There was a loud ringing of applause, cries of "Happy Birthday," and the orchestra began to play the traditional song. Everyone, except Travis, joined in to sing it to Alaina.

When the music ended, Jordan held up his hands for silence and everyone waited expectantly. "As on the occasion of my daughter Marilee's birthday," he announced jubilantly, "I present to Alaina one thousand acres of my prime land." Enthusiastic applause interrupted briefly and he waved for silence. "And, as with Marilee, Alaina now receives her generous trust fund as a gift from me and her late mother, God rest her soul." His voice broke effectively and Travis wondered if he was the only one who saw the show of dramatics for what it was.

Alaina dutifully kissed her father, then allowed herself to be swept into Stewart's arms as the orchestra began to play a lilting waltz. She was now, officially, an adult and a wealthy young woman in her own right.

Jordan turned to Travis. "My butler should have announced you, Marshal. I would have done so myself, but the moment, as you can see, belonged to Alaina."

"It doesn't matter," Travis shrugged. "I never cared for formalities. Don't blame your butler. He offered."

Jordan looked amused. "Alaina's entrance was another display of her constant struggle for independence. She is quite a little rebel when it comes to social decorum. Quite frankly, it will be a relief to see her married. Someone else can deal with her little insurrections."

Travis did not comment, and Jordan eyed him suspiciously, the smile fading. "Tell me, how much longer do you think you and the other marshal will be around? I must be candid and say that our people aren't exactly happy at having the government send in outsiders to deal with *our* problems."

A nerve twitched in Travis' jaw. "When local law can't deal with those problems, Barbeau, it's the government's duty to send in outsiders. Marshal Bucher and I will stay . . . until we are no longer needed."

A shadow passed over Jordan's face but quickly disappeared

as he gestured toward the door. "I am afraid I am not being a very gracious host, Marshal. Would you care to join me in my study for a glass of my personal stock of brandy?"

Travis nodded, and the two men left the ballroom to cross the foyer and turn down a short hallway which ended at a spacious, oak-paneled room. "Do you like it?" Jordan asked as they entered and he closed heavy double doors behind them. "I had everything shipped from England—the leather furnishings, sofas, chairs, chandeliers, and even the mahogany desk. I love this room. It's just as well. I spend much of my time here."

"It's very nice," Travis commented while silently wondering if a tomb could be much gloomier.

Jordan took a crystal decanter from a cabinet, poured them both a drink, then toasted to a "pleasant stay in Kentucky." He sat down in a large leather chair, crossed his legs, and looked straight at Travis. "So. Tell me. What have you decided since your arrival? That we are all a bunch of nigra-haters, out to destroy their race?"

Travis swished the amber liquid around in his glass, frowning as though considering the question. "I don't think everyone in these parts hates the Negroes, Barbeau, and it would be foolish for anyone to think they could destroy the Negro race. Let's just say that, after looking over the records in the marshal's office, I find too many reports of crimes. I intend to find out why these things happened, and to see that more do not take place."

Jordan looked amused. "That might prove difficult, Marshal. After all, you're dealing with some Southerners who will never bend to the will of the Yankee bureaucrats. Just because they have given freedom to the slaves does not mean that those very slaves suddenly have the intelligence to vote, to own land, to live like white men. You're a bright fellow. Surely you understand that."

"They now have the freedom to try," Travis said coldly. "It is a crime for anyone to stand in the way of their trying. Beating them, intimidating them, killing them will not be tolerated."

"Let the nigra learn his place," Jordan matched his tone. "Then we won't have any problems. If the nigras don't like not being able to run roughshod over the whites in Kentucky, then let them move farther south, to Georgia or Alabama. Perhaps they can do so there."

"Don't speak for all the whites, Barbeau. Let's be realistic. The ones responsible for the crimes that have been committed are members of the Ku Klux Klan, for the most part. I'm sure there are many decent white people in Kentucky who don't feel as you do."

Jordan's eyes widened, his nostrils flaring slightly. "*I* consider myselt decent, sir, and I am not a member of the Klan."

"But I imagine you know who is."

"Perhaps. I know everything that goes on around here. But that does not mean that I am necessarily a part of everything that goes on."

Travis took a sip of brandy, staring thoughtfully at him over the rim. "If you know everything that goes on, then you could tell me who I need to look for, couldn't you?"

"I didn't say that." Jordan's reply was swift. "And you should be aware, sir, that even if I do know whom you seek, I would never betray my neighbors. I'm afraid you are going to find yourself in for a very difficult time here. It could also be dangerous. The Kentuckians I know won't welcome you."

Travis looked at him steadily. "I'm not here as a goddamn goodwill ambassador. I'm here to do what I can to stop the mistreatment of the Negroes, and I intend to do my job no matter what," he added meaningfully, eyes unflinching as he met his host's angry stare. Travis paused, then continued, "As long as I'm here, there are a few questions I'd like to ask of you."

"Go ahead," Jordan snapped. "I won't promise to answer."

"To the best of your knowledge, just *why* are the Negroes being persecuted?"

Jordan smiled. "They're uppity. As I said, they don't know their place. Maybe the Yankees did set them free, but that does not make them as good as white people. No law can ever do that." He got up to refill his glass, inviting Travis to join him. "Frankly, Marshal, I don't like this conversation. I'm not involved in the Klan's activities, but I must admit to being sympathetic. I'm a businessman, a farmer, and I also have a family. It does not please me that you even consider me involved in this nasty business enough to question me."

"Look at it this way. I'm questioning you because you are

important around here, Barbeau. My job is to find out everything I can. So don't be offended."

"No offense taken." Barbeau smiled stiffly. "Now then, is that all you wanted of me? I do need to join my guests now that we've had time for me to make your acquaintance."

"I have one more question."

"Ask. Again, I may not answer."

"Stewart Mason. He's your foreman. You hold the mortgage on his property. It's common knowledge he wants to marry Alaina. I don't suppose you would tell me whether he has any dealings with the Klan."

Jordan was clearly surprised, both by Travis' knowledge of Stewart and by his audacious question.

"Come now, Marshal. Do you take me for a fool? Do you think I would allow my own foreman and future son-in-law to be a part of the Klan when you lawmen are out to get them? No. If Stewart is involved with the Klan, he is keeping it a closely guarded secret from me. I'm prominent in this state and well respected, and while everyone knows where my sympathies lie, they also know that I do not deal in anything illegal."

Travis rose. "Very well, then. I suppose I have no further questions."

Jordan also stood. "Then let's get back to the party. The cake is yet to be cut, and I have champagne imported from France especially for Alaina's birthday."

They left the study and were entering the foyer as Alaina came in from the ballroom, eyes searching. "Oh, there you are," she cried, scurrying forward and holding her dress with both hands to just above the tips of her satin slippers. "I want to dance with you, Marshal."

"Alaina, do you think that's very ladylike?" Jordan admonished her, his cheeks flushing slightly. "It isn't proper for a lady to ask a gentleman to dance."

"Oh, pooh, Daddy," she laughed merrily, taking Travis by his hand and tugging him gently. "It's my birthday. I can do anything I want."

"I've a feeling," Travis whispered as they moved away from Jordan's disapproving expression, "that you do what you want even when it's not your birthday."

"Of course." She beamed up at him as they entered the ballroom. Moving through the throng of guests, Travis took her in his arms and they began to dance. The other dancers did little to hide their curiosity.

"You dance divinely," she murmured, giving him a melting gaze. "I knew you would. I knew the first time I saw you that you're the kind of man who was born knowing how to please a woman . . . in every way," she added clearly.

He was amused. "And what do you know? You're hardly more than a child, Alaina."

"Oh, am I?" She feigned offense. "You've never known the likes of a woman like me, Travis Coltrane. Perhaps I will prove it to you."

He grinned at her crookedly. "You make that sound more like a threat than a promise."

"It could be both. You will just have to wait and see."

He chuckled softly, and, as the music ended, he released her. Stewart Mason suddenly appeared, quite annoyed. "Your father is ready for the champagne toasts," he snapped, ignoring Travis. "And the cake is ready to be cut. Come with me."

She slipped her hand in Travis'. "Come along and help me cut the cake. It's enormous. Daddy had it made by a baker in Louisville, and it took four men just to lift it from the wagon."

"Alaina, don't be absurd!" Stewart snapped furiously. "A stranger has no business helping you cut your birthday cake. Have you lost all sense of decorum?"

She whirled on him. "What do you know of decorum, Stewart Mason? You were nothing but a grubby redneck till Daddy picked you up and gave you a decent job!"

Stewart hissed, "How dare you, Alaina? Now, stop behaving like a spoiled brat or I'll—"

"You'll what?" she challenged him, still holding onto Travis' hand. "Now, stay out of my business, Stewart. The marshal is my house guest, and if I ask him to cut my cake, he will."

Stewart looked at Travis then, silently sending him a dare.

Travis took his hand from Alaina's. Damn, the last thing he wanted right then was a scene with Mason. Travis had never backed off from a fight, but he did not believe in provoking them, either, especially not silly ones. "Go along with Stewart," he said to Alaina, stepping back. "I'll see you later."

He turned quickly before she could argue and hurried through the open doors that led out to a vine-shrouded terrace.

With a sigh of relief, he stepped to the shadows and pulled a cheroot from his coat pocket and lit it. Watching the smoke spiral skyward into the purple night, he was grateful for a few moments of peace.

He reflected on the conversation with Barbeau and decided the man was lying. While Travis could not put his finger on exactly why he sensed the man was behind the Klan activities, it was a gut feeling that told him to be on guard. Stewart Mason, he felt, was very much involved. Alaina had said that he was nothing until her father took him under his wing. Why would Jordan Barbeau do that except to have a man he could trust? Someone to do his dirty deeds?

Suddenly a movement beyond the low stone wall surrounding the terrace caught his eye. He could just barely make out a woman in the darkness. She spoke. "Well, Marshal, what are you doing out here alone? I hope you're not trying to think of a way to cope with my precocious sister. It's a waste of time."

She laughed softly, stepping onto the terrace, then moved closer. "Forgive me. I wasn't spying. I like to walk at night, and I do get tired of all the noise and smoke of parties. I'm Marilee. Alaina's sister."

Travis saw a slight resemblance but nothing that would have told him the two were related. Marilee was taller and definitely older by at least three or four years, and he sensed that she had experienced more of the tragedies of life than Alaina. Perhaps it was Marilee's eyes, a dull brown that one day long ago might have sparkled. Her hair was chestnut, pulled back into a severe bun at the nape of her neck. He could tell nothing of her figure, for she wore a high-necked, bulky black dress, with long sleeves. The drab gown served to make her appear even more somber than she already was.

"My pleasure," he bowed slightly.

She laughed again, but the sound was hollow. "When Alaina is around, there is no room for anyone else. Oh, I don't mean to sound envious. I love Alaina dearly, but she does have her ways.

"I watched the two of you when you were dancing," she went on. "I know her, Marshal, and she has designs on you."

Travis felt uncomfortable.

"I know it's none of my business," she hastened to add,

"but I feel I must warn you that Alaina is trouble. So is her fiancé, Stewart Mason."

"Why are you taking the trouble to tell me this?" he asked, looking down at her curiously. Perhaps, he thought, she really was envious of her sister. By comparison, she looked like a spinster.

To his surprise, Marilee smiled as though she knew exactly what he was thinking. Then she astounded him even more by saying, "I'm not envious of Alaina, Marshal. Actually, I feel sorry for her. She's looking for something she will never find unless she discovers herself first. As for why I am telling you this, I feel obligated to keep you from being hurt."

"Hurt?" he laughed shortly. "Who is going to hurt me, Miss Barbeau?"

"It isn't 'Miss Barbeau,'" she corrected evenly. "It's Mrs. Traylor. But call me Marilee, please."

So, he thought. She was no spinster.

"Kentucky is a dangerous place for those who oppose the views of the Klan," she went on in a quiet voice. "I don't think you know how dangerous, especially around here. You have enough to do without becoming involved with Alaina."

"Suppose you explain just what you mean, Marilee."

For the first time, she appeared nervous as she answered. "If you don't spurn Alaina's advances, you will only provoke Stewart and my father. I'm telling you this for your own good. You're an outsider. You have come here to interfere. You aren't welcome, but that's not going to change whether my sister takes a fancy to you or not."

"You do get right to the point," he said. "But what about you? Do you also find my presence an imposition?"

"I couldn't care less, Marshal."

"And how about your feelings regarding the Negroes? Do you feel the lynchings and beatings are the best ways to deal with Negroes?"

Her eyes narrowed, and he saw that her hands were knotted into tiny fists. "I hate it. I hate all of it. But I have no voice. Our neighbors hate me enough as it is without my preaching to them about their sins against their fellow man."

Travis heard the bitterness immediately and urged her on. "Why would your neighbors hate you? I find you straightforward and honest. I see nothing to dislike."

She bit down on her lower lip, closed her eyes briefly, then forced a smile. "It doesn't matter about me, Marshal. I just wanted to warn you about Alaina. She is quite beautiful, and I'm sure you find her appealing. But you can't know her as I do . . . how cunning she can be. She stops at nothing to get what she wants."

Travis leaned against a vine-wrapped trellis and folded his arms across his chest. "Mrs. Trayler . . . Marilee . . . I find your concern for my welfare touching. But rest assured that Alaina is not the first desirable woman to come into my life. I think I can handle your sister."

Her face tightened. "Yes, I just imagine you can, Marshal." She lifted her chin. "Suppose I just leave you to handle your own . . . *affairs.*"

She whirled about so quickly that there was no time to see that Alaina had stepped onto the terrace. The sisters collided.

"Oh, Marilee, watch where you're going! You'll muss my dress!" Alaina cried, eyes darting to Travis, then returning to her sister. "Just what are you doing out here with *my* guest?"

"Being polite," Marilee replied nonchalantly, breezing by to disappear inside.

Alaina shook her head and hurried to Travis, who was still leaning lazily against the trellis. "Oh, that girl!" She glanced back over her shoulder in disgust. "I do wish she would find a beau of her own and stop flirting with every man who comes to call on me."

He raised an eyebrow. "She just introduced herself to me as Mrs. Traylor."

"She's a widow. Her husband was killed in the war. She will probably never marry again. She's turned into such a shrew. You should hear some of the fights she and Daddy have over her being such a nigra-lover. Just like Donald. When he got killed, Daddy said it was good enough for someone who would go off to fight for the damn Yankees."

"I fought for the damn Yankees, as you call them," he said drily.

She moved closer, placing her fingertips on his shoulders as she whispered, "I know. But that doesn't matter. You were just a soldier. Doing your job. You couldn't really have *cared* one way or the other."

"As a matter of fact, I did care. Very much. I still do."

She stood on tiptoes, her lips, moist and inviting, inches

away from his face. "Oh, Travis, do we have to talk of unpleasant things?" she murmured huskily, thrusting her breasts against his chest. "I think we can find more interesting things to do."

He felt the familiar burning in his loins. Damn, he wanted her. What man wouldn't? Beautiful. Desirable. And he could tell she was every bit as hungry as he was. Sheer masculine need moved him to gather her in his arms. His lips crushed hers.

Her fingers moved up to trail along his neck, body melding into his. He held her tightly for a moment, then withdrew. "I think we should return to your party. After all, you are the guest of honor."

Gasping slightly, she patted her hair nervously, face flushed. "Yes. Yes, I suppose you're right. Come. Let's dance." She led the way from the terrace.

It was during their second waltz together that Travis felt a hard tap on his shoulder. Stewart was standing behind him, grim-faced. With a mock bow, Travis stepped aside and headed to the corner table, where there were liquid refreshments.

He made small talk with the few men who introduced themselves. There was no mistaking the hostility directed at him as they asked questions about his investigation. He told them only that he was there to do a job and intended to do it. Looks were exchanged, and a few began to mutter to one another. He caught a glimpse of Marilee standing to one side, watching him with . . . what? Amusement? Anger? He could not quite fathom her expression.

He approached her and held out his hand, relieved to get away from the table. "Would you care to dance with me, Marilee?"

The smile she gave him was almost sad. "It's very kind of you to take pity on a wallflower, Marshal, but no thank you. I don't need your pity."

He laughed shortly. "Who said I felt pity for you?"

"It's in your eyes. I can always tell what a man is thinking by his eyes. No thank you, Marshal. I don't need your sympathy. I don't need anything from you."

She turned and walked away, leaving Travis standing there feeling foolish and angry. Who the hell did she think she was?

He had almost made up his mind to leave when a short, bald man walked up to him, acting nervous. He introduced himself as Norman Haithcock, a farmer. He darted anxious glances around the room, as though afraid someone was watching, and began to ask questions about "the investigation." Had Travis found any clues?

Travis was noncommittal, giving the standard answers, all the while observing Norman Haithcock. He seemed genuinely concerned. Here, perhaps, was an ally.

Travis was so engrossed in listening to everything the man had to say, about the weather or the government, that he did not realize the ballroom was nearly empty until Jordan Barbeau approached.

"Well, you two have really been deep in conversation," he said with mock joviality, his eyes glowering. "Seems everyone has left but you, Norman, and it's time I was showing the marshal to his quarters."

Norman Haithcock nearly stumbled in his haste to say good night and depart. Jordan watched him with pursed lips, then said, "I hope he did not bore you, Marshal. He's not very bright, I'm afraid. I invited him only because his land borders mine on the southeast, and I always try to be neighborly. Actually, folks around here don't have anything much to do with him."

Travis kept silent.

"Now then," Jordan went on, "my daughter tells me you are staying the night. Come along, and I will show you where you will sleep."

Travis followed him up the stairway to the second floor, to the third, and finally to the top floor of the enormous mansion. "I always put our guests up here in this wing," he explained as he flung open the door to a well-lit suite. There was a parlor, and to either side of the parlor were two bedrooms. "You have a splendid view of the mountain range to the east. It's quite lovely when the sun rises," Barbeau said proudly.

A young Negro woman emerged from one of the bedrooms, curtsied, and disappeared.

"Selma has turned down your bed," Jordan said, backing toward the door, his hand on the knob. "In the morning, I will have my personal valet bring your bath water. Breakfast is served at eight. I imagine Alaina will want to take you riding. I have some highly prized animals in my stables, you know."

"I've heard," Travis said politely, knowing it was expected. "Thank you for all your hospitalities, Barbeau."

Jordan nodded, just a hint of self-satisfaction on his face, and stepped out, closing the door behind him.

Travis walked around the room gingerly, quickly deciding it was far too ostentatious for his taste, going to the smaller of the two bedrooms, done in shades of blue and furnished with mahogany, he suddenly realized he had neglected to bring in his saddlebag. No matter. He hated nightshirts anyway and used one only when he was a guest in someone else's home.

He took off his clothes and lay down across the bed naked. He had not drunk very much but realized he was tired. It had been an interesting evening but a trying one. He just hoped he could do his job and get the hell out as soon as possible, go back to North Carolina, get little John, and then head to Nevada.

He did not like the anger he was finding in Kentucky, he mused sleepily. He did not need an involvement with the daughter of the man who might be running the whole Klan operation. All of this amounted to a very bad situation.

Travis' eyes flashed open to instant awareness. His years as a soldier had trained him well. He never had to grope his way out of sleep. He knew at once that someone had extinguished the lanterns, for he had left them burning. He felt, too, that someone was there in the room with him. In a flash, his hand snaked beneath his pillow to close about the gun he had put there before falling asleep.

"Don't be afraid, Travis. It's me."

He swore under his breath. "Damn it, woman, are you out of your mind? If your father catches you in here, there'll be hell to pay. . . ."

He sat up and realized she was already in the huge bed—and quite naked. She fumbled in the dark for his hands and placed them over her breasts. "Now then. Let's see if you still want to worry about Daddy," she challenged.

He allowed himself to fall back under her gentle push and she followed. Even before he knew what he was doing, his hands caressed the tender flesh she so freely offered, his fingertips gently bringing the ripe young nipples to taut eagerness.

His organ sprang erect, and she pressed it against her belly, stretching out on top of him. Their mouths met, then opened, and he touched her tongue with his own as he moved to clutch her buttocks and press her to him.

She began to undulate her hips against him and raised her mouth to gasp, "Oh, Travis, take me, take me, please. Don't tease me. . . ."

He kissed her again, harder, hands moving across her back to hold her tighter. As much as he wanted her, needed her, he knew from long experience that a woman needs time. He never rushed his partner, never wanted it thought that he sought only his own pleasure.

Suddenly Alaina's head jerked up and she sobbed, "Damn it, Travis . . ." Positioning herself atop him, she pleaded, "I want you now!"

Spreading her thighs, she lowered herself down onto his shaft, taking all of him with ease. She began to gyrate her hips, arms stiff, palms flat against his chest. He could barely make out her face in the dark room, but he saw that her head was thrown back, lips parted as she moaned in ecstasy. "So good. So damn, damn good!"

With one quick movement, he fastened his hands around her tiny waist and slung her over on her back without uncoupling. Then he plunged in and out of her again and again. He was glad she came quickly, for he could hold back no longer. It had been so long.

They clung together, bodies wet with perspiration, as they floated back to earth. Soon Travis moved to the side, chest heaving, breathing heavily. He felt her moving from the bed and asked where she was going. In a few moments, he knew, he would be ready once more. This time he would take it easy, savor each moment, and take them both to greater heights of ecstasy.

Chapter Sixteen

MARILEE Barbeau dared move only a few feet at a time. Hiding behind a tree trunk, she would press her body against the rough bark and listen, alert for any sound, before moving stealthily to the next tree, the next clump of bushes. It had been eleven o'clock when she left the mansion, and she needed to be at the meeting place by midnight. To ride in late was to draw attention to herself. That was dangerous.

There was only a quarter moon, and she moved along with difficulty.

As always, while darting through the black night, she thought of her father's reaction, should she ever be discovered. Probably disown her. Perhaps order a beating. But, she reminded herself with a vengeance, should this even cost her life, she believed in what she was doing. Donald had given his for what he believed in. She could do no less.

Thoughts of the husband she had adored caused tears to sting her eyes. Their love had been born when they were children, nurtured in adulthood, consummated in marriage, and terminated by the grave. At times, she felt that he was still with her, watching, protecting, urging her on.

So far, she calculated, she had saved fourteen Negroes from

beatings at the hand of the Klan, perhaps even saved their lives. Disguised as one of the Klan, she had listened to their plans and been able to warn the intended victims.

And while thoughts of the good she had done gave her a warm feeling, the warmth was quickly replaced by a heart-stabbing chill. To think that her father was part of it! Her eyes narrowed as she thought of him and of Stewart Mason. The two were behind it all. Father did the planning. Stewart carried out those plans.

Sadly, she thought of her mother, such a loving, caring person. Never had she mistreated any Negro slave. She had reacted furiously whenever she found out that Father's overseer was being cruel to a slave. Pneumonia had taken her to heaven two years before the war erupted, and Marilee grieved not only for her death but also that she was denied the satisfaction of knowing that the Negroes had been freed at last. Her mother would have known great pain had she been aware of Father's part in the Klan.

Just a short distance away, Marilee could make out the lines of the springhouse, hear the soft gurgling of water dancing among the rocks. Her timing had been good. She would be able to get to the mountaintop in time to arrive with the rest of the crowd. The white robe and hood had been hidden in a tree knothole. All was going well.

She reached the last sheltering tree before having to step into the clearing and cross to the path that would take her deep into the shrubs and weeds to where the horse waited. Pausing to listen one last time, she froze.

Voices. Whispered, frantic voices. A man and a woman. But who? And why were they here?

And then, as the sounds drifted to her on the night wind, she knew.

"Oh, Travis, darling, if only we didn't have to meet this way. I want the whole world to know that I love you . . . that you love me. . . ."

Alaina. Alaina and Travis.

Marilee's fists clenched, her nails cutting into her palms. Damn them! She had suspected something of the kind for the past several weeks, for she had often heard Alaina leave her room across the hall at night after everyone was asleep, returning sometime later. So Alaina had bedded the handsome marshal! That came as no real surprise, but their continuing to meet was a shock. Stewart Mason would kill the marshal if he knew. So would their father. Coltrane was a fool, she thought angrily. Just then he was hindering her efforts to do what he ought to be doing . . . protecting the Negroes from the vicious Klan.

"That's not possible," Travis' voice floated to Marilee, husky, thick with desire. "We both know it would be risky. Let's just take what we can."

"No!"

Marilee stifled a sigh of disgust. How often had she heard that petulant sound from her sister's pouting lips!

"I want you here and now, but I want more. I want to be yours for always and always. I don't care what Daddy thinks, or Stewart, or anyone else. I want to be yours, Travis. You can't deny you love me."

"I never said I loved you, Alaina."

"You don't have to. You've shown me in a thousand ways. No man can make love to a woman the way you do and not love her with all his heart."

Marilee heard his impatient sigh.

"Alaina, desire and passion have nothing to do with love, not the kind you're talking about. I told you I felt that for only one woman."

"I know, I know," she stopped him. "Your wife. But she's dead, Travis. And I'm alive. You can't love the dead. If only you would let go of all that."

He chuckled, amused. "You don't want me to let go of what I'm holding onto now, woman, and you know it."

"That's not what I'm talking about." Then she gasped and moaned. "Oh, Travis, it feels so good when you touch me like that. You . . . you're driving me crazy. Oh, don't stop, please."

Marilee pressed her face against the rough bark of the tree, revulsion sweeping over her. To stand there and listen to them make love was embarrassing. Disgust washed through her, and something else. What? Jealousy? Surely not. Yet, it had been so painfully long since she had lain in a man's arms, and there had only been one—Donald. She had tried to tell herself she would grow used to lying awake, thinking how wonderful it had been, her body on fire, wanting fulfillment.

As she stood listening to Travis and her sister she realized that it had never been quite like that with Donald. What they had shared was wonderful. Tender, soft, quiet. But he had never said to her what Travis was saying to Alaina, and she had never responded with such animal groans.

She felt her own body heating as she listened, and she was appalled.

What was he doing to her sister to make her respond that way? So wanton, so *vulgar*. And he seemed to like the way she was talking, answering her with endearments, telling her what a sensuous woman she was.

Then there was no sound at all save their cries and gasps.

Squeezing her eyes shut, clenching her fists even tighter, Marilee tried desperately to think of something else. Alaina's loud, piercing scream caused her eyes to flash open. Was he hurting her? Marilee took a step forward, forgetting herself. Her sister was hurting and she had to go to her.

But she stopped short when she heard Alaina cry out, "Travis, so good . . . do it again. Oh, Lord, never before has it been so good."

Marilee stepped back to her hiding place, ashamed. Alaina had only been crying out in ecstasy.

"Don't leave me," Alaina was saying, her voice weak. "I want you to hold me all night long."

"You know that isn't possible. I have to get back to town. I can't be away all night."

"But you'd like to, wouldn't you?" she coaxed him for reassurance. "You would love to take me again and again, wouldn't you?"

There was silence. Marilee took a long, careful breath. Good grief, what kind of man was he that he could make a woman scream out as though she were dying, then throw pride to the wind and beg for more? What secret did this man possess?

No matter, she thought angrily. He was a savage. If he were doing his job, she would not be on her way to a secret meeting of the Klan, perhaps endangering her life. He would wipe out the Klan. That was his job, wasn't it?

Then why didn't she tell him? she asked herself.

She knew the answer. Her father. She loved him despite everything. She did not want him sent to prison. She could not turn against him. If Stewart and the others were exposed, then they would surely point the finger at her father.

No, she could not tell, not now. She could do only what she was doing, and warn victims whenever possible.

She heard Travis urging Alaina to dress, saying that he would ride her as close to the house as he dared. She had to get to bed without anyone knowing she had been out.

"No danger of that." Alaina laughed. "The only person in my wing of the mansion is Marilee, and she goes to bed with the chickens and sleeps soundly till dawn. I never hear her. If I'd been that long without a man, I'd be pacing the floor."

"You probably would," Travis chuckled. "You enjoy it as much as a man, perhaps more."

"Is there something wrong with that? I have needs, needs only a man like you can answer. I won't let you go, Travis. I swear I will make you love me and want me for all time."

"That might not be as hard as you think."

"You tease me. I know you resent me because I didn't come to you a virgin, but I never pretended to be. You know I won't lie to you, and you know I'm telling the truth when I say that you're the only man who's ever satisfied me."

He laughed again. "I must have done something right. I think you ripped my back to pieces. I'm bleeding from those long claws of yours."

"You loved it and you know it."

Damn it, Alaina, let him go! Marilee fumed. *I'll have to ride like the wind to get there on time.*

Alaina rushed on. "This was a wonderful place to meet. It's better than the stable. It's so risky there."

Their voices were coming closer, and Marilee pressed herself harder against the tree.

"Tomorrow tonight?" Alaina begged.

Travis sighed. "I can't promise. I'll have to get a message to you."

"Good old Israel," Alaina laughed. "That old nigra will do anything for money, even slip a note to the fiancée of a man he's scared to death of."

Travis was suddenly very angry. "If Stewart Mason lays another whip to his back, I'll kill him."

"Oh, don't worry about Stewart. He thinks Israel is just running errands for me, keeping me from having to go to town. He likes that. He's so jealous he doesn't want me in town, around lusty men like you."

There was a long silence. They were kissing again.

Suddenly Travis cried, "Damn it, woman, you're in my blood. I swore I'd never let a woman get a noose around my neck again, but you've got such a fire in you! I can't get enough of you."

"Maybe one day you will truly love me for something besides my body, Travis Coltrane," Alaina whispered tremulously. "Maybe you'll want to make me your wife so you can have me all the time and in every way. I want you inside me every night and day of my life. I want your seed within me to make a child grow— *our* child—and I will welcome each pain as I deliver him into your arms."

Marilee felt sick. What was it about the man that provoked a woman so? She sounded like a common trollop. Never could Marilee say such things, not to any man, and to hear the words coming from her sister's lips made her shudder.

Finally their voices drifted away, and she moved cautiously from behind the tree, making her way as fast as she dared to the springhouse, then beyond to where the horse was tied. Reaching inside the hollow tree, she found the white clothing.

She pulled the white robe over her head and positioned the hood, peering out through the slits.

As always, when she was dressed in the white flowing robe of the Ku Klux Klan, Marilee felt like a traitor. She hated masquerading in the costume of cowards.

Swinging up on the horse, she guided him slowly through the brush and onto a path that would lead them up the mountain.

As she rode, the cool night air upon her face, white robe flapping, Marilee reflected upon the discovery that had led her to these secret missions. It had been accidental.

She had been bored one afternoon, and, as always, when her mind was unoccupied, thoughts of Donald haunted her. To keep from brooding, she had wandered into the little room that had been her mother's sewing nook, tucked comfortably beside her father's study. She lovingly touched the old machine that had made her dresses and Alaina's. Their mother had loved making clothes for her girls.

She wandered over to the old spinning wheel, the quilting racks, and she could almost hear her mother speaking to her once again, for they had spent long hours in the room, talking and laughing. Marilee stood before the huge wall mirror, blinking back tears as she remembered her mother down on her knees pinning in a hem.

Suddenly her eyes caught something she had never seen before. There were tiny little hinges on one side of the mirror which had been covered by ribbons. Yes, she was sure of that. Always, her mother had draped the ribbons she used in sewing down that side of the mirror. That was why Marilee had never noticed the hinges before that moment.

Curious, Marilee ran her fingers along the edge of the mirror opposite the hinges, then gasped as she touched a little hidden catch. When pressed, it caused the mirrored door to swing open.

She had laughed out loud. This was an entrance inside the wall that ran to her father's study. Suddenly so many memories came flooding back, times when her father had declared he had much work to do in his study and should Marilee or Alaina disturb him, they could expect a sound thrashing. At the same time, Mother would disappear into her sewing room, saying that she, too, had much to do and did not want to be disturbed. These were probably times when the two wanted to be together in private, without the servants whispering over their making love at such odd hours.

Smiling to herself, Marilee had groped along inside the wall in the darkness, imagining how excited her mother must have felt to have a secret rendezvous with her own husband. It was so romantic, so sweet, and she felt closer to her mother for sharing her secret.

Running her fingers along the wall, she wondered where the entrance to Father's study was located. Then, just as she felt a doorknob, she heard his angry voice.

"You shouldn't have hanged the sonofabitch with his family watching, Mason! That was stupid. Beatings are one thing, but to kill a man with his wife and children watching, well, the good people of Kentucky will not tolerate things like that no matter how much they hate nigras."

Marilee blinked. Killing? Beating? It was quite wrong to eavesdrop, but she stood there, unable to move.

"Look, boss, I can't always control that bunch."

Stewart Mason's voice sounded apologetic but, at the same time, belligerent.

"You wanted me to do a job and I did. We went to that

nigger's house, Billy Kiser, to teach him a lesson, 'cause he'd been shooting his mouth off about how the niggers had to join up and fight back, that the law was on their side. He came out of his house with a gun and started blasting away. He shot two of us before we were able to wing him.

"Peter Haskins got shot in the arm, and Wendell Cathcart got hit in the leg," he went on anxiously. "You think after that happened I could keep them from hanging that nigger? They wouldn't have cared if God had tried to stop them. They strung him up and hung him. It was all I could do to keep them from hanging his wife and kids, too. The only way I stopped them was to keep yelling that we had to get Haskins and Cathcart to a doctor. They did try to burn the house down, threw all our torches up on the roof of that rotten old shack, but the niggers put it out as soon as we left."

His voice rose. "There sure wasn't nothing they could do for Billy Kiser, though. His neck popped like a walnut when we kicked that horse out from under him. He was dead quick."

She had not remembered making her way through the wall that night and back into the sewing room. It had been too horrible a shock, the realization that her father was involved in the Ku Klux Klan . . . no, he was *behind* the Klan, giving orders to Stewart Mason.

For long hours she sat in her mother's sewing room, unable to move, her mind whirling. No matter what, she could not turn her father over to the law. But oh, Lord! the guilt she felt every time a Negro was killed.

In every other way, he was wonderful. Her mother had adored him and he had been a kind, loving father. True, he favored Alaina, who knew how to wrap him around her little finger, but Marilee had never really felt less loved.

No, she could not turn him in. There had to be another way. She had decided to disguise herself as a Klan member, infiltrate their meetings, and do what was possible. After all, even if she did turn her father in, that wouldn't stop Klan activities.

The Negroes knew she was involved. Without their help, her efforts could never have been so successful. They made sure her horse was waiting where she needed it, and when she returned from a night ride, someone was there to meet her. If she had news of an attack, then the person who met her went out to warn the intended victim.

She prayed that Donald would understand that she couldn't turn her father in.

Suddenly, ahead, a ghostlike figure floated from the forest to stand in the middle of the road. Flames from its torch cast a red glow over the road. Marilee cursed. A sentry was always posted, and she should have remembered and been prepared. Damn it, a few more mistakes and they would become suspicious.

"Halt, brother," the figure in white commanded. "Give the sign."

She jerked the reins. Then she crossed her forearms across her bosom, clenched her fists, gently pounding herself three times.

"Advance!" The sentry stepped aside.

Riding onward, she recalled the terrifying night when she had hidden in the bushes and watched as the sentry commanded each Klansman to give the signal. It was only one of many nights that she had hidden and watched, wanting to be sure of every procedure before going to a meeting. So far, she had been successful. They never removed their hoods and no one ever questioned her.

The red and yellow glow of torches beneath the shroud of trees and against the black drape of sky made an eerie scene. Marilee dismounted, tying her horse with the others, and made her way to where the crowd of white-robed figures was gathered.

It was, she knew, an excellent meeting place. One would have to know the exact location. This was not a site likely to be stumbled upon. *She* had not found it easily. In fact, it had taken three different attempts, after hiding in the wall outside her father's study and listening to Stewart tell of meetings, before she actually found it.

Dear sweet Lord, where was this all going to end? Would these nightmare meetings, the cruelties, ever end? Would she one day be able to live a quiet life?

She guessed attendance at around fifty people. The most ever had been close to eighty. But if a public roll of those who supported the Klan were taken, perhaps two out of three whites would say they did.

Even though he wore a robe and hood, Marilee had no doubt that the tall figure standing on the large rock was Stewart

Mason. He faced the crowd and began to speak.

"Let the light of justice be ignited!" he commanded.

Someone stepped forward with a torch. In an instant, a large cross about ten feet tall was engulfed in flames. It lit up the sky with a flash. Marilee bit down on her lip, determined not to shudder. She had heard the Negroes talk about the horror of awaking in the middle of the night to the sound of thundering hoofbeats, staring out their windows to see a burning cross in front of their homes. She could imagine their terror.

The crowd cheered when the cross was ignited, and Stewart waved his arms until they fell silent. "Tonight we're going to talk about a nigger named Tom Stanley," he cried. "He tried to sign up to vote the other day."

"No!" The crowd hollered in unison, some of them striking at the air above them with their fists. "No! No! No!"

"Damn right, no!" Stewart yelled back, pacing the flat-topped rock that set him slightly above them. "We're not going to have any niggers voting in this county. Give them the vote, and the next thing you know they'll be holding office! We've got to keep them in their place, and if they don't want that, we've got another place for them—in the goddamn ground!"

His voice rose to a thunderous yell and was matched by the crowd. He allowed them to cheer for several moments, then motioned again for silence.

"So what are we going to do to Tom Stanley?" cried Stewart, and the crowd called, "Hang the nigger! Kill him! Burn him out!"

Would there be time to warn Tom Stanley? She would have to return to the springhouse, tell whoever was waiting for her, and he would have to warn Tom.

She kept her head straight ahead, darting her glance around. Would anyone notice if she left? They were all fired up, waving their arms and yelling. Was there a chance she could slip away? It was chancey, but did she have a choice?

"Hear me out!" Stewart was yelling. "Listen to me!"

She took a few steps to her left, calculating that she could be in the woods and out of sight in the time it took for them to set up one more loud cheer.

"We need to discuss those new marshals," Stewart was saying.

Marilee froze.

"So far, all they're doing is asking questions and nosing

around. I don't think there's cause for worry. They seem about as stupid as the other four we ran out of town."

The ghostly figures swayed with laughter. A figure on her left turned to Marilee, his head bobbing gleefully, and she returned the gesture as though sharing his mirth.

Stewart continued, "I want all of you to keep your eyes open. If they start getting in our way, we'll just take them out and give them a beating. That should send them on their way. But we don't want to rush anything. The law will only send in more to replace them, like they've done in the past. I keep hoping we'll get lucky and get a couple in here that will just be content to sit back on their butts and do nothing except draw their pay."

The white figures laughed again.

Someone cried, "Yeah, and maybe we'll be extra lucky and get some in here that'll want to join up!"

This brought a resounding wave of laughter, and Marilee swiftly backed closer to the woods.

"Who are these new marshals?" someone shouted from the far side of the throng. "I ain't never seen 'em and don't even know what they look like."

That, Marilee realized gratefully, would occupy the crowd long enough for her to be on her way. With a pounding heart she moved quickly into the woods and groped her way toward the horses.

She had taken few steps toward the horses when a flowing white movement caught her eye among the stock. She crouched down in the brush, peering out anxiously. There was never a sentry among the horses. Why was anyone there? Was she under suspicion? Dread became a tight knot in her throat as she watched, waiting.

There was no further sign of anyone. Finally, she dared move from cover once more. But she did not stand up. Instead, crouching on hands and knees, wobbling along in ducklike movements, she scuttled toward her mare. *Don't get excited and whinny and bring them running,* she prayed to the horses. *Just let me get out of here.*

She found her horse, identifying the mare by the feel of the stirrups, which she had nicked in special places so as to be able to find her in darkness. Standing, she slipped an arm around her neck, whispering softly, "Easy, girl. Easy. Don't get excited."

She led the horse through the others, moving slowly, cautiously, not wanting to cause any stamping of feet.

Once deeply into the woods, she groped her way along the path. A quarter mile, she surmised, was how far she had gone on foot before daring to move to the road and mount and be on her way. A quarter mile more of walking the horse slowly, and she could spring to a gallop. Should the Klansmen break up and be on their way before she was far enough along on her own, she would merely dash into the woods on either side of the road and hide until they went by. So far, she had been lucky. Since they were prone to emotional discussions of their crusade against the Negroes, it was usually quite late before they dispersed.

Finally, she was able to urge the horse to ride as fast as she would go, giving thanks for being an expert rider. No sidesaddle feminine style for her, thank goodness. Let Alaina be the graceful flower. Marilee was grateful that Donald had taught her to ride and shoot. His theory had been that one day she might need to take care of herself. Well, she reflected pensively as she held on tightly for the fleeting ride, he had been right.

Reaching the springhouse, she swung down from the horse and called out in a hoarse whisper, "Who's there? Is anyone there? I have news!"

A voice whispered back, "I's here, Miz Marilee. It's me—Caleb."

"Caleb!" She gasped with relief, for he was a good rider. Turning in the direction of his voice, she cried, "Do you know Tom Stanley? Do you know where he lives? Is it far?"

"Yes'm," he was immediately frightened. "Is they after him, Miz Marilee? I been afraid they would be. He's been doin' a lot of talkin'."

"Does he live far from here?" she repeated urgently.

"A ways. I can get there, though. I got a horse waitin'. You want me to tell him to hide out for the night?"

"No! Tell him to leave the county. Get as far away as he can. Take his family with him right away. They aren't out just to beat him. They mean to kill him."

"Oh, Lawdy!" She could hear the man's terror. "I gotta go right now. If'n they get there a'fore I do . . ." his voice trailed off as he crashed through the brush.

In seconds, Marilee heard the sound of Caleb charging his horse away.

Wearily, she sank to the ground. He probably would arrive in time, and, for the time being, her efforts were not in vain. For the time being . . .

Suddenly she sat bolt upright. It was here, she realized with a warm flush. Right about here was where Travis had taken Alaina. They had lain here, and now she was here alone, aching.

Rolling on her stomach, she burrowed her face in her hands. Damn Travis Coltrane. Damn him for being the man he was. Until tonight, until she had heard the glorious raging fire between man and woman, the hunger had not rumbled so intensely within her.

It was terrible. Damn him! Why did desire, sleeping until now, have to awaken? In that moment, she knew that as much as she despised Travis she also envied her sister. Marilee was not the beauty her sister was. Marilee lacked not only the looks but also the feminine coquetry that seemed to drive men wild. Plain, ordinary, quiet, settled, Marilee would probably always have to be content with no more than she had already known in a man's arms.

Now, after hearing Travis cause her sister to scream, she knew what she had been missing, what she would probably always be missing.

And it hurt.

Chapter Seventeen

I'm not dull and drab! Marilee stared at her reflection in the mirror above the dresser, saw the glimmer of unshed tears in her coffee-colored eyes. Donald didn't find me drab. He said I was beautiful, beautiful and wonderful.

She turned slightly at the sound of the bedroom door opening. It was Alaina.

"Wear that olive green," Alaina said, pointing to the open wardrobe. She sat down on the side of the large canopied bed. "It's the brightest dress in your wardrobe. Really, Marilee, why do you keep wearing widow's weeds? Donald has been dead six years now. You can't stay in mourning forever."

Marilee looked at the strawberry pink chiffon gown Alaina was wearing, the skirt billowing with rows and rows of tiny ruffles, caught here and there with net rosettes of a darker pink shade. Her light brown hair was piled in ringlets, winsome curls provocatively dancing about her lovely pale face. How, Marilee wondered, could we be sisters when we look so different?

She pulled the olive green dress from the closet. The neck was high, edged with fine lace. The sleeves were long and tapered. The skirt was full, but not terribly so.

"You could be pretty if you tried," Alaina offered quietly.

Marilee turned to stare at her, stunned.

"You could," she rushed on. "You don't try, Marilee. I mean, you wear your hair pulled back in that awful bun, and it's not fashionable *or* flattering. You never use rouge or paint your lips, and the clothes you wear—" She wrinkled her nose. "It's almost as though you try to be unattractive."

Marilee sighed. "I don't work at it, Alaina. It just turns out that way."

"You didn't dress that way when Donald was courting you. I remember. You wore bright colors, and you washed your hair every day and brushed it till it gleamed. Even after you married him, you still tried to be pretty. You *were* pretty. You could be again, if you tried."

"Maybe I don't have any reason to try."

"If you don't start taking care of yourself, no man will ever give you a reason, Marilee." Alaina was becoming exasperated.

Marilee raised an eyebrow. "I can live without a man, Alaina, believe it or not."

"You're going to have to, the way you're going," came the snapping reply. "Look, I'm only trying to help. There are going to be lots of eligible men at Daddy's party tonight. Why don't you let me fix your hair and do your face. You can borrow one of my dresses."

"No!" Marilee shouted, then lowered her voice. "I'm sorry. I don't mean to be sharp with you. It's just that I don't need your help. I don't need anyone's help."

Alaina shrugged. "Suit yourself." She got up and walked to the double glass veranda doors, swinging them open to look out and allow the cool evening air to rush in. Without turning around, she murmured, "You know, Sam Bucher is eligible."

"Sam Bucher?" Marilee echoed. "You mean, Marshal Bucher? Why, he's almost old enough to be my father! Look, Alaina, you just take care of your own affairs. From what I hear—" She trailed off, ashamed. Alaina was, in her reckless way, trying to help.

Alaina whirled on her, cheeks coloring. "What do you hear? That I'm having a mad, wild love affair with Travis Coltrane?" Her eyes flashed with rebellious anger. "Well, you heard almost correctly. I say 'almost,' because I'm sure you heard that we have been meeting secretly. We have, but only because of Stewart. Neither of us wanted a confrontation. Now our love has reached a point where we no longer want to hide our feelings. We want the whole world to know."

Marilee turned back to continue dressing. She didn't want to think about Travis Coltrane. Too, she had things on her mind. Only a few hours earlier, she had hidden in the secret passageway and listened to Stewart and her father talk about there being a Negro sympathizer within Klan ranks.

"Travis is coming to the party tonight, and it's going to be our way of letting everyone know he is courting me."

Alaina's declaration brought Marilee out of her reverie. "Are you serious? Marshal Coltrane is going to court you, Alaina? But what about Stewart? Do you think Father would actually allow—"

"Father won't have any choice," Alaina cut her off. "When he sees how much we love each other, he won't want to stand in our way. As for Stewart"—she made a face—"if he knows what's good for him, he'll stay out of Travis' way. Travis is a hundred times the man Stewart could ever be, and I pity anyone who crosses him."

Marilee sank down upon the dressing table bench and looked her sister over, considering. She took a deep breath. "Do you truly love Marshal Coltrane, Alaina? Enough to marry him? He's older than you, and I hear he's a widower, with a child. Are you prepared to raise another woman's child as your own?"

Alaina shrugged. "Travis owns a silver mine in Nevada. He's rich. So am I. We'll be able to well afford a governess to take care of his son, just as we'll have someone to look after any children I might have. You know I'm not going to spend my life with babies tugging at my skirts. Why, Travis and I will be the toast of all Nevada. We'll build our own empire there. It's going to be heaven!" She stood and wrapped her arms about herself and whirled around and around the room, dancing.

Marilee shook her head. The match was not a good one. Alaina was far too immature and self-centered to be a mother, or to be obligated to just one man.

As for Travis, she thought that he would have a hard time tying himself to just one woman. Did he share Alaina's opinion of the seriousness of their relationship, or was she, as usual, seeing things the way she wanted to see them?

She watched as Alaina continued swirling around the room, eyes closed, an ecstatic expression on her lovely face. What could she say to her sister that she would understand? Headstrong, spoiled, she had never listened to anyone.

A sudden knock stopped Alaina in midtwirl.

"Marilee?" Jordan Barbeau called out jovially. "Is Alaina in there with you? I'd like to see both my lovely daughters for a moment before the guests start arriving."

Marilee tied her dressing robe around her and called to him to enter.

"Ahh, you are here, my darling." He kissed Alaina's cheek, then crossed the room to greet Marilee the same way. "And what are you two in here gossiping about? My, you look so serious, Marilee."

"Girl talk, Father," she responded, turning away so he could not see the worry in her face.

He smiled. "I see. Well, I won't interfere. I just came to tell you, Alaina," he turned to her, "that a very special young man will be here tonight. He was quite distressed earlier this afternoon when he found out there was a party going on and you had not invited him."

Alaina spoke up bitterly, "If you're talking about Stewart, Daddy, I wish you hadn't invited him. I have already invited someone as my guest. Stewart being here will only make things awkward." Seeing the quick flash of anger in his eyes, she lifted a hand and inspected her manicure.

"You . . . you invited someone," Jordan sputtered. "I had heard that you were seeing that rowdy marshal, but I told myself that wasn't possible, that the gossips were merely wagging over your disgusting manners at your birthday party. I told myself a daughter of mine would never lower herself to be in the company of a . . . a commoner."

"Commoner?" Alaina echoed, stunned. "Daddy, the man owns a silver mine! He's rich! He was also highly decorated during the war, publicly praised by General Sherman himself. He's a gentleman."

"A gentleman! He's a damn Yankee! And Sherman was a bloody marauder! Sherman, indeed!"

Waving her arms, Marilee pleaded, "Daddy! Alaina! Please. This is not the time to discuss the situation. The guests will be arriving at any moment. The marshal has obviously already been invited and will be here soon. Let's all make the best of this and not give the gossips any more reason to talk about our family."

Jordan glared at Alaina, who met his gaze defiantly. "You keep that man away from me tonight," he said between clenching teeth. "He's a troublemaker. It's men like him who would have the nigras running roughshod over the whites. You make sure he keeps his distance from me. And after tonight, I had better not hear of you seeing him again. Is that clear?"

Alaina stared straight at him, tight-lipped.

"Did you hear me?" he yelled, grabbing her shoulders. "Watch yourself around him tonight. Do not let me see any ridiculous behavior, or I'll say to hell with manners and gossip and throw him out the goddamn door myself. And so help me, if I hear of you seeing him again, I don't care how old you are, I'll give you the worst thrashing of your life."

Alaina broke into sobs as she backed toward the door. "I hate you for this," she cried. "I love Travis and he loves me, and you aren't going to come between us. Not now! Not ever! I'll run away first!"

She ran through the doorway, slamming the door behind her, the sound of her crying echoing in the hall.

"God, God, why?" Jordan ran nervous fingers through his tight gray curls. "Why would Alaina be attracted to such a . . . a barbarian? Whatever does she see in him?"

He shook his head from side to side, then looked at Marilee thoughtfully. "Lord, why couldn't I have been blessed with *two* sensible daughters? The only time you disappointed me was when you married a Union sympathizer and even then it was wartime, and emotions were running high. You had a right to make one foolish mistake."

Marilee snapped, "Father, stop it! I won't listen to you insinuate that my marrying Donald was a mistake. He had a right to his views and he believed in them so strongly that he gave his life for them. I knew what I was doing then, just as I know now. Don't call it a mistake."

"Of course, I'm sorry. Forgive me, dear. Donald was a fine young man. I always liked him. You know that. But it did upset me when he turned to the Union. All that is past now, and you are a lovely, sensible young woman who will one day fall in love and be a wonderful wife for some fortunate man. But Alaina . . ." he sighed and shook his head once more. "I fear her beauty and lack of judgment are going to cause all of us grief. I must stop this relationship between her and Coltrane before it gets out of hand."

Marilee could have told him it already was, but it was not her place to say so. If Travis Coltrane was smitten, that was *his* business. Let them work things out. She had all she could take care of trying to keep up with the Klan—which was, she thought resentfully, what Coltrane should have been doing.

"Will you see if you can get her calmed down?" Jordan said as he moved toward the door. "I must go on downstairs and greet the first guests. Tell her we'll discuss this tomorrow."

He opened the door, started out, then paused and said, "Remind her that I do not want her making a spectacle of herself. He will not stay here overnight. In fact, he'd best leave early."

Marilee sighed once more and turned to begin dressing. She held up the drab olive green dress, then hesitated. *Widow's weeds*, indeed, she thought. Flinging it aside, she reached to the far recesses of the cedar wardrobe and pulled out a bright yellow satin, forgotten for years. She had not worn it since the night her father had announced her engagement to Donald.

It was still beautiful, and since she was the same size she had been then, it would fit quite well. Feeling particularly daring, she ran to the braided bell cord and gave it a tug. With some help, she would feel pretty.

A little later, Marilee tugged at the bodice. Her breasts were fuller, and they were pushed high by the stays. Her rosy pink nipples showed just a little. "I can't wear this!" she cried.

"Oh, yes, you can," Rosa, her maid, spoke up. "It ain't no worse than what other women is wearing."

"But I'm a widow!"

"Well, you gonna stay one if you keep dressin' like you just come from the cemetery. Ain't no need in you lookin' like you do all the time. Now, I'll loosen that stitchin' under the arms just enough that you can tuck your nipples down good, and then it'll be just fine."

Marilee watched apprehensively as Rosa went to work, and, shortly, she looked in the mirror and agreed that, even though her bosom was displayed, there was nothing brazen about her appearance.

"With your hair all shiny brown, it looks just fine with that yellow," Rosa said, standing back with a satisfied smile on her dark face. "Now we gonna fix your cheeks, paint yo' lips, and you gonna be the prettiest lady at the party."

"I can't believe it's me!" Marilee cried a little while later.

"Well, it is you," Rosa beamed. "And you best be on yo' way, or you gonna be the last one to arrive. Maybe that's what you should do—make an entrance."

Marilee cut her off with a wave. "No. I've got to go to Alaina and see that she's all right."

"Yes'm. All the help knows about the fightin'. We could hear him shoutin', and we done been knowin' fo' some time when he found out about her and the marshal, he was gonna raise cain."

"That he did," Marilee said fearfully. "If only Marshal Coltrane would do his job and stop chasing after Alaina!"

"Oh, I think it's the other way around, missy."

Marilee looked at her, puzzled.

"The marshal, he's a'doin' his job," Rosa told her bluntly. "I can't tell you what I knows, any more than you tells my people evahthin' you knows. But I can tell you that he's doin' somethin'. As for him chasin' Miz Alaina, if you'd just look, you'd see *she's* the one a'doin' the chasin'. I hear all the gossip, and I knows how she makes old Bart take her into town in the middle of the night to get up with him, and old Bart, he say the marshal got mad a couple of times and sent her back home. Miz Alaina had one of her fits."

"Rosa!" Marilee stared at her, aghast. "That will just be enough of that. I won't have you repeating gossip about my sister."

"But it's so," Rosa whined defensively.

"I don't care. I won't have the servants talking about her. Now, please, go back to doing whatever you were doing when I called you."

Marilee hurried down the hall, truly worried now. Rosa would not lie. If what she had said was the truth, and if Alaina were chasing after the marshal, then the situation could become embarrassing. She took a deep breath and knocked on Alaina's door.

There was no answer.

"Alaina," she called, "I know you're in there. I want to talk to you."

"Go away!" The sobbing voice drifted through the closed door.

Marilee turned the knob and walked in to see her lying

across the bed in her chemise, the strawberry chiffon gown lying to one side. "Well, are you going to stay up here and pout and leave the marshal to Father's mercy?"

Alaina pounded the bed with her fists as she sobbed, "It isn't fair for him to tell me I can't see him. He can't break us up. I won't let him. I'll run away."

Marilee sat down, reaching to brush her sister's hair back from her forehead. Alaina was spoiled and willful and could be quite vexing, but Marilee still loved her fiercely. Damn that Travis Coltrane! Alaina was bewitched, that's what was wrong.

"Get yourself together," Marilee coaxed her. "You invited him here as your guest, and you know how Father feels, so it's up to you to keep him company. Just tell him the situation, and he'll probably leave early. If he doesn't, suggest that he does. You and Father can talk about it tomorrow."

She sighed and got to her feet, reaching for her dress. "I suppose you're right." Her eyes widened as she looked at Marilee, really seeing her for the first time. "What have you done to yourself?" She gasped. "I don't believe it! Your hair! Your face! That dress! Why, I haven't seen you look like this in years."

Marilee smiled brightly. "Maybe I'm tired of 'widow's weeds,' little sister. You were right, it's time I started thinking about fixing myself up."

"Well, isn't that nice." She stopped at the sound of knocking.

Rosa hurried in, looking nervous. "Missy," she cried, "the marshal, he's downstairs. He say he can't stay long. You better get on down there, 'cause yo' daddy looks like a watermelon what's laid out in the sun too long. He stomped off with Mastah Mason, and they went in the study, and I just knows Mastah Mason is raisin' cain about the marshal bein' here."

Alaina silenced her with a wave of her hand, turning quickly to Marilee. "You've got to go down there and keep him company till I can get dressed. Rosa will help me. I won't be long."

Hurrying downstairs, Marilee felt a rush of panic. If Father and Stewart were locked in the study, she needed to know what they were talking about. True, Stewart might just be furious over Marshal Coltrane's presence, but they might be discussing Klan business. But if she went to the secret passageway, she would not be able to keep the marshal company as she had promised Alaina.

She reached the bottom of the stairs and spotted Travis standing to one side of the foyer, annoyance clouding his gray eyes. He looked at her through half-closed lids, the sudden play of a smile on his lips, and she cursed herself for wondering what it would feel like to be kissed by him.

Walking toward him as gracefully as possible, she knew she really wanted to rush over, make her excuses, and hurry away to the secret passage.

"Marshal Coltrane, good evening," she greeted him pleasantly. Then, without waiting for him to speak, she said, "Alaina asked me to tell you that she has been detained. She'll be along shortly. Please have a drink and make yourself at home."

He caught her hand, raised it to his lips, but did not release her. She stared at him, surprised. "What's your hurry, pretty lady?" he whispered, eyes moving over her with pleasure. "It *is* you, isn't it? My, my, the lady has come out of mourning at last."

His tone was slightly mocking, and she was angry at once. Jerking her hand away she said quietly, "It is none of your concern, Marshal. Now, if you'll excuse me, I have things to tend to."

"I think first on your list of priorities should be keeping your sister's guest company until she arrives. Where are your manners, Marilee?"

"I told you I have things to do!" Her eyes were blazing at his mockery. "Now let me go."

He laughed softly. "Why are you afraid of me?"

"A—afraid of you?" she stammered, gasping. "Whatever makes you think so? How absurd."

"You're trembling."

"I . . . am not," she lied, forcing herself to meet his gaze.

"You have no need to be afraid of me. I won't bite. At least not here. There's a time and a place for everything."

"Sir!" she cried indignantly. Seeing that others were turning to stare, she lowered her voice to say bitingly, "Marshal, you are my sister's guest. She thinks very highly of you. I hardly think she would appreciate your forcing such a conversation on me. If you don't let me go, I'm going to scream, and that will bring my father. And while I hate to be the one to tell you this, he was quite upset when he heard Alaina had invited you here tonight. So let's not make the situation any more unpleasant than it already is."

She faced him, brown eyes icy with contempt for his blatant arrogance.

Unruffled, he continued to smile in that same infuriating way.

"I find your behavior distasteful, Marshal. Now, if you will excuse me, I will leave you to wait for my sister."

He stared at her in such a puzzling way that she asked bluntly, "Would you mind telling me just why you are looking at me that way, Marshal?"

He folded his arms across his chest, tilting his head to one side. "I find you an extraordinary woman, Marilee."

"What is that supposed to mean?" she asked, exasperated.

"For now, that will have to do. If you'll excuse me, I think I'll find myself a drink while I wait for your sister."

She shook her head, puzzled. But there was no time to dawdle. Pausing to exchange pleasantries with a few guests, she hurried as discreetly as possible, breathing a sigh of relief when, at last, she dashed into the sewing room and locked the door. Once inside the passageway, she moved slowly, noiselessly, groping in the darkness.

At last she heard voices.

"Damn it, Jordan, I don't like him hanging around Alaina."

Her father sounded annoyed. "I don't like it a bit better than you do, but that's not the issue right now. I'll take care of that. I told you, I've already put my foot down to Alaina. Just be glad he's been so busy running after her that he's forgotten why he was sent here. Now, look, are you sure you can get the Klan together on such short notice?"

Marilee's heart quickened. They were going to meet tonight. Something was up . . . something important.

"Yeah," came Stewart's confident reply. "All I got to do is ride up on Turkey Ridge and blow my whistle. Someone will pick it up and it'll be passed along till everyone rallies. It'll take maybe a half hour to get everybody together."

"You'd better get started."

She heard them leaving the study and turned to make her way back through the passageway. She was trembling. No matter that there was a party going on. She had to go to that rally.

When she entered the foyer again it was necessary to stop and greet newly arrived guests. All the while, she was trying to figure out how to take her leave without arousing suspicion.

She caught sight of Willis, one of the Negro house servants. She trusted him absolutely. Signaling to him, she drew him aside, pretending to sample the tray of tiny sandwiches he was passing. Hardly moving her lips, she told him the news and said, "See that a horse is waiting for me at the springhouse in fifteen minutes. I'll pretend I have a headache and retire for the evening."

He nodded. She wanted to tell him not to look so frightened, but there was no time for that. "See to it," she hissed, then turned away.

Halfway up the stairs, she met Alaina making her descent. "Please give my apologies," Marilee said hurriedly, pressing a hand to her forehead. "I have a terrible headache. I'm going to bed."

Alaina was concerned. "Is there anything I can do?"

"No, no. I just want to be alone. It will pass."

She started on by, but Alaina caught her arm. "Where is Travis?"

"Over there." Marilee stopped, surprised. Travis was gone.

"Perhaps he went to get another drink," she offered, just as Willis spotted them and began to move through the crowd.

"Miss Alaina," he said, reaching them, "the marshal asked me to give you his regrets. He say he have unexpected business to tend to, and Miss Marilee can explain."

"Me?" Marilee asked, surprised. "I know nothing about him having to leave."

"Oh, Marilee!" Alaina's eyes glistened with tears. "What did you say to him? You didn't tell him what Daddy said, did you?"

Silently, she cursed Travis Coltrane for putting her in this position. Taking a deep breath, she said, "I did tell him Father was upset, but he certainly didn't seem ruffled by that. He said nothing about leaving, only that he was going to have a drink and wait for you."

"Oh, this is terrible!" Alaina shook her head from side to side. "What am I going to do?"

Marilee patted her shoulder sympathetically. "You'll go on and have a delightful time. Don't worry about him."

"Oh, but I do worry. You don't understand, Marilee. I . . . I think I love him."

Marilee rolled her eyes. "You've thought you were in love before."

"This is different!" She stamped her foot, clenching her fists at her sides.

"What is going on here?" Jordan Barbeau appeared suddenly at the foot of the stairs, looking from one to the other. "Why are you two just standing there, and Alaina, why are you crying?"

When she did not reply, Marilee said, "The marshal left. She thinks it has something to do with what we discussed earlier."

"Well, this is absurd," he snapped. "Alaina, you get yourself together. I won't have a daughter of mine making a fool of herself over some scalawag."

"He is not a scalawag!" Alaina cried. "He's wonderful. And you aren't going to come between us."

"He can't be so wonderful if he just walked out on you," Jordan reminded her.

Marilee saw the effect. Her sister's chin lifted just a bit, enough to display the resentment he had provoked. Eyes glittering slightly, she said, "Where is Stewart? I won't be without an escort this evening. He will dance with me."

Marilee noted the anxiety in his voice as he replied, "I'm afraid he had to leave, too. Come along with me. As long as I'm around, you needn't worry about an escort." He gave her a stiff little smile.

Alaina continued down the stairs and Marilee lifted her skirts to rush on up to her room. Once there, she pulled the bell cord and waited, pacing nervously. At last Rosa arrived, eyes wide. "What's wrong?"

Marilee explained quickly. "I have to be there, Rosa. But how am I going to slip out of the house wearing this stupid gown? How am I going to slip out with all these people here, anyway? Damn!" she cried, exasperated.

"I's thinkin'. I's thinkin'." Rosa began to pace, wringing her hands. Suddenly she looked to the window and cried, "You can climb out!"

Marilee looked at her as though she had lost her mind. "Rosa, there is nothing for me to climb down on. No trellis. No tree. Nothing. Just a drop from the balcony to the ground that will break my neck."

Rosa ignored her protests, went to the closet, and drew out a plain muslin dress and tossed it at her. "Put this on. They'll have some trousers waitin' for you when you get to the springhouse. If you try to climb out with them frills on, you gonna get 'em snagged on somethin'. I'll make you a rope while you change."

"You are going to—what?" Marilee stared incredulously as Rosa yanked the satin coverlet from the canopied bed, then began jerking off the sheets and tying them in knots.

"Hurry up and change, missy. All you gots to do is just shinny down this. When you come back, I'll be waitin' downstairs. If the party is still goin' on and there's no other way for you to get in, I'll run up here and help you climb back up."

Marilee could only stare at her in disbelief, shaking her head slowly from side to side.

"It's the only way," Rosa urged her. "It's the only way you gonna get out of this house tonight without bein' seen. You ain't scairt, are you?" she added.

Marilee stiffened. Why not? Why not shinny down the rope? Could that be any more frightening than riding alone through the night, dressed in a white robe and hood, spying on a Klan meeting? Suddenly shinnying down a rope seemed like nothing.

She took a deep breath. "All right, Rosa. But if I break my neck, see that I have a nice funeral."

Rosa's eyes suddenly misted, and she stepped forward to give her a quick hug. "If'n anythin' happened to you, my people would never forget you. We'd declare a day of mournin' evah year, just to remember you. We owes so much to you."

Marilee turned away. "You don't owe me anything," she murmured.

This is why I do it, she told herself for the hundredth time. *Because there is no one else to help these people. And because I've got to feel like I'm doing something with my life.*

Chapter Eighteen

KICKING the horse with her heels, Marilee headed for the landmark, the skeletal tree, bony limbs clawing toward heaven as though in agony from the lightning bolt that had ended its life.

Willis stepped from behind the tree, only the whites of his eyes showing in the moonlight. Marilee reined to such a sudden halt that the horse reared. Willis lunged for the harness, bringing the animal back down.

"You find out somethin'?" he whispered anxiously as she dismounted. "Was it important?"

"Very!" She took a deep breath, exhausted. "You know the old man, Israel, who works for Mr. Mason? It's his son they're after tonight. Munroe. He's been hiding out. He knew they were after him because he's been stirring your people up.

"Well," she rushed on, "they know where he is, and I hope you do, because I imagine they're on their way by now. They mean to hang him, Willis. Not just beat him. They want him dead."

Willis pushed her aside as he leaped up on the horse. "I know where he's at," he cried. "And I can get there a'fore they do."

She watched as he cracked the reins across the horse's back, urging him into a full gallop as he headed into the woods.

She was alone. Above, the clouds parted momentarily and she looked up to see them tinged with silver as the moon shone down brightly. A cool breeze touched her skin, cooling after the hard ride.

Her fingertips moved up and down her forearms as she looked toward the springhouse. There. Her eyes fell on the gentle grassy slope beside it. Kicking off her shoes, she walked barefoot through the softness, feeling the silken tickling between her toes.

Staring down, a sudden rush engulfed her entire body. She felt bathed in a strange, purple light from the night, skin sprinkled with moondust. It was here where Travis had made love to Alaina. Here where they had lain together, Alaina in ecstasy.

Without thinking of what she was doing, she dropped to her knees, fingertips lovingly touching the grass, entwining it as she imagined what it must have been like, here on nature's special bed.

No, she realized suddenly, angrily, she could not imagine what it had been like. She tried to remember what it had been like with Donald, so long ago. It had always been over quickly, and he had rolled to one side and whispered he loved her, then fallen asleep. How many hours and how many nights had she lain awake wondering why she felt so empty? Now she knew that what she had been seeking was what Alaina felt with Travis Coltrane.

But what made Travis different from Donald?

Perhaps, she thought with a touch of shame, perhaps it was not Travis, had not been Donald. Perhaps it was she who was to blame. Maybe she just wasn't a passionate woman.

Her breath was coming in shallow gasps. It was so terribly hot. She slipped off the trousers and the shirt, absently thought about going to the tree where the muslin dress would be hidden. But the cool air felt good on her warm skin. No need to hurry. No one would see her.

Stretching out on her back, the grass felt delicious on her bare skin. What, she wondered dreamily, would it be like to lie here with a man beside me, a man like Travis Coltrane? So big. So handsome. So dashing. To look into his steel gray eyes was like falling in a whirlpool and being sucked down, down, but with absolutely no fear.

She ran her hands over her breasts, touching them gently, caressing.

"A lady should never do that when there's a man around to do it for her."

Her eyes flashed open, a scream locking in her throat. Travis Coltrane was lowering himself to the ground beside her. She lay there frozen in silence as he removed her hands from her breasts, replacing them with his own large hands.

She gasped, then found her voice. "You . . . you mustn't."

"Oh, yes, lovely lady, I must."

His voice was warm and rich, washing over her.

"You were here that night, the night I was with Alaina. You heard."

"Yes."

"You want me."

"Yes."

"Hang on, lovely lady," he said huskily. "I'm going to take you somewhere wonderful."

His lips touched hers, and she felt the strange sensation of his tongue entering her mouth. She touched him with her own, marveling at the delightful sensation. Strong, firm fingers moved to her breasts, massaging skillfully.

He moved to one side, using his knee to force her legs apart. He knew just where to caress. And she seemed to know where to caress him. How did she know?

Passion. This was passion. Savage, fierce, demanding passion. She felt spasms of joy she could not control. Her muscles were squeezing, straining to satisfy that wild, fierce longing.

He raised his lips slightly, breath hot on her face. "Please . . ." she whispered.

He lifted her legs, bending her knees as he locked them up and over his neck. Placing firm, sure hands beneath her bottom, he positioned himself, gazing down at her tenderly.

With one mighty thrust, he entered her. Her scream, of pleasure and of pain, was muffled by his lips. Again and again he threw himself into her, holding tightly to her.

Her nails dug into his flesh as she sought to get closer, closer. She wanted . . . wanted . . . and then there was the sun falling through her, to melt and consume her. All things glorious were hers.

And she was spent.

Slowly, his fingers released her. He withdrew, moving to one side. She turned to stare at him, gasping.

He was smiling. "A man always knows when a woman wants him."

"I don't understand any of this." Suddenly she was horribly embarrassed. She struggled to sit up, but he held her back.

"I was watching you," he went on quietly, holding her tightly. "I saw you walk to this spot. In the moonlight, I could see your face and knew you were remembering that night I was here with Alaina."

"You knew I was here that night?" she cried, stunned. "How could you have continued—?"

He chuckled softly. "I didn't know until later, after it was over. Believe me, I'm not the kind to perform for spectators."

"Oh, but I couldn't *see*," she told him quickly. "I could only hear. Oh, dear!" She struggled in his arms.

"Don't be coquettish with me now, Marilee. That's one of the reasons I find you so appealing. You're candid. Mature. I like that in a woman."

She felt dizzy. "This isn't real. I'm going to wake up soon and find it was all a dream."

"Why can't it be real?"

"Because this isn't me. I've never been with a man except my husband. It was never like this. I've never behaved *wantonly*."

"That was his fault."

She looked at him sharply. His gray eyes shone with warmth and his lips curved into a smile that made her shiver from wanting to touch them.

"Yes," he nodded, "it was your husband's fault. How could he expect you to feel like a woman if he did not act like a man?"

"I don't think it's nice of you to speak of him that way," she responded tightly. "You did not know Donald, and he's dead. He cannot defend himself."

"I mean no disrespect," he said honestly. "As for not knowing him, I don't have to. Making love to you is all the evidence I need. It was like opening the door to a cage and letting out a wild tigeress. Donald never opened that door, Marilee. It's too bad, but maybe he did not know how."

She struggled against him once more. "Please. Just let me

go. It's over. I would be lying if I said I didn't enjoy it, but it *is* over."

"It doesn't have to be."

She faced him once more. "No moment can last forever, Travis. We both know that. I was lonely, and I'll always treasure the feelings I had in your arms, but it can never happen again. I happen to love my sister, and I don't feel very good knowing that I made love to her fiancé."

He sat up very slowly, his eyes never leaving her face. *"Fiancé?"*

She shrugged. "Perhaps that's premature, but I know the two of you are quite serious."

Travis sat facing her. "Now, let's get something straight, Marilee," he said evenly, tensely. "I have never discussed marriage with Alaina. The only serious conversation we ever had was the first time she came to my room in town, late one night. She had a servant convey her in.

"We talked and agreed there would be no commitments. She said she understood. When you told me tonight that your father was objecting to our relationship, I was a little surprised. Evidently, she saw more in it than actually existed."

"Why didn't you tell my father that instead of running out on Alaina?"

"You do say what's on your mind, don't you?" He reached to tousle her hair playfully, but she jerked away. "Actually, I wasn't running out on Alaina, Marilee. I had business to tend to."

"Then why are you here?"

"I might ask you the same thing."

"This is my father's property. I have a right to be here."

"A bit strange for you to be here at this time of night, wouldn't you say? Especially when you come riding up dressed in men's clothing, a Negro meets you, takes your horse, and then goes riding off in a panic."

She had never liked feeling defensive. "Marshal Coltrane, what we just did together was a mistake. I owe you no explanation for being here, but I think I have the right to hear one from you. Why were you spying on me?" She struggled as he grasped both her arms. "Let me go."

"We haven't finished our conversation."

She glared at him. "I have nothing further to say to you."

"The last time I saw you, you were dressed in an exquisite gown. I'm curious as to what has happened since then."

"Then be curious," she said bitingly.

"Why are you here so late?" he prodded.

"Why aren't you out doing the job you were sent here to do?" she countered. "I think you are only interested in seeing how many women you can charm. You care nothing for the plight of the Negroes, and need I remind you that *is* why you were sent here? You aren't even trying to stop the Klan. You forget your place, and you forget your duty, and you are a disgrace to the badge you wear."

"Damn it, Marilee, you're one hell of a woman," he growled. "I've known only one other woman with that kind of courage. I told myself I'd never..."

He shook his head, muttered, "To hell with it," and then kissed her, long and hard. He whispered, "Damn you, woman, don't fight me. You know you want me again, just as I want you, and I'm going to have you."

She moaned softly. She could not deceive herself. She wanted him. Oh, yes, she wanted him, and soon she was sobbing with wonder as she locked her legs around his back, gently digging her heels into his buttocks to urge him onward ... onward ... onward.

Repeatedly he thrust into her, and each time she erupted in the greatest of all joys he would gently rock her for a few moments before starting his savage movements once more.

The explosion was coming. He was about to consume her in sweet-hot flames. He took her all the way, rocking her to joyful satisfaction, and even then he did not stop. She felt the flames lick high, higher, burning low once the awesome feeling spread within her. But the flames did not die out. He took her upward again and again, and she peaked the crest again and again.

Later, she would look back and try to remember when he had stopped, but could recall only being in his arms, held close, feeling deeply cherished.

He grinned down at her. "You're one hell of a woman, Marilee," he murmured huskily.

She turned her face away, but quickly, almost roughly, he cupped her chin and jerked her about to meet his gaze. "Don't ever look away from me again. Not after tonight."

"You gave me something I will always remember, Travis.

Now I know what it means to be a woman. I'll never forget."

"No. You won't forget. Because there will be other nights just as wonderful." He raised up on one elbow, his eyes glowing in the purple darkness. "You've got fire and spirit and courage. Perhaps those are the greatest qualities a woman can have."

"I also made love with the man my sister loves."

He snorted. "Will you stop being dramatic? It isn't like you. And we both know Alaina doesn't love me. She just wants me because she knows she can't have me. I've told her that."

The words leaped out so quickly there was no time to hold them back, and she hated herself for crying, "And I suppose I can have you? I suppose that's what you are telling me now!"

He was silent for several moments, and though she fought an inward battle, she could not tear her gaze from his.

Finally he took a deep breath and whispered, "I can give you everything but my heart, Marilee. Never my heart."

She forced herself to recover. "I'm not asking for your heart or anything else." She made her voice light, breezy. "What we had was lovely. As I said, I'll never forget it. But it's over. Now may I leave you? I do need to be getting home before I'm missed."

He looked toward the eastern horizon, where the first hint of dawn streaked the sky with waves of pink and coral. She followed his gaze.

"Oh, my God! Is it that late?" She leaped to her feet, found her clothes, and began putting them on. Would Rosa still be waiting? Would she have become frightened and perhaps alerted Father? No, surely not. Rosa was loyal and smarter than that. But Marilee had to hurry.

Travis stood, tucking in his shirt. "I'll ride you almost to the house. I've a horse nearby."

"No. Someone might hear us. It's best I just walk. I've time to get there before it's light."

She started to move away, but he reached and caught her arm.

"You never did tell me what you were doing out here in the middle of the night, dressed like a man," he said. "I'd like to hear it from you, Marilee."

"I . . . I like to walk at night," she stammered, thinking wildly. "I dress in these clothes so as not to draw attention. Who would wonder about a man walking around at odd hours? But a woman, dressed in a ball gown, now that would attract notice." She laughed but the sound was not right and she knew it.

"Who would be around here to see you?" he persisted, still holding her arm.

Suddenly she was desperate. "People like you, Travis Coltrane, who sneak around at night preying on women. Is this what the government pays you to do?"

His hand fell away and a strange shadow crossed his face. "You said something like that before. I'm doing what I get paid to do. Why don't you tell me why you're doing what you *aren't* paid to do?"

She challenged him with her eyes. "I don't know what you're talking about. And now may I go, or will you grab me again?"

He nodded. "You may go, but you *do* know what I'm talking about."

She gave her long brown hair a toss, for it had long since fallen wildly around her shoulders. "You're a strange man, Travis Coltrane. I think I shall forget this night ever happened. I suggest you do the same. Whatever you and my sister are to each other is between the two of you. I regret my weakness. Or should I say, my madness? It won't happen again."

His smile was infuriatingly arrogant. "If it doesn't happen between us, lovely lady, then it will surely happen in your dreams. You enjoyed it far too much to forget it."

"Well," she retorted angrily, taking several steps backward, "*You* won't ever know about it, that much I can be sure of." She turned and ran away, his laughter ringing in her ears.

Travis watched her disappear. He felt the old, familiar loneliness consuming him once again. For a little while, he had almost held her close to his heart. It was as near as he had come to loving.

Kitty.

He doubled up his fist and sent it slamming into the nearest tree trunk. But feeling the pain didn't help.

Marilee had almost the same spirit Kitty had possessed, the same unchallenged spirit. What other woman would dare infiltrate the dangerous Ku Klux Klan?

Yes, he knew. He knew a hell of a lot of things. Pieces of the puzzle were slowly beginning to fall into place. It was not a nice picture. He did not like what he was finding, did not like it at all.

But he did not want to think about that just then. He wanted to remember the way she had felt in his arms, the genuine responses. The passion.

Like Kitty.

But she was not Kitty. There would never be another Kitty. There was no point in looking for his fiery redhead, his one true love.

Yet there was something fascinating, something unique about Marilee. She would never possess the ethereal beauty of Kitty, but there was an aura about her that he found irresistible, though he could not quite define it.

She was not at all like her giddy sister. God, he would never forget that first night when she came to his bed right in her own house. He would not want Marilee to know about that escapade.

He also recalled a night less than a week after that first time, when Alaina had come to his office, asked Sam to leave, and, once they were alone, scooped her breasts from the daring bodice of her dress and taunted, "Have you had dessert tonight, Marshal?"

Well, he was, after all, only a man. Hell, he didn't want to come right out and tell her he could never feel anything for her except physical satisfaction. He sighed.

The usual warning signs had been there, the ones that surface when a woman gets to thinking about something permanent, but he had ignored the signals. Now he wished he had taken notice and put a stop to it. Had he led her on, he asked himself harshly? Had he been that selfish?

With a weary sigh, he began to move to where he had left his horse. Damn, he was tired. And there would be no time to sleep. Too many things were starting to happen.

He froze at the sound of a twig cracking. Instinctively dropping to his knees, he pulled his gun.

"Don't shoot, Marshal. It's me, Willis."

He saw the black man rise cautiously from the scrub brush just beyond the springhouse, and he sighed with relief and called out, "You better learn to yell out quicker than that, or you're going to find yourself holding a bullet."

"I didn't know you could hear me walkin'. I was waitin' till I got closer." He stepped into the clearing, panting, his shoulders heaving. "I didn't know you'd still be here. I went to the house, and Rosa was hidin' out in the bushes, scairt plumb to death 'cause Miz Marilee ain't back yet. I knowed you was here when I left her, and I come runnin' back here to tell you somethin's happened to her."

"Nothing has happened to her, Willis," he said quietly, not missing the wide-eyed look the Negro gave him. "She just left. She's probably almost to the house by now."

"All this time?" Willis cried, then, realizing he was treading on business that did not concern him, ducked his head and glanced away.

Travis decided it best to change the subject. "Did you find Munroe? Did you get there in time?"

The head bobbed up and down, and he grinned broadly. "Oh, yassuh, I found him. I helped him get away. We had to do some fancy sneakin', 'cause the Klan won't too far behind, but we made it."

"Good," Travis smiled, relieved. "It seems Marilee has once again come through for your people."

"Yassuh, she sho has," he chimed in, then said cautiously, "You won't nevah tell her I tol' you what she was doin', will you, Marshal? I mean, she'd be very mad."

"I won't let her know you told me, Willis. When the time comes, if it does, I'll make her think I discovered what she was doing on my own. Don't worry. You were wise to confide in me. She's been doing something very dangerous. I don't care if she is a woman, or if her father is rich and powerful. There are some vicious bastards in the Klan, and if they found out a mere woman had penetrated their security, they would deal with her just like she was a man."

Willis shuddered. "You gonna make her stop?"

"I think it will soon be time. But you let me handle that. Just keep on dealing with her as you have always done until I tell you otherwise."

"Yassuh. I will, suh. And I'll let you know what's goin' on. I'll be in touch, just like I have been."

With a wave, Travis turned and walked away, disappearing behind the springhouse.

No moment can last forever, Marilee had said. But other moments could happen, moments just as wonderful.

He had not lied to her. He could give her everything he possessed except his heart, for he had no heart to give.

His heart was buried in a grave in Nevada.

Chapter Nineteen

TRAVIS was feeling no pain. The straight Bourbon whiskey had settled in his stomach like a large warm blanket. He lifted his head now and then to stare around the saloon. His vision was slightly blurred, but this was the first night off he had allowed himself in weeks, and if he wanted a little booze, then damn it, it was his business.

The image floated through his inner vision, the image of golden-red hair, lavender eyes. Kitty. She was smiling in that special way, the secret way that said *I want you*.

And oh, God, how he wanted her. Forever.

He had not realized how tightly he was holding the glass. His fist was squeezing . . . squeezing. Suddenly the glass shattered and he felt a stinging sensation as whiskey and blood ran down over his hand in rivulets.

Sam left the bar and sat down opposite him. "All right," he spoke softly. "What happened to start it up again?"

"Start what up again?"

"The drinking."

"Damn it to blazes, Sam. This is the first time I've taken some time off in weeks. Can't a man have a few drinks in peace without somebody being on his back about it?"

"I'd say something is eating you. Time off or not, I know you. Something's eating you. What is it? Alaina?"

Travis stiffened. "Just get me another goddamn glass, Sam," he snapped. "I'd get it myself but I'm bleeding."

"I know you're bleeding. And I ain't getting you no glass. You've had enough to drink." He paused, sighing. "Say, before you bleed to death, satisfy an old man's curiosity and tell me what's wrong. Alaina? Or is it Kitty?"

Travis snarled, "You know, Sam, you're a nosy bastard. Always have been. I don't know why I've stuck by you as long as I have."

"It's the other way around," Sam said with a lazy grin. "Now you're either going to talk to me, or we're gonna get that hand fixed. Which will it be? You want to talk or you want to bleed?"

"Neither one."

Sam shrugged. "Then I'll sit here and watch you bleed to death over Alaina Barbeau. It surprised me, though. I figured you had control over yourself better than that. Mind, she is a fine-looking piece, real fine. If I was younger, I'd give you a run for your money and go after her myself. But since I ain't, there's nothing I can do but watch you make a fool of yourself."

"Shut up, Sam," Travis said harshly, holding his bleeding hand against his chest.

Sam pursed his lips. "It ain't her, Alaina, is it? It's Kitty you're aching over."

Travis struggled to his feet, gripping the edge of the table with one hand. He knew Sam only wanted to help. But there were times when nobody could help. "Sam, I appreciate your concern, but . . ."

His voice trailed off as he looked up into the blazing eyes of Stewart Mason, who was standing very close to Travis.

"I'd like a word with you, Marshal. And I'll tell you here and now it don't make no difference that you're wearing that badge." His eyes went to his bleeding hand. "And it don't make no difference that you've already been in one fight tonight, either."

Sam started to speak, but Travis quickly replied, "If you got something to say, Mason, say it. Don't worry about the badge or the blood."

Sam got to his feet. "Travis, I don't think—"

"Stay out of it, Sam. We're on our way back to the office, Mason. If you want to talk to me, you can come along."

Sam and Travis moved through the swinging wooden doors and out, leaving Stewart Mason behind.

Out in the damp night, Sam shook his head, murmuring, "Damn it, what's he all riled up about?"

"I'm plenty riled up, old man," Stewart yelled, lunging through the doorway after them. "Get out of my way." With one shove, he sent Sam sprawling to the boardwalk.

Travis turned in time to see the punch coming. His injured right hand was of no use, so he brought up the forearm to block the blow while hitting Mason with a left uppercut to the chin.

Mason staggered, and Travis hit him at his midsection, doubling him over. Mason fell to his knees. In the dim shadows, Travis was barely able to see the quick movement Mason made to his holster, but he caught it in time and lifted his right foot to kick Mason's face. As Mason fell backward, Travis brought out his own gun. By the time Mason's head hit the ground, he was upon him, the cold steel barrel pressed against his neck.

"Now what in the goddamn hell is this all about?" he asked through gritted teeth as a crowd began to tumble from the doors of the saloon. "What's got you so riled up that you're about to get yourself killed?"

Mason's eyes glittered, his body trembling with rage as he spat, "You know what it's about, you sonofabitch! You know what you did to Alaina! You better go ahead and kill me while you got the chance, 'cause you're a dead man if I ever get up from here and get my hands on a gun."

"The hell!" Travis roared, holstering his gun. With his left hand, he reached to jerk Mason to his feet. "My gun is holstered," he challenged. "You want to draw on me, you do it!"

Mason spat blood, then wiped his mouth with the back of his hand. He glanced up at the onlookers, thinking of the gossip that would run rampant about Alaina, thinking, too, that this was not the time to kill Coltrane. "Not now," he muttered, glaring at Travis.

Travis took a deep breath. "Come with me to the office. We're going to talk."

"I ain't going nowhere with you."

"You'll come if I have to pull my gun again, Mason. Make it easy on yourself."

Mason glanced around once more. His mouth was still bleeding, and he knew the crowd was not going to break up if he kept standing there. They were waiting to see what was going to happen. He moved forward, Sam and Travis following close behind.

Once in the office, Sam motioned Travis to the chair behind his desk and snapped, "You two are gonna have to wait to settle this thing till I see to that hand."

"We'll talk while you work on it," Travis said quietly.

Sam gathered a pan of water, rags, a needle, and a small knife. He sat down next to Travis and pulled his hand forward. "Just grit your teeth, you goldanged fool. It's gonna hurt, but you ain't got nobody to blame but yourself."

Travis bit his tongue. He was not about to show any pain no matter how damn much it hurt. He saw Mason watching with a gloating expression. "All right. Start talking."

Mason's upper lip curled. "You know what it's about. Alaina." He sat on Travis' desk, glad to be looking down at the marshal.

Travis raised an eyebrow. "What about her?"

"She told me. About you and her. She says she won't marry me 'cause of you. If you think I'm gonna let a fucking Yankee take my woman away, you're full of—"

"Hold it, you redneck sonofabitch!" Travis jumped to point the finger of his left hand as Sam cursed and struggled to keep his other hand still. "Don't start telling me what I can and can't do. If Alaina were 'your' woman, she wouldn't be seeing me. I will continue to see her as long as it's what *I* want and what *she* wants. You must have a wish to die if you're thinking of telling me what I can do. Now suppose you just back on out of here while you're still in one piece."

The two locked eyes, standing only a foot apart.

Sam looked from one to the other, then said, "Why don't you take his advice, Mason? There's been enough trouble for one night."

"She's going to marry me," he said quietly. "Alaina's young and flighty. She always has been. Her old man spoiled her, but I'm the one who knows how to handle her. She's just using you to try to make me jealous."

"I would say she has done a fine job."

"It's going to stop," Mason yelled. "Her daddy told her she couldn't see you no more. You keep on messing with her and, marshal or not, you're gonna wind up dead, if not by my hand, then by her daddy's. If your hand wasn't cut up, I'd take you outside right now and we'd settle this in the street. But it ain't gonna be said that I drew on a man with his gun hand messed up."

"How do you look in white?"

Mason blinked. "What?"

Travis smiled. "You seem like the cowardly type who would wear the white robe and hood of the Klan. Why don't we talk about that instead of Alaina?"

Mason fought for control. Forcing a feeble smile, he said, "You ain't gonna goad me into drawing, Marshal. Not here. And the Klan ain't none of your business."

He leaned forward to place his knuckles on the desk. "You been in town long enough to know by now, Marshal, that you ain't never gonna find out nothing about the Klan. Why not clear out before you wind up hanging from a tree like a nigger?"

Travis looked over at Sam, who was still picking glass from his hand. "Sam," he said in a calm, deadly voice, "get him out of here or let me have my hand back so I can strangle the sonofabitch."

Without looking up, Sam thundered, "Mason, get the hell out or I'm going to kill you myself. You're lucky you're still breathing."

Mason stepped toward the door. He was almost out when he whirled around and bellowed, "You ain't seen the last of me, either of you. And if you know what's good for you, you'll both clear out of town. People around here don't want you nosing in what don't concern you."

"It concerns us when cowards hide behind masks to hurt innocent people," Sam said, still not looking up. "We won't be leaving till we stop you, Mason. Carry that back to the Klan."

Mason's laugh was taunting. "You dumb shitheads really think you're gonna bust the Klan? You're crazy. You're gonna get yourselves killed, that's all you're gonna do. Running your mouths like them dumb niggers. The only reason you're still alive is because the Klan knows you're too dumb to know anything. Keep talking like that, and they'll take care of you."

Travis laughed. "You'll tell them, right, Mason? The next time you put on your robe and your hood, you'll stand up and tell them."

"You can't prove I got anything to do with the Klan," Mason snarled. "I may know what's going on 'cause I know everything that goes on around here, but you can't hang nothing on me."

Travis sighed. "I'm getting bored with you, Mason. I'm not going to tell you again to get the hell out of here."

Mason's lips worked nervously for a few seconds, and then he stepped outside, slamming the door behind him with a crash.

Sam gave a long, low whistle. "Boy, you sure do get yourself in some messes. You just had to start fooling around with the Klan leader's woman, didn't you? That's about the dumbest thing you've ever done."

"She brought it to me, Sam. I didn't go after it."

"I can't recall you ever going after it, but I *can* say that you've turned down a few. Why couldn't you have done the same thing with her? Now you've gone and gotten yourself all involved."

"I'm not involved," Travis interrupted sharply. "Not the way you think."

"Then why am I picking glass out of your hand?"

"Kitty."

Sam was contrite. "I might've known." He was silent for a moment, then said, "You can't go on this way, Travis. It won't bring her back."

"I don't want to talk about her," he said shortly.

"All right, then. Let's talk about Alaina. How come you've gone and gotten yourself involved with her? We've known for quite a spell that Mason's the ringleader of the Klan. This could complicate things."

"Not really. We'll move on Mason and his followers when the time is right. I'm still not sure he *is* the leader, though."

Sam raised his eyebrows. "What makes you say that?"

"It's simple," Travis shrugged. "He's not smart enough. It's got to be somebody else, somebody smart enough to call the shots *and* keep his identity secret so nothing can be traced to him."

"You said you saw Mason get up in front of the Klan rally the night you dressed up like one of them and slipped in."

"I did. But that doesn't mean that he was acting on his own. I think he was just following someone's orders."

"And who do you think that someone is?"

"Jordan Barbeau."

"Goddamn!" Sam yelped, straightening. "Are you sure?"

Travis nodded. "I can't figure out a better reason for Marilee to be spying on the Klan."

"Now, wait a minute." Sam held up his hands, knife in one, needle in the other. "You better explain."

Travis did, and soon Sam bent over and began working on his hand once more, shaking his head in astonishment. "I found this out from Israel.

"Anyway," he paused to grit his teeth as Sam went after a particularly deep sliver of glass, "I followed her a couple of nights ago."

"That's quite a story," Sam said and whistled. "So you think Marilee is doing all this to help the Negroes instead of going to the law with the truth about her father?"

"That's bound to be at least the biggest reason. I think it's safe to say that Barbeau is behind all of it. Mason is just his puppet."

Sam held Travis' hand over a pail and poured a bottleful of whiskey over the wounds. Travis cursed and jerked his hand back. "It needs a bandage," Sam told him.

"Never mind that. It won't bleed much more."

Sam shrugged. "It's your hand. There's still some glass in there, but I can't get it all out."

"It'll work out sooner or later. Hell, with you picking at it, it's really starting to hurt."

"So what are you going to do about Marilee?" Sam wanted to know. "It's damn dangerous for her. She may be Barbeau's daughter, but if she gets found out, that won't help much."

"Exactly," Travis said grimly. "That's why I want to bust this thing wide open as soon as possible. I want her out of this mess."

Sam was thoughtful for a few moments, watching Travis pace. After a while he asked, "How much longer do you think it's going to be?"

"We've got to move slowly."

"I know that. I also know it's time we moved on, Travis. You've got a son back in North Carolina who needs a father. You've got that silver mine out in Nevada that is probably making you a rich man. Hell, you've never even been there to look at it. You need to see to both. Staying here only means trouble, especially now that you've got yourself involved with another woman. That's a match I can't see."

Travis turned to stare at him, a stunned expression on his

face. He laughed. "There's no way I'm ever going to be serious about a woman like Alaina. So there's not going to be any match."

Sam decided to let it all out. "I've known you a long, long time, Travis. I've seen you involved with more women than I can count. But there's been only one time . . . one time, mind you, that I've seen that look on your face, and that was when you fell in love with Kitty. Now, I'll be the first to say Alaina Barbeau is not your type, just as I was the first to say Kitty was. This whole thing's got me puzzled. Maybe you don't realize it, but you think more of Alaina than you're admitting."

No, Travis began to realize. It was coming back to him. Just before the glass had shattered, Kitty's face had faded and been replaced by Marilee's. Not Alaina's.

Marilee's.

He closed his eyes. Spirit. Courage. These were what had drawn him to Kitty. Marilee lacked Kitty's ethereal loveliness, but her grit was almost equal to Kitty's.

"It isn't Alaina," he said quietly with finality.

Sam had been watching him carefully, and suddenly he wondered why he hadn't realized it before. "Marilee?"

Travis nodded. "Yeah. She's quite a woman."

Sam took a deep breath, then let it out slowly. "I think, my friend, that you've outdone yourself this time. You're involved with two women, both of them a daughter of the Klan leader, and one of them the fiancée of a Klansman. I'd say you're going to be in quite a mess if we don't hurry up and finish our business and get the hell out of here."

Travis gave him a wry look. "Have you ever seen me in woman trouble I couldn't get out of?"

"Yeah," Sam replied grimly. "Kitty. You fell in love."

"Never again." Travis sat down at his desk. "I can handle it. Right now I'm more concerned about winding up the business at hand."

Sam pulled up a chair and they began to talk, planning strategy, losing track of time. Suddenly there was a soft rapping on the door. Travis murmured, "What now?" sighed, and got up to answer the door.

He found Willis standing outside, twisting his straw hat in his hands, a worried look on his dark face.

"What is it?" Travis asked, reaching to draw him inside. "Trouble?" Sam hurried over.

"You can call it that, Marshal." Willis looked apologetic. "I didn't want to bring her here. You told me not to no more. But she made me. Said she'd see her daddy kick me out if I didn't do what she said."

"Goddamn it!" Travis slammed his left hand against the door sill in disgust. "Where is she this time?"

"Same place as before. I rode her into town in the back of the wagon, covered up with a blanket. I took the wagon into the livery stable and left it. Nobody's around. She said for me to come get you."

"Alaina!" Sam spat out the name contemptuously. He had known plenty of women who chased after Travis, but never that boldly. "That's all we need right now."

Travis was rubbing his forehead thoughtfully. It was late. He was tired. His head was beginning to ache. No doubt Stewart Mason was still in town. Probably in the saloon getting drunk. It was risky to go to the stable, but if he didn't, Alaina would come storming into his office. And he knew why she had come to see him. He had left the party without explanation and had not talked with her since. After riding all the way into town at this hour, she would not return without seeing him. There was nothing to do but go to her.

Sam cried, "You aren't going, are you?"

Travis ignored him, saying to Willis as he passed, "You'd best be at the stable in a half hour to take her home. Don't you be late."

"Yassuh, Marshal, yassuh," Willis bobbed his head up and down.

Travis hurried through the night, down the empty streets, glancing around to make sure he was not being seen.

The stable was at the edge of town. He entered the dark recesses and stood silently, listening.

"Travis, is that you?" came her whisper from a stall to his left.

"It damn well better be me," he growled, moving toward the sound. "Woman, are you crazy? I told you not to come into town like this. It's dangerous."

"Well, if you'd come to me, I wouldn't have to be so bold, would I, darling?"

She was naked, and despite his anger, he was instantly aroused. It made him even angrier.

He struggled for control. He wanted to talk, make her see

reason. Ignoring his urges, he gripped her slender white shoulders and said harshly, "Listen and listen carefully, Alaina. Stewart Mason almost got himself killed over you tonight. He's mad as hell about us. Your father doesn't like it, either. Now it's no good. It's got to stop."

"It can't," she cried. "You love me and I love you."

"Wait a minute!" He pressed his hand over her mouth. "I never said I loved you. I told you from the very first that what we had together was just desire and nothing more. I never promised you anything else. And now it's got to end."

"But why can't you go on seeing me this way? It . . . it's better than losing you, Travis. I can't stand the thought of losing you."

"You never had me to lose, Alaina. Be reasonable. You're taking chances, and you're going to cause Stewart to get killed."

"He doesn't own me."

"So he doesn't own you. But if he's going to get himself killed over you, it's not going to be by me."

Her voice rose shrilly, angrily, and she struggled in his grasp. "You bastard! You used me!"

He clapped his hand over her mouth. "Alaina, shut up! Someone is going to hear you," he commanded harshly. "And don't be foolish. I did not use you. You knew how it was. If you saw things that weren't there, it was your doing. I never misled you."

Slowly he removed his hand. "Now are you going to be quiet or bring the whole town in here?"

"I'll be quiet," she hissed, body quivering with rage. "But I promise you this, Travis Coltrane. You're going to pay for this. You made a fool of me."

He looked at her and she was forced to look away. "Alaina," he said quietly, "you and I enjoyed each other. I didn't make a fool of you and you know it. Now the thing for you to do, if you don't love Stewart Mason and you don't plan to marry him, is to tell him. Straighten all that out before you start up with another man."

"You never loved me, did you?" she asked, voice quivering with emotion as he turned away. "None of this meant anything to you."

He turned, barely able to make her out in the darkness. "I loved your body, Alaina. I took pleasure and I gave pleasure. I never promised more."

"Bastard!" she screamed as he hurried on. "I'll get you for this. I swear I'll get you."

He walked out of the stable as quickly as possible without breaking into a run. All the way back to the office he cursed himself for becoming involved with her in the first place. In the future, he made a vow, he would be more discreet. As Sam had said, he had gotten himself into quite a mess.

Lost in thought, he was unaware . . . did not sense the men hiding in the shadows as he entered the alley leading to his office.

He felt only a sharp crack on the back of his head, and then he felt nothing at all.

Chapter Twenty

THUNDER rolled across the majestic Kentucky mountains, lightning cracking against the skies. Branches whipped, fighting the storm.

Marilee trembled, dismounting and moving through the shadows. Her long, flowing white robe twisted around her legs as she stepped carefully through the weeds and brambles. Soon the skies would open and the rains would fall. She hoped by then to be on her way to meet Willis.

The flames of the burning cross lashed back angrily at the beating wind, casting a red glow across the white hooded figures. A gathering of ghosts, she thought.

She stood to the rear of the gathering near the woods, as always, so she could slip away. As always, her eyes scanned the sea of white robes. Who were these people? Neighbors? Friends? Had she dined with them? Were they decent people out of disguise, turning into hoodlums and murderers here in the hysterical air of the gathering?

Where, dear Lord, was it all going to end?

She thought of Travis. Where was he? Why wasn't he here, doing his job?

Her thoughts turned to the way Alaina had behaved all day.

When she had refused to come out of her room for breakfast, Marilee had not thought about it. But when the lunch hour arrived, and Rosa reported she would still not come out of her room, it had been time to do something.

Marilee had found her bundled up in bed, eyes red and swollen from crying.

"Whatever is wrong?" she asked in alarm.

"I don't want to talk about him," had been the tearful, angry reply. "Not now. Not ever. I wish he were dead."

Travis. And there was nothing to be done, Marilee thought, for it was best ended. So Marilee had sent a tray to her sister's room and made excuses to their father and instructed the servants to leave her alone. Time was the only thing that would help. Alaina might spend many days in her room, suffering alone.

Something caught Marilee's attention, bringing her back to the present. A name. Whose? She strained to hear, admonishing herself. This was no time for woolgathering.

". . . and we've had too many slipups lately," shouted the man standing on the rock and overlooking them. "By the time we get there, the nigras are gone. Something's wrong! It's almost as though they're being warned that we're on the way!"

Marilee trembled. They were suspicious. She had known it would come to this. After several of their victims had escaped, they would start to wonder.

"Tonight the sonofabitch isn't going to get away!" The man on the rock was yelling. "And we've got something special planned for him, too. Tar and feathers!"

The crowd cheered, and Marilee was sick. She had once seen a man after hot tar had been poured over him. She prayed never to see another. A layer of skin had come off with the tar, and she had heard his screams of agony.

"What'd the bastard do?" someone called out.

A hush fell as everyone waited for the leader to answer. Finally, in a strained voice, he said, "He helped a white man persuade a white woman to sneak off where she shouldn't have gone. I say a nigger ain't got no business getting involved with white man's business."

"No!" the robed figures shouted in unison.

"We're going to teach him a lesson . . . set an example for other niggers."

Someone cried, "Who is it? Who're we after tonight?"

"That nigger that works for Barbeau! Willis!" the leader shouted back.

Quickly Marilee turned away, checking herself immediately. There was an urgency, yes, but she had to remember to be cautious. With short, hesitant steps, she moved sideways toward the woods.

The leader was saying that a brother had an announcement to make concerning problems in another county. Another Klan group needed assistance. It would give Marilee a little time.

She quickened her pace, daring to run the last few steps, breathing a sigh of relief as she reached the cover of the foliage and stooped down. Thank God, she thought as she began to crawl forward on her hands and knees, she knew the way by heart.

She groped for the familiar landmarks, knowing the horses were nearby. All she had to do was lead her own mount away, out of hearing range, leap upon him, and thunder through the night to Willis, who would be at the springhouse. He would have to go far away and probably not return. He had been a good friend, and she would miss him. Perhaps one day law would be restored and he could return. She would cling to that thought. There were so pitifully many just like him who had been forced to run, leaving family behind, leaving their homes.

Fighting tears, she found her horse, dread rising in her. She could never deny fear of the ride. Only when it was over could she breathe easily.

She walked the horse to a safe distance. Suddenly, with an explosion of thunder and a brilliant flash of lightning, the skies opened and the rains poured down. But, she thought frantically, that would not so stop the Klan, so it must not stop her.

Thoughts jumbled together, blurring, as she walked faster, her robe soaked. Her only advantage was that the others had no way of knowing where Willis was.

The winds were screaming, whipping the rain to a slashing fury. Walking was becoming almost impossible. She had to mount the horse. It would be difficult in the mud, but by God, she had to try.

She had her left foot in the stirrup and was about to swing her right leg up and over when she felt something hard and cold jammed into her back.

"Just hold it right there or I'll blow you to hell," the harsh voice growled.

Terror washed over her. She stared straight ahead, praying that when the gun exploded, it would be over quickly.

"I been watching you," the man behind her snarled. "We knowed we had a traitor, and when I seen you sneak off tonight, I knew I had you, you goddamn nigger-lovin' bastard."

He yanked the hood from her head, then gasped. "A woman! Shit! A woman! Hey, Higgins, c'mere! I got him, only *he's* a *she*."

Heavy footsteps crashed through the woods and her captor clamped a beefy hand on her shoulder to spin her around. Lightning streaked across the sky, lighting up the night for an instant. "I'll be damned! Marilee Barbeau! What in the hell you doin' out here, woman?"

She pulled her wet hair back from her face and stared up at the hooded man defiantly. Looking right at the slits in the hood, she said firmly, "I'm here because somebody has to stop you lunatics! Yes, it's me, but I'm not a traitor. I never belonged. I never swore to secrecy. It goes to show how damn stupid you really are, that a woman could penetrate your secret meetings."

"If you weren't a woman, I'd blow you away here and now," he growled, pushing the gun into her stomach threateningly.

"Hey, leave her be!" The other man appeared. Then he recognized her and swore, "Damn! It can't be you!"

"It is me," she matched his voice with his large build. "And it's you, Tom Higgins. I might've known you would be involved in this. You always were a scoundrel! Donald despised you, and so do I. It's going to give me great pleasure to see you behind bars."

"You keep talking like that, and you won't live to see nothin', little lady." He jerked off his hood and faced her. The man holding the gun reached for his hood, also, but Tom snapped, "Don't. She don't know who you are. No need in her knowing any more than she already does."

"Okay. But what do we do with her? I ain't never killed a woman before."

"You mean there's an atrocity you haven't committed?" She threw all fear away, anger replacing terror. "I find that hard to believe. A man who hides behind a hood and terrorizes Negroes will not stop at killing a woman. Go ahead and pull the trigger. Show what a big man you are."

She did not see Higgins' blow coming and when his hand cracked across her face she reeled. She would have fallen but he grabbed her arm and squeezed painfully. "Now you just shut your goddamn mouth, bitch. We've got to figure out what to do with you, and we might just lose our patience if you keep yapping."

She tasted blood but her anger never diminished. "Go ahead and kill me! Go ahead!"

He slapped her again, this time hard enough to knock her to the ground.

It was difficult to focus her eyes or to hear, and she struggled to keep from drifting away as dizziness overtook her. She became aware that someone else had arrived. Their conversation sounded thick, muted, as their voices reached her through the fog settling over her.

"What'd you hit her for?"

"Hell, you should've heard what she was saying. Goddamn hysterical female!"

"Barbeau's daughter. Who'da ever thought she'd do this to us?"

"Things make a lotta sense now . . . all them niggers that got away. She was here. High-tailin' it outta here to warn them."

"But why?"

"Her husband fought for the Yankees, remember? I've always heard her and him both were nigger-lovers."

"But how'd she find out about us? How'd she know our secret signals? How'd she know where we were meetin'?"

"How did she know *when* we were meetin'? That's what bothers me. Someone told her. How many more spies we got? This is bad. Real bad."

"We don't have time to worry about the others, not now. We've got to deal with her."

"You gonna kill her?"

There was a long silence.

"No. Her old man would kill us." The voice held authority, and Marilee at last recognized it as belonging to Stewart Mason. Stewart was not going to let them kill her.

There was movement. Marilee kept her eyes closed, not wanting to let them know that she had heard. The ringing in her ears was getting fainter now, and the pain was not so bad. She could hang on.

She felt herself being tied, arms jerked behind her back and wrists bound together. A wet rag was tied across her mouth. She was lifted roughly and tossed across her saddle. The impact hurt, but she kept quiet, wanting to hear as much as possible.

The horse began to move, and soon their voices became too distant to understand. The ride seemed endless, and several times she felt as though she were going to roll from the saddle onto the ground. They were moving uphill, over rough terrain.

Where is brave Marshal Coltrane? she thought bitterly. Down by the springhouse making up with Alaina? There was still that jealousy, for Alaina had known many nights with Travis, while she had known only one.

The horses were stopping. She tensed. She heard Stewart's voice coming closer. "We'll leave her here, and since she already knows about you, you can guard her."

"For how goddamn long?" Higgins protested. "I got land to tend. I can't stay up here."

"You've got to. Just till I can get word to the Klan in the western part of the state and ask for their help."

"What can they do? Kill her for us?" came Higgins' sarcastic response.

"I don't want her dead. I just want her out of the way. Right now, she can only tell on you, Higgins. Sure, she knows the secret signals and where we meet, but we're going to change all that."

"I'll get the western Klan to take her off our hands," he continued, then paused to laugh. "They'll find something for her to do."

Higgins snickered, catching on. "You mean, they'll find something to do *with* her. She's a fine-lookin' woman. I wouldn't mind havin' some myself."

Marilee heard the sounds of scuffling and Stewart shouted furiously, "You lay one hand on her that way, goddamn you, and I'll kill you myself, Higgins." Silence. Harsh breathing. Then Stewart said, "All right, now. We understand each other. The thing is, we can't have Jordan Barbeau's daughter around here for long because once she turns up missing, he's going to want these mountains combed inch by inch."

"So why not kill her and be done with it?"

Marilee tensed, for Stewart fell thoughtfully silent. "No. She's good-looking enough that the western Klan will make use of her. Once they've got hold of her, then it's out of my hands. I won't have her fate on my conscience."

As if you ever had any conscience, you bastard, Marilee fumed. It was all she could do to keep still.

She felt herself being lifted from the saddle. The blindfold slipped down. "I'll stay," Higgins was saying reluctantly, and she realized it was he who held her, "but not for long. You make the arrangements and make 'em fast, 'cause I ain't staying but a couple of days."

Stewart snapped, "You'll stay till you hear from me."

The sound of footsteps faded, and she knew Stewart was gone. Higgins began walking, grumbling to himself. She dared to open her eyes just as a brilliant flash of distant lightning danced across the sky. She could see a large, black, gaping hole just ahead. They were headed straight for it. A cave. She had no idea where they were except that it was somewhere in the mountains.

A bobcat screamed from up above, and she was unable to control the sudden jerking of her body. Higgins laughed, "So, you're awake, are you? Well, you got yourself in a peck of trouble. Bet you wished you'd minded your own business, huh?"

He snickered, gazing at the gag. "Well, I promise you that before this night has ended you'll talk plenty. Maybe somebody I can't name is willing to send you off without finding out all you know, but not me. Uh-uh. You're gonna tell me plenty. Or wish you had," he added with an evil chuckle.

Higgins must have realized that they were alone. In one rough movement, he tore the rag away from her mouth. It dangled around her neck.

She could no longer suppress her contempt. "I'm not telling you anything. And you're the one who's in trouble. If I could find out about you, how long do you think it will take the marshals to do the very same thing? They'll arrest all of you."

He dropped her to the ground, and she fell clumsily, still bound by the ropes. "That's what I aim to find out. How come you know so much and they don't? Of course, I ain't worried about them two fool marshals. I 'magine after what happened to them last night, they'll be high-tailin' it away from here about as fast as they can."

Fear shot through her. "What . . . what did you do to them?"

"Beat the shit out of 'em," he laughed. "I mean beat 'em up good. I think the old one's got a busted leg, and Coltrane's face is all broke up. Them two won't be getting around for a spell, and when they do, they best get out of here. We let 'em know that next time, they'll die!"

"You stay here," he ordered. "Don't try to get out of those ropes 'cause you won't get far. I'll be back directly and get you fixed up all nice and cozy so we can have our talk."

He left, and she allowed herself to think her own thoughts. Travis and Sam injured! No! She shook her head wildly from side to side. Travis' face swam before her, the firm set to his jaw, the eyes, not blue nor black but a sheen almost the color of silver. What had they done to his face? And how badly had they hurt Sam?

Deep inside, a terrible remorse began to build. She had kept still about the Klan because of her father, and now, because of her silence, the situation had gotten worse. Travis was hurt. Sam was hurt. And she was in trouble.

Higgins returned carrying a burning torch in one hand, a bottle of whiskey in the other. "Now we can see," he grinned down at her. "You can look around at what'll be your home for the next few days. Like it?"

The flame cast a sickly yellowish glow around the inside of the cave, shadows dancing ominously off the mold-covered walls. It was cold and damp, and the sound of water rushing could be heard faintly from somewhere in the cave.

"Like it?" he taunted.

She did not reply.

He approached her, taking a knife from his back pocket. With one swift movement he cut the rope from her wrists. Quickly she brought her hands forward, rubbing the sore, bruised flesh.

"I'm not stupid enough to take off the ankle ropes. Get your clothes off and be quick about it." He grinned.

She jerked up her head in horror.

"Go on." He grinned. "Unless you want to leave here naked when they come for you, 'cause I'll rip 'em to pieces getting them off you if you don't take 'em off yourself."

"No . . ." She shrank back against the rough cave wall. "You can't."

"Yeah, I can," he said matter-of-factly, tipping up the bottle for a long drink. "I've got some nice plans for you, honey.

Whether you enjoy 'em or not depends on you. I want to hear all you got to tell me."

She swung her head from side to side. "I won't tell you anything. You can rape me . . . kill me . . . I won't tell you anything."

He cocked his head to one side and stared at her thoughtfully for a moment, then said, "I believe you've got just enough spunk that you're going to be a real challenge. But not for long. Now get them clothes off!" With a loud bellow he swooped down on her, grabbing the front of the white robe and ripping it and the shirt beneath from her body.

She attempted to cover her naked breasts, but he jerked her arms away, laughing, "Let me see! Oh, they're nice, they're real nice. When you get through telling me what I want to know, me and you are gonna have a fine time."

"You go to hell," she screamed, kicking her bound ankles at him as he reached down to yank at her trousers. He backed away in time to keep from getting struck, laughing as he tore and pulled until her trousers were off.

"Now get up!" He wrapped his fingers in her hair and gave her a painful jerk. And when she was on her feet, he shoved her deeper into the cave.

"Here!" he shouted. "I found something."

Fearfully, she followed his gaze upward, and saw the gnarled, twisted, roots protruding from the cave's roof, snaking horizontally like cross beams. He pulled the rope that had bound her hands from his belt, grabbed her arms, and began to bind her wrists once more.

She struggled and fought, but he was much too strong for her. Suddenly she found her arms being stretched high above her head, pulling her body painfully upward until only the tips of her toes touched the ground.

"Please, please, don't do this to me," she begged.

His eyes moved up and down her tightly stretched body. Licking his lips hungrily, he came closer and reached out to run his hands up and down her quivering flesh. "Nice," he murmured thickly, cupping her breasts and squeezing. "Oh, baby, you're real nice.

"We're gonna have time to pleasure ourselves later, baby, but right now we got business to tend to. Now, if you'd like to go ahead and talk, I'll cut you down. All you gotta do is tell me how you found out where and when we were meeting, and give me the names of the niggers and anybody else who helped you out. You're also gonna tell me who else knows about us."

With a movement so quick as to catch him off guard, she lifted one leg and kicked him in the side of the head so sharply that he staggered backward. "I'll never tell you anything, damn you," she shrieked.

He rushed forward to clutch her buttocks, digging his fingers cruelly into the flesh as he bit down on her breast. Then he stood back and roared, "You snotty little bitch. I never liked you nohow! So high and mighty! Marryin' a goddamn Yankee! And if the boss don't like it, then he can kiss my ass, 'cause I'm gonna fix you good!"

He picked up the torch, then looked around the cave until he found a long stick with a forked end. Mumbling to himself, he disappeared into the recesses of the cave.

Marilee felt her heart leaping wildly. Never had she known such panic. What was this madman going to do to her? Her arms ached terribly from hanging, and she struggled to touch the floor with her toes, trying to take as much weight as possible from her body.

"Well, well, I didn't have far to look," she heard him call triumphantly. Soon she saw the glow of the torch as he returned from around a curve. "Seems we've found these critters' hide-out. . . ."

A long, piercing scream escaped as she saw the deadly, writhing snake he held tightly just below its diamond-shaped head.

A rattlesnake!

He dropped it to the ground about four feet away from where her toes dangled. The snake coiled, rattling angrily, swaying from side to side, anticipating his strike.

Higgins backed away, grinning. "Here's how we're going to play this little game. I'm gonna ask you a question, and if I don't get the answer I want, I'm gonna use this stick and push our little friend closer to you. He's gonna get mad every time I poke him. And sooner or later he's gonna take a bite out of them pretty legs. So you better be real good at this game.

"Or," he continued, cackling with anticipation, "once you finish talking, I'll do away with him. Then you and me'll have us some fun. How's that sound?"

She did not speak but kept her eyes riveted on the coiled

rattlesnake. Judging by his size, he was already close enough to strike.

"The first thing I want to know," Higgins began, "is how you knew where we were meeting."

When she did not answer, he grasped the stick and thrust it at the snake, pitching him a few inches closer to her. She screamed as the snake struck in Higgins' direction, missing Higgins by only inches.

"Aw, now, you shouldn't've yelled," he said. "Now he's heard you and knows you're there. He's apt to get pissed off 'cause he can't get me, and go for you."

Squeezing her eyes shut tightly, she clamped her teeth together, bracing for the fatal strike.

"Here he comes!"

Her eyes flashed open as the snake was shoved closer. Her toes were less than two feet away.

"It's gonna be a shame to see a pretty thing like you die," he sighed. "'Course, I'll just take off the ankle ropes and tell the boss you tried to run away and got snake-bit. It's really a waste. And all you gotta do is talk. I just can't believe you're willin' to die."

He had positioned the torch between two large rocks, and the scene looked, she thought, like a vision from hell. Shadows of her body, hanging from the roots, danced eerily over the cave wall. Higgins' large, hulking body hovered to one side. The hissing, rattling snake swayed in the middle.

Higgins was watching her with narrowed eyes, his chest heaving as he fastened his gaze on her breasts. "No," he said suddenly. "We got time later for all this. Right now, I've gotta have me some of you."

Quickly he swung the stick, scooping up the rattlesnake and sending him sailing through the air into the back of the cave. "Gonna have you," he grunted, rushing forward to cover her nipples with biting kisses in between hungry flicks of his hot, eager tongue. She shrieked in protest and he jerked his head back and shouted, "Let's get you down, baby. Let's get you stretched out on the floor where I can get at you good."

He leaped up, moving quickly behind her to tug at the ropes that held her.

That was when his scream turned her blood to ice.

"Goddamn, no!" He staggered away, slumping to his knees. "No! No! No!"

He was clawing at his right leg, and she twisted around, trying to see. She froze, silently screaming at her body not to move, for there, below her, coiled and ready to strike again, lay a rattlesnake.

This was their cave. They were probably all around.

Higgins was jerking up his trouser leg, screaming as he saw the twin puncture marks in the flesh of his calf. He leaped to his feet, bolting for the mouth of the cave. "Gotta have help . . . gotta have help. . . ." he cried hysterically, his voice growing fainter and fainter as he ran.

He was going to die. She recalled her father's many warnings about snakebites. When a person panics and runs, he had said, the poison moves quicker. Death is certain. She could hear Higgins' faint screams as he ran ever closer to his own grave.

She forced her breathing to slow down, told herself that, for the time being, there was nothing she could do but endure the pain of hanging there, the stark terror of knowing the snake was close by.

Then a movement caught her eye, to her left, near where the torch was propped. Another snake was slithering along the cave floor. He inched his way closer and closer, and her eyes widened in horror as he approached.

He stopped, looked up at her with beady black eyes. She bit down on her tongue, tasted blood, concentrated on the pain and bit harder, harder. She could not, would not scream as the snake's flesh touched her own.

Around and around he moved, warming his cold body on her warm flesh.

She closed her eyes, and then suddenly the movement of his flesh against hers stopped. She opened her eyes again and allowed herself the faintest of movements as she looked down.

The snake had coiled himself around her feet. Mercifully, she fainted.

Chapter Twenty-One

THE screaming whine of the rifle shot reverberated inside the cave, bringing Marilee to sudden consciousness with painful jerks. Horror claimed her and she looked down, willing her body not to move.

A gasp of joy escaped her as she saw the huge reptile lying inches from her feet, its head blown away.

"Hang on, sweetheart. I'll have you down from there in a minute."

She turned her head, daring to hope that this was not a dream. Then she saw the battered face. She cried, "No! No! Oh, my God, Travis! What have they done to you?"

He propped the rifle against the cave wall and pulled a knife from inside his boot. He sliced through the ropes around her ankles and then the ones holding her to the exposed roots above. She collapsed in his arms. "Don't try to move," he cried. "I don't know how long you've been suspended there like that, but you're probably too stiff to walk. Damn. Your wrists are bleeding. Got to get you out of here. This place is a snake pit."

His voice trailed off, but before there was time to wonder what was happening, he had rolled her into the crook of his left arm, holding her tightly as he stooped to pick up his rifle and fire from the hip, all in one flashing movement. There was another snake, now dead, about five feet away.

"He . . . he didn't even rattle," she whispered, slumping against him. He hoisted her up and over his shoulder.

"They don't always play by the rules." He glanced anxiously from side to side as he backed toward the cave entrance.

Once they were outside, Marilee blinked gratefully at the dawning sun. The sky was streaked with pink and purple wisps of clouds, and all around them birds were chorusing praise to God. Silently she praised Him also, for allowing her to live to see the dawn.

Travis placed her gently on a bed of pine needles, then quickly stripped off his shirt and used it to cover her nakedness. Kneeling beside her, he touched her wrists and asked, "Are you hurt anywhere else? Did he do anything to you?"

She knew what he was referring to by the tone of his voice, and the way he averted his eyes. "No," she replied, "but he was about to when the snake bit him."

He nodded. "He's dead. He was still alive when I found him, but he didn't last long. Obviously he'd panicked and run around, causing the poison to spread quickly. He mumbled something about a snake pit in a cave. I've spent some time combing these mountains, so I knew where there was a cave nearby."

She reached to touch him but drew away, afraid she might hurt him. One eye was swollen almost shut, and there was a cut along his cheekbone.

"Don't worry about my face, sweetheart." He smiled. "It might be what attracted the ladies in the beginning, but it's not what kept them coming back."

She could not help laughing. "Only you, Travis Coltrane, could think of such things at a time like this. But are you sure you're going to be all right? And what about Sam?"

"Sam's got a broken leg," he said grimly. "They jumped me in the alley outside my office night before last, then got Sam when he heard the commotion and came running out. They did a good job on us. I woke up in Doc Humboldt's office and realized I'd been unconscious all night and all day, too."

She was bewildered. "But how did you find me?" she cried. "Way out here, and—"

"I think," he said quietly, "it's time we leveled with each other."

She watched as he sat down and crossed his legs, could not help marveling at his handsome chest, bare, muscular, covered with a thick down of black hair that would trail all the way down to . . . She felt the warmth in her face, and hoped he could not tell what she was thinking.

He picked up a pine straw and chewed it thoughtfully for a moment as he stared at her, then drew in his breath and said, "I have known for quite a while now that you were spying on the Klan."

"How?" He had hinted at this before, during their night together.

He continued matter-of-factly. "You passed information along to Willis and others and they confided this to me. I asked them not to let you know that I was aware of what you were doing. You were doing a good job, dangerous though it was, and I figured if I kept you covered, stayed close by, things could continue till I was ready to make my move."

She moaned. "All this time I thought you just weren't doing your job." She shook her head in disbelief. He grinned at that, then continued, "I wasn't aware the Klan was meeting last night. I just wanted to check on things. When I got to the springhouse, Willis was there and told me you'd gone out but had not returned. He was pretty upset. We waited around, and I was about to leave and try to track you down when Israel came and told us what had happened."

"Israel?" she cried. "How did he know?"

Travis laughed softly. "I told you. I had you covered. Israel perched up in a tree and kept an eye on you when you were at the Klan meetings, just in case something happened. He told me the direction they'd taken, so I followed the trail."

"They were after Willis last night," she cried suddenly, remembering. "Did they—"

"No," he assured her quickly. "Israel told us. Willis is safe now. He's going to stay out of sight until I get word to him that everything is all right. I told him it might be a while.

"Anyway," he went on, "I trailed you. I saw Mason coming back, but since you weren't with him, I let him pass without letting him see me. Then I kept tracking till I found Higgins. I knew you had to be close by."

"Then you know Mason is involved?" she asked.

He looked straight at her and said quietly, "I know everyone who is involved, Marilee."

She told herself he could not know about her father. There was no way. And she was not about to tell him, even now. "Mason didn't want to kill me," she explained. "I heard him talking when he thought I was unconscious. He was going to get a Klan group from the western part of the state to take me and keep me prisoner. He said he knew my father would have a search party out combing the mountains for me."

Travis raised an eyebrow. "Does Mason know that you know he is their leader?"

She shook her head no. "He thinks the only Klansman I recognized was Higgins."

"And now Higgins is dead," he murmured thoughtfully. "Then you're in no danger for now. You're going to have to go home and pretend you don't know anything at all. The Klan will, no doubt, change their meeting place, but you won't be slipping in anymore, anyway."

"Higgins tied me up to torture me," she said, hoping that talking it through would help her forget. "He wanted me to tell him who knew about my spying, but I didn't say anything. He got bitten by that snake, and then ran out. Then another snake crawled out and wrapped itself around my feet."

"I know," he interrupted, smiling slightly. "That's how I found you. I was afraid if you woke up suddenly, you'd startle him, and he'd strike. So I shot him," he said simply.

She sat straight up. "You shot him while he was still . . . *coiled* around my feet?"

He nodded. "It was either shoot him or leave you both hanging there, sweetheart," he grinned. "I've got work to do. I can't waste a whole lot of time rescuing damsels in distress."

"Well, thank you, kind sir," she said sarcastically. "You know, I could have been shot, too."

"You weren't," he said simply. "I don't shoot unless I plan to hit what I'm aiming at. You saw the snake."

She could only stare at him in silent wonder as he stretched, muscles flexing tautly in his shoulders and chest. "Now then, I think we'd better get you home. We've got to get some clothes for you, though. Can't have you walking in naked. Tell your father you got thrown by your horse in the storm when lightning scared him. You had to find your way home when your horse ran off. I'll ride you just so far, and you can walk the rest of the way."

"But what about Stewart?"

"I don't consider him a threat just now. And he doesn't consider you one, since he doesn't know you're on to him. He'll go out to check on Higgins and find him dead of snakebite and assume you just managed to escape by yourself."

"But won't he wonder why I'm not telling my father everything?"

He looked at her thoughtfully for a moment, then said, "He'll know that you don't want your father to realize you're on to him."

She gasped, hands flying to her throat. "You know that, too? I wanted to talk to him, to reason with him. You can't arrest my father, Travis."

He took her hands and held them, studying the wounds. "You'll need to say that you got yourself caught in the reins when you fell from your horse. That'll explain these cuts. Fortunately, they aren't serious."

"Travis, you aren't listening to me!" she screamed. "I must save my father from prison and disgrace! You can't ruin it for me now. I won't let you."

He continued to hold her tightly. "Sweetheart, I know how you feel, but I think you already realize it just isn't going to work out the way you want it to. I haven't cracked down on the Klan yet, because I wanted to identify the brains behind it. I'm going to get him, but I want to do it in my own way and have enough evidence to send him away. Your father is a smart man, and he's covered his tracks well. It hasn't been easy to come even this far. I don't want to spoil it all now."

Tears were streaming down her cheeks. "No. I won't let you do this to my father."

"You have no choice," he snapped, then cupped her chin in one hand, forcing her to look directly into his eyes. "Listen to me. It has to be this way. I know you love your father, and your loyalty is admirable. But it's too late. I've too much on him already."

"Why can't you take Mason and the others and leave Father alone?" she cried. "If they're in prison, there won't be enough left to form a Klan."

She stopped as he shook his head. "You know that's not right. Why should they be punished while your father goes free? Hate me if you will, but I can't let him go. And if you warn him, I will still get him. Do you understand me?"

She squeezed her eyes. "I suppose I have to."

"Stop blaming yourself. Your father knew what he was doing all along. He did this to himself."

"And what about Alaina?" she asked pointedly. "You arrest our father, and she will hate you even more than she already does."

"I'm not responsible for Alaina's emotions. I am responsible for upholding the law."

"You made her fall in love with you," she accused. "How can you not care if she hates you?"

"I didn't ask her to fall in love with me."

Suddenly she could not stand any more. It had all been too much—being caught, the snake, finding out that Travis knew about her father. What difference did it make how much he knew? "That first night you stayed at our house, I heard Alaina slip up to your room," she exploded. "And you know I heard the two of you making love down by the springhouse that other night. I know about Willis taking her into town to meet you. So you see, I know what she meant to you. How can you be so callous to say you feel nothing for her?"

"I gave her the only thing I ever promised her," he said simply.

"And what was that?" she cried angrily.

"Satisfaction," he said, not looking away. "She got what she really wanted, which is all her kind of woman wants from a man, anyway. The love and romance is what they tell themselves they want. It gives them the respectability society demands. I call it bullshit. If a man and woman want each other, who says they have to be married . . . or in love . . . or any other damn thing? They should take their pleasure and to hell with what people think."

She took a deep breath, let it out slowly. "I was right. You are a savage, Travis Coltrane."

He sprang forward, clutching her shoulders and pushing her down into the sweet-smelling pine needles, falling on top of her, his lips only inches from hers. With an amused smile he whispered, "So you think me a savage? Well, then, just what does that make you? I seem to recall you enjoyed it when we made love."

"Go on and take me!" she challenged, bitter tears stinging her eyes. "Damn you!" she cried. "Go on and rape me! That's what you do to your women!"

"I don't rape women, damn you," he growled. "I don't have to. And I'll tell you why—because I can make them beg for me. Can you understand that, you conceited little bitch? I never had to force a woman in my life."

His lips crushed down, and she fought to jerk her head from side to side but there was no way to escape. He rolled her to one side, pinning her arms behind her back and holding her tightly with one hand. Despite herself, she responded to his kiss, arching her body toward his. She was already forgetting to hate him.

He raised his lips and whispered, "Say you want me to stop! Call me a savage! Tell me to go away."

She moaned, and he chuckled. He released her arms, and she wrapped them quickly around his back to pull him tighter against her. "Please, Travis, don't stop. I want you."

"But it's wrong to just take our pleasure this way, isn't it?" he mocked. "It's wrong."

Her fingers were digging into his buttocks, pulling him closer. "I don't care about the right or wrong of it, I know only that I want you!"

The hurricane winds of pleasure blew across her body, taking her up and away. Thousands of tiny stars cascaded across her as she bucked against him. It was all things wonderful . . . all things sweet . . . all things forbidden, and she knew then that the sins of the flesh were sweeter than any nectar of the gods.

Travis rode in thoughtful silence, aware that Marilee was holding onto the saddle, not to his waist. She was mad. Okay. She had asked for it. Damn, he hated women who played games of virtue. Now she was angry. What damn difference did it make to him?

A hell of a lot, a little voice deep within admonished him. There was something about her that made him want more of her, and he was frightened by that. The last thing he ever wanted to do was get seriously involved with another woman. He had not meant it to happen with Kitty, but it had happened. Sure, they had enjoyed good times together, but there had been pain along with pleasure. Her reckless love for him was what had driven him to Haiti and set up her own fate with Luke Tate. Had he been there when she needed him, she would still be alive. Little John would have a mother. He would have a wife. Now he had nothing, and it was best, by damn, to keep it that way. "Nothing" demands no responsibilities. He was free. He had to keep it that way.

God, would he ever forget golden-red hair, violet eyes, lips as succulent as strawberries? Would the memory always torment him?

Marilee's voice brought him out of his painful stupor. "We're almost there. Stop and let me signal to one of the field hands to find Rosa."

He reined the horse to a stop and dismounted, helping her down. She watched him crouch down and call softly to someone, and in a few moments one of the Negroes hesitantly approached. He gave him the message, and the Negro scurried off toward the big house.

Travis returned. "He'll have Rosa here in a short while with clothes. I'm going to leave you now. I can't be seen around here. You know what to say and not to say. I know you won't warn your father. You've seen the cruelties of the Klan, and you want them stopped as much as I do."

"When will I hear from you?" she asked. "When do you plan to make your move?"

"I'll decide that after I talk to Sam. Try not to worry. And remember"—he tapped the end of her nose with a fingertip—"no matter what you overhear, no matter what the Klan is planning, stay out of it from now on. Things could get dangerous. You could be killed. They know you've been spying on them, but they aren't sure how much you know. They're going to be watching you. So be careful."

"Don't you tell me what to do," she snapped. "I've gotten along quite well without you hovering over me, Marshal. I didn't need your masculine protection before and I don't need it now."

"Don't get haughty with me, Marilee." He grinned.

He grabbed her and kissed her, long, hard, leaving her breathless. "Let me go!" she cried, struggling in his arms.

"Oh, hell, woman, I'm tired of playing."

He pulled at her shirt, finally getting it off of her. "What are you doing?" she protested, trying to cover her nakedness with her arms. "Give me back that shirt!"

He put it on and began to button it. "What am I supposed to do? Ride into town bare-chested? Now, that would cause some raised eyebrows, wouldn't it?"

"Well, what am I supposed to do? Stand here naked?"

"Hide in the bushes," he replied simply, swinging easily up onto his black stallion once again. "Rosa will be along soon."

She placed her hands on her hips, no longer caring that she was naked. "Thanks, Marshal!" She glowered at him. "Thanks a hell of a lot!"

See?" he cried, reining his horse around. "I knew I could make you say thanks."

He kicked the horse into a gallop. Behind him he could hear her shriek of outrage.

Yes, he told himself, amused, she was one hell of a woman. If he were ever to get involved again, she would be a likely choice. But no. He was free. He wanted to stay free. Marilee was a passing fancy and nothing more.

Once he had told himself that only fools fall in love. Wise men used women, took their pleasure with them, then walked away to freedom without a backward glance. He was determined to stay wise, despite Marilee.

Chapter Twenty-Two

"YO' daddy is fit to be tied!" Rosa declared as she poured another pail of hot water into the tub. "He say if'n you don't hurry up and get downstairs, he's gonna come up heah, and he don't care if'n you are takin' a bath."

Marilee sighed and slipped deeper into the soapsuds. How could she face her father, knowing he might be arrested any minute? How could she pretend nothing was wrong when their whole world was about to collapse?

Suddenly she noticed how nervous Rosa was and asked sharply, "You didn't say anything, did you? About the way you found me?"

Rosa made a face. "You knows me better than that. I told him just what you said to tell him—that you got throwed by yo' horse and got all turned around in the storm and got lost. I didn't tell him you was out there hidin' in the bushes naked as the day you was born!" She sniffed with disapproval, adding spicily, "And you can't tell me you lost yo' clothes in the storm, neither!"

"Rosa, that is none of your business," Marilee just managed to stop herself from shouting. "You just forget all about that, and you better remind the field hands to forget anything they might have seen, too."

"They ain't gonna say nothin'. 'Ceptin' to me. I already knows it was the marshal what called Matthew over and sent him hightailin' it to the house to find me. And I done told Matthew not to dare open his mouth, that ain't nobody supposed to know nothin'—'specially that the marshal was around here." She narrowed her eyes suspiciously as she asked, "Just what was you doin' out there with him naked, anyways?"

"That is none of your business."

Rosa laughed. "That man. He sho' do get around. He keeps it all in the family, though. First Miz Alaina, and then you. And then just the other night, Miz Alaina went to town and—"

Marilee sat up so quickly that the sudsy water spilled onto the floor. "What night?"

Rosa pursed her lips, eyes widening. Had she said the wrong thing, she wondered frantically? Did one sister not know about the other?

"Rosa," Marilee said slowly, "you better start talking. And don't worry about giving Alaina away. I know all about her affair with the marshal. I want to know about her going into town."

Rosa let out her breath in relief, then said, "If'n you knows 'bout the affair, then you oughtta know about Willis takin' her into town to meet him. He did that a couple times, I reckon. But he say night before last that when he brought her back, she cried all the way home. He say she sit in the carriage and carry on somethin' fierce fo' a li'l while, and then she get mad and cuss the marshal. He didn't know what was goin' on, and he won't about to ask. You know what a temper Miz Alaina got."

"That was the night they were attacked," she whispered thoughtfully.

"Yes'm. Everybody's talkin' about the marshals gettin' beat up. Matthew, he say he got a good look at Marshal Coltrane's face, and he was beat up bad. Shame, too. Him bein' so handsome. But he'll get well. And Willis, he say he saw the marshal comin' outta the liv'ry stable after meetin' Miz Alaina, and he was all right then, so he musta got jumped a li'l while later."

"The same night," Marilee mused. Stewart Mason had somehow known that Travis had met Alaina, and it was his way of getting revenge—having him beaten. Sam, too. Stewart wanted to run both men out of town.

She slapped the water with the palm of her hand. Damn the Ku Klux Klan. Damn Alaina for chasing after Travis. Damn him for being unable to resist her. Damn her father for being involved in all this. "Oh, damn them all!" she cried, jumping up to reach for a towel. "I'll be glad when it's over."

"What you talkin' about?" Rosa asked fearfully. "And what you so mad about?"

There was a knock on the door and Marilee snapped, "Never mind me. See who's there. If it's my father, tell him I won't be long, but don't let him in."

Rosa hurried around the brocade dressing screen, and Marilee heard the sound of the door opening, then Alaina's voice as she rushed into the room. "Where is she? I just heard. Oh, my God, thank heavens you're all right!" She came around the screen and embraced Marilee, not caring that she was still wet from her bath. Then she stood back to look at her, eyes shining with tears. "Do you know what a fright you gave us all? Whatever were you doing out there in such wretched weather? You could have been killed."

Marilee patted her shoulder and smiled. "Just calm down, Alaina. I'm fine. There's no need to fret." She took the robe Rosa held out to her.

Alaina turned away, wringing her hands, a worried look on her face as she cried, "What is happening to everyone? You almost get killed in the storm. Daddy is behaving so strangely. And I can't find Willis to slip me into town. Someone said he ran away. I've got to go to Travis. I heard he was beaten." She whirled to face her sister, clutching the front of her pink dressing robe. "Marilee, you've got to help me. Daddy listens to you, because you're so sensible. He won't hear of me going into town, but I must. With Willis missing, there's no one to take me in. Talk to Daddy and tell him I just have to see Travis."

Turning her back, Marilee said quietly, "If Travis wants to see you, Alaina, he will come to you. Have some pride."

"It's not a matter of pride," Alaina wailed desperately. "I have to know he's all right. Can't you understand that he's the only man I've ever truly loved, Marilee? I can't live without him."

She covered her face with her hands, then threw her arms in the air. "How can I expect you to understand? How can I expect anyone to understand? You had to be there to know.

You had to taste his kisses, feel his embrace, or you could never understand how much I love him!"

Marilee said unsteadily, "I can imagine, Alaina, but let me remind you that you have declared yourself to be in love at least a dozen times since you were fourteen. This little romance with Marshal Coltrane is no more important or lasting than any of the others. You'll see."

"I won't see!" Alaina faced Marilee, fists clenched at her sides. "You'll see."

"Then why did he end it?"

Alaina gave her head a toss, sending her curls dancing. "We had a lovers' spat. That happens, you know!" Her eyes narrowed. "But then how would *you* know? You married the only man who ever came to court you. And there hasn't been another. What do you know of romance? Donald never struck me as the kind to set a woman on fire."

Marilee stared out the window, determined not to let Alaina get to her.

Rosa, on the other hand, exploded. "Miz Alaina, that's a terrible thing to say to yo' sister, 'specially after what she went through last night. Lost in the storm. Wanderin' around all night tryin' to find her way home. Now you just hush up that kind of talk. You got a mean tongue."

Alaina lifted her chin. "Perhaps it was mean, but it is true. No one can understand the feelings I have for Travis Coltrane."

"Well, it don't make no never mind," Rosa quickly told her, "'cause yo' daddy done put his foot down and said you ain't seein' him no mo'. And you told me the marshal won't gonna see you no mo'. So you just stop actin' like a baby. You got plenty menfolks what wants to court you without gettin' mixed up with somebody yo' daddy don't like."

Alaina glared at her, furious. "And I thought you were my friend, Rosa."

Rosa shrugged. "Sometimes friends has to tell you when you doin' wrong. I only do it 'cause I love you, and I hate to see you hurt y'self and hurt yo' sister just 'cause you finally run up on a man you can't wrap around yo' little finger."

Alaina sniffed. "Maybe I'll just go ahead and marry Stewart Mason and move out of this wretched house. Then I won't have to put up with either of you anymore."

Marilee could not help but laugh, "You aren't that stupid. Stewart doesn't mean a thing to you. You've only led him along because Father pushed him on you. So why don't we stop all this nonsensical talk and let me get dressed?"

Alaina turned toward the door with a swish of her skirt. "You'll see!" she said tremulously. "Both of you will see!" She left the room, slamming the door behind her.

Marilee reached for the cream-colored taffeta morning dress and pulled it over her head. Soon she was ready to face her father.

He was waiting in his study, tight-lipped and grim. After a quick embrace, he settled into his high-backed leather chair, lit a cigar, and commanded, "All right. Tell me what you were doing out in that blasted storm last night. I want to hear the whole story."

Her heart pounded as she looked at him, struggling to remain calm. Dear Lord, why did he have to be involved in the Klan? Her own father!

His fist pounded the desk, causing her to jump. "Damn it, girl. I'm getting sick and tired of my daughters gallivanting around the countryside at all hours of the night."

She told him the story she had rehearsed, about wanting to get some fresh air before going to bed, about the storm, and about her horse bolting in fear.

"I'm still angry with that stupid nigra, Rosa. Why she waited till almost 3:00 A.M. to wake me and tell me you were gone, I'll never know. Said she fell asleep!" He grunted. "How could she sleep knowing you were out there in that goddamn storm?"

Marilee closed her eyes. Rosa assumed she was still out on Klan business. She had been instructed never, ever to report Marilee missing until the last possible moment. She surmised that, to Rosa, three o'clock in the morning had been the last possible moment.

"It's bad enough," his voice rose, "that Alaina has all the gossips wagging over her little escapades into town at night to see that damned marshal. I don't know what's come over that girl or what kind of power that man holds over her. I've a mind to sic the Klan on him and teach him a lesson. He's a fool if he thinks . . ."

His voice trailed off as he saw the expression on Marilee's face. "What's wrong with you? Why are you looking at me like that?"

She folded her hands in her lap and stared at them. "Could you do that, Father? Could you send the Klan after someone?"

"Well, of course," he replied, sputtering. "I have connections."

"That's what I'm afraid of. Your connections." *Damn,* she cursed herself silently, *why couldn't she keep her mouth shut?*

He bounced back instantly. "What are you talking about? Afraid of what? What are you trying to say?"

She took a deep breath, searched wildly for the right words, then plunged ahead. "I'm afraid you have too many connections, Father. I don't want to see you in trouble."

"Now wait a damn minute!" He rose swiftly from his chair and rushed around the desk to tower above her. She continued to stare down at her clasped hands as he continued his tirade. "I don't know what you're implying, but I will not stand for it. Of course I have connections. I have connections with everything that goes on in this county, perhaps in the whole goddamn state. But that does not mean I am directly involved in, or responsible for, what goes on? Do I make myself clear?"

She squeezed her eyes shut. She had known it would be like this if she ever tried to talk to him about it. Father could not be reasoned with. Not now. Not ever. She whispered, "If the law ever breaks the Klan, and you are involved in the slightest way, you could go to prison."

He chuckled. "Do you think I'm that stupid, girl? Do you think I have become one of the richest and most powerful men in the state of Kentucky by being an idiot? I don't know what has caused you to entertain these worries, but I suggest that—"

Loud pounding on the door interrupted him. Before he could call out, Stewart Mason rushed in. "I heard you found her," he cried, then saw Marilee. His face turned the color of flour. He worked his lips silently for a few seconds before choking out the words, "How . . . how are you?"

It sounded ridiculous, even to her, but she kept her composure despite the loathing she felt for him. "I'm fine, Stewart, thank you."

He looked terrified, and she struggled to restrain a smile as she recounted the same story she had just given her father. "So you see?" she ended brightly. "It was just an unfortunate evening, but thank heavens, I'm all right."

He cocked his head to one side, as though waiting for her to begin screaming the truth. It was obvious his mind was churning with questions. How had she escaped? Where was Tom Higgins? Why was she lying about what had really happened? And most of all, did she know he was involved?

To her father, she said, "I understand that Willis is missing. You don't suppose the Klan had anything to do with his disappearance, do you?"

His lip curled back in a snarl as he shouted, "Don't concern yourself with nigras and keep your nose out of Klan business. Now get out of here. Mason and I have things to discuss."

She stood slowly, blinking. Hurt from his outburst washed over her. He fumbled impatiently with papers on his desk, ignoring her. Stewart watched her every move. Realizing there was nothing to do but leave, she hurried from the study.

But she did not go upstairs. She turned quickly toward the sewing room. Whatever the two were about to discuss, she was determined to hear it.

Once inside the secret passageway, it was with great effort that she forced herself to move slowly, lest there be a sound to expose her. She could hear her father's muffled voice. Little did he know that she stood inside the wall, listening to everything.

". . . time has come to stop him once and for all!" he was saying. "That beating you and the others gave him didn't do a damn bit of good. It only served to make him all the more determined. Now you tell me that Willis disappeared last night, just before the Klan was going to tar and feather him for taking Alaina into town to meet the sonofabitch. That's not good. Not good at all. There's a spy around, and I've got suspicions that Coltrane is behind it all. I've got too much at stake, Mason. So have you."

Mason replied sharply, "Hell, yes. He's turned Alaina's head, taken her away from me."

"He hasn't taken her away, you fool," he said in disgust. "Turned her head a bit, maybe, but he hasn't taken her away, and he won't. I'm tired of his interfering in my business and interfering with my family. I want him dead, Mason!"

Marilee could not suppress her gasp of horror.

"What was that?" her father asked suddenly, alarm in his tone.

"I didn't hear anything." Stewart shrugged. "Hell, I tried to tell you weeks ago we should go ahead and kill him and

Bucher. There's no telling how much they know. I told you Coltrane's been seen slipping around here at night, but I figured he was coming to meet Alaina."

"I think he was. He can't know much or he would have moved by now. But I don't like the way nigras keep escaping. I'm afraid Coltrane knows more than he's letting on. The safest thing to do is kill him and be done with it."

Marilee pressed her hands to her trembling lips. She pressed closer to the wall, swiped at a cobweb, and shuddered as a spider scurried over her hand. No time to be female and scream. Travis had to be warned, and the only way to warn him was to hear their plan.

Bitter bile rose in her throat along with the reality of just how ruthless her father really was. Was this cold man really her father? She forced herself back to their conversation. This was not the time to go to pieces.

She heard her father say, "It must look like an accident. The Klan mustn't be implicated. That would only mean more trouble with the law. It's one thing to kill nigras and another to kill federal marshals."

"What if the niggers kill them?" Stewart said triumphantly.

There was a pause, then, "How do you propose to arrange that?"

"Simple. We think we've located that troublemaker, Munroe. Now, everybody knows what a rabble-rouser he's been. We'll kill Coltrane and Bucher and make it look like Munroe did it. We'll say they were going to arrest Munroe and he shot them. Then some good, God-fearing citizens happened along, and the nigger tried to run, and the good citizens shot him as he was trying to escape. More lawmen come in to investigate, and all they'll do is sympathize with us and our problem with the uppity, trouble-making niggers. It'll make us look good, and we'll be left clean. And no more Coltrane and Bucher."

He sounded quite proud. "Congratulations, Mason. That's about the best idea you've ever come up with. Who knows? One day you just might be smart enough to run things by yourself."

Mason sounded bitter. "Everybody thinks I do already."

"Well, we know different, don't we?" Her father chuckled. "When do you think you can locate this Munroe? I'd like to get them out of the way as soon as possible. I'll rest easier once it's done, and I also won't have to worry about the gossip about Alaina."

"I want that more than you do," Mason snarled. "I'll know by midafternoon if we've got our hands on Munroe. The only thing is, Bucher's got a busted leg and he's laid up. I hate to set things up in town. It's risky. But that's the only way we can get both of 'em."

"No, you fool. That's asking for more trouble. Set it up wherever you locate Munroe. I don't care where that is. Have someone Coltrane won't suspect of being involved get a message to him that the Klan is about to hang a nigra. He'll come running. Then you can ambush him and kill the nigra.

"As for Marshal Bucher," he continued matter-of-factly, "just have someone quietly persuade him to go with them, once Coltrane has headed out of town. When you get him to the scene, shoot him, too. It would be too risky to kill him in town. Of course, all of this is going to take place well after dark."

Good Lord, thought Marilee, how could he sound so methodical, so pitiless? She heard the sound of a cabinet opening, the tinkling of glasses. They were having a drink. She thought of leaving at that very moment to run and warn Travis, but dared not. There might be more. She could not chance missing anything.

"You should have key people in the Klan in public places tonight," her father went on brusquely. "That way, anyone suspected of being involved with the Klan will have an alibi. You are going to have to leave the killings to the 'drones.' That means you can't be involved, either. Make sure you're at the saloon, playing cards. Be sure you are seen by plenty of people."

"Boss, I can't do that. If I take all our leaders and leave the job to the ordinary Klan members, there's sure to be a slipup. Plus, you're involving a lot of people who shouldn't know what's going on. The more who know, the worse the chances of keeping it a secret. Why, some of those stupid bastards would even brag about having a hand in killing the marshals. We can't risk that."

Silence. The sound of her father's sigh. "All right. You will have to do it. I will lock myself here in the study tonight. As soon as it's over, report to me. I will leave a side door unlocked so you can slip in. If anything happens, I will swear that you were with me all evening. But just you make sure nothing goes wrong, damn it," he warned.

"Don't worry," Mason laughed. "I've been looking forward to this too long to make any mistakes."

"Good. Soon all we'll have to worry about is whether or not there actually is a spy within the Klan. I'd hate to think we have neighbors who would betray us."

Marilee drew in her breath and held it. What was Mason thinking at that moment?

"We'll look into that, boss. You can be sure of it," she heard Mason respond. "Right now, let's just get through tonight."

The sound of a rapping on the door startled the men and Jordan called out irritably, "Yes, who is it? I asked that I not be disturbed."

"Sorry, Mistah Barbeau," came Rosa's meek voice, "but they is a man at the back door what says he's got to see Mistah Mason right away."

Marilee had to strain to hear Mason say, "That will be Lonnie Bruce Burnham. He's the one who was checking to see if we located Willis."

"All right," Jordan called out, "bring him in here." Then he lowered his voice once more and said, "I'm going to leave the two of you for a few minutes. Some goods I bought when I was in Paris last spring arrived by train yesterday, and I sent men to town to bring them out by wagon. I need to check on them."

"Sure, boss. Go ahead. I'll talk to Lonnie Bruce."

Marilee heard the study door open and close. Soon she would be able to leave and warn Travis, but not yet. It would be far too risky to attempt to get out of the house now, and she wanted to hear where Munroe was hiding. Travis would need to know.

Marilee waited nervously as the minutes ticked by. Lonnie Bruce and Stewart drank and talked of inconsequential things. As she waited in the musty darkness, she planned her every move. First, she would tell Rosa what was happening. Then . . . Marilee heard the scurrying sound of tiny claws on the wood just above her head. A mouse? A rat? Merciful heaven, and she could do nothing . . . make no sound, or they would hear her. Her father might remember the secret passageway, open the door, and there she would be!

The animal was moving closer, and then something touched her hair, swung down across her forehead. A rat's tail! He was on her head. And he was not moving, just standing on her head.

She dared not move. If she raised her arm to shoo him away, then he might make enough noise to alarm her father. Or he might bite her and then she would lose control and scream.

Concentrate. She ordered her wildly dancing brain to concentrate on something that wasn't there.

Travis. She saw his face. The silver-gray eyes. The shining black hair. He was smiling. Oh, that melting smile. Sometimes arrogant, sometimes teasing.

The rat moved.

Concentrate! Think!

Why did she care for Travis? She silently challenged her pounding heart. What was there about him that thwarted her every attempt to dislike him?

He was splendid. He was glorious. He was afraid of no man, no thing, and he had taught her, mystery of mysteries, what it was like to be a woman.

The rat's tail whipped across her forehead once more, this time tickling the end of her nose.

Recite! She commanded. Slowly, a verse came to her. It reminded her of Travis. In the finishing school in Louisville, she had read the words of Sir Richard Steele, and they had stayed with her, waiting for the day a man would coax them forth.

"Of all affections which attend human life," her heart whispered, "the love of glory is the most ardent."

Love of glory . . . love of splendor. Travis was all those things to her, and she was not going to let that damned rat make her scream and give herself away and thereby cost him his life. "Of all affections . . ." she repeated to herself.

Beyond the wall, she could hear the men talking. There in the dark recess Marilee could only command herself to recite, recite and remember sweetness and passion. Memory took her away to a place where she could hide until the nightmare was over.

Rosa pushed open the door to the sewing room and stepped to the side, making way for the two men carrying the large crate.

"I reckon it'll be all right in here," she said, glancing around the room. "Mistah Barbeau, he say to get it out of the way till he has time to see it's unpacked right. What is it, anyway?"

The man closer to her swore under his breath. "The manifest says it's small marble statues, but it's heavy enough to be marble tombstones. Woman, will you tell us where you want it? We can't keep holding it."

She placed a fingertip against her lips thoughtfully. Miss Marilee came in here sometimes, she knew, and she would not want such a big crate in her way. There was no telling when Mister Barbeau would get around to unpacking it.

"Woman, please!" The second man groaned, staggering under the weight. "You tell us where you want it, or so help me, I'm putting it down right here."

She snapped her fingers suddenly. "There! It won't be in nobody's way right there, no matter how long Mistah Barbeau takes gettin' around to unpackin' it."

She pointed to the spot directly in front of the mirrored door.

Chapter Twenty-Three

IT was midafternoon and hot. No breeze stirred. The streets were deserted.

Travis sat tilted back in the chair, his booted feet propped casually on the windowsill as he stared out into the quiet day. This job had, he reflected, taken much longer than he had anticipated. Gaining the confidence of the Negroes had taken a long time. Then, when the truth began to unfold and he realized just what he was up against, caution had to be exercised.

He shook his head slightly, thinking of Marilee. The woman had guts. Spying on the Klan was something Kitty would have done. He chuckled silently. Only thing was, Kitty would probably have lost her temper and pulled a gun on the Klansmen. Marilee was more reserved. That was all right. No two people were ever alike. And, he reflected with a pang, no woman could ever be just like Kitty.

Sam stirred and Travis turned to see that he was awake, watching him.

"Damn this infernal bed," Sam cursed, striking the air with angry fists. "I want out of here, Coltrane. You go tell that stubborn doctor that I want some crutches so I can get out of here. I ain't got time to lay in no damn bed."

"In due time," Travis murmured quietly, nodding. "You always were an impatient old cuss, Bucher."

"I wasn't always *old*. You didn't used to talk to me like that. You knew I'd bust your head."

"Well, you're the one who's busted now, old friend. We both have seen better days. They gave us quite a going over. I've been wondering why they didn't go on and kill us."

Sam snorted. "You know as well as I do what they were trying to do—scare us into leaving town. Just like you know who they were—Mason and his bunch."

"Oh, yeah, but we can't prove that, can we?"

"Hell, no. They made sure of that. I never knew what hit me. Sonsofbitches. I want a shot at them so damn bad!"

"You may not get your chance, Sam. It looks as though I'm going to have to make a move soon."

He proceeded to tell Sam of how Marilee had been discovered spying on the Klan. "It's just getting too damn dangerous," Travis declared firmly. "What if I hadn't just happened to decide to check on things last night? She said they were planning on sending her to one of the Klan groups in the western part of the state. You and I both know what misery she would have suffered. White slavery!

"I don't have much on Barbeau," Travis said worriedly. "Maybe not enough to convict him. But at least I can bust up what's been going on here. To wait and try to get the goods on Barbeau would be too dangerous for the Negroes here."

Sam nodded thoughtfully, then cried, "I want to go with you. You ain't got no business doing this on your own. There's too many of them. And you'll have to walk right in on them when they're meeting. You're a damned fool if you don't think they'd blow your head off."

"Sam, give me credit for having a little bit of sense, will you?" he grinned at his partner. "I didn't get through the goddamn war by being a hothead, did I?"

Sam grumbled to himself awhile, then waved his hand. "All right. Go on. Tell me the plan. You obviously can do just fine without me and don't give a shit about what I think, but I'm curious. I'd like to know how you plan to pull this off by yourself."

Travis grinned at the crotchety friend who had seen him through so much. "All right," he said finally. "The first thing I've got to do is find out where and when they have a meeting.

They'll change locations now that they know Marilee found out about their old one. I've got about a dozen Negroes staked out in the mountains, keeping an eye on things tonight. They'll be sure to see any gatherings."

"Them are big mountains, Travis."

"These people know those mountains, Sam. And they'll be perched up in the top of tall trees. They can see for miles. When a cross is fired up, they'll see the flames. But I'm hoping they'll know the location of the meeting before that."

Sam snorted. "So you'll just go charging in, eh? Well, I'll tell your boy what a brave fool his daddy was, and I'll go on to Nevada and take care of your silver mine for you. And I promise ever' so often to have a drink just for you." He swung his head from side to side in disgust. "Travis, you're a dead man."

"I asked you to give me a little bit of credit for having some sense, remember?" Travis was enjoying his reaction but decided the game had gone on long enough. "I've deputized twenty of the Negro men. They'll be ready to ride with me when I give the signal."

Sam slapped his good knee and bellowed, "Oh, Lordy, would I love to be there when they go riding in with badges on, totin' guns. Them cowards in their robes and hoods are gonna head for the hills and never come down."

"We'll round up as many as we can. The main thing I want to do is get Mason. He's the one I want. I've a score to settle."

"Break one of his legs for me," Sam grinned. "Damn-a-bear! I want to be there."

"Well, you can't be there." Travis stood, the chair legs hitting the floor with a thud. "You're going to stay right where you are and let that leg start healing proper before you start getting around on it. Once this mess is taken care of, we're going to North Carolina."

"Miss the boy, don't you?" Sam's eyes grew soft. "Me too. I'll bet he's growed a foot by now. Mattie Glass is gonna cry buckets when you take him away from her. She probably thinks he's one of her own by now. But a boy needs to be with his father."

Travis drew a deep breath. "What makes you think I'm going to take him away from Mattie? A boy John's age needs a woman's care."

Sam clasped his hands together, popping the knuckles. "I

reckon if you had a wife you could take him wherever you went."

"A wife!" Travis cried, eyebrows raised. "You beat everything, Sam. Here we are, talking about busting the Klan, and out of the blue you start trying to marry me off. Did you have anybody particular in mind or do you just want to pick somebody off the street?"

Sam plunged bravely on. "I got somebody in mind. So've you, if you'd realized it."

Travis shook his head. "There will never be another Kitty, Sam. I'm not even going to look."

"She's gone. You're here. Life has to go on."

"Seems to me that I've heard that piece of philosophy before."

"Yeah, and you'll hear it again as long as you stay around me. Little John needs a mother."

"So I'm supposed to get married for that reason and that reason alone? Oh, no, my friend. I'm struck with wanderlust. Always have been. I'll see that my son is well cared for, always. But I will not marry someone I don't love just to provide him with a mother. I'm too selfish for that."

"Hell, boy, how do you know you don't love her? Have you thought about her without thinking of Kitty? Without comparing them? Maybe Marilee isn't the raving beauty Kitty was, but Marilee has spunk, courage, spirit—all the things you admired. You might grow to love her if you'll bury Kitty."

Travis strode toward the door. He was becoming angry, and he did not want to lose his temper. Not with Sam. Sam meant well. But Sam also had a way of pushing to the limit. Telling Sam he would check on him later, Travis left and returned to his office.

It was cool in the office. He walked to the desk and sat down to begin going through the work waiting there. Routine matters. Boring. His head began to ache slightly. The doctor had warned him that might happen as a result of the beating. Possible concussion, he had said. It would wear off soon, but when the pain began, it was best to lie down. Travis obliged, moving to the small room adjoining and his narrow cot.

He lay down on his stomach, turning his head to one side. Thoughts of Marilee came to mind. Maybe he shouldn't have teased her, but damn it, she shouldn't have taunted him.

If, he thought drowsily, *if* marriage ever entered his mind again, someone like Marilee would do very nicely. Very nicely indeed.

His eyes closed and he slept.

The sound of the office door opening and closing softly brought him to instant awareness. He reached for his gun, drawing it without a sound. The room was almost totally dark, and he realized that he had slept a long time.

Tense, his eyes remained riveted on the doorway. Suddenly he saw the intruder and cried, "Damn it, Alaina! What in the hell are you doing here?"

He quickly holstered his gun and leaped to his feet as she rushed forward. She threw her arms around him, but he caught her wrists tightly, holding her back.

"I had to see you." She was crying softly. "I heard you were hurt, and I had to find out how you are."

"I'm fine," he said coldly. "Now just turn around and get out of here."

"You can't mean it. Not after all we've been to each other." She struggled in his grasp, tears streaming down her cheeks. "I love you, Travis, and you must love me."

He sighed. "Alaina, listen to me. You don't love me. I don't love you. What we had together was nice, but it's over. I've told you a dozen times that I never promised you anything *except* nice times. That's what we both got, and now it's history."

"It's not history! I don't believe you, Travis."

"Alaina, I never meant to hurt you. You just saw things that weren't there. Now, please, go home. You've caused me enough trouble. Who do you think was behind my being beaten up? Your fiancè!"

"Stewart?" Her eyes widened. "Don't be ridiculous. Stewart would never commit violence," she said primly.

"Well, it doesn't matter what you think. I'll settle with him when the time comes, but I don't need you here provoking the situation in the meantime."

"What makes you think Stewart had anything to do with it? I don't like you spreading lies about him. It's true that I don't love him, but he loves me, and that makes me loyal to him."

"Loyal?" he echoed with a burst of harsh laughter. "You call it being loyal when you made love with me? Oh, Alaina! You really are amazing. Now please, go home."

"I am not leaving until you tell me why you blame Stewart. If he really was behind it, then I will tell my father."

"You won't tell your father a goddamn thing!" His humor faded in a flash. "You'll get out of here right now, or so help me, I'll throw you in jail."

"I must know why you blame Stewart."

"You—" He froze at the sound of the office door opening. "Don't move!" he hissed. "Don't make a sound."

He crept across the room with the stealth of a lion stalking prey, right hand inches from his gun. Just then he saw an old man glancing nervously around the office. "Who are you and what do you want?" Travis called, stepping into the office.

The stranger's eyes bulged fearfully. He reached for his hat with trembling fingers, dropped it, and stooped quickly to retrieve it. He spoke in a high, quivering voice. "Marshal, there's trouble."

"Who are you?" Travis said again.

"Lloyd Perkins. I live out near Blueberry Ridge. I'm a God-fearin' man, Marshal. I'm too old for trouble. Don't like trouble. A man's a human bein', no matter what color his skin."

"Get to the point," Travis said evenly. He judged the old man to be close to seventy. His face was deeply lined, the knotted veins visible through translucent skin. His shoulders were stooped, his hair gray. The eyes were yellowed with weariness and age.

Lloyd Perkins swallowed hard, Adam's apple bouncing. "It's the Klan, Marshal. They're after a young buck nigger named Munroe. He's been hidin' up on Blueberry Ridge for weeks now. His daddy, Israel, been slippin' up there to take him food. The Klan musta spotted Israel. I seen some of 'em, heard 'em talkin'. They're gonna get him tonight."

Travis' eyes narrowed. "Why would a white man like you betray the Klan?"

"I told you," the old man whined. "A man's a human bein' no matter what color his skin, and I don't hold with hurtin' anybody, black or not. The Klan's gonna kill that boy tonight. I just know they are. They been wantin' him for a long time."

That much was so, Travis was certain. Still, he was not completely comfortable with the notion of this man coming to him, not a white man, not here.

"You do what you want!" Lloyd Perkins said suddenly, angrily, yellowed eyes blazing. "I done my part. I'm old, and

I can't take up a gun and fight. You're the law. It's your job. Now I done what I came here to do. I told you the Klan knows where that nigger, Munroe, is hidin' out. If'n you don't want to do somethin' about it, then that's your business. I ain't gettin' involved no more than what I already have. And if you tell anybody I was here, I'll call you a bald-faced liar."

Travis responded coolly. "I mean no offense, Perkins. It just seems a bit odd that a white man would come here. I haven't had much help from white people in this county."

"What reason I got for lyin'?" he bellowed indignantly. "Hell, I never shoulda come here. What's one more dead nigger? I just feel sorry for old Israel. Known him a long time. He loves that boy. Shit, you do what you want to do. I'm gettin' outta here before somebody sees me."

He backed toward the door, placed his hat on his head, and with one final, blazing glare at Travis, walked out.

Travis stared after him thoughtfully. It was strange, but he would have to check the story out. Blueberry Ridge was a half-hour's ride. He returned to the back room and said to Alaina, "Forget you heard any of that. And get out of here and go home. How did you get here, anyway?"

"As if you care," she sniffed. "It's none of your business, but I brought myself. I know how to ride a horse."

"Well, it's dark. Head home at once and make sure you stick to the main road and don't get lost. I've business to take care of."

He went to his desk drawer, took out a box of ammunition, and began to load cartridge slots on his gun belt.

"Are you going to tell me why you said what you did about Stewart?" Alaina asked frostily.

"No. Just get out of here."

"I might just tell him what you said."

"Suit yourself."

He walked to the gun rack, selected a rifle, grabbed up another box of bullets, and walked out without another glance at her.

Alaina stood there a moment, hands on her hips, watching the door. Damn him. He could push her away, accuse Stewart of terrible things, then go running off because someone told him a nigra was in trouble. She laughed out loud. She could have told him that Lloyd Perkins was the biggest nigra-hater in all of Kentucky, but let him find out for himself. It was probably just a prank to lead him on a wild-goose chase. Good enough for Travis Coltrane!

She flounced out of the office and made her way down the alley. A cup of tea at the hotel would be nice. As she walked, she heard her name being called and she saw Sam Bucher leaning out the window of the doctor's house.

"Alaina, come here, please. I need to talk to you."

She sighed and walked over. "Yes, what is it?" she responded. "I'm in a hurry."

"I just saw Travis ride out of town," he called anxiously. "Come up here and tell me where he was going."

She started not to, then decided it might be fun to gloat over Travis being such a fool. Smiling, she hurried inside the house, not bothering to knock. Doc's house was like a hospital, and people came and went all the time to see the patients he bedded there.

At the top of the stairs, she turned to the room at the front, shoving the door open to find Sam next to the bed, hopping on one leg. "You're going to fall, you ninny!" she cried. "I heard your leg is broken."

"It is, but it ain't gonna keep me down," he snapped. "Now, where did Travis go? I saw you coming from down that way and figured you'd been pestering him again. Woman, you are sure a lot of trouble."

"Maybe," she grinned, tilting her head to one side, "but I'm not *stupid*. I don't go chasing out of town because some old fool tells me a silly story."

He looked at her sharply. "What do you mean?"

"Travis is a fool. Lloyd Perkins came and told him that the Klan knows where the nigra Munroe is hiding, and he took off with his guns. I could have told him Lloyd is a nigra-hater. Some say he's in the Klan. He's just playing a trick on Travis, and I say he deserves it after the nasty things he said about my Stewart."

Sam bellowed, "Hand me my boots over there, and my pants."

She blinked in disbelief. "Why? You can't go anywhere."

"The hell I can't. Do as I say."

She handed him his clothes and watched in amusement as he dressed right in front of her.

"Now hand me my holster—over there, and my gun. You're gonna help me down to the livery stable to get a wagon."

"So you're going to go riding off, too," she giggled, enjoying it all. "My, my, no wonder the Klan still does as it pleases. With two ninny marshals like you and Travis—"

"You little fool!" he snapped. "Ain't you got sense enough to see it's a setup? An ambush? If what you say is true, and this Perkins is a Negro-hater, then Travis is walking straight into a trap!"

Her hands flew to her mouth as she squealed, "Oh, my God, no!"

"Oh, yes!" He nodded, hobbling toward the door. "And you could've stopped it if you hadn't been so dadblamed ignorant and stubborn. Now I've got to go to him. Where did he go?"

"Blueberry Ridge. Lloyd Perkins said that nigra, Munroe, is hiding up on Blueberry Ridge. It's about half-hour's ride, I suppose."

"He's got a good ten-minute head start already," Sam said, his brown eyes dark. "Hurry up. Help me downstairs and to the stable."

Struggling beneath his weight, Alaina held on tightly as he threw one arm around her shoulder, and they moved from the room. The stairs were hard and difficult, but Sam bounced along as quickly as one leg would carry him.

Out on the street, he told her, "You go get the wagon. Grab the first one you see. I'll wait here. It'll only take longer if I go with you. Now run, girl, run, and don't tell nobody nothing. No telling who all's in on this."

She took off, lifting her skirts so she could run. Soon she was back with a wagon and a strong brown gelding.

He ordered her to help him up, and, once he was in position, told her to get down and go home.

"I want to go, too," she said with a stubborn set to her chin. "I want to help."

"You've helped enough. I can't take no woman along. It's too dangerous. Get down quick and keep your mouth shut. Go home and pretend nothing's happened. Move!"

When she made no effort to obey, he gave her a rough shove, almost knocking her to the ground. "Damn it, girl, I said move!"

She scrambled to the ground, leaping back out of the way as he whipped the horse into an instant gallop.

She stood there only a moment before going off to find her own horse. If Travis was heading for an ambush, then it was her fault for not telling him her suspicions about Lloyd Perkins. She had to go, to make sure he was all right.

And dear God, she prayed as she hurried along, *let him be all right*.

Through the wall, her father's infuriated voice reached Marilee's ears: "Rosa, where the hell is Marilee? Where is Alaina? What's going on around this damn house?"

"I don't know," Rosa sounded frightened. "Honest, Mastah, I ain't seen Miz Marilee since she first come down this mornin', and the last time I saw Miz Alaina was when she said she was goin' for a ride this afternoon."

"Well, damn it to hell, it's dark outside, and both my daughters are not in this house. I want them found."

Rosa shook her head worriedly and walked into the sewing room. Her mistresses were going to feel the brunt of their father's wrath, she knew, when they showed up. But where were they? Alaina was probably off chasing after that marshal, but it was not like Marilee to disappear without telling Rosa.

Something was going on, too. She could just feel it. Something with the Klan. Whenever Stewart Mason got that glow in his eyes, he was up to something.

She stared at the crate. It would be a while before Master Barbeau got around to doing something about that, she knew. But it was not in the way, and, at the moment, it was the least of her worries.

She turned to leave, then hesitated. What was that sound? It came from nearby, but was muffled. Eyes wide with fright, she stared at the wall. Ghosts? She shook herself, ashamed. Won't no such thing as *ghosts*.

She started out once more, but heard a sound again. It was not her imagination. The crate! Was it coming from the crate? She tiptoed closer, cautiously.

Suddenly she knew it was coming from behind the wall. A little cry escaped her lips, and she backed away.

Marilee threw caution to the wind, "Rosa? Rosa? Is that you?"

Rosa froze. "Who dat?" she whispered fearfully.

Marilee beat on the door. "It's me, Rosa! Me! Let me out!"

Rosa sprang forward, using every bit of strength she could muster to shove the heavy crate to one side. Then she watched, astonished, as the mirror swung outward. A door! The mirror hid a secret door! And Rosa had never known, never even suspected.

Marilee fell into her waiting arms, hair disheveled and hanging limply about her dirty, tear-streaked face. "Something terrible is about to happen. I couldn't use the door to the study because Father's men are still in there. And this was blocking my door."

Marilee straightened, met Rosa's fearful gaze, and whispered, "Please, God, just don't let me be too late."

But as her eyes lifted to the window, seeing the black night, she knew she might be far, far too late to save Travis' life.

Chapter Twenty-Four

THE sound of thundering hooves echoed against the hills surrounding him. Soon, Travis knew, he would have to slow his horse, dismount soon after, and go the rest of the way on foot. Blueberry Ridge was dense with undergrowth of berry bushes and vines, and the trees grew close together. It was a good hiding place for anyone on foot, but no good for riding.

He wished Sam could have come along and knew he was going to be rip-snorting mad when he found out about this later. He also wished there had been time to alert Negro deputies, but if the deputies were doing their job of spying, they would already know what was going on. The idea of facing the whole damn Klan was not appealing but, by God, if he had to do it, he would. He was thoroughly sick of it all, the cowards in their robes and hoods terrorizing Negroes, Alaina chasing after him, and the mixed feelings smoldering within him for Marilee. Sam was right. It was time to move on. Go back to North Carolina and spend some time with John, then head for Nevada.

He thought of the letters he had received from the lawyer handling the operation of his silver mine. It was doing well, damn well. He was on the way to being rich. Sadness descended as he reflected on the irony of it. Being so poor and struggling so hard might have contributed to his getting the wanderlust. Had it not been for that, Kitty would not have plotted to get him to go to Haiti with Sam. And Luke Tate would never have taken her away. He never would have gone to Nevada and never become a rich man because of an inherited silver mine. He wished he were behind that goddamn plow again . . . poor, weary, anything as long as Kitty was alive.

John was all he had left of their love. He wanted to do right by the boy. John was better off where he was, with Mattie Glass. Later, when he got older, Travis could make a home for him.

He pulled back on the reins, slowing the mighty stallion to a walk. A quarter moon, peering down from behind golden-edged clouds, lit the first rising slopes of Blueberry Ridge. Travis knew where Munroe was hiding. Israel had told him about the old shack near a creek. Travis recalled how hard he had tried to convince Israel to get his son to leave Kentucky, or at least leave the area, but Munroe had refused.

Travis rode as far as he dared. Several hundred yards ahead, the ridge would peak. Just beyond, the land would start to slope once again, leading to the creek and the cabin. He dismounted, tied his horse inside a tight clump of hickory trees, then took his rifle and began to move very quietly through the woods.

After about twenty minutes of careful walking, the cabin came into sight. It was dilapidated, leaning precariously to one side as though a good, strong wind would send it into the oblivion it seemed to long for. How anyone had used that for shelter for any length of time was amazing.

Squeezing down on his stomach between two close trees, Travis positioned his rifle, pointing straight at the cabin door. The stupid Klan, he smiled derisively. White sheets would make them perfect targets in the moonlight. All he had to do was wait.

There was no warning.

He was lying there watching the glimmer of moonlight on the grotesque shack when a twig snapped behind him, to his right. He rolled over quickly onto his back, gun pointed, cocked, ready.

But it was too late. He found himself staring up at the leering faces of Stewart Mason and a man whose face he knew.

"Well, we got you, Marshal," Mason crowed. "And you

know what? It wasn't hard at all. We just had to watch and wait, let you settle down all comfy thinking you had us by the balls, and then make our move. Won't half as hard as we thought it'd be. I guess you aren't as smart as I gave you credit for."

Travis felt the fire of fury flow through himself. Goddamn it, this was his own fault. He had walked right into a setup, and had helped things along by being so damned cocky.

They each held a gun on him. He was trapped. Mason's partner snatched his rifle away.

"Don't try anything," Mason warned, reaching to take Travis' gun from his holster and toss it into the bushes. "Now get up off your ass real slow. No sudden moves, or you're dead."

Travis' mind was whirling as he slowly obliged. There had to be a way out. There was no reason to think others were around. Why weren't Mason or his partner wearing their Klan outfits?

Mason snapped, "Now turn around." He gave Travis a nudge with his gun.

Travis grinned. "Well, at least now you're not hiding behind a robe and hood. Where's the rest of your cowardly friends? Am I going to be treated to seeing them face-to-face, too, before you shoot me in the back?"

The other man gave him a rough shove and snarled, "It ain't gonna make no difference, you bastard. Just shut up."

"I'll handle things, Bruce," Mason spoke quickly, angrily. "Shut up and do as I tell you."

To Travis, Mason said, "Turn around and start walking toward the shack, or I'll shoot you right here."

Travis began to walk slowly down the ridge, talking all the while.

"It would seem I've been set up."

"Yeah, and it's worked out just fine. See, me and Lonnie Bruce here, we came out earlier while Lloyd Perkins was in town telling you a story."

"Where is the rest of the Klan?"

"We didn't need them for this. The less who know about this, the better off we are." Mason put a firm hand on Travis' shoulder and stopped him, then stepped to the door ahead of him and pushed it open. Walking a few steps inside, he looked at something Travis could not see and grinned. Reaching for a lantern, Mason pulled a match from his pocket, struck it on the seat of his pants, and in a few seconds the room was filled with a soft, mellow glow. Holding the lantern high, he beckoned Travis inside the shack.

Travis' heart skipped a beat when he saw Israel lying on the floor, wrists and ankles bound tightly together. His yellowed eyes were wide with fear, silently pleading for help. A rag was stuffed in his mouth.

Munroe lay beside his father, also bound and gagged, but there was no terror in his eyes, only rebellious rage. Mumbling against his gag, he struggled frantically. Mason saw what he was doing and gave him a swift kick in the back of his neck. "Stop that, nigger!" he ordered. "We don't need no rope burns to make folks ask questions."

Munroe moaned, dazed by the kick.

Mason turned to Travis. "You see, Marshal, this is what has happened here. This boy"—he pointed to Munroe—"is a known troublemaker. The whole town knows that. Well, he robbed Lloyd Perkins' chicken house tonight. Stole some of his best hens. Lloyd didn't get out there in time to stop him, but he did get a chance to see who it was. He would've shot him, but his old musket misfired."

Mason grinned slowly, evilly. "What happened next was that Perkins rode into town to get you. He, like a lot of other good, God-fearing citizens in these parts, wanted to put a stop to this worthless nigger's stealing. So you rode out here to the shack, where Perkins told you he thought Munroe was holed up. You tried to arrest him, but there was a fight, and you got killed. He was about to get away when Perkins came riding in with some of the neighbors. Good citizen that he is, he got to worrying that Munroe might have other niggers up here, and you'd be riding into an ambush."

He paused to smile down triumphantly at Munroe, who had opened his eyes to stare about dazedly. "Poor Munroe. He was trying to get across the creek and escape. Perkins and the others yelled out for him to stop, give himself up, but he kept on going. They had to shoot him, and he drowned."

Travis knew he must stall for time. "What about Sam? You think he'll believe that?"

Mason and Burnham exchanged snickers, then Mason said, "Sam should be on his way here now. Of course, we had to handle that part carefully. We have someone bringing him in a wagon. It will look like Munroe got him, too. By now, he ought to be dead already."

Mason's words hit him full force, and Travis reacted blindly, lunging for him. Mason anticipated the attack and leaped to one side as Lonnie Bruce slammed his shotgun butt down onto the back of Travis' head. Travis fell to his knees, groaning as needles of fire shot through the base of his skull and down his back. He struggled to stay conscious. *Sam.*

"Now, before I kill you," Mason said calmly, "it would help a whole lot if you told us just how much you know about the Klan."

"Go to hell!" Travis murmured, swaying as he struggled to stand. "No one is going to believe your story. There's someone who knows the truth . . . who knows Perkins told me the Klan was about to get Munroe and never said a word about stealing chickens. One person heard what really happened."

Mason looked at his partner nervously, holding tightly to his gloating smile. "You're lying, Coltrane. Nobody was with you when Perkins talked to you. He's got better sense than that."

It was Travis' turn and he forced a grin, even though the pain across the back of his head was excruciating. "Perkins didn't think about the back room. He didn't know I had . . . a woman back there."

Mason's eyes narrowed and the smile disappeared. "What woman? I still think you're lying." He took a step toward Travis. "You start talking, goddamn you, or I'm going to start chopping up that old nigger over there, bit by bit." He slowly slipped a knife from inside his left boot and held it poised menacingly over Israel's face.

Travis kept his calm appearance. "Tell me, Mason"—he flashed another arrogant grin—"what was the problem between you and Alaina? *I* never had any problem satisfying her. She sure kept coming back for more, just like she did this evening."

Mason's face twisted with rage. "You lying sonofabitch! She wasn't there. Barbeau put a stop to your hounding her."

"She was there, all right," Travis said quietly. "Frankly, I always make it a rule never to talk about my ladies of pleasure, but I couldn't resist letting you know that the one person you can count on not to lie for you if you kill me was listening all the while Perkins was spinning his web."

"Hey, if he is telling the truth," Lonnie Bruce interrupted

worriedly, "then we got problems. Everybody knows she's got quite a yen for him, and when she finds out he's dead and hears the story going around, she's gonna scream to high heaven. You said we wouldn't get the blame for this, Mason. Killing a nigger is one thing, but if somebody fingers me for killing a U.S. marshal—"

"Shut up! Just shut up!" Mason screamed. "He's probably lying. If he isn't, then I'll have to deal with Alaina in my own way."

Travis gave him a big smile. "It looks like your way of dealing with Alaina sent her straight to my bed."

"I'll worry about her later," Mason retorted. "I still think you're lying."

Lonnie Bruce waved his gun and cried, "Come on. Let's get it over with. Go on and kill the nigger."

Mason smiled slowly. "Yeah, let's get on with it. I can't wait to pull the trigger and blast him straight to hell. Keep an eye on him while I drag this nigger outside."

He stepped toward Munroe and Travis said quickly, looking at Israel, "What about him? What's your story going to be when he's found dead, too?"

Mason cracked, "He got in the way of the bullets. Don't you worry about it, Coltrane. You just be thinking about how much you're going to tell me before I finally kill you. I can make it quick and easy, or I can drag it out and let you suffer. It's up to you."

He put the lantern down and reached to cut the rope around Munroe's ankles. Grasping his shoulders, he pulled the Negro to his feet. "Outside," he snarled, giving him a hard shove toward the door.

Munroe stumbled, falling to his knees, and Mason kicked him, cursing. "Get up, damn you," he yelled, "or I'm going to shoot your black ass right here and now."

"Hold it, Mason!" Lonnie Bruce cried, leaping forward to stomp down on Munroe's head, forcing him to lie still. He stared out into the darkness. "Listen! You hear it? Somebody's coming."

Travis saw his chance. He lunged for them both at once, throwing his arms out wide, catching their heads in the crook of his elbows and bringing them crashing together. He drew them apart to slam their heads together one more time. They crumpled to the floor.

Grabbing Mason's knife, he quickly slashed at the rope around Munroe's wrists, freeing him. Travis nodded toward Israel as Munroe jerked the gag from his mouth. "Untie him," Travis said quickly. "Then you two get the hell out of here."

"But what 'bout you, Marshal? They gonna get you fo' sho'," Munroe cried as he hurried to untie his father.

Travis reached for Lonnie Bruce's gun. "Not without a fight, they won't."

"Ain't gonna be no fight!"

Travis froze at the sight of Sam framed in the doorway, Lloyd Perkins beside him, holding a shotgun pressed into Sam's stomach. Lloyd grinned. "Naw, there ain't gonna be no fight. It's a damn good thing I decided to ride on out here and watch the fun. Caught this big bastard tryin' to make it through the woods on a busted leg. Just drop that gun, Marshal."

Travis did. "And you, nigger." He waved his shotgun at Munroe. "You just drop that knife and back up against that wall yonder. Ain't nobody goin' nowhere. Soon as they come around, we're gonna get on with it."

At Perkins' feet, Mason moaned, stirred, and lifted his head a few inches from the floor.

"Come on, Mason," Lloyd said. "Get up."

Travis did not fail to notice the frenzy in his voice. Lloyd Perkins was an old man and not at all confident that he could handle the situation alone. Good.

Travis looked at Sam, who barely met his gaze. Sam was ashamed. He thought he had failed. "How'd you know what was going on?" Travis asked him quietly.

"Alaina," Sam answered dully. "I saw you ride out of town, and she passed by, and I asked her where you were going. Damn it, I knew I wasn't going to be much help with this damn leg, but I had to try."

"You didn't know anyone would be hanging around watching. Don't blame yourself. I'm the one who walked into a trap, and it's no one's fault but my own that they slipped up behind me."

As he spoke, Travis was trying to send Sam messages with his eyes, darting his glance to Lloyd, who was slowly letting his guard down as he focused his attention on trying to wake Mason.

Quickly, Sam understood what Travis had in mind. Sam was supporting himself on a crooked stick, holding his weight off his broken leg. It was an awkward position, as old Perkins was balancing on the side of his makeshift crutch.

Travis nodded, signaling Sam slowly, and right then Sam made his move, lifting his arm off the supporting stick and giving Lloyd a vicious shove that sent him reeling to land on top of Mason and Lonnie Bruce. But the movement had knocked Sam off balance, and he fell forward to sprawl helplessly on top of the others.

Mason came alive, screaming with rage. He grabbed for Lloyd's gun as all of the men thrashed about wildly. Travis had grabbed his own gun, but did not fire for fear of hitting Sam.

"Move, Sam," Travis yelled. "Get out of the way."

Sam groaned in pain as he tried to move on his injured leg.

Suddenly Mason came up out of the melee, raising his arm to fire. Travis knew he was taking a big chance, but there was no other way. He fired, striking Mason squarely between the eyes. He was so close to Sam that blood splashed onto his partner's face.

Travis fired again, this time hitting Lonnie Bruce in the chest.

Lloyd Perkins screamed, flinging his arms above his head. "Don't shoot! Don't kill me! I lived too long to die like that. Please, please, don't shoot!"

Sam slapped him, sending him sliding across the floor. "Get the hell out of my way!" he roared, reaching for his homemade crutch. "Damn old fool! We wouldn't waste a damn bullet on your wrinkled old hide."

Travis laughed. There weren't that many years between the two, but Sam was grizzled and tough, and that made the difference.

Travis walked over and helped Sam to his feet, then turned to Munroe, who had quickly finished untying Israel. "You two all right?"

"Yassuh!" Munroe shouted gratefully. "We gonna be just fine. You done saved both our lives. Praise the Lord!"

He turned to Sam. "How bad did you hurt your leg? You may have messed it up good."

Sam shook his head. "It hurts like hell, but it'll be all right. Don't worry about me. What's going to happen now?"

"Munroe won't have to worry about the Klan anymore. I don't think anyone will. It's over. At least in these parts. With him dead," he nodded at Mason's lifeless body, "that leaves just the big boss. I'll get you back to the doc's, and then I'll go pick him up."

"You think you've got enough to send him away?" Sam asked skeptically. "Influence and money could save his hide."

"I'm well aware of that, but at least we can put him out of business."

"There's more," Sam said quickly, giving Lloyd Perkins a black look. "He told me about the plan as we came through the woods. He said I saved them the trouble of coming after me. Hadn't we better be on the lookout for the ones who *were* going to bring me out here? When they find out I'm already gone, they're liable to come riding out here."

"I doubt it," Travis said, shaking his head. "We aren't going to hang around here, anyway."

Perkins was watching him with wide, fearful eyes. "You gonna kill me, Marshal?" he cried suddenly, tears spilling from his veined eyes. "You wouldn't shoot an old man in cold blood, would you? I wasn't gonna kill you. I was just bluffin' . . . waitin' for Mason to get up. You know I wouldn't kill nobody."

Travis blinked thoughtfully. "Tell you what, Perkins." He walked over and hunched down beside him, propping his elbows on his knees as he pressed his hands together. "You did a very serious thing when you set up a U.S. marshal to be murdered. You're in a lot of trouble. I'm not going to kill you, but while you're rotting in jail for the rest of your life, I imagine you're going to wish a thousand times over that I had."

Lloyd Perkins swung his head from side to side, crying harder, his whole body convulsing. "No. No. You wouldn't do that to an old man."

Travis stared at him without blinking. "Now, what makes you think not, Perkins? After all, you knew you were setting me up to be killed when you walked into my office with your lies. And when you saw Bucher slipping in to try to save me, you drew a gun on him and brought him here knowing full well Mason would kill him, too. So why should I show you any pity?"

Lloyd covered his face with gnarled hands. "Have mercy," he sobbed. "Don't do what I did. Have mercy!"

Travis sighed and pulled the old man's hands away from his face. "Perkins, I'm going to give you a break. You're old. I wouldn't like to send you to prison to die. With Mason dead, the big leader of the Klan about to be arrested, the real power of the Klan is gone. You would be no threat to anyone if I just let you get up and walk out of here."

Lloyd's eyes bulged hopefully. He started to get up, but Travis easily pushed him back.

"Don't be in such a hurry," Travis snapped. "You aren't leaving here unless you tell me the name of everyone you know who is a member of the Klan."

Lloyd gasped in horror. "They'd kill me. They'd figure who told when I went free. I can't do that."

"You can," Travis nodded confidently. "And you will. I will also expect you to testify that you know for a fact that they are members. They are going to jail, and they won't be around to bother you. You can leave here, take a new name, disappear. That's up to you. But I promise you one thing, Perkins. You don't cooperate with me, and you'll die in prison. Make up your mind."

Lloyd glanced from Travis to Sam with growing desperation. Sam was watching silently, expressionless, from just inside the doorway. Munroe was grinning, enjoying Perkins' predicament. Israel listened in silence, still shaken from his ordeal.

Perkins' eyes went back to Travis'. Perkins swallowed hard and said in a croaking voice, "All right. I'll tell you what I know. But you gotta protect me. You can't let them kill me." He was nearly hysterical.

"Start talking," Travis ordered.

Lloyd began to name names, slowly at first, and then words were toppling out on top of each other and he cried, "That's it. That's all I can remember. If I think of more later, I'll tell you. Just let me go. Let me get out of here and go hide. Everybody is gonna know it was me what talked. You gotta let me go."

Travis stood. "All right, leave. But—"

He was interrupted by Sam's urgent cry, "Somebody's coming, Travis." He pointed his gun into the woods beyond the shack. Then a startled look appeared on his craggy face. "Well, I'll be damned. She did follow me."

Travis rushed across the narrow room, cursing at the sight of Alaina atop the horse, long hair flying in the wind.

Munroe came forward, holding the lantern as she reined to a quick stop and slid quickly to the ground. "You're all right!"

she cried, throwing herself against Travis' chest, face flushed, eyes sparkling. "Thank God! Thank God Sam got here in time!"

She fell silent as she saw the blood, shiny in the lantern's glow.

She moved away from Travis, and he let her go. Better to let her find out right then, he figured, find out and get it over with.

She stepped inside the doorway, and he watched as she covered her face with trembling hands. Her scream pierced the night. Throwing herself to her knees, she ran her hand over Stewart Mason's lifeless body.

"No!" she shrieked, leaping up to run to Travis. "No! No!" Her fingers arched to claws as she attacked his face. He grabbed her wrists but not before he felt the painful ripping of his flesh beneath her pointed nails.

"You killed him, you bastard! You goddamn bastard! You killed him! Killed him!"

Travis gave her a rough shake, then slapped her sharply. She staggered backward, and he grabbed her wrists and pinned them together behind her back. "Listen to me, woman. I had no choice. He was going to kill me. Now get hold of yourself."

When a moment passed without her making any effort to attack, he released her. "It's time we all got out of here," he said. Then to Sam he said, "Let Munroe help you get back to town. Israel can go along with you. Just stay there till I get back. Since Alaina and I will be heading in the same direction, we can go together."

"What do you mean by that?" Alaina hissed.

He ignored her, speaking to Lloyd Perkins, who was sneaking around the corner of the shack, trying to disappear. "Go home, Perkins," he called. "Don't say anything about tonight to anybody, hear? I'll send someone for the bodies tomorrow."

Perkins made no answer as he moved swiftly, disappearing into the night.

Munroe supported Sam as they began walking into the woods, carrying the lantern.

"I'm not going anywhere with you," Alaina said, beginning to sob. "I loved him! I never knew it till now, but I loved him. And I'm not going to leave him here like this. I hate you, Travis Coltrane. I'll see you dead for this."

Suddenly Travis realized he'd had more than enough. He

pointed his finger at her and bellowed, "Damn it, Alaina, you do whatever the hell you want to. Stay here and cry over Mason's worthless body. Get home any way you can."

He turned and began walking away in long, angry strides.

"And where do you think you're going?" she cried in a high-pitched voice. "You just killed the man I love, and now you think you can just walk away?"

He whirled around. "I think you've got it wrong, Alaina. I killed the only man who loved *you,* and now you realize that. Even a bastard like Mason was better than nothing, wasn't he?"

"Liar!" she screamed. "You goddamned cowardly liar. You loved me, too. You couldn't have done what you did if you hadn't loved me."

Turning, Travis walked as fast as the underbrush would allow, making for his horse. He would ride out of there . . . even out of the state if he could.

He was sick of Kentucky.

He was sick of fighting.

He was sick of women like Alaina Barbeau.

Why—his voice broke as he whispered into the ethereal darkness—*why, Kitty, did you have to die?*

Chapter Twenty-Five

HE had made a mistake that night that had almost gotten him killed. Travis Coltrane was not about to make another.

His senses alert, he reined up his horse quickly and slid from the saddle. Pistol in one hand, rifle in the other, he dove into a thick bramble of blueberry bushes and waited. Obediently, his horse trotted for cover.

Travis did not know what had made him do that. Perhaps it was just nerves.

Then he heard it, the steady clip-clopping of hooves. Distant, but headed toward him. Listening intently, he decided there was one horse, one rider. Raising to his knees, he aimed both weapons at the road and waited, both gun hammers cocked. But in a second his keen eye caught the hint of long, flowing hair.

A woman.

With a deep sigh of relief, Travis stood. He waved his arms over his head and stepped out into the open road. Marilee jerked the horse to a halt.

"Travis," she gasped, stunned and overjoyed.

He reached up to clasp strong hands around her waist and set her on the ground. "What in hell are you doing out here?"

Quickly, she told him all of it. "I came as soon as I could," she finished raggedly, exhausted from the frantic ride. "Thank God, you're all right. Tell me quickly what happened."

He did, finishing quietly, "I'm on way now to arrest your father and get it over with. Don't try to stop me. I understand how terrible this is for you, but he—"

She pressed a fingertip against his lips. "No," she whispered tremulously, "don't tell me what he has done. I know only too well. But don't put it into words. Do what you have to do."

She tried to step back, but he held her firmly. "Marilee, listen to me," he whispered huskily. "I admire what you have done. And you weren't doing it just for your father. I admire your courage. I can imagine how all of this has hurt you. But please remember that it was all his choice and his doing. No one forced him. He has a great deal to answer for."

She bowed her head. "I know. And I'm glad it's over. But if only I'd gotten there in time tonight, maybe no one would be dead. It's time all the horror ended."

"It may end here, for now," he told her quietly, "but the hatred will continue long after you and I are dead, Marilee. We can only do our part to make some kind of peace while we walk the earth."

Cupping her chin in his large hand, he forced her to meet his gaze as he murmured softly, "There's something else."

Her smile was sad. "I think I can take anything now. Tell me."

He took a deep, slow breath, wondering fleetingly why he felt the need to tell her just then. "I didn't know until now just how much you mean to me. I want you to know I'll miss you . . . and I'll never forget you."

She cocked her head to one side, forcing a smile. "Like I always try to tell you, Coltrane, no moment can last forever. This one won't either. You'll forget all about me. What we had together, you've had a hundred times before with a hundred different women. Who knows how many more the future holds for you?"

Something snapped deep within Travis Coltrane. He jerked her roughly against his chest, arms holding her tightly.

His lips crushed hers and his tongue slipped inside her mouth. He felt the shuddering sigh of her submission. Her arms entwined him, pulling him closer.

After a little while, they moved apart. This was not their time.

Travis whistled and his horse came trotting out. When he and she were mounted and riding side by side, he stole a sideways glance at her and saw the deeply thoughtful expression on her face. Funny, he thought, how people change . . . or maybe you really don't see them at first. He had once thought her drab. Now he knew that, far from drab, she was surpassed by only one woman.

That woman was dead.

They rode the rest of the way in silence, lost in their separate thoughts, until at last they approached the house, ablaze with light. A groomsman standing in the driveway saw them and signaled frantically to someone standing on the porch. In a few seconds, Jordan Barbeau appeared in the doorway.

As he reined to a stop at the gate, Travis looked up and saw Barbeau's anger. Well, he thought, the man was going to get a hell of a lot madder before the night was over.

As Marilee's feet touched the ground, and she turned toward him, Travis gazed deeply into her mellow brown eyes. He took her arm and began to lead her up the wide marble stairs.

Travis nodded curtly. "Barbeau. Good evening."

Jordan's face was grim, his cheeks flecked with red. "I don't think it's a good evening at all, Marshal," he snapped, then turned to Marilee. "Just where in hell have you been? How dare you ride out alone after dark? And where is Alaina? I would appreciate someone telling me what is going on in my own house!"

Travis pointed at the door and said, "Let's step inside and get this over with."

"Marilee, go to your room!" Jordan yelled as they entered the mansion. "I will speak to you later."

"No." Travis kept a firm hand on her arm. "She stays. She wants to hear everything said between us and I have agreed. Let's go into your study."

Jordan's eyebrows shot up. "You dare to tell me what to do in my own home, Marshal? I think you forget your place."

Travis sighed, his hand moving from Marilee's arm to a ready position inches from his holster. The action was slow, deliberate. Jordan's eyes widened. "Just what in hell is going on? What's this all about?"

Travis responded quickly, "I haven't forgotten my place,

Barbeau. I am a U.S. marshal, and you're under arrest."

Jordan laughed. "What kind of prank are you playing, Coltrane? I've been worried to death over my daughters, and I assure you I have no time for foolishness."

"You know it's not foolishness. You know very well why I'm here." He gave Jordan an impatient nudge toward the study. "Get on in there unless you want to put on a show for the servants."

They stepped inside and Travis kicked the door shut behind the three of them. "Alaina should be here soon. She stayed behind with the bodies. Stewart Mason and his sidekick are dead."

Jordan went white. He made a croaking sound, twisting his head from side to side, staring at Travis. "Mason?"

Travis grinned humorlessly. "You thought you had everything too well planned for that, didn't you? I guess it is hard for you to believe your right-hand man was killed after you had *me* all set up for that." He paused, upper lip curling back in a deadly snarl. "An ambush to have me killed!"

Travis gave Jordan a rough shove toward his desk and yelled, "Get over there and sit down and don't make any funny moves or you'll be burning in hell with Mason."

Jordan stumbled, righted himself, and hurried to sink down into the brown leather chair behind the desk. He wiped nervous hands across his face, body quivering.

Travis walked over to the shelf where bottles and glasses were set out and poured himself a drink. "It's over, Barbeau. I know all about how you've called the shots for the Klan, how Mason carried out your orders. I know you planned for me to die tonight . . . me *and* Sam." He picked up the whiskey bottle and set it down on the desk with a thud. "I think this will do you more good right now than a gentleman's brandy."

Jordan stared at the bottle, then lifted red-rimmed eyes to his daughter. "You *knew?*" he asked hoarsely. "You knew about . . . the Klan?"

She nodded wordlessly. "Meet your spy, Barbeau," Travis said. "Meet the one who's been masquerading as a Klansman, slipping into the meetings, and then riding out to warn victims. No telling how many Negroes are alive tonight, thanks to her."

"You?" Jordan gasped, swaying in his chair. "You did that? You're the spy?"

She nodded. "The night of the storm, when I told you I was

thrown from my horse and got lost, I was actually discovered by one of the Klansmen. Tom Higgins hit me. They thought I was knocked out. I overheard Mason telling them they had to get rid of me, but he didn't want me dead." She paused, Travis gave her a sip of the sour mash as Jordan looked on in horror. Then she spoke again, telling of Mason's plan to have another Klan group take her away, and of how that was foiled when Higgins died and Travis rescued her.

"God, no." Jordan slammed his fist on the desk. "To think Mason was going to do that. No! Not to my daughter!"

Suddenly he stopped and looked up at her sharply. "How were you able to know about our activities?"

She lifted misty eyes to Travis, who nodded. Pointing to the bookcase, she whispered, "The secret passageway. There. Behind that wall. From there to the sewing room. I discovered it by accident one day and overheard you talking to Stewart, planning a meeting. I was shocked and hurt, but I couldn't turn you in. I decided the best I could do was to try to thwart your plans."

"That's right," Travis interrupted, sensing how close she was to a breaking point. "She's your spy, but she never gave you away. The only way I found out about it was when some of the Negroes came to me for help. They were afraid for her, afraid the Klan was getting suspicious."

He gave Jordan a look of contempt. "God only knows what hell this girl has been through trying to protect you."

Jordan's words were barely audible as he stared at her. "I would rather be in my grave than hear that my own daughter spied on me, that you denounce what I was trying to do for you, for all of Kentucky. I had to try to stop it. The white man was meant to have supremacy!"

"But you ordered *Travis* killed, Father! I could pity you for your ignorance in trying to preserve your way of life, but Travis is white! Where would you have stopped?" She took a step forward and waved her arms wildly. "That's what you felt, wasn't it? No one must interfere with your wishes."

Jordan pointed a shaking finger at her. "You say you spied on me but you wouldn't turn me in. You think that makes you loyal?" His voice rose. "You would have been loyal to warn me. But this lecherous bastard lured you to his bed and turned your head. He did it with you and your sister."

Travis stepped forward as Marilee backed away in horror,

her hands covering her face. "That's enough, Barbeau!" he yelled.

Suddenly a scream filled the room. "What he says is true, damn you to everlasting hell!"

All eyes went to to door. Alaina stood there, her face a grotesque mask of hatred. In her hands she held a shotgun pointed straight at Travis. "You did lure me to your bed," she whispered quietly, ominously. "You're evil, Travis Coltrane. You are evil, and you must die . . . just as Stewart died."

"No!" Jordan screamed, throwing himself across the desk just as Travis shoved Marilee to one side and hurled himself to the floor.

The gun exploded. Alaina fell backward from the recoil, landing on the floor, screaming.

Jordan Barbeau slumped across the desk unconscious, blood gushing from what was left of his right arm.

Alaina fainted.

Marilee ran forward, crying, "Father! Father! No! No!" as Travis got to his feet and ran to lift Jordan and place him gently on the floor. "Get a blanket!" Travis cried. "Send someone for a doctor. Get me a rag. Anything. I've got to try to stop the bleeding or he'll bleed to death!"

As Marilee leaped quickly across her unconscious sister, Travis marveled at her ability to function at a time when other women would have done just what Alaina had—passed out.

He placed his ear against Jordan's chest, heard his heartbeat and knew he was still alive. A hasty examination told Travis what he had guessed. The right arm was blown away almost to his shoulder. Had Travis not leaped to the side, he would have caught the rest of the blast.

For the second time that night, Travis Coltrane wondered why he had been spared.

Chapter Twenty-Six

TRAVIS sat behind his desk, cleaning his gun for want of anything else to do. At the sound of the office door opening, he glanced up casually. A clean-shaven young man walked in carrying a rifle. He wore a badge on his tan buckskin vest.

"Marshal Coltrane?" he asked, leaning across the desk to extend his hand, "I'm Welby Abbott. I'm to be your replacement."

"Yeah, I know." Travis shook his hand, then continued cleaning his gun. "Marshal Bucher should be hobbling in here any minute. He went by the doc's to have his leg checked. Pull up a chair and sit down."

Welby looked around and saw only one other chair in the sparsely furnished office. Dragging it across the room, he decided the place was terribly drab. He did not like the location, either, tucked back in an alley. He would investigate the possibility of relocating as soon as possible.

"You don't like the office."

Welby looked up in surprise. "How'd you know what I was thinking, Coltrane?"

"You better learn to look at a man and know what he's thinking, Abbott, or you won't live to see thirty. How old are you, anyway?"

"Twenty-six," the younger man replied with a defiant lift of his chin.

Travis nodded.

Welby propped his rifle against the wall and sat down. He watched Travis for a moment, then asked, "How soon do you plan to leave? I was told you were anxious to be on your way to—where is it? Nevada?"

"I'll get there sooner or later. The first place I'm headed is to see my son. If I had my way, I'd ride out of this place as soon as Bucher gets back, but we'll wait till morning and get a fresh start."

Welby laughed. "It's that bad here, eh?"

"Not now it isn't. I've just got a lot of bad memories. Besides, I've been sitting around twiddling my thumbs for two months since it all ended . . . waiting for the grand jury hearings."

Welby snorted. "That was a farce, wasn't it? Who would have thought Barbeau would get off?"

"I'm not surprised." Travis shrugged. "The only man who could really testify that Barbeau did indeed run the Klan is dead. Barbeau's daughter wouldn't testify against him, not after his other daughter blew his arm off and nearly killed him."

"I heard she meant to kill you."

Travis threw him a grin. "She did."

Welby scratched his blond head. "Well, I still don't think he should have gone free."

"He's not free. He'll be in his own prison for the rest of his life. His right arm is gone. His good name is also gone. The important thing is that the Klan is dead around here, I'm sure of that."

Travis continued to work on his gun, and when several moments of silence had passed, Welby attempted conversation once more. "I hear you've got a big silver mine in Nevada. Are you going to turn in your badge? I figured a man with your reputation would never be able to give up being a lawman."

Travis did not respond.

Welby leaned forward, eyes shining with excitement. "If I were older and more experienced, like you, I'll bet I could be sent someplace where there's some action. It'll be dull as hell here now 'cause you've cleaned everything up.

"I'll bet," he rushed on, "I could even be sent to California.

Things are busting wide open out there, what with the 'Yellow Peril' and all."

Travis paused and looked at him. "What are you talking about?" he asked quietly.

Welby grinned, glad he had finally found something to interest the famous Travis Coltrane. "The Chinese," he explained eagerly. "You know how they've been coming over in droves. They work cheap. Railroad building out West has brought in a bunch of coolies, but now there's too many of them. They're taking jobs away from white men, and the white men are accusing employers of bringing the coolies in to hold wages down.

"There's all kinds of violence because of it," he continued. "Why, one night a mob hanged twenty-three Chinese."

Travis sighed, gave his pistol one last swipe with a rag, and returned it to his holster. "I wonder," he mused, "if I will ever see peace in my lifetime. If it's not Negroes it's Chinese. God, will it ever stop?" He leaned back in his chair and folded his arms behind his head. "No, Abbot. I won't be going to California to look for excitement. I'm going to look for peace. I may not find it, but I'm damn well going to search for it."

Welby dropped his voice, a sympathetic expression taking over his face. "I heard you've been through a lot, Marshal. I hope you do find some happiness."

Travis flashed him a wry grin. "Didn't say I was looking for happiness. Just some peace."

The door opened then and Munroe walked in, grinning broadly. "Marshal! How you doin'?" he greeted him, holding out his hand. "I swear it's gonna be an awful time around here when you leave. Me and my people, we can't stand the thought of you goin'."

"Well, you'd better learn to stand it fast," Travis told him quickly. "I'll be leaving tomorrow. This is your new marshal, Welby Abbott." To Welby he said, "This is Munroe, and if you ever need a job done, call on him. He's a good man."

They shook hands, then Travis asked, "What brings you into town? I thought Barbeau had given you a good-paying job that was keeping you real busy. Part of his way of reforming."

Munroe grinned, head bobbing up and down. "He did. I got a fine job now. He even lets me live on the place, and my daddy, too. But he let me off to ride into town to bring you a message. He heard the new marshal was comin', and he said he didn't want you leavin' without talkin' to him. He said for me to come ask you would you ride out to the house and have dinner with him tonight?"

Travis started to say no, but Munroe rushed on quickly, "And Miz Alaina, she say she gonna talk to you before you leaves. She say if you don't come hear what she got to say, then she gonna come to town. She's waitin' fo' me to get back and tell her what you said, 'cause if you ain't comin', then she say she gonna make me bring her back to town to see you."

Travis thought for a minute. He had not spoken with Alaina since the night she shot her father. She had not showed up at the grand jury hearings. Marilee had not been there, either, but he had gone out to see her. She had been coolly withdrawn, and he had made up his mind to leave Kentucky without seeing her again.

"What do they want to see me about, Munroe?"

Munroe smiled, gesturing helplessly. "I don't know. Things is different out there, Marshal. Mastah Barbeau, he ain't the same. He been saved. You didn't know that, did you? The parson, he come to the house one night . . . at least that's what Rosa told me. She say the parson come and he prayed with Mastah Barbeau, and Mastah Barbeau, he give his life to the Lord. Rosa say he a changed man, a good man. She say she hears him in his study cryin' lots of nights.

"And Miz Alaina"—he paused to take a deep breath before rushing on—"Rosa say she changed, too. She got saved, too, you see. And she hates herself fo' blowin' her daddy's arm off, and Rosa say she hates herself worse for meanin' to blow your head off."

Travis could not help glancing at Welby.

Munroe saw the looks they exchanged and his smile faded. "Now don't you all go to makin' fun o' me. I knows what I talkin' about, 'cause Rosa told me, and Rosa knows evahthin' what goes on in that house. You come on out there tonight and see fo' yo'self that evahbody has changed," he finished indignantly.

Munroe began to tap his foot impatiently. "Well, you just make up yo' mind. Now Rosa, she'd be tickled to death to see you. And Willis. You made lots o' friends around here, Marshal, and it ain't right you should just ride off and not say good-bye. How come you won't come on out and eat just one meal with Mastah Barbeau?" He paused to give Travis a piercing look. "Sho', he sinned," he said quietly, pointedly, "but if the Lord Jesus can fo'give him, how come you can't?"

"Your Lord Jesus is in the business of forgiving," Travis snapped. "That's not my job."

Munroe looked aghast. "Why . . . why, that's . . . that's blas'my! The Good Book say to fo'give yo' enemy, and that's just what you gotta do."

"I don't *gotta* do anything, Munroe." Just then there was a sound at the door, and Travis glanced up to see Sam fumbling with the latch. Travis quickly jumped to his feet, swinging the door open and holding it back so Sam could hobble through on his crudely carved crutches.

Sam nodded to Munroe, then spotted the stranger wearing the familiar badge, and a grin spread across Sam's bearded face. "Well, well!" he cried, lowering himself into the chair Travis had vacated. "You must be the new marshal. Good! That means we can be on our way first thing tomorrow."

"Welby Abbott," Travis made the introductions. "Abbott, Sam Bucher."

Welby stepped forward to clasp the older man's hand. "I've heard a lot of good things about you men. My job will be easy, thanks to the one you two did here."

Sam snorted. "I don't know about that. There will still be those who want to make trouble, both whites and coloreds, and—" He paused, looking at Munroe. "What's the matter? What are you doing here? Don't tell me something's happened."

Munroe quickly explained while Travis turned his back on them to stare at the wall.

"I's goin' now," Munroe finished. "And I gonna tell the truth. That Marshal Coltrane just didn't wanna come. And Miz Alaina, she be here soon. She got somethin' she wants to say, and she seems mighty set to say it."

Sam rolled his eyes. "Goddamn it, Travis! Do you have to be so stubborn? Why don't you ride out there and see what everybody wants so that woman won't come charging in here?"

Travis whirled on him, eyes narrowed. "I have nothing to say to any of them."

"Even to Marilee? Don't you want to say good-bye to her?" Sam asked harshly.

Suddenly Welby Abbott could restrain himself no longer.

He laughed and said, "I've heard what a ladies' man you are, Coltrane. Go on and ride out to say good-bye to the ladies and leave broken hearts. I can take care of things here. I've never been one to stand in the way of romance." His voice trailed off as he caught the look on Travis' face.

Munroe stepped back toward the door, wanting to get out of the way.

Sam muttered, "Oh, hell!" under his breath and shook his head.

In a tightly restrained voice, Travis said, "Abbott, the only reason I'm not rearranging your teeth is because you don't know any better. Just keep your mouth out of my business. And anything you may have heard about me, you can keep quiet about too."

"I . . . I'm sorry," Welby whispered, swallowing hard. "I was just trying to be friendly."

"Sometimes that can get you killed."

Travis sat opposite Jordan Barbeau in the familiar study, sipping brandy, puffing on a cigar, and wishing the moment would end. He still had to speak with Alaina, had not seen Marilee, and time was passing very slowly.

"So I have seen the folly of my ways," Jordan was saying, "I asked the Lord to forgive me, to teach me to love my fellow man and regard him as a brother, no matter what color his skin. And if I can live with myself now, then I don't care what other people think of me, Marshal. I've got peace with the Lord."

He cocked his head to the right, indicating his missing arm, his coat sleeve carefully pinned under the stump just inches from his shoulder. "This is what I hate most of all," he said emotionally. "Not for my sake. I consider this a penance for my transgressions. It's for Alaina that I regret it. She hasn't forgiven herself, and I don't think she ever will. It's a terrible thing to look at your father every day, see him maimed, and know you are responsible. I love her dearly, but I will be glad for her to marry and move away so she will not be tortured by looking at me."

Travis downed the rest of his brandy, grateful for the opening. "Speaking of Alaina," he said quickly, "I understand she wanted to see me, and I do need to be on my way back to town soon."

"Of course, of course." With his left hand, Jordan picked up a tiny silver bell from his desk and gave it a jingle. "I appreciate your taking the time to ride out here, Marshal. I wanted to make sure there was peace between you and me."

Travis held up his hands. "Everything is fine between us, Barbeau. It's over as far as I'm concerned. Now if I could speak to Alaina . . ."

The door opened and Willis appeared, pausing to flash a friendly smile at Travis before addressing himself to Jordan, "Sir, you wanted something?"

"The marshal would like to speak with Miss Alaina."

"She's waitin' in the settin' room."

Travis rose and walked to clasp Jordan's remaining hand. "I'll say good-bye then. Good luck with your new life." He turned and walked swiftly from the room, not giving the other man time to make further conversation.

Alaina was sitting on a red velvet sofa, staring pensively into the fireplace. When Travis entered the room, Willis closed the door softly behind him, leaving them alone.

She rose, brows furrowed in worry. How would he receive her? She pressed her palms together beneath her bosom, which spilled provocatively from the daring cut of her white taffeta gown. Travis' eyes swept over her appreciatively. She was still one hell of a beautiful woman.

Her face was haloed by the sweeping brush of her long, flowing light brown hair, and the emerald eyes she lifted to him were moist as she whispered, "Do you hate me, Travis?"

"No," he said shortly, walking across the room to stand before the fire. She followed his every movement. "I don't hate you, Alaina. You were hysterical that night to the point of insanity. But if you hadn't missed," he added with a sardonic smile, "I probably would."

She tried to smile also but instead lowered her face to her hands and burst into tears. He made no move to comfort her. This was her business, not his.

After a few moments, she regained her composure. "I love you," she said quietly, surely. "Only you. If I had killed you, then I would have taken my own life. You're the only man I have ever truly loved, Travis."

She took a step forward, gesturing pleadingly. "If you will only give me a chance to prove what I feel for you, Travis, you'll realize—"

"No!" He held up his hands to fend her off, his expression grim. "No more, Alaina. You're a beautiful woman. You have everything a man could desire. But I desire you only in bed. That's not the kind of love a man and woman should share for long. There has to be more."

Her face twisted. "There can be more. I'll make more."

"No!" he repeated sharply, an edge to his voice. "I don't love you, Alaina. I never have and never will. I'm not trying to hurt you, but I have to be honest."

She started to speak, but he quickly covered her lips with gentle fingers. "Don't say more," he said softly, kindly. "You will only regret it later. I don't like taking a woman's pride any more than I like her tossing it aside. Let's part friends."

She drew in her breath, closed her eyes, and nodded. He removed his fingertips and murmured, "I wish you well, Alaina. I regret much of what happened. Don't look back. Just go on from here. You'll meet someone else."

"No one like you," she choked, fighting to hold back the tears. "No one ever like you, Travis Coltrane."

He chuckled softly and smiled, "One day you may give thanks for that."

"No hard feelings?" she asked, desperately wanting reassurance. "I have enough to live with, knowing I caused my father to lose an arm. I don't want to think you hate me."

He touched her cheek in a gentle caress. "No, Alaina. I don't hate you."

He turned to leave without another word.

He opened the door and stepped outside, closing it quickly behind him, hearing her sobs but not turning back.

Willis was standing in the foyer.

Travis took his hand, squeezed it in good-bye, then asked, "Would you tell Miss Marilee I would like to speak to her before I go?"

Willis looked apologetic. "She left 'fore you ever got here, Marshal. When she heard you was comin', she just walked out. I don't know where she was goin'. You want me to give her a message?"

Travis shook his head. He believed he knew where she had

gone. Forcing his voice to be bright, he slapped Willis on the shoulder and said, "Take care of yourself and your people."

Travis left the house, taking the marble stairs three at a time. Mounting his black horse quickly, he headed down the driveway, headed into the night and towards destiny.

He spurred the horse into a gallop, wanting to hurry, wanting to put as much as distance as possible between himself and whatever force was drawing him back.

His horse slowed, finally coming to a stop. Travis stared straight ahead, immobile. Why? Why had he not gone charging ahead?

Because . . . a voice called, echoing from within the deepest recesses of himself . . . *destiny sometimes lies behind.*

Reining the horse around, he found he knew exactly where he was going. It took him only moments to get there.

She was bathed in moonlight, her face sparkling with starlight. She was sitting on the grassy slope leading from the springhouse, wearing a simple dress of blue muslin. Her legs were doubled, chin resting on her knees, a melancholy look on her lovely face, her fingers interlaced around a wild flower. Pressing her nose against the gentle yellow petals, she inhaled the sweet fragrance, staring into the blue velvet cloak of night that surrounded her.

Her lips trembled as she pursed them to kiss the flower.

"You have me to do that for you." The husky voice startled her. He knelt, pressed his lips against hers, then moved back, smiling. "Flowers don't kiss back, sweetheart. I do."

Her voice was so gentle he could barely hear her. "Why have you come here?"

He sat down beside her and reached to push a strand of chestnut hair back from her face. "Because I knew you would be here. I asked to see you at the house, but Willis said you ran out when you knew I was coming. Why?"

She glanced away. "I couldn't bear to see you again."

"Why?" he demanded tersely. "Why couldn't you see me? Did you want me to go away without saying good-bye? Is that all we meant to each other?"

"I have no illusions." She met his gaze boldly. "What is one more good-bye to a man like you?"

"I think," he murmured thoughtfully, "there are things you should know about me, about why I can never love another woman."

"You don't have to tell me," she said. "I know. I talked to Sam. He told me about Kitty."

He felt himself go tense. "When did you talk to Sam?"

"It's been weeks ago. I went to see him. I felt there was something I should know. It seemed there was. Don't be angry with him, Travis. He's your friend. He did me a great favor, because after he told me everything, I knew that I could mean only one thing to you." Suddenly she clasped the bodice of her blue dress and ripped it down.

He gasped. Her bare breasts gleamed in the moonlight. He lightly touched the firm, warm mounds. "My body," she whispered, "is all you will allow me to give you. So take it, Travis. It's yours. Let me give you this, at least, and I will treasure tonight for as long as I live."

She began crying, her body trembling as she undressed him, then pulled off her dress. She lay down, naked on the grass, the moonlight on her naked body.

He stared down at her in wonder, but there was no time for pondering. Her thighs were parting. She was positioning herself beneath him, placing her hands on his hips, then pulling him toward her.

"Take me, Travis," she commanded. "Right or wrong, I love you and I want you. I must have this moment."

She began to cry harder. He thrust himself against her, entering, and then her tears stopped and she wrapped her arms around him, pulling him closer, hugging him with all her might.

He held her around the waist, felt her legs touching his back. He drove into her hard, knowing she was eager. There was no yesterday or today or tomorrow, only that moment, and he would give her all he had to give.

He felt her nails clawing his back, saw her arching as she lifted higher, meeting his every thrust. Again and again he plunged.

He felt himself coming into her, could not wait to see if she was ready, then felt her teeth sink into his hard shoulder.

They took each other to that magnificent peak, riding the wind to the stars. There was no glory but this. And as she screamed his name, he knew that a part of him had crept from the grave. Not his heart, perhaps, but something like it. And if that was his only escape from the grave, then so be it.

Afterward, he held her for a long, long time without speaking. Gradually, the night sounds returned to them . . . an owl hooting, a bobcat wailing. A breeze shook the leaves above, danced through the grass around them.

After a long time, he spoke.

"I came because I had to see you, Marilee. I think I wanted to tell you what Sam had already told you. I wanted you to know about Kitty, the great love we shared."

He released her and sat up, staring straight ahead into the woods. Damn, he had sworn it would never happen again. But it had. Not as intense, of course. No, never that intense.

He looked at her and saw that she was watching him. "I'm leaving in the morning, going to North Carolina to see my son. Then I'm heading for Nevada."

"I wish you well," she murmured, glancing away. "Sam says you have a fine son. He needs his father. I hope you take him to Nevada with you."

"He's just a little boy. He can't go shuttling across the country without a woman to take care of him."

"Then you will leave him behind," she snapped. "You can't keep running, Travis."

"Remember what you said once?" he sounded surprised and there was a stunned expression on his face. "About how no moment can last forever?"

She nodded, smiling sadly. "Yes."

"No moment can last forever," he said, more to himself than to her. "So we just have to make more moments."

She stared at him, her eyes devouring him.

He pulled her into the strong circle of his arms. "I'm asking you to make more moments with me, Marilee," he whispered huskily. "Go with me. Be my woman. Be a mother to my son.

"I'm asking"—he paused to take a deep breath—"I'm asking you to be my wife."

She began to cry again, hating herself for the show of weakness. Flinging herself against his broad chest, she held to him tightly. To release her hold could mean the end of the dream.

He laughed and gave her a quick shake. "Hey! Does this mean you're saying yes?"

She nodded, fighting the impulse to scream her joy. "Yes, Travis. Oh, yes, yes, yes."

He got to his feet and pulled her along with him. He kissed her there in the moonlight and held her for a long, long time before they dressed, preparing to face the future together.

And Marilee told herself it would have to be enough. She

could not ask that he love her . . . could not be downcast because he did not.

All she *could* ask for, she told her furiously beating heart, were more moments. It would, she promised herself, be enough.

Chapter Twenty-Seven

AROUND him the bank was alive, a beehive. He stood by the window, staring out. To his left and across the street, he could see the four-storied Virginia City Hotel. Soon, he thought with satisfaction, he would no longer call a hotel his home. He wanted a better life for his son . . . and his wife.

His wife.

Travis took a deep breath and let it out slowly. Even after four months it was still hard to realize that he was married. The best thing about the marriage was the way John and Marilee had taken to one another. Marilee had said John was the kind of little boy a woman couldn't help but want for her own. Travis smiled with pride as he thought of his five-year-old son. He was quite a little man. His hair was black, like his father's, and his eyes were the same deep gray.

Mattie Glass had been more than good to the child who was not her own. John seemed undisturbed by his father's long absence, though ecstatically happy to have him back again. Travis had arrived at a good time, for Mattie Glass had found a new husband, and while Thomas Petula had vowed he would take care of the boy until Travis returned, it was not fair to ask the newlyweds to keep John. Besides, Travis had missed him terribly.

Travis swallowed hard, suddenly reflecting on how, looking into the boy's steady gaze he could somehow see the woman who still held his heart.

He forced himself back to the present and Marilee. Was it such a bad life for her? he wondered. Hell, he was good to her. With the money that had been piling up from his silver mine, there was nothing he could not buy her. As for affection, well . . . maybe he didn't say all the things she would've liked, but he had never been the romantic kind.

The fires of passion had dwindled a little. He took her less and less frequently and he could hear her crying in the night sometimes. What could he say to her? He was tired. There was a lot of business. Wasn't that why? There were no other women. And as long as there were no other women, then he felt she had no real complaint coming.

He tensed, recalling the night when she had shyly asked him if he had ever tired of Kitty. Too much liquor had made his response cruel. "What I had with Kitty is none of your goddamn business!"

He had fallen asleep to the sound of her broken sobs, and the next morning felt rotten. They made love slowly, tenderly, and he made sure she was pleasured not once, not twice, but three times before he let her go. She had seemed happy, content that there was, after all, a place for her in his life. But since that night when he had lashed out at her, there had often been a shadow in her smile. He had resolved never to be so brutal again.

It was about then, he realized, that she had begun to get involved in the new world around her. One day he had returned from his mine to find her in a rage over what she called "the unforgivable Indian situation." He had listened to her rant about the government, no one seemed to care whether the Indian children were educated or not. A week later she informed him with a "don't you say a word" look that she had gone to the Indian agent and gotten permission to start a school for Indian children on the outskirts of town in an abandoned Mormon Mission.

He had stared at her silently, incredulous as she talked excitedly of her plans. He decided that after all, it was good. It would give her something to do. Travis shook his head slowly, thoughtfully. He had thought many times that it might have been best for Marilee if he had not married her. Maybe that was true. He just didn't know.

There had been no time for a honeymoon before the newlyweds and Sam left for North Carolina. But Marilee had been good-natured about it, saying how many women could tell their grandchildren they honeymooned with two men?

Sam had been in good spirits, too, till the night Travis drank too much. The next day Sam got him way away from Marilee and raised hell. "You're a goddamn fool if you think I'm going to stand by and watch you mistreat that woman!" Sam roared. "Damn it, I know you don't love her like you loved Kitty, but you can't treat her like she's just somebody to have around when you feel like it.

"And you got a son to look after. You've got an obligation to John and to your new wife. So don't start grubbing in booze again. Get on with your life."

If anyone else had talked to him in such a way, Travis would probably have killed him on the spot. But Sam was Sam. And he was also right.

Travis' eyes narrowed resentfully as he continued to stare at the hotel. Marilee liked it just fine there. They had a fancy suite with two bedrooms, a parlor, and a dining room. The decor was exquisite—furniture imported from France, carpets from the Orient, oil paintings, velvet and lace drapes, every luxury a woman could want. There was even a separate dressing room with an ornate porcelain tub. The pull of a bell cord brought a maid with buckets of hot water, bath salts, and thick, thirsty towels.

Food was brought in just as easily, delicacies of every kind. The sumptuous meals were placed on the table with wine and fresh flowers, then removed discreetly later.

There was also someone to collect their laundry and bring it back washed and pressed, just as maids cleaned their dwelling each day and changed their sheets and made their beds.

It was, he knew, the kind of life Marilee had always been used to, and he was glad he could afford it. But things were going to change. He was sick of feeling like he lived in someone else's home. He wanted a real home—a house and land. Lots of land. And he wanted cattle, sheep, horses . . . a place where John could grow up without being cramped.

After today, Travis smiled to himself, that place would be

a reality. It was his surprise. He had picked out the land, a thousand acres bordering the Carson River. It was a perfect place for raising animals, with lots of grass and water. And the house was already there. Oh, not much of a house, not yet, just a two-room cabin. About a week of repair work, and it would be good as new. He would have a little kitchen built on. And later, when the barns were built, and the storage sheds, and the cattle and sheep herds were well established, there would be time to start building a new house. He would let Marilee have whatever she wanted.

Right now all he wanted to do was get the hell out of Virginia City and into the peaceful plains and buttes of Nevada. He couldn't wait to tell Marilee what he'd done. He looked around and saw Sam pushing his way through the people.

"I been looking all over for you, Travis," he called. "Thank God I tracked you down."

"What's the problem?" Travis sighed.

"Accident at the mine."

He came alive at once. "Tell me! How bad?"

Sam held up his hands. "Hold on. It's not that bad. Goddamn cave-in. Nobody's dead, but Horace Rigby, one of the new workers we hired last week, got hit when a beam collapsed. I just come from the hospital. They're checking him out now. He'll probably be all right. Maybe some broken bones." He paused, chest heaving, then rushed on. "What I came to find you for is to tell you we need to get back out there and oversee the laying of a new tunnel. We've got to get some support beams put up quick in the one that collapsed. Otherwise we could have another cave-in. If we dig a new tunnel into the old one, we've got to hit it in just the right place or it's going to be dangerous as hell. You studied the maps Odom made when he laid the place out. So you've got to be out there when they start the new dig. I've borrowed some men from Sacks' mine, and I sent somebody over to Youngblood's place to see if he'll loan us a crew. We need to get on this right away."

"Aw, hell!"

"Travis, there ain't time for you to get riled. What if this had happened when we was back in Kentucky? You're the only one who knows the layout of the way Odom dug that mine, and you've got to get your ass out there."

"Can it wait a little while?" he asked quietly. "I've got business to tend to here, with the bank."

Sam hesitated, then said, "An hour. No more. I'm going to get some things we'll need, and I'll wait for you at the hotel. But hurry, Travis."

He rushed out.

Fifteen minutes later, the old Latford place paid for, Travis tucked the deed in the inside of his brown leather coat and left the bank. He was going to tell Marilee.

When he entered their suite, he found her sitting on the floor of the parlor, papers and books scattered all around her. She flashed him a big grin and said, "I'm so glad you're home early, Travis. I want to show you these materials that arrived today all the way from Boston. They are just what I need for the children! The latest history books . . ." Her voice trailed off as she saw the strange way he was looking at her. She scrambled to her feet and ran to slip her arms around his neck.

He pushed her aside gently and walked over to seat himself on the sofa, patting the place next to him. "Come here. There's something I've got to tell you. It's good news. And I hope you're going to be just half as happy as I am."

She hurried over, heaving a sigh of relief. "Thank heavens it's not anything bad. Really, Travis, you have a funny way of bringing good tidings." She laughed and kissed his cheek, then withdrew as she realized he was still being guarded.

Taking the deed from his coat, he handed it to her without a word. Slowly, almost hesitantly, she took it from him, unfolded the crisp sheets, and began to read it. He watched as her eyebrows raised, lips parted slightly, and then she gave a little cry and stared at him in horror before exclaiming, "Travis, why did you buy land so far from town? I mean, this is on the Carson River. That's a good way below us, and you'll have a long way to travel to keep an eye on things. Goodness"—she paused to laugh nervously—"it's bad enough that you have to travel back and forth so far to the mine, and—"

"Marilee, listen to me!" He spoke sternly yet gently, for he knew she had already guessed the truth but was not willing to accept it. "The land is up near Silver Springs. And that is a long way from here. Too far for me to travel just to 'keep an eye on things,' as you say. I didn't buy this land to keep an eye on it, anyway. I bought it to live on."

"Live on?" she echoed, stunned.

"Me, you, and John. There's a cabin on it now, and I'm having it fixed up. We should be able to move there next week.

Later we'll think about a house. A nice house. As big as you want. The main thing is to get out of this hotel."

She rose to her feet stiffly, face set, brown eyes flashing like red coals. "You can't do this to me, Travis," she said, unwavering. "I came with you all the way out here to this . . . this wilderness. I left everything I've ever known behind me. You never knew how miserable I was."

"Marilee, listen to me." He stood and reached for her, but she jerked away, giving him a look so furious that for an instant he was shocked into silence.

"No!" she hissed. "You listen to me. I never told you how miserable I was. How homesick. I love you. I love your son. I think of him now as *our* son. I have tried to be a mother to him. I have tried to be a wife to you, even though you refuse to forget another woman. *God knows I have tried!*"

She clenched her fists, took a deep breath, and rushed on. "I finally found something that gave *me* happiness, real happiness. The Indian school. They need me as much as I need them. You can't take that away from me. You can't make me move miles away to live on some godforsaken wilderness just because you feel smothered by town, smothered by society, smothered by decorum, and—"

"Marilee, stop it!" He grabbed her shoulders and shook her. When she was quiet he made his voice gentle. "This is for the best, believe me. Virginia City is no place to raise a child. A hotel is no place for a family. We are not going to a wilderness. We're going to an empire, an empire that you and I are going to build together. We will have hands to help with the livestock. We'll have servants to work in the house. There will be people around us. It won't be a wilderness. All we've got to do is get out there and work."

"The school . . ." she moaned, swaying.

"Hell, Marilee!" He was losing patience fast. "Start another school out there. There are Indians all over the place."

"I love some of these children."

"You will learn to love others just as much." He stepped away, running his fingers through his thick black hair. Whirling, he cried, "Damn it, woman, you're my wife. You're going to do as I say. And I don't have time to argue with you about it anymore."

Her eyes sparkled once more, and he knew sadness was being covered by anger. "You don't have any regard for my feelings at all, do you?" she said in a deadly voice. "And what about John? Have you asked him how he feels about moving so far out? Leaving his friends? He loves it here as much as I do, and it isn't fair to keep uprooting him. He needs a home."

"I'm building one for him. And for you, too," he cried. Damn it, he hated it when he felt himself getting this mad. He knew all too well the consequences of losing his temper. He squeezed his eyes shut, reminding himself that there was, after all, no point in arguing. The decision had been made. The land was his. He was going.

His eyes flashed open. He stared at her thoughtfully for several moments, then murmured, "You don't like it here, Marilee. You have never been happy as my wife."

"Yes, I've been happy as your wife," she spoke up quickly, making a move toward him. Then she checked herself. Clasping her hands at her bosom she said cautiously, "Even though I know I live with a ghost and always will."

A nerve jumped in his face. "You knew that when you married me."

"You might have tried a little harder, Travis. I found out all too soon that there was no love for me in your cold heart. You find things in me to admire. You enjoy my body—perhaps not as much as before, but you find satisfaction with me. Other than that, you feel nothing for me."

He cocked his head to one side, as though understanding all of this for the first time. "You really believe what you're saying?"

She nodded. "I also fulfilled a need for your son."

"You have been a good mother to him, Marilee," he said readily. "I can't fault you for a thing."

Her smile was sad. "Except that I'm not Kitty. And you'll never love *me*. You'll never care about *my* wants."

Suddenly he faced her with the look of a man who has finally come to terms with himself. Taking a deep breath, he said with finality, "I think you should go home, Marilee. I think we should get a divorce."

"Divorce?" she echoed, hands moving to clutch her throat. "But why, Travis? Because I don't want to move to the desert or give up teaching the children? I don't understand."

"I can't make you happy, Marilee. Not the way you deserve to be. And I don't like seeing you miserable."

"I... I haven't been miserable," she whispered softly. "I

have loved you with all my heart, Travis . . . the way I have prayed you would one day love me. You can't want a divorce." She began to shiver but he didn't see it. He stared down at the carpet for a long time before looking up again.

He gestured at her. "Look at you. You don't look healthy. You're pale, sickly. Look at what this life is doing to you.

"As for John," he went on, feeling like a heartless bastard but unable to help himself, "in time, he'll understand. Maybe in the summer he can visit you."

Without quite looking at him she whispered painfully, "This is what you really want? For me to leave you?"

Suddenly he knelt before her, both hands reaching to clasp her hands in his. "No," he answered honestly, "it isn't. I care for you. But I don't want to hurt you."

She bit down on her lower lip, forced her eyes to meet his unwaveringly. Taking a deep breath, she said, "I am not leaving you, Travis. I will not divorce you. I will give up the school and move to the desert with you, and I will continue to do my best to make you happy. But I will not leave you. Not now. Not ever."

He knew she meant every word. With a deep sigh, he got to his feet and walked over to the window. It was not, he knew now, ever going to work out. He would spend the rest of his life worrying over his inability to love her, fearing she was being hurt, always unable to do anything about it. But she had said she would not leave, and he could hardly force her. But damn it to hell, where did all this leave him?

He realized she was speaking. Very slowly he turned, head tilted slightly as he realized that he had heard her correctly.

"I'm going to have your baby," she repeated.

Outside the door, Sam stood, rigid. He had been about to knock, but had heard them fighting.

He shook his head from side to side and struggled against the horror rising within him.

Marilee was going to have a baby. Dear God in heaven, how could he go ahead and tell Travis what he had just found out? He couldn't. He turned away. He could not tell his friend. He would have to carry the heartbreaking secret all by himself. It was, he told himself sternly, the only way.

Chapter Twenty-Eight

TRAVIS glanced over at Sam as they rode out of town to the mine site, clouds of dust swirling around the horses' hooves. Sam did not look well. "You sick?" Travis called out.

"Hell, no," Sam retorted, staring straight ahead.

"Something's wrong. Did the doctor give you a bad report on Rigby?"

Sam winced. "He's going to be okay. A few broken ribs. Plenty of bruises. A few cuts. He was lucky."

"Then what is it?"

"Nothing. I'm worried about getting that new shaft dug."

Travis continued to stare at him. He had known Sam too long not to know when there was something eating him. "Sam, what in hell is going on?" he asked sharply. "I know there's something."

Sam kicked his horse, moving him into a faster gait, but Travis kept up. "Will you slow down?" he cried, annoyed. "It's too hot to run these horses like this."

Sam slowed, but only a little.

"Marilee is going to have a baby."

Sam nodded.

Suddenly, Travis reined to a sharp halt. Damn it, what was wrong with the man? He waited until Sam realized he was no longer beside him and stopped.

Travis kneed his horse to a trot. "You didn't say a goddamn word. Now just what the hell is going on, Sam? Something is wrong, and I want to know what."

Sam took a deep breath. He could not, would not, tell him. "I'm just worried about what happened at the mine," he lied. "I also overheard you telling Marilee you wanted a divorce. I was about to knock when I heard you yelling, and I guess I just eavesdropped. I'm sorry."

Travis shrugged. "I would have told you sooner or later. I do think we'd be better off if we went our separate ways. It was a mistake and it's worse for her than for me. But it's too late now. If she's going to have my baby, then that settles everything. I'll just have to try harder to make things work out."

"Didn't you love her at all?" Sam suddenly exploded, and Travis stared, aghast. "I thought you did. Hell, I knew you'd never care for her the way you did Kitty, but I was sure you felt something. If she hadn't told she was in the family way, would you have kicked her out?"

"I don't like putting it that way, Sam," Travis said, shaking his head. "I would have sent her back to Kentucky. She's wealthy, but I would never have let her lack for anything. As for loving her—no, I don't. I never will. I care for her, respect her, admire her. That's as far as it goes. Being the mother of my child will naturally cause me to feel something more. But love? No."

Sam's eyes narrowed. "Are you happy about the baby?"

Travis had not really thought about it. He nodded slowly as he began to let it sink in. "Yeah, I am, Sam. I never thought of myself as a family man, but I love John and I will love another child just as much. Maybe now that I think about it, it happened for the best. Marilee deserves better, but I'll just try to treat her better.

"One thing is for certain," he continued fiercely. "I'm not going to hurt her or let her be hurt. No matter what happens."

No matter what happens. Sam mouthed the words silently to himself.

"We better get moving," he said gruffly. "I guess I was just worried about you two."

Travis smiled. "No need to worry. Everything is going to be fine. I'm going to build her a mansion on that land, Sam. Now let's go take care of the trouble at the mine."

They rode on in silence. As they reached the site, a worker charged out to meet them, a horrified look on his face. "Coltrane, there was another cave-in," he cried. "Just now. About ten more feet are gone. One more and the whole dig's gonna go."

The site came alive. Travis took off his shirt, grabbed a pick, and started slinging it along with all the others. Time moved with maddening slowness. Now and then they stopped for water, to gasp for a little air. Then they started in again.

Soon it was dark and they worked by lanterns. Dirty, sweating workers appeared ghostly in the light, as though working to dig a grave large enough for all. Support beams were placed, hastily but carefully, as work progressed digging a tunnel into the earth.

Hours later Travis turned at the sound of a wagon approaching. He blinked in disbelief at the sight of Marilee struggling with the reins of the team of horses, her eyes like black coals as her face was struck by lantern lights.

"What in the hell are you doing here?" he called, throwing his pick aside and walking swiftly over. "I've never known you to drive a team of horses."

"Don't fuss at me, Travis," she smiled, nodding toward the two women beside her. "We knew you all would be hungry, so we've brought food. Sandwiches. Soup. Coffee."

He reached to clasp her waist and set her down on the ground, pausing to kiss her forehead and give her a grin. "You're amazing, you know that, woman? But you shouldn't have done it."

She laughed, her pale face coloring. "You can scold me later. Right now we're going to set up this food and feed everyone."

Walking to the rear of the wagon, she turned and gave him an impish grin. "I'll make a pioneer woman yet, Travis Coltrane. Just you wait and see."

He laughed. Maybe, he thought, suddenly elated, everything would work out for them. She loved him and he liked her, and damn it, that was better than nothing.

He turned back to his work, much encouraged.

A half hour had passed when Marilee urged him to go and

eat. "Everyone else has finished. I've saved plenty for you, but the soup and coffee are going to get cold. Sam hasn't eaten, either."

"Find Sam," he said between gasps and swings of the pick. "We'll take a break and eat together so we can talk about our progress so far."

She walked away but came back just a few moments later, looking worried. "I can't find Sam, Travis, and no one has seen him lately."

He threw his pick aside and went over to where Gilbert Sacks stood sipping coffee from a tin mug. "You seen Bucher?"

Sacks nodded toward the old shaft. "He went in about a half hour ago, I guess. Said he wanted to keep an eye on things while the men who'd been posted there went to eat. They're back now, though, so Bucher should be out."

Travis ran to the partially collapsed tunnel. "Where's Bucher?" he cried, grabbing one of the men by the shirt. "Was he out here when you got back from eating?"

The man's eyes widened. "We figured he went to eat," he cried, shaking his head wildly from side to side. "We ain't seen him."

Travis released him and grabbed a lantern, staring into the tunnel entrance.

"Hey," the man called to him, "you can't go in there. It might collapse!"

Travis ignored him. Stepping inside, he smelled the sharp dank odor of deep earth. He called out, "Sam? Sam, damn it are you in here? Answer me!" He ordered himself to be calm If Sam was inside the shaft, and if there was another cave-in then he was in grave danger.

Travis held up the lantern, freezing at the sight. It was another cave-in, closer to the entrance than the last one, a cave in he hadn't known about. Why hadn't they heard it? Had they been eating?

And then he saw something that made his heart stop.

Sam's battered old hat.

Turning, Travis ran back to the mouth of the shaft and shouted, "Bring picks. Supports. Lanterns. Hurry. We've got a man down here."

Marilee ran forward, but he motioned her back. "This is no place for you. Stand by the wagon. We're going to need it to get him back to town." He yelled to the men, "Come on, god damn it. Move! He's suffocating, and I haven't even located him yet."

Gilbert Sacks appeared, brow furrowed. "Coltrane, you can't take those men down there! You start digging around in there, and it'll trigger another cave-in for sure. And this time the whole damn mine could go."

Travis snarled, "Don't tell me what I can't do, and don't get in my way! I'm getting Sam out of there if I have to dig him out with my bare hands." He gave him a rough shove to the side and pushed by Gilbert to enter the shaft again.

Travis threw himself on his knees and began to claw at the dirt with his fingers, calling all the while, "Can you hear me? I'll find you, Sam. I swear to God, I'll get you out of here." He choked on a sob. Dig, damn it, dig. Every second could mean life to the man who had been more than father, more than brother. *Dig*.

There was a low, ominous rumbling, very slight, but enough warning to send the four men who had started after Travis scurrying back out to solid ground.

"You can't make it!" someone screamed to him as a shower of dirt cascaded down on Travis' head.

"Come back, Coltrane!" yelled Gilbert Sacks from the mine entrance.

"It's gonna go any second. Get the hell out of there, man, while you've got a chance!"

Travis ignored them, swiping at the dirt caking his eyes and then starting to claw once more. Damn the cowards.

"Coltrane!" called Sacks. "He's probably dead. You're gonna kill yourself for nothing. Get out of there!"

Travis felt something and dared to hope. Sam's heel. He had found his heel! He clawed faster, harder. "Can you hear me, Sam?" he screamed. "Please, God, answer me."

Sam moved. Ever so slightly, but he moved. Travis inched his fingers upward from the heel along his legs, his buttocks, finally reaching his waist and digging in with all his strength to yank backward.

"Help me, God," he muttered as he dug frantically. "I've never given a damn whether you existed or not, but if You're up there, help this poor sonofabitch, and I'll never doubt You again."

Suddenly he fell backward, still holding Sam. He was out of the dirt, free!

Travis did not stop to see whether Sam was still breathing, or to offer up a prayer of thanks, for in that instant the earthen roof above gave way and fell over his legs. All about him, dirt was running down. "Hang on, Sam!" he cried, using every muscle in his body to inch his way forward on his belly, dragging Sam beside him. "We're gonna make it, boy!" he gasped, coughing.

Gilbert Sacks scrambled forward on his knees to reach for Sam, grasping his shoulders. Another moved in to grab Travis' hand.

Just as the three men moved free of the shaft, dragging Sam, there was a great roaring from deep inside, and in a thundering cloud, the mine collapsed.

Kneeling beside Sam, Travis brushed furiously at the dirt caked on his mouth, then leaned over to press his ear to his chest. "He's still breathing!" he cried triumphantly. "Get the wagon over here. We've got to get him to a doctor."

Marilee came with a blanket and stood by helplessly as Travis and Gilbert loaded Sam very carefully into the back of the wagon. Then Travis turned to her, hair and face streaked with grime, only the whites of his eyes showing. He clutched her shoulders and whispered, "You and the women stay here, sweetheart. I'll send a wagon back for you if I don't come for you myself. We're going to have to ride like hell, and I don't want you jouncing around."

"I'm fine, Travis." She was touched by his tender concern. "I want to go with you."

"Damn it to hell, no, Marilee!" he yelled, wiping his hand across his dirt-streaked face. "Don't argue. I'm not taking a chance on your losing the baby. Just wait here. I'll be back."

"Yes. Yes, of course, you're right." She stepped back, embarrassed that others had heard.

She watched as Gilbert Sacks hoisted himself up into the wagon to take the reins. Travis climbed in the back beside Sam. With a pop of the whip, Gilbert turned down the road, into the black night.

She loved him. The dear Lord above knew how much. He was everything a woman could dream of in a man and more.

But he did not love her.

She would never admit it to anyone, but the notion of leaving him, setting him free, and going home to Kentucky had been quite strong . . . till she found out about the baby.

Marilee had to accept things as they were, for now. With his baby growing inside her, there was no turning back. She could only give thanks for sharing his life . . . if not his heart.

The bright lights of Virginia City pierced the purple shroud that engulfed them. Gilbert shouted over his shoulder that they were almost there.

"He's about half awake," Travis yelled back. "Mumbling something, but I can't make out what he's saying. I'm afraid he's hurt on the inside. There's blood coming from his nose."

He kept his hand on Sam's chest, feeling his heartbeat. It had become stronger once Travis had cleared his nostrils and mouth of dirt, but he did not like the oozing blood.

They could hear noise from the city, piano music and boisterous singing wafting toward them, shrill laughter, a curse. With over a hundred saloons, Virginia City made a lot of noise every night.

Gilbert pulled up the horses in front of the two-story clapboard building with the painted sign, "Virginia City Hospital," lit up on both sides by gas lanterns. "I'll go in and get some help and a stretcher," he called, jumping from the wagon and running up the steps two at a time.

"You're going to make it, old boy." Travis patted Sam's shoulder gently. "Just hang on. You've been through tougher things before and come out of it."

Sam moaned, head lolling.

Travis glanced up as two drunks shuffled by. Across the street, a woman in a red-sequined dress called out to them boldly. The drunks ran their hands down into their pockets, laughed, and hurried over.

Gilbert returned with two men and a stretcher.

"Be easy," Travis ordered as they climbed up in the wagon bed. "He seems to be in a lot of pain, and I don't know how badly he's injured."

"What happened?" one of the attendants asked, picking up his feet while his assistant caught hold of his shoulders. "Gunfight?"

"Mine shaft collapsed on him. I dug him out. He may have been under there fifteen minutes or so. It was mostly sand. A few rocks. He may have been crushed by one. He's been trying to talk, but he's bleeding from his nose."

They placed him on the stretcher, then maneuvered it carefully down from the wagon.

"Will you please hurry?" a woman called from the doorway impatiently. "I've got a gunshot wound waiting, and I'd like to check this one before I start operating."

Travis looked up to see her framed in the doorway in a halo of mellow light. She wore a plain white dress. The two men carrying Sam on the stretcher disappeared through the hospital doorway, and the woman in white turned to follow. He fleetingly took note of golden-red hair before bellowing to Gilbert, "What the hell is going on here? A woman doctor?"

"Hell, Travis, I don't know," Gilbert said wearily, leaning against the wagon and pulling a flask from his pocket. Taking a long drink, he handed it to Travis. "Maybe she is a doctor. You heard what she said."

"A woman doctor!" Travis spat the words in disgust. "I don't want Sam looked after by a woman doctor." He took a swallow of the whiskey and handed the flask back.

Gilbert laughed. "Well, that's progress, old man. Just be glad there's a doctor around at all."

"There's always a doctor around here," Travis said angrily. "With everything that happens in this town, there has to be. Someone is always getting shot or cut up. And there's bound to be a man doctor in there. That's who I want looking after Sam."

He ran up the steps and pushed the doors open to find a long, empty hallway lined with doors on either side. Damn it, which door had they gone through? He started into a door on his left and ran into a heavy-set nurse with the build of a man who charged straight for him, elbowing him back out into the hallway.

"Who do you think you are?" she hissed. "This is a hospital, not a saloon. Now you get back out there and wait your turn."

"Where'd they take the man injured in the mine accident?" Travis demanded, allowing himself to be pushed only because she was a woman.

"I don't know," she snapped. "This is a busy hospital. You just wait out there, and someone will speak to you later."

She started back into the room, but he called out, "Wait. Just answer one question. Do you have women doctors working here?"

She gave him a sour look. "One. What about her?"

He knew he was going to see trouble for this, but he had to ask. "Is she any good?"

"Yeah, she's good!" The nurse folded her arms across her chest. "You want to know anything else?" she asked irritably. "I got a patient to tend to."

"What's her name? She's treating my friend."

"Dr. Musgrave. Your friend is in good hands. Ask anybody she's ever treated, male or female." She turned once more, then paused to flash him an arrogant leer. "I don't like your attitude, mister. If you ever come in here as a patient, just hope you don't wind up with me for a nurse."

"Don't worry," he muttered, turning away. What kind of place was this? A woman doctor and a nurse who acted like a man!

Gilbert had come in and was watching him, snickering.

"What are you laughing about?" Travis demanded hotly, ready to take out his frustration on the handiest person.

"You've met your match with that woman, Travis." He nodded at the closed door. "That's Miss Cannon. Her patients lovingly refer to her as Cannonball. She's hell."

Travis silenced him with a wave. "I don't care, Sacks. I'm worried about Sam. I want the best care for him." His eyes narrowed and he stared thoughtfully at the green wooden floor. Something wasn't right.

He held out his hand to Gilbert. "I could use another drink if you don't mind."

They sat down on the wooden benches lining the hallway. There being nothing left to say, they fell silent, finishing the whiskey. Travis propped his elbows on his knees, his face resting on his palms, staring at the hardwood floor. Absently, he thought of Marilee waiting back at the site. Someone would see to it that she got home all right in a wagon. She didn't look good at all. It would have been best for everyone had she not become pregnant. She didn't seem healthy enough to carry a child.

It was not, he silently declared, that he did not care for her. He did. But he just didn't want to be married to her. Well, he sighed wearily, it was too late for that.

At the sound of footsteps clicking down the hallway, Travis glanced up sharply. The woman in white was coming. Gilbert had slumped down on the bench and was sound asleep, snoring softly.

"Are you with the man who was in the mining accident?" She approached Travis, her brow furrowed.

Travis could only stare. His heart refused to beat, lungs refused to breathe. He felt himself growing dizzy. There was a ringing in his ears.

"Sir"—her impatient voice cut through the gray mist enshrouding him—"sir, are you with the man who was in the mining accident?"

"Yes, yes," he gasped, struggling to stand up.

"He has some broken ribs," she was saying, gazing at him strangely. "We will continue to keep a close watch on him to see if other problems develop. You may see him for a few moments now, and then he needs to rest."

She turned to leave, but his arm, acting on its own, shot out to grab her. "Who are you?" he screamed suddenly, unable to control his voice. "Goddamn it, who *are* you?"

"Let me go!" she cried, jerking away angrily, her voice breaking. "What is wrong with you? Are you drunk?"

He gripped her tighter. "I want to know who you are!" he demanded, pulling her face up closer. "Tell me who you are!"

Gilbert had awakened and leaped to his feet. "Travis, what're you doing? Let go!" He began to pull at Travis' arm but Travis only tightened his grip, staring at the doctor without blinking.

Doors opened and people came running. The first to arrive was Miss Cannon, who slammed her beefy arms against Travis and knocked him off balance just long enough that he lost his hold on the terrified woman. "Don't pay him no mind, Doc," she roared. "He just don't like lady doctors."

"I assure you"—the doctor straightened, smoothed her skirt, and patted her red-gold hair, which was twisted back in a severe bun—"that I am quite competent. If you feel strongly adverse to my treating your friend, sir, then I shall take myself off his case and refer him to one of the men doctors."

She turned to go. Travis lunged forward, but the nurse and Gilbert held him back. "Just tell me who you are!" he screamed as she ran down the hall. "I just want to know your name."

She turned around slowly to stare at him, her violet eyes dark. He moaned. It was the eyes that had done it, the eyes.

Only one woman in the whole world had purple eyes!

"I'm Dr. Musgrave," she whispered, then turned and hurried away.

Travis slumped, suddenly unable to stand. He stumbled to the bench and sat. Nurse Cannon shook her head and hissed, "I oughtta throw you out of here. Another outburst like that, and you'll be barred from this hospital. You might even get yourself arrested."

"Forget it!" Travis snapped, standing as quickly as he had sat. "I'm going to see Sam before I leave. The doctor said I could."

As Nurse Cannon led them to Sam, Gilbert sighed and murmured, "I've never seen you act this way."

Travis decided not to try to explain. There was no way to explain about the red-gold hair and those violet eyes.

The nurse led them up a flight of stairs to a ward filled with beds. The room was quiet and almost totally dark. "He's in the third bed on the left, near the window," she whispered. You make any noise and wake up any of the patients, and you will go to jail." Then she strode from the room.

Travis told Gilbert to wait outside. "I want to see him alone." He moved to the bed and found Sam lying on his back, eyes closed. Crouching on the floor beside the bed, Travis reached out and gently touched his shoulder. "Sam. Sam. Can you hear me?" Travis whispered.

Sam's eyelids fluttered open and Travis could see the tears glittering. Sam's lips moved silently for a moment, and then, in anguish, Sam moaned, "I saw her, Travis. I was going to tell you today, but when I heard you and Marilee talking about the baby"—he paused to catch his breath, then went on raggedly—"I couldn't. It's best you didn't know, but you saw her. I know you saw her. I can see it in your face."

Travis' head dropped. "It can't be her, Sam. She just looks like her. She didn't know me at all."

Sam struggled to sit up but fell back. "She didn't know me, either, but it was her, Travis. I don't understand, but that woman is Kitty!"

The silence hung between them. Finally Travis stared down at Sam and said, "Yes. It's Kitty. God made only one woman that beautiful." His voice broke.

They were silent a little longer, and then Sam asked the

inevitable question. "What are you gonna do, boy?"

Travis spoke more to himself than to Sam, as he said, "Find out why she doesn't recognize either one of us. Find out how she got here. But before I do that, I want to find out just who *is* buried in that grave. I've got to move slowly. I can't let anyone know what's happening, certainly not John, or Marilee."

Sam touched his arm and softly asked, "Then what? What are you going to do about Kitty?"

Travis drew in a deep breath and held it, then let it out slowly as he got to his feet and forced a smile. It was a very sad smile. "The only thing I can do, Sam," he replied quietly. "Nothing."

He turned and left the ward.

Chapter Twenty-Nine

HE was a big man but not fat, his shoulders broad. The slight graying at the temples and the few lines around his eyes told Travis that Dr. Ambrose Watkins was in his forties.

There was no more time for studying the man. He looked up from the paper he was reading and frowned impatiently. "Yes? What is it?"

Travis sat down though he had not been invited to do so. It was best to get right to the point. "I want to ask about a doctor here at the hospital. Dr. Musgrave."

Dr. Watkins' expression changed from impatience to suspicion. He glared and said, "What about Stella Musgrave?"

"I would like to know where she studied medicine. I believe a person has the right to ask that question of a doctor."

Dr. Watkins laid his paper aside. "I believe I have the right to ask why you want that information," he replied tightly.

"Is that confidential information?"

"No . . . so why don't you ask Dr. Musgrave herself?" Dr. Watkins countered. "Just who are you, mister?"

"Coltrane. Travis Coltrane. I own the Odom mine."

The doctor's face split into a wide grin. He jumped up, ran around the side of the desk, and clasped Travis' hand. "I don't believe it," he cried. "Captain Coltrane, *sir*. I have always wanted to meet you. God knows, I kept up with your magnificent exploits during the war. I was with the medical corps under General Grant, himself."

"Sir," he beamed down at Travis. "You did the Union proud."

Travis murmured "Thank you," clearly unwilling to discuss the war.

"Well, now, back to business," the doctor smiled. "You asked about Dr. Musgrave. Now that I know you're not some overamorous suitor, I'll be glad to tell you what I know."

He returned to his seat, then gestured helplessly. "Actually, Captain, I don't know exactly what to tell you." Suddenly he leaned forward and whispered, "This will, of course, be confidential?"

"Of course," Travis nodded grimly.

The doctor rolled his eyes, sighing, the light blue eyes troubled. "Heaven help me if it ever got out that she is practicing medicine without a license." He looked hard at Travis. "But there is no danger to the patients, believe me, Captain. That woman knows almost as much about medicine as me or any other doctor on my staff, but I don't assign her any difficult surgery. She handles gunshot victims, stabbings, that sort of thing, mostly at night. I tell you, this town is so damn wild at night that it strains our capabilities here to answer the needs."

"When did she come here?"

"It's a long story, Captain."

"I've waited a long time to hear it."

The doctor looked at him strangely, then settled back in his chair and began. "She was brought here as a patient, almost two years ago. She had a very high fever and was quite sick. As frail as a newborn chick and just as weak. I didn't think she was going to make it."

"Who brought her?" Travis was struggling to keep himself composed.

The doctor thought a moment. "I honestly can't say. When she did get better, she could not tell us who she was. Didn't know a thing about herself. I thought perhaps it was a result of the fever, her weakness. As time went by, it became obvious that she had a severe case of amnesia. She still does. I thought eventually someone would come looking for her, but no one ever did. So I let her start doing odd jobs around the hospital to earn her keep. Little by little, she began to help out in the treatment rooms, and I was amazed at how much she knew about medicine.

"Oh, I asked her a lot of questions," he went on. "She remembered medicine. Who knows why, but she did. Yet she remembered nothing else. There was only one name that she recalled—Doc Musgrave. She couldn't explain that, either."

"Doc Musgrave taught her all she knew," Travis told him tonelessly. "She followed him around when she was a little girl. She worked in hospitals during the war, for both sides. Get her to perform an amputation for you sometime. You would be amazed."

"You . . . you know her then?" the doctor cried, incredulous. "My God, man, why didn't you say so? Is she really a doctor?"

"I'm afraid not, not really, but she does know as much as a doctor knows, maybe more. I imagine she remembered Doc Musgrave's name because he meant so much to her. She always wanted to be a doctor. But why do you call her Stella?"

"I had a daughter named Stella. She died," he answered quietly. "This young woman came to be like a daughter to me. My wife and I took her into our home. She's one of the family."

Travis thought a moment, trying to absorb it all. "Have you seen any change in her at all? Do you think she will ever remember who she is?"

The doctor spread his hands helplessly. "I can't say, Captain. I wish I could. Amnesia follows few patterns. We know so little about the intricacies of the mind." He looked at Travis thoughtfully. "You know her. Has she seen you? Does she know you?"

"No. It was as though she had never seen me before."

"Well, how close were the two of you?" the doctor asked carefully.

Travis saw no point in being evasive. "I'm her husband."

The doctor slowly swung his chair around to face the wall. After a while he turned back and faced Travis, pity in his gaze. "Captain, I realize you have another wife. She is a patient of mine, and she is expecting your baby in a few months. What happened? Did you think Stella was dead?"

Travis told him all of it. When he finished he could only shake his head in despair. "I still love her. But there's nothing I can do about it."

"Kitty Wright Coltrane," the doctor mused. "Abducted from

home by a ruthless bastard who put her through so much horror that her mind could not stand what she was being forced to endure. So her mind withdrew.

"This Tate fellow," he hurried on as the pieces began to fall together, "must have decided she was demented. He also wanted to cover his tracks in case anyone came looking for her. That was why he took you to her grave."

"I killed him on top of that grave, Doc"—Travis ground out the words—"in cold blood."

"Well, you needn't worry about my saying anything. I think I could kill him myself."

"I went to the grave after I left here last night," Travis said. "I opened it. There was nothing there—no coffin, no bones, nothing."

The doctor stretched his arm across the desk to touch Travis' folded hands. "What are you going to do, Captain?"

"There's nothing I can do. She has to know me, know her son. It can't go on this way."

"Captain, listen!"

He spoke so sharply that Travis was startled.

"Your wife is my patient. She is going to have a baby. It isn't easy for me to tell you this now, on top of everything else, but Mrs. Coltrane is not a strong woman. I'm worried about her. Whatever you do about your first wife, please don't do it now. Not while your present wife is in the condition she is in.

"As for Stella"—he paused, shook himself—"Kitty, nothing has changed. She still does not know who she is, who you are, or anything else about herself. It must go on that way. I know what you must be going through. This has to be a terrible, terrible shock, but for the present Mrs. Coltrane's sake, you must do nothing. Things can go on as they are for now."

Travis rose. "Of course. I won't do anything. We'll just wait and see what happens."

"I doubt that anything will happen, Captain," the doctor said remorsefully. "Stella can go on as she is for the rest of her life. And you, you are going to have to live with things as they are. You have other obligations now."

"I don't have to be reminded, Doctor," Travis said wearily, turning toward the door. Suddenly he paused. There was one last question that had to be asked. "Does she . . . see anyone? Is there a man?"

The doctor smiled, shaking his head. "No. This hospital is her whole world. There is no man, Captain. Oh, they ask to court her, you can be sure of that, but she just isn't interested."

Travis walked out and closed the door behind him.

He found Sam propped up in bed, his chest bandaged, demanding a drink of sourmash and a cigar. A young nurse was arguing with him and when Travis appeared, Sam fell silent.

As soon as the nurse scurried away, Sam asked anxiously, "Did you talk to her again? I saw her this morning, and I tried to ask her a few things . . . where she was from, stuff like that. She acted like she didn't even hear me."

"Sam, don't be asking her any more questions," Travis said sternly, drawing up a chair and sitting. Leaning forward so as not to be overheard, he told Sam of his conversation with Dr. Watkins.

When he had finished, Sam was crying, unashamed. "Oh, Lord, son, what are you gonna do? It'd almost be better if she *was* dead."

"Don't say that!" Travis shouted, then lowered his voice. "She's happy. She's doing what she loves doing. She's got her life, and I've got mine, and that's the way it has to be."

"You know you can't live here, in this town with her. You won't be able to stand it."

"I have to, Sam. I've got Marilee to consider. None of this is her fault, and she's going to have my baby. If she finds out about this, it could be very bad. Dr. Watkins says she's not in good health. That's just what I've been afraid of. She looks terrible."

"What if Kitty gets her memory back? What if she recognizes you? What then?"

"I'll have to face that when and if it happens. Damn it, Sam," he cried, fists clenched, "I don't know if I can even face Kitty again."

Sam's gaze moved beyond him. Lips grimly set, he whispered, "Well, we're about to find out."

She was walking through the door, golden-red hair loose about her face, sparkling in the bright daylight spilling through the windows. She was wearing another white dress, this one fresh and crisp, skirt swishing as she walked between the rows of beds, bodice stretched tightly across her large bosom.

Pausing to speak to the patients, she smiled, lavender eyes glowing with the misty lights Travis had always adored. His memory flashed back through the years to the first time he had ever seen her. Long, silky hair that ached to be touched, eyes that could swallow a man alive in their shadows, their dark fires. Her skin, so soft. Her legs, long, shapely, tapering to slender, delicate ankles. Hips firm to the touch, buttocks curving saucily and begging to be squeezed.

God, she was beautiful, the most beautiful woman he had ever known.

Suddenly he found himself staring once more into those deep lavender eyes, wanting to drown in them. But her gaze held not desire, but defiance. "Well, it's the man who dislikes women doctors," she greeted him coolly. "Tell me, sir, were you surprised to find your friend still alive this morning?"

She was looking at the chart she held in her hand, and when he did not speak, she glanced up. "Well, were you so surprised that you can't find your voice, sir?"

Travis grinned a huge big grin. It was the same old Kitty! Never intimidated. Afraid of no one. Ready to meet anything. The same old Kitty! "Yeah, I guess I was," he said, still grinning. "But if I were in his place and had a beautiful woman like you waiting on me, I'd fight to hang on, too."

Her chin tilted upward in that familiar characteristic that told him she was getting mad. "Sir," she snapped, "I do not wait on any man hand and foot. That is not my job. My job is to try to make them well. I succeed most of the time. In your case"—her eyes flicked over him with distaste—"I might not waste my time."

Sam had been watching every movement. Suddenly he could not resist the temptation to blurt, "This is Travis Coltrane, Doctor. He was a mighty fine cavalryman in the war. A captain. Did you ever hear of Coltrane's Raiders?"

Travis shot him a angry look.

Kitty's expression did not change. "No. I try not to think about the war, Mr. Bucher. Dwelling on the past only shadows the future."

She pushed Travis aside to get closer to Sam's bed. "How do you feel this morning? Is there much soreness here?" She touched his chest gently, and he winced. She nodded and made a notation on the chart. "You are going to be laid up for a while. So you just relax and let us take care of you."

"By the way," she frowned, "I hear you have been badgering

the nurses for whiskey and cigars. You will have neither while you are here. Understand?"

She turned sharply to Travis, her eyes glittering. "And you, sir. Don't be smuggling in anything to him, or I will see that you are not allowed to visit anymore. You strike me as the kind who would take great joy in defying rules."

"Whatever you say, Princess," he smiled.

She walked to the next bed, dismissing Travis.

Travis' eyes followed her every move, a stricken look on his face. "It was like the first time," he whispered wretchedly to Sam. "We were at war with each other then."

"You better just stay away from her. I sensed the sparks between you two, and it can only lead to trouble."

"I've got to leave now." Travis stepped back from the bed. "I haven't been back to the hotel. I was up all night, and I don't even know if Marilee got back all right. I'll look in on you later."

He hurried from the ward, unaware that Kitty was watching him leave.

However arrogant he appeared to be, she could not deny she found him attractive. The smiles he gave her were taunting, as though he knew she found him appealing. She cursed herself for suddenly wondering what it would be like to feel those sensual lips on her own. The firm set to his jaw, hair the color of the raven's wing, eyes neither blue nor black but a sheen in between that was devastating. A handsome man, but dangerous. She sensed that at once. Tall, husky, she was sure that, had he been bare-chested, she would have seen the thick mat of hair trailing down to . . . she felt herself blushing. She could almost see *that* part of him as well.

He had called her *Princess*. It was somehow familiar, as though the name belonged to her.

Nonsense. She must shake herself out of this. What was the matter with her?

Travis found Marilee standing at the hotel window, looking out at the street. The face she turned to him was even more pale and gaunt than before.

For a moment, he could not speak. He looked at her, feeling what? Pity?

"Travis, whatever is wrong?" she called to him in a wistful

voice. "You never came back for me last night. Martha Troby's husband finally brought a wagon for me. Mr. Sacks came back and told us Sam was going to be all right, yet you didn't come home all night."

He went into the bedroom and threw himself across the bed. He felt Marilee sit beside him, her cool fingertips smoothing back the thick, unruly hair from his forehead. "Travis, what's wrong?" She spoke so sweetly. "Please tell me."

"Please," he whispered hoarsely, "please, Marilee. Just leave me alone for right now. I've got a lot on my mind."

"You aren't sorry about the baby, are you?" she persisted. "I don't think you really wanted me to leave you, Travis. I was wrong to try to stand in the way of moving to the desert."

"We aren't moving to the desert. Not now."

She gasped, startled, jerking her hand away. "I don't understand."

"We're staying in town until the baby is born. Then we'll move."

She touched him again, and her voice was thick with relief. "Travis, you are worried about me, aren't you? And you're staying in town so I can be near the doctor. I love you for that. I do, Travis."

He turned suddenly and pulled her into his arms. She did love him. He knew that. She was his wife. Nothing had changed. Nothing could ever change. He knew that, too.

He pulled her down beside him and moved his hand to caress her breast gently.

And all the while they made love he thought of violet eyes and golden-red hair and a love forbidden to him.

Chapter Thirty

IT was cold. An icy wind blew across the desert, and Travis shivered despite his heavy shirt and coat. He stood on top of a ladder, nailing planks into what would be the first of several barns.

Casting a wary eye to the northwest, he could see the bank of grayish black clouds moving in fast. Snow, and a hell of a lot of it. Damn winter, he cursed, moving down the ladder. He had wanted so badly to finish the barn before bad weather descended on them.

Stepping from the bottom rung onto the ground, he looked at the few cattle standing in the pen. Brood stock, they had cost plenty, and he wasn't about to leave them outside all winter. The small shelter he had repaired from old ruins would be better than nothing.

He picked up a stick and began to round them up, herding them through the rail gate and into the rickety stable. The clouds were moving faster, and it was getting dark far too early. Once the stock was safely tucked away, he headed for the cabin. The wind had picked up ferociously, and despite his size and strength, he found himself struggling against the whipping force.

Finally inside, he slammed the door and bolted it. Glad now

that he had thought to store some wood inside, he set about starting a blaze in the fireplace. Once that was done, there was only food to think about. He wasn't really hungry, though. It seemed he had no desire to eat anymore.

The flames crackled and popped, and he stared into them pensively, reflecting on the past few months. He had been unable to keep his vow to stay in Virginia City until after the baby was born. Having Kitty nearby became too much for him.

Strangely, Marilee had taken the news of his move to the desert calmly and quietly, and when he finished explaining the need to get things settled before the baby arrived, she had agreed. She seemed quite content to remain at the hotel, near Dr. Watkins, and she wanted John to stay with her.

Sam understood the hell Travis was enduring, but he offered no sympathy. "You can't change nothing. And you sure as hell can't hurt Marilee. You said so yourself. So there's nothing to do but try to forget it."

Forget it? Travis laughed, but it was an unsteady laugh. Forget what it was like to hold Kitty close to him and play his fingers on her warm, eager body? Forget her defiant spirit? Forget Kitty?

Sam was still in town, but had mended and was traveling back and forth to the site and the new diggings. He had promised to keep an eye on Marilee—and Kitty, but Travis doubted he would relay much news of Kitty.

Outside, the wind screamed and icy snow pelted the windows. A draft blew down the chimney, sending the flames skittering wildly. It was cold. Damn, but it was cold. He got up and found a blanket and wrapped himself in it and wished morning would hurry and come. If the snow wasn't too deep, he would make the trip into town for supplies and see John . . . and Marilee. And he silently promised himself not to go anywhere near the blasted hospital.

He pictured the expanse of land outside, *his* land, the cabin, the small cattle barn. He realized he would have to ride to Gilbert Sacks' place in the morning and ask him to feed his livestock in case he stayed a day or two. Gilbert was sure to be around. His wife was also expecting a baby any day, and he wouldn't be straying too far from home.

Gratefully, Travis felt his eyelids finally growing heavy. Turning on his side on the narrow cot, he pulled the blanket tighter around himself and allowed himself to drift away, hoping that the dream would not come to him again, the dream of lavender eyes and golden-red hair and a body a man would die for.

He heard the sound from far, far away and told himself it was only the storm. Pulling the pillow over his face, he struggled to stay asleep in the other world. Then suddenly he sat straight up. It was not the storm. Someone was calling him. A woman's voice.

"Captain Coltrane, please let me in! Please! I'm freezing!"

He shoved the blanket back and leaped to his feet. What in blazes was a woman doing out here in the middle of a damn blizzard? Rushing to the door, he fumbled with the latch and the door flew open. She fell into his arms, covered with snow and shivering with deep, jerking spasms.

He struggled to carry her to the fire, and when the firelight caught the spun red-gold of her hair, he gasped, "Kitty! My God, girl, what are you doing out here?"

Her frosty eyelids fluttered open. The lilac eyes stared up at him in fright. She tried to pull away from him, arms flailing. A fingernail caught his cheek and she screamed in agony, a sound such as he had never heard.

"Hey, hey, hold on!" he yelled, struggling to catch her wrists, holding them tightly by her sides. "It's me. Coltrane. What's wrong?"

She looked up at him with such desolation that his heart swelled. "Are you hurt? What's happened to you? And what in hell are you doing out here in this storm?"

She turned her face to his bare chest, and he saw that he was wearing only his underwear.

"Uh . . ." he stammered, swallowed hard, telling himself not to call her Kitty. "Dr. Musgrave," he made his voice crisp, "if something's wrong, I wish you'd tell me. How about if I get you a drink? I think you could use some whiskey."

"Yes," her voice was muffled. "Yes, yes." She pulled away, turning her back to him as she sank slowly to the floor.

Travis hurried to find the bottle and took it back to her. "Sorry I don't have a glass," he muttered, quickly moving to find his pants and slip them on.

After throwing another log on the fire, he sat down next to her on the floor. Hesitantly, he gestured to her wet clothing. A long blue woolen cape covered her white dress. Both were sodden. "I think you'd better take those off and let me dry them in front of the fire. You can wrap up in a blanket. It's not good to sit around wet."

Wordlessly, she got up and went behind him. He could hear the rustling sounds as she undressed. He did not turn around. He did not have to. He knew every inch of that luscious body, what it looked like and how it felt.

She returned, handing him the wet garments with one hand while she held the blanket wrapped about her with the other arm.

"Are you hungry?" he asked above the roaring in his head. Damn, what was she doing out here? "I haven't thought much about food. I've been pretty busy trying to fix things up."

"I ate at the Sacks' earlier," she said in a small voice. "I delivered Wilamina's baby tonight."

He exploded. "You mean Gilbert let you ride out on a night like this? He's crazy."

"I insisted," she told him quietly. "He wanted me to stay over, but I thought I could make it. Then the snow got worse, and I was afraid of getting lost. I remembered passing here on my way out there yesterday."

"You knew I lived here?"

"No."

She spoke sharply, *too* sharply, he thought. It was as though she did not want to acknowledge his existence.

He felt the sudden need to prod. "You called my name. Captain Coltrane. You knew I lived here."

"Yes. No. I—" She shook her head, sunshine-red hair flying about her face. "I may have heard Mr. Sacks say something about you living around here. I don't remember."

He took the bottle from her, saw how her fingers were trembling. Where was her spirit? The usual arrogance? Why did she seem terrified of him?

Trying to set her at ease, he gave her a lopsided grin and cracked, "Look, Doc. I'm sorry I gave you a rough time when my partner was injured. I guess I'm not used to lady doctors. I wasn't myself that night, anyway. Hell, I thought Sam was a goner."

She took a deep, shuddering breath. "It's all right, really." She turned toward the window. "I wonder if it's let up. I could be on my way soon."

"Are you out of your mind?" he roared. "It's about a three-hour ride to town in good weather. You'd never make it. You're staying here."

She looked back at him, and the old familiar sensation of wanting to drown in those limpid violet eyes swept through him with a terrifying force. "I don't think it's quite proper, Captain Coltrane."

"Propriety!" he laughed. "It's a matter of survival. You're safe with me."

She bowed her head. "I'm sorry," she murmured, "I had no right to insinuate that you would behave as anything except a gentleman."

"I'm no gentleman," he told her candidly, recalling saying those same words to her a long, long time ago. Quickly, he added, "But I always respect a lady."

She began to speak nervously, casting about, he knew, for conversation of any kind. "I'm sorry I woke you. You were sleeping, weren't you? I knocked on the door several times and called to you over and over before you came. The wind is so terrible. Nevada can be so brutal in the winter. I should have stayed with the Sackses, I know, but I wanted to get back to town, to the hospital. Nights are our worst times there. You wouldn't believe what goes on. Shootings. Cuttings. Men are brought in looking like they've been in a war. Virginia City must be filled with the worst kind of people. They come looking for silver, gold . . . adventure. I know there are good people there, too, but the rowdies far outnumber the decent folk. It's not quite as bad as it used to be, though. I think the adventurers are moving on."

She paused to catch her breath and he reached over to place his fingertips against her lips. "Doc, I think we should both go to sleep now. You take the cot. It isn't much, but it's all I've got."

"I can't let you sleep on the floor," she protested. "It's your house."

"I've slept here on the floor so many times I've lost count," he laughed, getting to his feet and reaching to pull her up. He prayed that she did not sense the way he was reacting to touching her.

He stepped back, releasing her. "I'm planning on riding into town tomorrow myself. I'll go with you—if the snow isn't too deep, that is. And I meant to ask, where did you leave your horse?"

"I found your stable and shoved him in there with your stock."

"That's fine. Get some sleep now."

He found another blanket, wrapped up in it, and lay down in front of the fire. He could hear her settling down on the cot. Soon silence, except for the howling wind, settled over the cabin.

He stared into the fire. Something was not right with her. Something was troubling her deeply.

Behind him, six feet away, he could hear her tossing and turning. He sipped from the whiskey bottle, hoping the liquor would work its magic and take him away to that land of oblivion. God, how he wanted her. With every beat of his heart, with every breath, he wanted her desperately.

He dreamed the old dream again.

She was naked in his arms, snuggling closer. Her fingers danced through the curling hairs on his chest, trailing downward. His teeth bit gently into one taut nipple and he sucked hungrily as she cupped his manhood with both of her soft hands.

God in heaven, he loved her even more than he realized, more, if possible, than when they had been together.

But the dream had to end, and it did.

He opened his eyes, stiffening at the sight beside him.

Kitty lay in his arms on the floor before the fire, gazing up at him, tears sparkling in the firelight.

"Please." She touched his cheek gently, her body trembling. "Please don't say anything. Just hold me."

He held her. And finally, they slept.

He awoke suddenly, alone, and the memory washed over him. He looked around. The cabin was empty. Her clothes were gone. He ran to the door and jerked it open, stepping ankle-deep into snow before realizing he was barefoot and naked. Rushing back inside, he jerked on his pants and boots and then hurried out again. He could see her footsteps in the snow, leading to the stable. And as he ran, he could see more prints, hers and a horse's, leading toward the road.

He went back to the cabin and finished dressing. Then he took precious time to leave feed for the stock, enough to last them a couple of days. If they ate it all at once and then starved, he couldn't help it. He could not take the time to ride over to Sacks and ask him to look after them.

He had to find Kitty!

He was grateful that the snow was only about three inches deep. The sky was still overcast, and probably more snow would be dumped before the day was over. Riding as fast as he dared push his horse, he reached town in just over two hours. The horse was lathered and exhausted. Pausing long enough at the livery stable to tell the boy to walk him down and rub him carefully, Travis headed straight for the hospital, running all the way.

As luck would have it, the first person he saw when he pushed through the doors was Dr. Watkins.

"Why, Captain Coltrane. What brings you out so early?" His eyes narrowed. "Is it Marilee? I'll get my bag. It isn't quite time, but I've been afraid something might happen."

"No, no, it isn't Marilee," Travis cried, then stopped as the doctor's words sank in. "You've been afraid something might happen. Is something the matter with her? The baby?"

"She's weak," the doctor said bluntly. "I don't know what's wrong." He and Travis walked down the hall toward the hospital dining room. "Come have some coffee. Stella just got back from the Sacks place, where she delivered a strong baby boy. Though how she got back here in the snow I don't know."

"I'm glad you came by, Captain," Dr. Watkins was saying, as they neared the dining room. "I have been wanting to talk to you about Marilee's condition. I think you should plan to stay in town till the baby comes. She seems so wistful and sad. I've tried to get her to talk to me about what's bothering her, but she won't. She seems to be wasting away. The baby is growing, but she's losing weight. I might even put her in the hospital to see if we can force her to eat."

As they entered the dining room, Travis saw Kitty sitting at the table, eyes wide, face pale.

"I need to talk to you," Travis whispered to Kitty as he and the doctor walked by.

Dr. Watkins looked from one to the other and asked sternly, "What is going on?" Quickly pushing Travis back into the hallway, he whispered angrily, face reddening, "You haven't tried to tell her who she is, have you? You'll only make things worse for Stella and your wife."

"No, it isn't that." Travis shoved the man away. Kitty had

run through the doorway and down the hallway.

"Wait, please!" Travis yelled to her. "All I want to do is talk to you!"

She turned to look at him over her shoulder, her face pale. She did not see the little boy running toward her from the other end of the hallway and he crashed right into her. Travis cried, "John! What are you doing here, son?"

John saw him and pushed by Kitty, sobbing wildly. "Daddy, Daddy, you gotta come quick," he screamed, throwing himself into Travis' waiting arms. "Mommy's real bad sick. She sent me to get the doctor. I ran all the way, but she's bad sick. She's bleeding all over the floor and—"

Travis snatched him up and turned to find that Dr. Watkins was already running to get his bag.

Kitty called out to Dr. Watkins, "I'll get my bag and come with you, Ambrose."

Travis was already heading down the hall, holding John tightly against him, running as fast as he could.

They reached the hotel, and Travis took the steps three at a time, still holding John, who was crying wildly. The door to the suite was open, and the first thing he saw when they rushed in were the pools of blood all over the floor.

"Did she fall, John?" he asked, setting the boy down gently.

"No," he sobbed. "She was bleeding and said for me to run and get the doctor."

"All right. You go sit down on the sofa and don't get up till I tell you to." John obeyed, and Travis headed for the bedroom.

She was lying on the bed, the sheets stained crimson. Her face was drained of color, and her eyes were closed. Hurrying to her side, he called gently, "Marilee, sweetheart, can you hear me?"

She did not respond and, terrified, he felt her pulse. It was weak, but she was alive.

Dr. Watkins rushed in just then, pushing Travis aside. Travis turned and went back into the living room. He was only in the way.

He froze at the sight of Kitty kneeling before John, holding the little boy against her bosom. Mother was comforting son, only neither knew that. It was a sight Travis would never forget as long as he lived.

"She's going to be all right, John," Kitty was murmuring

as she smoothed back the unruly black hair. "If God wills it so, your mommy will be all right."

John sniffed. The lady's warm, violet eyes had made him feel much better. Suddenly deciding he should be a man, he wiped his eyes. "She's not my real mommy, you know," he told her. "But I love her like a real mommy. It feels like she is."

He paused to hiccup and went on, "My real mommy died and went to heaven. I hope God doesn't take this mommy, too."

His small body convulsing with a sob, he whimpered, "I don't want my mommy to die!"

Kitty pulled him tightly into her arms, burrowing her face in his hair, and they cried together, mother and son, sobbing their fears for the lady in the next room.

Chapter Thirty-One

TRAVIS sat in Dr. Watkins' office, sipping the strong coffee someone had brought him earlier. How damn much longer was it going to take? They had taken Marilee into the hospital over three hours ago.

He looked at the clock again. Fifteen more minutes and, by God, he was going out there to find out what the hell was going on.

The desk clerk at the hotel had taken John to his wife to look after. Travis had been adamant—John was not to go to the hospital. Kitty had come to the hospital with Dr. Watkins and Marilee, carefully avoiding Travis' eyes all the while.

The sound of footsteps made him leap to open the door. Dr. Watkins came in and Travis recoiled at his blood-stained white coat. Marilee's blood!

The doctor waved away his questions and hurried inside the room, closing the door behind them. Sitting behind his desk and urging Travis to sit down, he took a deep breath and said, "All right, Captain Coltrane, I'm going to tell you as much as I can at this point. Your wife is still alive. The bleeding has stopped. She is stable for the moment."

"The baby?" Travis croaked.

Dr. Watkins shook his head. "She is not even in labor."

"Then why in hell was she bleeding to death?" Travis yelled. "What is going on?"

"I believe that the afterbirth has been separated from where it is supposed to be attached inside her body. That is the reason for the bleeding. As I said, the bleeding has stopped."

"Can't you give me some idea of how long it's going to be this way?"

"The baby isn't due for another six weeks. I only hope she can carry it that long. I just can't say. I'm afraid doctors don't know much about this type of situation, Coltrane. I wish I could tell you more. Hell, I wish I could *do* more."

"Is she in any pain?"

"No, none. When I left her, she was sleeping. You can see her in a little while."

Travis rubbed his forehead, wondering what in hell to ask next that the doctor could answer. "The baby," he said suddenly. "If you went ahead and took the baby, then she would be all right, wouldn't she?"

The doctor's brown eyes darkened. "They might both die. We would have to take the baby surgically, and it is a very dangerous operation. I would rather she go into labor prematurely and deliver. As much blood as she had already lost, she would surely die if I operated." He shook his head firmly, folded his hands before him in a gesture of finality. "No. I won't do it. I'm going to wait and see what happens."

He cleared his throat and stared at Travis for a moment, pondering. "Why were you in such a frenzy to see Stella this morning, Coltrane?"

Travis shook his head. "It doesn't matter."

"Hell, yes, it does matter!" Dr. Watkins slammed both fists on his desk and stood up, glaring at him. "I have seen to it that that girl is going to fulfill her greatest desire. She will be a real doctor."

Travis stared up at Dr. Watkins, afraid of what was coming.

"I have made arrangements for her to study at the finest medical school in Europe, with the finest doctors. When she returns to America she will not only be a fully qualified doctor, she will also be a surgeon."

Travis refused to react, to show his feelings even to himself. It was best that she leave, he knew that. And Watkins was right. She would make a great doctor. For her sake, for *all* their sakes, Travis was glad she was going.

"She must never know about you, or about your son," Dr. Watkins said in a strained voice, sitting down carefully, trying to gauge his reaction. "You cannot stand in her way. You cannot deny her this wonderful future."

Travis snapped, "Why are you telling me all this now? I've got enough on my mind—"

"Because of this morning!" Dr. Watkins shot back. "Because I think you are still in love with her, and I won't have you hurting her."

"Doc," Travis grinned ruefully, "what's going to happen to Kitty when she remembers one day? Do you think she will just pretend her son and I don't exist?"

Dr. Watkins shook his head. "Maybe she'll never remember. If she does, I hope she will turn away from the past. Just don't stand in her way now. Let her get the training she needs," he added in a warning tone, his eyes fixed on Travis' face.

Travis leaned back and closed his eyes. "I just hope she's leaving soon. The sooner the better—for all of us."

"She leaves tomorrow."

There was a long, startled silence, and then Travis got up and walked to the door. "Fine. Now I'm going to the hotel to see my son and tell him to pray for . . . his mother. I'll be back in a little while to see how she's doing. If you need me, you know where to find me."

John was watching from a window and ran through their second-floor suite, meeting Travis at the door. Flinging himself forward to wrap his arms around his father's legs, he cried, "Is Mommy going to be all right? Can I go see her?"

Travis scooped him up. "I don't know, son." He pressed his lips against his forehead and carried the child into the living room. "The doctor is doing all he can for her. We must pray for her. As for you seeing her, I don't think that's a good idea right now. She needs a lot of rest."

"Miz Martin cleaned up," John explained as Travis set him down. "She cleaned up everything. I offered to help, but she wouldn't let me."

"She's a nice lady," Travis said absently, suddenly wishing he were anywhere but here. Damn the waiting. He would rather be out at the ranch, or anywhere.

"I liked that other lady, too," said John, walking to the

window to peer out. "Daddy? You know who I'm talking about? The lady with the pretty hair and the funny-colored eyes."

"That was . . ." Travis stopped himself, took a deep breath. "Dr. Musgrave."

"Wasn't she pretty?" John persisted. "And what color are her eyes? I've never seen eyes that color—"

"Lavender," Travis replied sharply, too sharply. Quickly, he apologized, "I'm sorry, son. I don't mean to snap. I'm just tired. And worried."

"Well, you must take a nap," John announced importantly. "I'll be here if anybody comes to see you, okay?"

Travis nodded and headed for the bedroom. Throwing himself across the freshly made bed, he squeezed his eyes shut. Damn, he wished John had never seen Kitty. Somehow, he felt his son would always remember the "pretty lady" with the "funny-colored eyes."

Travis felt himself dropping away and gratefully allowed his weary body to succumb.

"Travis, damn it, wake up!"

He sat straight up, instantly alert. "What the hell's going on?" he cried. "Is it Marilee?"

"I'm afraid so." Sam handed him his boots. "Somebody rode out to the site and told me what happened, and I came to town and went straight to the hospital, figuring to find you there. I ran into Doc Watkins. He was just about to send somebody over here for you."

Travis looked past him to where John stood clinging to the doorway, his small body shuddering with the sobs he so manfully tried to hold back. "John," he said softly, "I want you to go to Mrs. Martin's. Now. Don't argue."

"Yes, sir," John sniffed, then turned and disappeared in a clatter of tiny footsteps.

Sam swore under his breath. "Marilee's started bleeding again. Real bad. The doc says the baby is coming."

Travis was heading for the door, Sam right behind him. "Travis, is it bad?" he asked as they ran down the stairs. "Is she gonna make it?"

Travis did not answer. He just ran.

Marilee lay very quietly, eyes fixed on the ceiling above. Now and then a pain would squeeze down like a pair of giant, rushing hands, and she would gasp, holding her breath till it assed.

"Don't fight it, Marilee," the soft voice at her side com-ianded. "Go along with the pain. We want you to have this aby now so you will both be all right."

"The baby will be all right," Marilee murmured in a thin 'hisper, her voice barely audible. "God will let my baby live. know it."

"You are both going to live," the voice beside her said rmly. "You just hang on now." Marilee smiled at the voice. brooked no argument.

"Do you want a boy or a girl?" the warm voice asked.

She looked up to see the woman bending over her, saw the iolet eyes fringed with the thickest lashes she had ever seen. nd the hair. No, there was no mistaking that hair.

"You're her, aren't you?" Marilee asked simply, awed yet, omehow, not surprised. Nothing surprised Marilee anymore.

"I'm Dr. Musgrave," the woman said. "I've been with you ll along."

Marilee gasped for breath, then whispered. "I think I knew while ago, but now . . . I know for sure."

"Know what?" Kitty smiled and brushed Marilee's damp hestnut hair back from her pale forehead. "You feel feverish, ut don't fret. It will all be over soon, and you'll have a fine, ealthy baby. A bit small, but we'll take extra good care of im."

"You *are* her," Marilee exclaimed, trying to raise herself or a better look.

"No! No, you don't!" Kitty pushed her back down. "You are oing to lie still if I have to tie you down."

Another pain rolled over Marilee's body, and she felt herself ontorting, bearing down, screaming for the first time. When had passed, she slumped against the mattress and struggled force the words past her parched lips. "It's you. I knew. I new when he called out your name in his sleep that you had be alive."

Kitty's hands fluttered over the woman, tucking the sheet ound her. "Stop talking. You need your strength to get this aby born."

Another pain bore down. Marilee screamed over and over. tty cried above her voice, "The baby is almost here. Bear wn, Marilee!"

Marilee's world had shrunk to just this room, then to jus this bed. A great black cloud sought to engulf her, but she hel on. An hour later, or perhaps it was only a few minutes later she heard a faint cry. "A little girl, Marilee!" Kitty cried ju bilantly. "A beautiful little girl. Oh, she's gorgeous!"

"What on earth!" Dr. Watkins entered the room, eyes bulg ing. "Lord, she's had her baby!"

"Yes, and it's a perfect little girl. Wait. Let me take car of the cord. There. See?" Kitty held up the baby for Marile to look at.

Marilee tried to lift her arms but found she could not. Kitt moved forward, holding the baby close.

"My husband," Marilee cried suddenly, her eyes riveted t the baby. "Please. I must see him."

"Not now," Dr. Watkins said crisply. "We've still got som work to do."

"Now!" she screamed with the little strength she had left "Now! Please! There's no time!"

Dr. Watkins exchanged a worried glance with Kitty, wh nodded. "I'll stay with her," she whispered. "You send fc him."

"You shouldn't be talking," Kitty chided gently. "Rest. will all be over soon. You will pass the afterbirth, feel a fe more pains, and then you will sleep and wake up to you beautiful new daughter. And your husband."

Turning to Nurse Cannon, who had been sent into the roo by Dr. Watkins, she silently handed her the baby. Nurse Car non was smiling happily as she left the room, cuddling th baby close to her.

A moment later Travis bolted into the room, hurrying t lean across Marilee and gaze down into her white face. "You' going to be all right," he said quickly, raggedly. "We've g a little girl, and you're both going to be fine."

"No," Marilee was quite calm, her face beginning to tak on a serene, Madonna-like expression. "You and Kitty a going to be fine."

"Kitty?" he echoed, swaying as though thunderstruck.

"You know, Travis. She knows, too, my beloved." H gaze went to Kitty, who was openly crying now. "She knov who she is . . . who you are. . . ."

"And I"—she paused to gasp, feeling the worst pain y

uilding within—"I knew when I saw her. I knew I had to
ave the baby and . . . leave you."

Travis realized what she was saying. Marilee wanted to get
ut of the way so they could be together. "This is crazy," he
ried furiously, almost wanting to grab her as if he could shake
ome sense into her dying body that way. "Now stop talking
nd rest, Marilee. You don't know what you're saying."

Weakly she lifted her hand to touch his dear cheek. "Re-
nember what I told you, darling?" The pain was growing,
aking over her body, squeezing her chest, and making it hard
o breathe, but gathering everything left within she forced her-
elf to continue. "Remember I told you, that no moment lasts
orever."

"And you," she swallowed, "you said to make more mo-
nents. Make them, my beloved . . . make them with the only
voman you ever truly loved. . . ."

The pain consumed her and the blood came in a fierce gush.
'his time they could not stop it. Travis flinched at the sight
f it all, and turned away in soul-wrenching agony as he saw
Aarilee's sightless eyes lock in a gaze of eternity upon his
ace.

The next moments were a blur. He beat his head and fists
gainst the wall, crying "No-no-no" over and over until he felt
his own blood begin to ooze from his forehead and the torn
flesh across his knuckles. Strong hands were pulling at him,
wrenching him from his self-destruction. They dragged him to
the hall, then into another room, and held a bottle of whiskey
to his lips. He drank. Swallowed. Drank some more. And
through the maze he saw Sam's tear-streaked face staring down
at him in sorrow and pity.

But Sam moved away. Travis blinked and saw the blood-
spattered skirt before him. He dared finally to look up. Golden
hair tumbled about the most beautiful face he had ever seen,
one he once feared he'd never see again. "She died for us,"
Kitty whispered as she knelt beside him. "Ambrose told her
to stay in bed or she would start bleeding again. She got up
and made herself bleed. She wanted to die, Travis; she wanted
to die so we could be together."

He touched her face gently, as though afraid if he did not
feel her, she would prove to be an apparition that would fade.

"There was something about you," she went on quietly,

"I didn't know exactly what. You made me angry, yet excite
me in a way that seemed familiar. And then you called m
'princess,' and little by little it all came back."

She lay her head against his chest and he folded her in hi
embrace as she went on. "It was no mistake I came to you las
night. I wanted to know your love just once more before I left.

"And you would have gone."

"Yes, I would have gone. You had a wife expecting you
baby. I had another life. I was no longer a part of yours. Bu
she knew somehow. And when she was finally sure, she jus
died."

Kitty lifted her face to gaze at him steadily. "She gave u
a part of her that will live on, Travis. She gave us her daughte
yours and hers. And I will raise her to know what a wonderfu
woman her mother was.

"I feel," she whispered, "awestruck, as though I've bee
touched by an angel."

"I know," Travis murmured, kissing her tenderly, then look
ing at her with all the love he'd held so long within. "And
feel like God has given you back to me. And this time, I'
never going to let you go."

Their lips touched once more.

There would be time for grieving for the woman who ha
died so they could love.

There would be time later to plan the future . . . together.

The present moment would, somehow, last forever.

Re-Entry Into Faith

"Courage—be not afraid!"

by Catherine Doherty

Madonna House Publications

Combermere, Ontario, Canada

Madonna House Publications®
2888 Dafoe Rd, RR 2
Combermere ON K0J 1L0

www.madonnahouse.org/publications

Phone: (613) 756-3728
Email: publications@madonnahouse.org

For more information about the Servant of God Catherine Doherty and her cause, see:

www.catherinedoherty.org

Cover Art: Helen Hodson "Peter coming to Jesus through a storm"

Library and Archives Canada Cataloguing in Publication

Doherty, Catherine de Hueck, 1896-1985

Re-entry into faith : "courage—be not afraid! " / Catherine de Hueck Doherty.

ISBN 978-1-897145-34-0

1. Faith. I. Title.

BT771.2.D643 2012 234′.23 C2012-901997-6

Dedicated to Father Gene Cullinane (1907-1997)

Pioneer priest of Madonna House Apostolate

Man of strong faith

Why should I want to do this? Faith, my friends, faith! Simple, unadulterated, idiotic, superb, beautiful, enticing, holding up, lifting up, pulling down, full of challenge, full of crises, full of excitement, alive faith!

Catherine Doherty

Table of Contents

About the Author

Catherine Doherty's long life spanned most of the 20th century. Born in Russia in 1896 and falling asleep in the Lord in Canada in 1985, she personally experienced and suffered through many of the cataclysmic events of that century. The Holy Spirit used these events, and her experiences and suffering, to communicate graces to her for the enrichment of the whole Church.

Catherine was born and raised in a wealthy and deeply Christian family. She served as a nurse with the Russian Army in the First World War, but after the Communist Revolution was forced to flee her homeland—she and her husband and son immigrated to Canada as refugees. For some time she worked at menial jobs to provide for her family, which gave her an experience of poverty, but also, as she would later say, deepened her faith and dependence on God.

Through a chance meeting, her talent as a public speaker was discovered, and in the 1920s she was a successful lecturer throughout North America, speaking about her life in Russia and her experience of the Revolution. Her marriage was disintegrating, however, and later was annulled.

Living in comfort again with the success of her lecturing, Catherine found herself pursued by Christ's words, "Sell all you possess, and come follow Me." This was the time of the Great Depression, and with the blessing of the Archbishop of Toronto, Catherine gave away her possessions and went to live a life of prayer and simple service to the poor in the slums of Toronto. Others came to join her, and the work developed into an apostolate she called Friendship House, which provided food, clothing, and spiritual support to those in need.

Because her approach was so different from what was being done at the time, she encountered resistance, and Friendship House closed in Canada. Soon Catherine was invited to open another in New York City's Harlem. Catherine was horrified by the injustices she saw done to black people, and she used her speaking gifts to travel the country decrying racial discrimination—in this she was a forerunner of the movement for civil rights in the U.S. The Great Depression was followed by World War II. Although Catherine remained in North America, she was aware of the suffering of her own mother and siblings in war-torn Europe.

Again due to misunderstandings, Catherine was forced to leave Friendship House. In 1947 she returned to Canada, to the village of Combermere, with her second husband, newspaperman Eddie Doherty. What seemed like the end of the road turned out to be the most fruitful period of Catherine's life. Her example of radical Gospel living became a magnet for men and women in search of a way to live their faith. The community of Madonna House was born, and has grown into a family of lay men, lay women, and priests, living under promises of poverty, chastity, and obedience.

Catherine sensed and witnessed the de-Christianization of the Western world as the 20th century unfolded, and over time exemplified and communicated a faith vision for the restoration of the Church and our modern culture. The Madonna House training center in Combermere offers an experience of this Gospel life to guests who come—they participate fully in the daily life of the community. In this Madonna House way of life are the seeds of a new Christian civilization.[1]

During the many years of her apostolic life, Catherine's voice and her pen spoke out. In

---

1 For further information about Madonna House see our website at www.madonnahouse.org

lectures and talks up and down the North American continent, and in a ceaselessly flowing river of articles, letters, and books, she penetrated the lives of Christians with the unwavering message of the need to live the Gospel. She insisted that the core of the Good News is God's love for us.

Catherine's faith was greatly challenged in her experience of some of the most significant events of the 20th century. As she lived through them, her faith and her love grew stronger and more mature. As a wife and mother, writer and lecturer, as one whose experience and gifts could form a whole community of men and women, she was involved in the myriad facets of existence. God taught her much wisdom through her long life, and she grew ever closer to him. The intensity of her union with God could shatter the mediocrity of those who encountered her, and many people who met or heard her speak only once found their lives radically changed by that single, powerful, and charismatic encounter.

The depth of her spiritual legacy stems both from her personal gifts, and from the extraordinary range of experiences through which God finely honed and forged them.

She serves as a sure guide for others in the life of faith.

Part I

I live in faith … in the Son of God
who loved me
and sacrificed himself for my sake.

Gal 2:20

We must not forget that very many people, while not claiming to have the gift of faith, are nevertheless sincerely searching for the ultimate meaning and definitive truth of their lives. This search guides people onto the path that leads to the mystery of God. Human reason, in fact, bears within itself a permanent summons, indelibly written into the human heart, to set out to find the One whom we would not be seeking had He not already set out to meet us.

Pope Benedict XVI: *Porta Fidei*, Para.10

God's Gift to Us

Doing the works of God is this:
believing in the One whom he has sent.

Jn 6:29

The other day I was sitting with a priest who came to visit me on my island. It was one of those beautiful, cold, sunny days that Canada is so celebrated for. The river was a sheer, lovely blanket of snow, tinted pink by the setting sun. I think that Russians and nature automatically go together. We live in its symbols and its delights.

The priest was talking about faith. Strangely enough, I had been meditating on faith for quite awhile. It seemed that faith wanted to clarify itself for me so that I might clarify it for others.

The priest said to me, "Catherine, people often believe faith to be a set of moral obligations. Many lay people, clergy and religious see it this way. Oh, yes, we believe, but it is mostly with the head that we believe."

I looked at the snowy expanse of the river, now tinged with the blue shadows of the evening and cried out, "But that's not faith!"

Faith is a gift, a gift given by God to man. We receive the Christian faith through Baptism, when we are immersed in the death and resurrection of Jesus Christ. As we grow into adulthood, faith is assented to again and again. It is the *fiat* or *yes* of one who, as he grows to maturity, continues to say, "I believe."

Faith is a country of darkness into which we venture because we love and believe in the Beloved, who is beyond all reasoning, all understanding, all comprehension. And at the same time, paradoxically, is enclosed within us: the Father, the Son, and the Holy Spirit. Faith must go through this strange dark land, following him whom it loves.

Christ, our Beloved, becomes the door, the way into and through this darkness. And suddenly our heart knows that if we will pass through the door and walk along that way, we will see the Father.

What does it mean to see the Father? It means to assuage that hunger that has been put in man's heart by God himself, the hunger of finally meeting absolute love. We yearn for it. All of us do. We arise and go on a pilgrimage, guided only by faith that we must journey toward the face of perfect Love—because for this we were created, to be one with that Love.

If we embark upon this quest, into the land where we may not be able to hear, may not be able to see, may not be able even to speak, suddenly we will be mysteriously visited. A hand will touch our ears and they will be opened, not only to the speech of man but to the speech of God. A hand will touch our eyes and we will see, not only with our eyes, but with the sight of God. A hand will touch our tongue, and we will speak, not only as men do, but as God speaks, and we will become prophets of the Lord.

True, on the road to the Father we shall fall, for we shall sin. We may turn away from God, we may leave the Church, we may think that we have left everything. But faith being a gift of God, it does not desert us; we desert it, but it follows us. We leave the Church, but the Church—which is part of faith, for it is part of Christ—does not leave us. We turn away from God, but God never turns away from us.

You Are Loved

I am the good shepherd:
the good shepherd is one
who lays down his life for his sheep.

Jn 10:11

When I was a young wife in Petrograd, the city was in chaos as the communists took over. My husband Boris and I were sleeping on the floor after everything was taken away from us. I said to him, "Boris, I am afraid." He yawned and said, "Why? You are a Christian." That was a pretty good answer; I never forgot it. If I am a Christian, can I give way to hopelessness? No. The resurrected Christ is in our midst.

What we have to battle in this day and age is our own hopelessness. Many people are depressed. They are depressed by the image of themselves. They don't think they're doing much. Well, the picture they see in the mirror is cockeyed.

Then, on top of this depression, and in it and over it, comes a terrible loneliness. This applies to lay people, to priests, to everyone. The answer to it is so utterly simple, almost childlike. The answer is faith. A very small word, but one of such immense power that it can lift you to the very feet of God. Faith in who you are, what you stand for, where you are going.

These days, who of us does not need faith, love, peace, compassion, understanding? Especially since many people cannot escape from their fears that bay like a pack of wolves at their heels. They are fearful of everyone in authority, frightened of themselves, filled with inferiority that they should not exist.

Let us stop listening to these nonsensical fears. We don't have to worry about our sinfulness. Forget all this nonsense about being ugly and unlovable. Throw yourself into the arms of God who incarnated himself to become like you and me.

Faith tells you that you are loved by God. Without it, you go down into the pit of your own hell. The wrong self-image puts you right into this pit. When you think of your own image, stop! Look in a mirror and repeat the words from Genesis, "and God saw all he had made and it was very good" (Gn 1:31).

When you have an inferiority complex—and who of us hasn't—you say things like, "I just don't believe that what God made is good. Look at me, I'm a louse." Don't dare to challenge God like this. Everything he made is good, including yourself. Don't listen to that serpent who is giving you apples that look red on the outside and are full of inferiority complexes on the inside. Don't eat that apple, or else you are going to go down into a pit prepared by Satan for you for your whole life.

How can you have a wrong image of something or someone that God touched? God touched you and he created you. You passed through his mind and you were begotten. Anyone of us that passes through God's mind, anyone of us that God touched, cannot be this horrible person we think we are. No! Each one of us is beautiful—we're beautiful because he touched us.

Sometimes this is very difficult for us to accept. We look at ourselves and say, "He made us in his image, equal to himself in a manner of speaking, heir to his Son? This just can't be. He hasn't looked into my heart. He doesn't know what I'm made of!" We say those silly things because our evaluation of ourselves is very poor. We haven't looked at ourselves with the merciful, tender, compassionate eyes of God. So we walk in despair half the time. As a result, the ability to realize that God is both in our midst and in us—a realization that is the fruit of faith—fades and disappears.

This is the main reason, it seems to me, why the Father sent his Son to us, why the Word was made flesh and dwelt amongst us as one of us. The Father, having given us the fantastic gift of faith, wanted to help us accept this awesome gift. He sent his Son Jesus Christ so that we, unbelieving, might believe. We are like children; we need to touch.

Every human being is a mystery. The mystery of man enters into the mystery of God, and bursting forth with great joy, comes faith and understanding. When faith is there, all is clear, and a love relation with God enters into your heart. When you have faith, it is such a simple thing to accept his love, even if you do not understand why he loves you.

Prostrate Before Him

Blessed are the poor in spirit.

Mt 5:3

The only way to approach faith is on our knees, through prayer. We should not only kneel but be prostrate before him, falling on our faces, imploring, crying out for growth in faith, so that we may believe ever more firmly, not only in God but also in one another—we who are fashioned in God's image.

Yes, we can reach God very simply when we prostrate ourselves before him. When I come before God like this I am transformed. And I need to be transformed.

Here I am, an arrogant and proud human being, capable of walking on the moon, of making fantastic instruments that send us pictures of other planets. In my arrogance and pride I am once again polishing the apple to eat, so to speak, to prove I am equal to God.

Suddenly, I realize my works are but nothing. God is God, and I am not. I am his creature, the poor man of the Lord, the poor man of the Beatitudes. I realize that he really meant what he said: "Without me you can do nothing" (Jn 15:5).

Prostration is humility. It's an acknowledgement of who I am, and who he is. A "prostrated Church" is a Church of what I call the *humiliati*: the poor, the forgotten, the lonely. It includes the widow who put her last two cents into the temple collection, and the prostitute, and the thief.

The *humiliati* is the working-class mother who doesn't know how to get her money together—there's not enough of it to feed and clothe everybody. All those who sorrow, all those who seek, all are turning their faces to God. All these enter into faith. All are prostrated before God. All experience God.

It is inconceivable that we shall reach God through books. We shall reach God as he reached us, by covering our brokenness with his incarnation. By incarnating himself, he has made us divine. We partake of this incarnation through prayer and through the deep silence of the prostrated Church. It is not the silence of passivity, but the silence of fire and flame that possesses any person who approaches the invisible.

Faith grows with each prostration of ours. Faith grows with each acknowledgement within us of the Father, the Son, and the

Holy Spirit—the one in three and three in one—within us.

Only children can talk of mysteries as if they were realities. As we lie prostrate before God we have to cry out in faith, "Lord, give me the heart of a child and the awesome courage to live it out as an adult." Then, when we arise from this strange, humbled position, we, like children, can dare to explain the unexplainable. As the Lord said, "It is to such as these that the kingdom of heaven belongs" (Mt 19:14).

Portal to Faith

As soon as Jesus was baptized
he came up from the water,
and suddenly the heavens opened
and he saw the Spirit of God
descending like a dove
and coming down on him.
And a voice spoke from heaven,
"This is my Son, the Beloved;
my favor rests on him."

Mt 3:16-17

It is strange, but when I talk about faith I hear water. I hear little waves splashing on the sand. Then, quite suddenly and inexplicably I hear footsteps, and I am filled with awe. I know that Christ is approaching to be baptized. Nothing is as profound as the baptism of the Son of God.

Just look and listen. A man stands naked to be baptized, and that man is God. He enters into his creature, which is water, and he is baptized by his creature which is man. He immersed himself in that water so that you and I, and all of us who follow him, could go through the waters of baptism. Faith is given to us in baptism, that we might grow in it. Then, slowly, as a child grows, we enter into the mystery of faith.

In baptism you are joined to the Mystical Body of Christ. When you become part of his body, one of his people, a sheep of his flock, faith whispers to you about the resurrection: "Open your eyes and see. See the dazzling light that comes forth from the East. It is our Lord rising from the dead." As you behold the light of this mystery in the darkness of faith, light and darkness are mingled together, and you can almost faint from what is pouring into your heart. Jesus died for us and rose as he promised so that we might have this faith. I often think that Niagara Falls is a puny little stream compared to the rushing waters of baptism that lift us up to the feet of the Father.

St. Paul says, "When we were baptized in Christ Jesus, we were baptized in his death. In other words, when we were baptized we went into the tomb with him, and joined him in death, so that as Christ was raised from the dead by the Father's glory, we too might live a new life" (Rom 6:2-11). St. Paul visualized baptism by total immersion as is done in the Eastern Church. By immersion, we enter into the death of Christ. In the Roman rite, water is usually poured over the child's forehead, symbolizing this entry into the death of Christ.

St. Paul felt very strongly about this meaning of baptism. It was also understood in this way by the early Christians, and by the Church through the centuries. This is the essence of our life, those of us who believe deeply, who walk in faith. I come together with the death of Christ at my baptism. Something fantastically, incredibly awesome, beyond all imagination, happens to me and in me, in baptism.

Just think for a moment: Father, Son, and Holy Spirit now truly abide in me. God dwells in me. Christ said it: "My Father and I will come and abide in you" (cf. Jn 14:23). The mystery of the Trinity dwells in the mystery of man. I come together with the death of Christ at my baptism. Something encompassed only by faith, not by the intellect, has happened to me and in me.

To Believe and To Love

"Faith is the assurance
of things not yet seen"
Heb 11:1

The tragedy of our modern world is that it wants proof that God exists. There is no such proof. No amount of books, libraries, erudite people, or marvelous speakers can convince us that God exists. We enter into the unseen mysteries of our faith, the mystery of God, through an experience, an event, a happening, a miracle.

Once upon a time the second person of the Most Holy Trinity walked this earth. Somewhere there is a spot of land that has kept his footprints. You might not see them but they are there! To make all things clear the Son died for us. Before he died he brought us a new covenant, a new contract if you like. After he died he resurrected! At that moment faith exploded like a thousand stars, or suns, or moons. Love became a platter and presented itself to each of us carrying faith.

This pits our peanut-brain against the mystery of faith. We want to tear apart the very thin veil of faith, to see if we can weigh it, measure it. Faith always eludes us when we approach it this way.

Those of us who have been baptized have received faith as a grace of God, a very special gift. This gift has to be constantly reaffirmed. It is so important to continue to ask for it, to implement it and to act as if I believe. Then the whole of the world is in me and I am in the whole world because God belongs to me and I belong to God.

Through faith we are able to turn our faces to God and meet his gaze. Each day becomes more and more luminous. The veil between God and man becomes less and less until it seems as if we can almost reach out and touch God.

Faith is a pulsating thing; a light, a sun that nothing can dim if it exists in the hearts of men. That's why it's so beautiful. God gives it to me saying, "I love you. Do you love me back? Come and follow me in the darkness. I want to know if you are ready to go into the things that you do not see yet, on faith alone."

Then you look at God, or at what you think is God in your mind, and you say, "Look, this is fine, but you're inviting me to what? An emptiness? A nothingness? There is nothing to see. I cannot touch you. I cannot feel you." Then God goes on to say, "I invite you to a relationship of love: your love of me, my love of you."

Yes, God comes to us as an invitation to love. True, his invitation to love is crucifixion. In a strange and incomprehensible way the pain of the crucifixion that we foresee blends into the joy of an alleluia of his resurrection. As he is crucified, so he is risen. So, too, do we die and rise. No sooner is he taken off the cross and put into the tomb than the stone is rolled back. He is not there. Here is where faith enters. With Mary Magdalene who was the first to see him, we cry "Rabboni! Master!"

At this moment love surges in our heart like a tremendous sea that takes us in and lays us in the arms of God whom we haven't seen but in whom we believe. Across the waves we hear, "Blessed are they who have not seen and yet believe" (Jn 20:29). Now I walk in the darkness of faith and I see. I see more clearly than is possible with my fleshly eyes.

Now I am free because I believe. That's true freedom. Believe without end, believe without frontiers, believe without any kind of proofs, any kind of walls. Just believe.

Mother in Faith

"I am the handmaid of the Lord,"
said Mary,
"let what you have said be done to me."
And the angel left her.

Lk 1:38

I love to meditate on Our Lady. I've written a lot of poems about her. I believe she holds my heart in her hands. I like to think about those hands that embraced all the household tasks: cooking, sweeping, weaving. The hands that embraced God.

Imagine a fourteen or fifteen-year-old girl having an angel stand before her and say, "Hail, full of grace, the Lord is with thee" (Lk 1:28). How does it feel to be addressed by an angel? Strange as it might seem, this woman-child answered regally, simply, directly, without false modesty. She said, "How can this happen to me for I do not know man?" (Lk 1:34) Then she was told that the Holy Spirit would overshadow her. She responded by saying, "Let it be done unto me according to his will" (Lk 1:38). What faith! She simply said yes to the impossible. The strange, incredible, unbelievable faith of a young girl. Faith that gave us God.

Now that's something that should penetrate our hearts. Do you feel it penetrating your heart?

You see, she was a person, a human being just like you and me. Isn't that amazing? True, she had certain graces given her, but she did not understand many things. No, she didn't understand them. She put these things in her heart. She plunged into faith.

This child took a plunge into faith so deep it gives me goose bumps. When you have difficulties in faith, turn to her. She will help you say, "Let it be done according to his will."

Joseph, too, seeing her become large with her Child and, no doubt, seeing the neighbors looking askance, had to trust in the dream he was sent. He, too, plunged into faith. He, too, will hear your prayer.

I bow low before this little girl-woman. She is truly the mother of all those who believe. She had a faith beyond our understanding. I invite you to enter into that solitude of faith that Mary had. Close your mind and open your heart. Enter the solitude of faith. Do not worry about going apart to a quiet place. The solitude of faith is at this very moment, whether you are on a bus or sitting at a table. Do you really believe? All you have to do is what Mary did. Enter the solitude of faith and say yes. That's all.

Part II

That Christ may live
in your hearts
through faith.

Eph 3:17

A Christian may never think of belief as a private act. Faith is choosing to stand with the Lord so as to live with Him.

Pope Benedict XVI: *Porta Fidei*, Para. 10

What the world is in particular need of today is the credible witness of people enlightened in mind and heart by the word of the Lord, and capable of opening the hearts and minds of many to the desire for God and for true life, life without end.

Pope Benedict XVI: *Porta Fidei*, Para. 15

The Mercy of God

One of the criminals hanging there ...
said, "Jesus, remember me
when you come into your kingdom."
"Indeed, I promise you," he replied,
"today you will be with me in paradise"

Lk 23:39, 42-43

This word to the good thief is a consolation for all who feel guilty because of their sins. Let guilt be wiped out. If any one of you feels guilty and you know that you deserve it, fear not. Look at Jesus Christ. You only need to say, "Have mercy on me." Then, with the eyes of faith that I have tried to tell you about, see an unseen hand wipe out all your sins and misdemeanors. You will realize you are in paradise because he who is merciful dwells in you. Where he is, there is paradise. It is as simple as that.

After confession of sin, guilt should be totally alien to the Christian who has faith. Faith permits us to know the mercy of God. It enables us to read and absorb what God said in torment while he was dying: "Today you will be with me in paradise."

I had a patient in a hospital, and this patient told me that he didn't believe in God at all.

As his sickness progressed he got worse and worse. So he took my hand in his and said, "Nurse, do you believe in God? Do you believe that he is present?" I said, "Yes, I do." He said, "Well, all my life I said he wasn't present. I didn't believe in him. What do you think he will do to me?" I said, "He will embrace you. God understands all things."

Faith assures us that when we come close to God with sorrow in our heart, his consuming fire cleanses everything in us. His arms reach out and take us in and rock us back and forth. We rest against his breast and are lulled by the heartbeats of God.

The Mystery of "Uselessness"

Whoever remains in me,
with me in him,
bears fruit in plenty.

Jn 15: 5

Sometimes, due to sickness or an accident, we find ourselves unable to participate in the normal activities of every day. Then we are greatly tempted to say things like: "Oh, I'm not doing anything! I've been sick for two weeks, a burden on my family, on my community; a burden, period." You can be sure the devil is nearby, rubbing his hands together and saying, "Here I come!" We leave ourselves wide open to him when we do not understand the usefulness of uselessness.

Look at a crucifix. On it is a man, a person like you and me—flesh, muscles, blood—crucified. The nails penetrated his hands and his feet. He was stretched out. People look at this and wonder how useful was he hanging there for three hours? Why didn't he walk around and do a few miracles? That would have been a lot more useful.

This kind of thinking doesn't go with faith. We fail to grasp that by his three hours of suffering the Son of God redeemed the whole world.

Faith convinces us that when we are useless, we are most useful to God. There is such a depth to our usefulness that it shakes me to think about it.

When I was nursing I always told people about it. I said, "Look, here you are, lying immobile with your leg in traction. You're a Christian. You went to Communion. Offer it up. Let this pain go to the world. Take it in your hands like your hands were a chalice. Lift it up. Then you become a most powerful person."

We had a staff worker here who died from cancer. She offered her life for priests and for our apostolate. That was some years ago, and I still get letters from priests who heard about her or who met her for a fleeting instant. It was during the years following Vatican II and many priests were leaving. In the midst of all this uncertainty and confusion and pain, this ordinary woman was lying in bed doing absolutely nothing except telling God she offered him her suffering for priests. A priest wrote, "I had heard about the woman offering herself for priests and she entered into my heart. I stayed in my Order."

Now she didn't meet him, he never came here, so what happened? God happened. God picked up those sufferings and used them. The usefulness of uselessness.

Be on the watch for doubts about this kind of thing. They're natural, they're human, but they're not of faith. Gather up the doubts, the temptations. Make a nice little bundle of them and at night put them at the feet of Our Lady. She will dispose of them as only a mother can. Then you will arise with fewer doubts, and you won't leave yourself open to the promptings of the devil.

Face to Face

Whoever comes to me,
I shall not turn away.

Jn 6: 37

God passionately desires to give us faith. He wants us to ask for it, for only he can give it to us—that is, of course, after his original gift to us in Baptism. He wants us to ask for faith again and again, ask for an increase of it, for a constant increase of it.

When we ask for faith it seems we are, as it were, turning our face toward his face. It seems that God desires this very simple action to happen so that he and we are face-to-face! He wants to look at our face; he loves to see our face facing him. Yet so often we avoid this simple act. Even while we beg him for various favors, we somehow close not only our physical eyes but the eyes of our soul, strangely avoiding looking at him. But we need to remember that he always looks at us, looks at us with deep love.

Faith is that God-given gift that has healed so many who believed in God: the leper, the blind man, the woman with the issue of blood, the servant of the Roman soldier—and millions of others who are not mentioned in the Bible or outside of it.

Faith—the father of love and of hope, as well as of trust and confidence. Faith—that sees God's face in every human face. As it grows and as we pray and beseech God for it, faith identifies us with Christ. Faith heals by asking God to heal. Faith heals others because of the faith I have in the Lord.

Faith walks simply, "childlikely", between the darkness of human life and the hope, the knowledge through faith, of what is to come. "For eye has not seen, nor ear heard what God reserves for those who love him" (cf. 1 Cor 2:9).

Faith—an incredible, fantastic reality, untouchable, unweighable. Faith—contact between God and man. In faith the eyes of God meet the eyes of man, until there is such a little veil between us and the reality that is God, it seems we can almost touch Him.

Faith breaks barriers. Faith makes out of love a bonfire. Faith is contagious when shown by any one of us to the other.

We certainly must pray for faith, especially to preach the Gospel with our lives. Without faith we cannot do it. We must enter into trust and confidence with quiet steps but without hesitation, without cerebration. Truly, here is the moment of the heart, not of the head. The head will rationalize. The head will turn its face away from faith, from love, from hope. The head will put its hand behind its back, so as not to touch the martyr, the prostitute, the publican.

If we have faith in God, we have faith in men. Even the most evil one of us has some redeeming feature, and faith will seek it out. Faith is fundamentally a type of folly, a folly that belongs to God himself.

It is so important to have faith in each other; for it is only through faith that we can communicate. Without faith there is no communication, and there is no love. Without faith, our love will be ill, thin, and tired, and our communication will be just as miserable. Faith alone will restore it.

God's Will—True Life

What we ask God is that
through perfect wisdom
and spiritual understanding
you should reach
the fullest knowledge of his will.
So you will be able to lead the kind of life
which the Lord expects of you.

Col 1:9-10

How do we know the will of God? Well, the first thing is to get your own will out of the way. That means you have to pray and you have to have faith.

To enter the total darkness of faith is something that very few people want to do these days. They want to manage themselves. "I can lead my own life. Nobody is going to tell me what to do." That's what the average person feels like. They are in charge of their life. They decide it all.

A very small group says, "Lord, I have received my life from you. You died so that I might live. I throw my life at your feet and sing. It's such a small thing. Now it's yours to do with as you wish."

Many people have looked me straight in the eye and said, "I have not wanted to look at God's will because I was afraid of it." They are afraid that God is going to ask them to do something that they do not wish to do. Well, at that stage, there is no faith.

Faith presumes belief in a person. The person of Jesus Christ who is Love incarnate. The one who came to do the will of his Father. The one who gave up his life for you and me.

You see, you will find the will of God when you stop thinking about your own will. Just "close the wings of your intellect" and enter the darkness of faith.

It's as if you're walking through an absolutely dark night in an unknown country. Your feet are bare and you step very carefully along the path. Your toes are grasping every inch of ground so as not to fall through a crevice. Your hands are outstretched to feel the way. You can't see anything. That's like faith. God has laid out a path for us but he wants us to follow it in darkness. There is fear in entering darkness, but not in the darkness of faith. At the end of the journey there is the Lord waiting for you.

Sometimes this path has fantastic difficulties along it. A man wrote me a letter after he had visited here at Madonna House and said, "Catherine, you lied to me. You told me that God was love and this sort of thing and I arrive home and my mother is dying from cancer. Things are terrible. You're a liar."

Well, I'm not a liar. He hasn't understood what suffering means. Faith, like love, walks hand in hand with suffering. Even though you may be a genius and understand everything, you have to become like a child in order to believe.

We have to throw ourselves at God's feet and say, "Lord, what you are asking is totally impossible!" Then he bends down and picks us up and says, "Child, with me, the impossible takes five minutes more. Come." Now faith, like a lance, goes straight through you. You feel shattered by what you are facing, but you are able to move. You know God will take care of you.

Our Lord died on a cross. You could call it stupidity. I call it the folly of love. He was so in love with you and me that he was willing to die in that fashion with all his intellect perceiving what was going to happen. Faith is like that.

To know the will of God is to enter into that kind of faith and say to God, "*Credo,* I believe! Against all odds, I believe!"

When you believe, when you have faith, wisdom enters. Some call it discernment. With this wisdom you begin to understand the will of God. It becomes clear.

Courage to Witness

When the Advocate comes,
whom I shall send to you
from the Father,
the Spirit of truth…
you too will be witnesses.

Jn 15:26-27

This is the age in which we must transmit and lavishly sow faith into a technological society against all odds, especially intellectual ones. Sow faith into a society demanding that everything be measured, weighed, collated and put into cubbyholes.

In the midst of this, we are called to sow the seeds of faith in the souls of men, for in each there is still left a field, a hill, an old garden that demands re-seeding. But man doesn't want to be put into a cubbyhole; he needs the open spaces to live, to be himself. He especially needs the spiritual "open spaces" for which he hungers. These are the spaces where God dwells, for it is for God he hungers.

This is the age of faith to be given, not only to those who have lost faith, but to those who have wrapped it up and buried it somewhere deep within themselves. So deep that perhaps there are moments when they forget that they ever had it, or where they have hidden it.

It is up to us Christians to show by our lives that God is with us. It is for us Christians to be a light to others' feet, and to put those feet on a path where they will find the faith they think they have lost, but which they have simply put aside. This path is a path of prayer, both for them and for us.

For us, so that we will have the courage to recognize this age of faith that is in *diaspora,* to sow that faith by incarnating it in our lives, by living the Gospel, by praying and by becoming pilgrims of it—pilgrims with an eternal lantern in our hands: the lantern and light of Christ.

Temptations Against Faith

You can trust God
not to let you be tried
beyond your strength,
and with any trial he will give you a
way out of it
and the strength to bear it.

1 Cor 10:13

We say that we believe. And yet do we? At the slightest difficulty, we cry to God, and if he doesn't answer our prayer within the next five minutes or ten, or twenty-four hours, we begin to doubt. We need to get our heart in tune with God's heart.

Because, you see, he's a lover, and he wants us to love him back. For this, he incarnated himself, lived as a man for a number of years, and died a martyr on a cross, all for me. And, by so doing, reconciled me with his Father. I believe that this is so.

When I believe, I am like a tree standing by the water, and I shall not be moved. Yet a tree can be hit by lightning. But for a man or a woman of faith, the lightning passes through them and doesn't touch them, because their faith is strong as God is strong. God doesn't abandon people.

You can say to me, "Well, how do I get that kind of a faith?" On your knees. (Maybe not literally on your knees, although kneeling can be a good position!) You ask for it. The God who has given you faith in Baptism, when you died in Christ and resurrected in Christ, is not going to say "no" to your request. If there is one request that he says "yes" to all the time, always, it's a request to grow in faith.

Now and then we all feel tremors begin to shake our faith. Then we must ask God, implore him, beg him, to give us faith, to increase our faith. We can simply say to him, "Look, Lord, I need this faith, because unless I increase in faith I won't increase in love". Now, wouldn't that be disastrous, not to increase in love? And if my faith is wobbly, and I murmur against God, and so forth, what happens to hope? I need faith so as to have hope.

When doubts come, as come they will because we're human; when mistrust comes, because it will, for we're human, why don't we look this whole thing straight in the face? From where do we have those doubts? From where comes this shakiness? Take, for instance, myself. Seventeen times I've said to God, "I've had it, I can't hack it anymore, it's too much". And seventeen times I've gone into a church—which of course was my undoing, and at the same time the right thing to do—because once I entered a church I understood from whence my temptations came: Satan.

A heart that is in love with God radiates light. One doesn't know this oneself, but others do. But one creature really knows, and that's Satan. When he sees a person from whom light radiates, he comes and attacks through every little chink in that person. He is pretty clever and will use weaknesses of all kinds in order to squash the light—because that light brings people to God. So take a look inside of yourself, and ask yourself, "Is Satan tempting me?"

When pain comes, we cannot help complaining sometimes. Remember that Christ came, and he did something to pain: he made it holy. What is most extraordinary, he made it joyful. That is the whole difference.

Now it all changes and the light grows greater. The devil comes, but he has no chink to enter, because we have understood—by the grace of God and through prayer, in our asking for growth of faith—that temptations are permitted by God; we understand that we should refuse them. Then each one of them becomes a stepping-stone up the mountain of the Lord.

Part III

What matters is faith
that makes its power
felt through love.

Gal 5:6b

The "door of faith" (Acts 14:27) is always open for us, ushering us into the life of communion with God. To enter through that door is to set out on a journey that lasts a lifetime. It begins with baptism (cf. Rom 6:4) and it ends with the passage through death to eternal life.

Pope Benedict XVI: *Porta Fidei*, Para.1

Faith and Self-acceptance

I have not come to condemn the world,
but to save the world.

Jn 12: 47b

You are—in your person—an instruction, a catechism, an icon, a light to your neighbor. And in order to be all these things you have to love yourself. Love yourself, because you are called to witness the Good News, witnessing not so much through speech but through *being yourself.*

Initially it is very difficult to love ourselves. For what exactly does it mean to love oneself? The moment we ask this question we enter into the realm of faith. For without faith, we cannot love ourselves or anyone else.

This faith was given to us by baptism; and throughout our life we must grow in it. And we grow in it by praying to the Most Holy Trinity, beseeching them to give us an increase in faith. God is our Father, from whom our faith stems. Jesus Christ is our brother who brings us that faith through his life, death, and resurrection. And the Spirit is given to us by the Father just for that—to help us grow constantly in faith.

There is God and there is myself, and the two mysteries meet—God and man. Now this is what it is all about, this loving of oneself.

The wind blows where it will, says Jesus, and nobody knows where it comes from. So it is with the soul or heart. If we love, the Wind, the Holy Spirit, will take us wherever he goes, and the one who holds such a fantastic fire will teach us to begin to love ourselves as God wants us to love ourselves. Factually, what we are going to do is to love God in us.

As we begin to love ourselves, we will understand why we are loveable: we will begin to see how beautifully we are created and how lovingly. And as we think of that, we will touch God again. We will love ourselves because we constantly will see God in ourselves. Christ died to make us like God, and all this will come to us ever more clearly if we continue to beseech the most Holy Trinity for growth in faith.

But we don't know ourselves and don't love ourselves, for we don't believe in the mystery of ourselves. And that leads us inevitably to lose part of our faith, all of it.

No matter what happens to our family, what type of lifestyle we might have to change, what dangers beset us, we must begin to love ourselves. Yes, we must work toward this, and this is a tremendous work! It is almost staggering to think that one has to engage in it. Yet, it is a strange thing, for if I begin to love myself, if I begin to turn inward and look at myself—not psychiatrically speaking, not intellectually speaking, but spiritually speaking—if I turn inward and look at myself, at that very same moment I have already turned outward and loved somebody else!

Because I believe in God I believe in me, for God is in me. And once I believe in me and trust God and myself, then I can believe in everybody and trust everybody. The roots of my love for my neighbor, and for the trusting of the untrustworthy, lies in my love for myself and a trust in myself. It is a long road to travel.

Direct your attention to two points: attention to your person and attention to other persons. Unless you give attention to yourself, lovingly, with the deep realization of who you are, who made you, of your mystery and of that mystery contacting the mystery of God, you will not be able to contact and love, in a personalized way, your neighbor.

I repeat, what I am talking about isn't a psychological analysis of who we are, nor is it an attempt to discover our own identity. Far from it. What loving ourselves really means is that we become a little more quiet about our guilt and our shame. Our mind and our heart simply sink to where God is, and we begin to understand gradually how much he loves us. That is who we are. If you ask me who I am, I would answer, "I am a person beloved by God".

But coming back to faith. I am talking about that fantastic faith that means being in love with God, and really seeing God in every person, including oneself. This faith holds you and never lets you go. Faith in which you cry out to God, "Teach me to grow in faith more and more so that I may love you more and more. And so that I may love, more and more, those whom you love."

Show Your Faith

"Do not be afraid to speak out,
nor allow yourself to be silenced:
I am with you."

Acts 18:9

It seems today that young people are in despair. So many have a negative approach to life. Many commit suicide. Why? Because there is a lack of faith.

Somehow, we have allowed those in youth, and middle age and old age, to lose their faith. How does this happen? It happens because we do not practice it ourselves. When you see somebody practice their faith, you come and touch them. You want to be like them. You are interested.

Often those of us who have faith don't show it. We don't want to proclaim loud and clear, "I believe in God."

One day I was sitting on the subway reading a detective story and the lady next to me asked me quite directly, "Do you believe in God?" I said, "Yes, I do, thoroughly." She said, "Do you tell other people that you believe in God?" I said, "Of course I do." "Oh," she said, "so few people do."

People hunger for God as they never hungered before. They hunger for belief in him, but cannot come to this belief if no one shows them how to love God.

Let us examine our conscience very thoroughly because this is not something you write off and say is not important. It is the most important thing in our life. How do we act toward God? Do we really believe in him and take pride in acknowledging him? Or do we hide our belief away?

This is something to really pray about. Can anybody see the light of Christ through our eyes? Through our speech? Through our behavior? Do we wish to remain in darkness, and, by doing so, keep others in darkness, too?

When I pass a Catholic church I make the sign of the cross because I believe that the Blessed Sacrament is there. This lets everyone know I am a Catholic. I do it very often. It is a simple way of proclaiming my faith. In the past, even children knew that they should bless themselves in front of a church. It is something people don't think about doing, but we need to think about it.

Lately I am afraid for us Christians. It is as if we are being called to make a last stand, to proclaim the Good News that God has come on earth, that he was born, that he died, and that he resurrected—that he is our Savior. That proclamation today cannot be done only by words. It must be done is by living it.

These days terrible events are taking place in the world. They are even more terrible when they happen to people who do not believe. We have to show our belief now, because so many people will not believe in God if we don't. We have to show the face of Christ. We must be very definite. Think about the power we have to revive the faith of a soul or to kill it. What a terrible responsibility it is.

Yes, it is by touching someone who lives by the laws of Jesus Christ that men and women gather faith.

Faith in a Child

There is a child born for us,
a son given to us …
and this is the name they give him:
Wonder-Counselor, Mighty God,
Eternal Father, Prince of Peace.

Is 9:5-6

Each year we ought to celebrate the coming of Christ with a gallant faith. It should be a faith that stands up against the whole hellish world that surrounds us today.

I know that Our Lord was born in a hell: the Romans occupied his homeland and there was great injustice. Yet, as I meditated on this, an immense peace came upon me. I want to share this peace with you.

The birth of Christ is like a gentle call. In the midst of this infinite tragedy that is the world today—its pollution, its killings—there is one consoling thing: the cry of a Child. This cry rises higher and higher than any noise of battles, any noise of cities. It rises higher than any noise and turmoil that we carry within ourselves.

It is that kind of cry that brings peace. It seems strange that a little Child can give so much peace. If you meditate on his coming you realize it is because this Child is God himself.

I came to understand a little better what faith is. From this faith in a little Child stems an inner peace that quiets the very essence of our beings whenever we feel rebellious, when we want to ask questions about these paradoxes that fill the Gospel and our lives. Very slowly, the cry of a Child begins to be the cooing of a Child. Hope is born in a manger. Above all, love, the immense fruit of faith, covers the earth.

A Living Faith

"Faith without works is dead."

cf. James 2:17

We remember what the scriptures say. Well, if faith is dead without works, then naturally we want to practice the works of mercy for our salvation. But unless there be a tremendous love, an immense delicacy, a tact beyond computing, and the ingenuity of love that turns its imagination to delicate ways of serving those in need, we will not make great dents in helping them. Love is austere. It is a two-edged sword and it can cut fine.

We run a soup kitchen. Our friend Murphy, for example, is a ne'er-do-well. He is a lousey, dirty, stinking hobo knocking at the door of Marian Center. There is nothing attractive about Murphy. In fact, everything repels you. You feel like vomiting from his stench, you detest his dirt because you are fastidious, he is a hopeless drug addict. And he is drinking himself to death. He is that kind of character. And he comes to eat! Now, why should you receive Murphy? Where does love enter into Murphy? From the will, from reason! A reason illuminated by faith that reminds us of the teaching of my Lord whom I serve, "You must love the Lord your God ... and your neighbor as yourself." (Lk 10:27-28)

Who is my neighbor? Do you remember the parable of the Samaritan? Somebody down and out, somebody up and high—all are my neighbors. And the Stranger with an Aramaic accent comes across the centuries and says, "What does it matter that you love your friends? So do the pagans. You who belong to me must love your enemies!" Then comes: "I was hungry... I was thirsty... and you never gave me anything". (cf Mt 25:31-46) Like a flash, as I behold Murphy shaking fleas and lice at my doorstep and stinking, all this passes through my head. And the gift of faith begins to act: I do believe that this man, Murphy, is Christ, and that I must love him as myself for the sake of my love of God.

My faith is at work and I act on that knowledge. I now look at Murphy with different eyes. Unless I help Murphy, I shall not fulfill the commandment to love my neighbor. These considerations are not emotional; they are intellectual and they are of faith and of grace. Love is something that comes to us from faith.

Understanding that my faith and my salvation are bound up in this character at my doorstep; seeing a rich, selfish person and yet loving him; spending yourself on a family who needs you—that is love. There is absolutely no 'liking', no emotional feelings, no success, no nothing. You do it because you love God.

Now, saints went to great degrees to make love just that—of the will directed by reason and illuminated by faith. These irrational things that come and go, such as liking or disliking are emotions. Examine yourself how through the day you live on likes and dislikes. "I don't like how he talks to me." "I don't like how he looks at me." "I don't like what she said." I, I, I, like, like, like—how can the light of love grow in all this? Unless there is a tremendous love, it is not enough. We need to implement the faith sixty seconds of every minute, sixty minutes of every hour, 24 hours a day, 365 days a year and throughout our life.

Part IV

Let us not lose sight of Jesus,
Who leads us in our faith
And brings it to perfection

Heb 12:2

In Christ, all the anguish and all the longing of the human heart finds fulfillment. The joy of love, the answer to the drama of suffering and pain, the power of forgiveness in the face of an offense received, and the victory of life over the emptiness of death: all this finds fulfillment in the mystery of His Incarnation, in His becoming man, in His sharing our human weakness so as to transform it by the power of His resurrection.

Pope Benedict XVI: *Porta Fidei,* Para. 13

A Loving Hand in Trials

Through your faith,
God's power will guard you …
even though you may for a short time
be plagued by all sorts of trials.

1Peter 1:5-6

One of the most hopeful books in the Bible is Job. His story is very simple. You remember how Satan said to God, "Look at that guy. He has everything: children, servants, flocks, good health. He has never really been tempted by miseries." So God said, "Go ahead and tempt him. I believe that he will trust in me and love me." Satan begins to tempt Job to make him give up on God. The worst things happen: all his herds and flocks are destroyed, and his children and servants have all died. Then Job himself is covered with horrible sores and ends up in the ash pit, so ugly and smelly that no one can bear to be near him. Job was absolutely down and out. And he told God how he really felt about it all. Still, he had one thing: faith! Under all kinds of difficulties he continued to believe. Now that is the yardstick of Christianity.

To believe when everything is fine, to trust when all goes well, is normal. However, to see in trials a loving hand, to believe in that fantastic mystery who is God—that takes faith. It is a strange thing, my friends. Faith shines in darkness. It comes forth under trial. It sings its song under pain.

Take my own life. I went through World War I and the revolution in Russia, and came to Canada with my husband, Boris, who was still experiencing the effects of being shell-shocked and gassed. Then our son was born. All I lived by was faith. There was nothing else to live by. I was making $7 a week. You don't go very far with a baby on $7 a week. Yet faith, like an immense tree with roots sunk deep into the underground waters of the earth, kept growing and growing within me. I could rest under the shadow of its branches. No matter how I was pushed around, I could rest. That is faith, and I'm not exactly a person who has enough faith. I should have more.

Faith walks simply, like a child, between the darkness of human life and the hope of what is to come. Faith is fundamentally a kind of folly, I guess, the folly that belongs to God himself.

There is joy in suffering when you understand and believe why you are suffering. To us Christians it is simple. For example, a woman in her thirties was diagnosed with cancer of the lungs. When the doctor told her the diagnosis, her face lit up like the sun and she said, "Thanks be to God. I now can offer something for my family, the world, and for everybody." She offered up her suffering, and the joy in her was something you could touch. Yet the pain was there, too.

Sometimes we cannot help complaining. However, anytime we are in physical or emotional pain and we accept it for the love of Christ and our brethren, something happens that is very mysterious. It is so deep, so high, so wide that nobody can measure it. Into that pain enters a power—the power of the Trinity. We are filled with the Father who gave his Son to pain, the Son who took pain upon himself to reconcile us with his Father, and the Holy Spirit who keeps hovering over us to remind us about the Son and the Father.

Look at the revolutions that have passed before our eyes and what people have had to suffer. Many had a fantastic faith and offered themselves for others. During World War II, Father Maximilian Kolbe told the Germans who were about to kill a man, "I will take his place if you let me. He has a family and I am a priest." So they killed him, and the other man survived. Years later, at the canonization of Father Kolbe, who was there in the first row? The man he had died for. That is faith.

Faith allows us to enter peacefully into the dark night that faces every one of us at one time or another. Faith is at peace and full of light. Faith considers that its precariousness and its finiteness are but the womb in which it abides, moving towards the plenitude and fullness of the eternity which it desires and believes in, and which revelation opens to it.

Faith brings into our lives such freedom, such love, such peace, and such joy that there are no words in any language that can explain it. You have to have it in order to know it. You have to experience it in order to understand it. Faith liberates. It liberates love and hope. If I am free to love and free to hope, what more do I want of life?

Love Your Enemies

"Lord, how often must I forgive?
as often as seven times?
Jesus answered, "Not seven, I tell you,
but seventy-seven times."

Mt 18:21-22

Lately I have been confronted by the misery and tragedy that surrounds us these days. Many innocent people die every day in terrible situations around the world. How much faith must I have to stand before this slaughter of the innocents? We have to look at it and still believe that the God we worship is real. Even more, my faith tells me I must love my enemies.

Why should I love my enemy? Most people believe we should kill our enemy, get rid of him. Why should I love him?

You see, when we come up against this kind of situation we are entering into a fantastic, incredible depth of faith. We are called to make a terrible act of faith in the midst of our modern society. Youth is destroying itself with drugs. Cities are in turmoil. The churches are nearly empty. Everything is a mess.

It is out of this mess that a little seed comes forth, somewhere, someplace. A small group here is trying to live the Gospel. Somewhere else others are trying to love one another. The little seed begins to grow. Eventually it will become a big tree: a tree of faith, hope and love, provided we believe. We have to believe. Every day we need to say to God, "I believe, help my unbelief!"

When I first began Friendship House in Harlem in the 1930s, I started hating the whites. I considered it to be a just hate. It shook me: the more I lived with the blacks in their poverty, and saw the discrimination, the more I shook. I lectured all over the U.S. about racial injustice. One priest said, "You went through the States like a sword of justice." After each talk, I felt like I had spent all of myself in the cause of the black people.

At that time, you couldn't imagine people in a worse situation than those who lived in Harlem. Humanly speaking I should have been a heroine, travelling around, being one of the few Catholic voices speaking about interracial justice. However, for the first year I wasn't any voice at all. The Lord was deaf to my voice because I hated the whites.

Then one day I began a retreat. I went into the church and prostrated myself as I usually do. Suddenly I saw that everything I had done was wasted because I hated the whites, hated them with a passion. I had not fulfilled what the Russians consider to be one of the great commandments of the Lord: I had not loved my enemy. In my heart, I was not at all ready to lay down my life for any white person. I wept and wept. I wept because I had alienated myself from God. I had not loved at all.

After my retreat I began talking to white people. We began to have dialogues. As time went on, changes started to happen. They happened because I was no longer alienated from God by my hatred. At Friendship House, we loved both the white and the black. It was not a superficial thing that happened overnight. It was a question of faith and of depth. We worked at it and prayed for it.

You have to love your enemy no matter who he is or how you feel. The only way it can be done is through faith.

You see, faith removes from your eyes the veil that was before them. Now you constantly see a figure on a cross who died for his enemies, and hear him say, "Father, forgive them, for they know not what they do" (Jn 23:34).

The Ordinary is Sacred

The life and death of each of us
has its influence on others.

Rom 14:7

I feel very deeply that the Lord is giving us an increased gift of faith because he knows that we need it. Yes, an increased gift of faith. This gift holds so much of God's mystery. It is of this "mystery" that I want to talk to you.

When I say faith, I mean a land of darkness and a land of pain, in a manner of speaking. For it is not easy to walk in darkness wondering about the abysses and crevices and pitfalls that might be wide open at our feet! It is not easy to walk in faith, in total belief in the Trinity: in the love of the Father; in the sustaining, warm and divine love of the Son; and the strange, incredible love of the Holy Spirit who is both Wind and Fire. It is not easy when we see the trembling of the Church, which at times seems to be poised over earthquakes. But this is the only way that is open to us. God will give us that faith, and we have to continue to pray for it so that, full of hope, we might love.

So many of us desire to console the world, to ease its pain, to do something to help it. I suggest humbly and simply, let us begin by paying attention to "our own". There are so many lonely people amongst us. Let us drop the barriers of fear, rejection, and so forth, and let us cross the divide and offer ourselves to others in our own family. There are so many lonely ones in our midst—let us go toward them, let us reduce their loneliness with the warmth of our faith, our hope, and our love. Only then can we console the rest of the world.

Our daily work—ordinary, exciting or unexciting, monotonous or un-monotonous, routine or non-routine—is, in itself, part and parcel of that faith that I talk about, that hope, that love. This workaday world of ours is the outer shell of a deep inner grace that God gives us. It is because we believe, we hope, and we love that we can do the things we can do.

Most of us still evaluate life by results, or by what we think has been achieved. Achieved in what you might call the social justice or the spiritual realm—the things that newspapers and magazines, both Christian and non-Christian, talk about. We think the routine of everyday isn't enough; we need other "important" things added.

Stop here. Please stop. Fall on your knees, pray, and listen. The darkness of faith, the walking slowly—only because we believe in the Trinity, because we hope and because we love—that, my friends, is the essence of Christianity. That is the heart of the Church; the rest flows from it. But this is to come first.

Strange as it may seem, it is the fruit of that faith and hope and love that the Lord bends over and picks up, picks up and changes the world, and allows his Church to expand because one, two, three or more people believe, hope and love.

I know the sacredness and "sacrament" of the ordinary day. I use the word "sacrament" because each day is a sacrament. Each day is a mystery. We are walking in a fantastic mystery. Don't try to figure it out. Just open your heart so that the mystery of God will meet the mystery of you. And somewhere, the two mysteries will blend. When you allow that to happen, you have peace, a fantastic peace that no one can take away from you.

The Keys of Faith

"The mysteries of the kingdom of heaven are revealed to you."

Matt 13:11

Deep in the heart of faith—which is a gift from the heart of God—lies this fantastic understanding of who we are. This awareness is transmitted to us through the sacraments that God has given us. The sacraments sing of this faith. Each sacrament calls us to love, each sacrament calls us to hope, and each sacrament calls us to serve. These are the keys faith gives us. The keys of the sacraments.

Let's reflect on the sacrament of Baptism. Look at people who have just been baptized. Can you see the glory within them? All their sins are forgiven. They enter into the death of Christ when they enter into the strange, dark, holy waters that he himself once entered. These waters could be a sea, they could be little lapping waves on the sand, they could be any kind of water. All waters became holy after he entered them.

God the Father baptizes us and his Son is next to us, bringing to mind his own baptism. The crimson dove, the Holy Spirit, hovers over us. We enter the holy of holies, the holy Catholic Church. That is, factually, the beginning and the end of faith. A baptized newborn who dies minutes later is like a star shining in the heavens of the Lord, and goes directly into his heart.

I bow low before the sacrament of the most holy Eucharist. Faith will give you the key to this sacrament, too. Try to understand it, try to understand what is not understandable. A piece of bread, a cup of wine, the ordinary things of human life for generations upon generations. That is what people ate and drank around the world. Then Our Lord took a piece of bread in his hands. He broke it and he said, "Take this, all of you, and eat it. This is my body which will be given up for you." And he raised the cup. "Take this, all of you, and drink from it. This is the cup of my blood, the blood of the new and everlasting covenant. It will poured out for many so that sins may be forgiven. Do this is memory of me" (cf. Mt 26:26-28).

Do you realize that because you believe and I believe we can move toward an altar to receive the Eucharist? It makes no difference what kind of an altar it is. It might be a stone, it might be the bed of a Nazi prisoner. It makes no difference. A man who is a priest takes a piece of bread, takes a little bit of wine, and lo and behold, faith sings a song that you can hear. You eat and drink and you have enough courage now for the next twenty-four hours to face anything and to stand firm against all that is not true or right or good.

Man sins. And Christ came to restore sinners. He became the one who took upon his shoulders all our sins, from the beginning of time to the end of the world. We are the beloved, his beloved, the ones he rescued from sin. Being the weak vessels that we are, we fall along the narrow road. Temptations, like boulders, are strewn along the path. So we come back to Christ again. We say to him, "Lord, kiss our sins away." And that is what the sacrament of Penance, confession is—the kiss of Christ. Now we are able to hear the Lord say, "Your faith has made you whole" (Lk 8:48).

Faith grows in you and me. The Church helps us along the road by giving us the beautiful sacrament of Confirmation. What does it confirm? It confirms the gift of God, confirms our faith. It makes our faith strong and immovable. Yes, it is a confirmation of depths unplumbed and mysteries unknown and yet familiar to us all. Now, hope, love, and all the seven gifts of the Holy Spirit follow.

There are other sacraments that lie in your hands: Matrimony, Holy Orders, Anointing of the Sick. As you look at your hands with the keys to the sacraments, they all suddenly change. You can hear the voice of God speaking to your heart. When he is there, love is there. When he is there, faith is there.

Now it is up to us to grow in our love and belief in him. Through our Baptism and all the sacraments, we will grow into an immense tree of faith so that people who are tired and heavy of heart will have a place to come and rest under.

Jesus Is Here

Make your home in me,
as I make mine in you.

Jn 15: 4a

I knew a little boy, Jimmy, who died at the age of fourteen. I saw him just two weeks before his death. I think of his simplicity. He said to his parents, "Oh, I have to go see my Father. My real Father who begot me. God the Father." Then, before he died he said, "Jesus is here! Jesus is here!"

That is the kind of faith we need to have: faith that is deep, profound, unsinkable, unbreakable. It is a faith that surmounts everything. It is a faith that really loves everything and everybody. Think about it.

Many nights when I'm alone I say a little prayer or two and I ask God that we would all have that faith, that simplicity of faith, that directness, just like little Jimmy. "Jesus is here. Jesus is here." That is exactly what happens. Close your eyes for a second, open them and Jesus *is* here. Jesus is in each one of you. Jesus has come in a big way. What joy that is. Yes, close your eyes, open them and say, "Jesus is here."

Fiat — Yes

The angel said to her,
"You are to conceive and bear a son,
and you must name him Jesus." …
Mary said to the angel,
"But how can this come about,
since I am a virgin?"
…"Nothing is impossible to God."

Lk 1:30-37

Our faith—how deep, how wide is it? I think that our f-a-t-e depends on our f-a-i-t-h, because there is so little drive to practice faith. Faith may sometimes be all we have. But that means we have God. And all things are possible to God.

I keep going back to Our Lady. When the angel told Mary about her becoming the Mother of God, she said, "yes". Her *fiat* is a booming "yes," so big that we still talk about it. It carried God's reverberations. What struck me is her complete natural and supernatural acceptance of God's will. She realized fully well, in the Jewish context of that era, what it meant to be pregnant when you weren't married. What faith did it take to do that?

My attitude to Our Lady is one of awe and love. And—because she's a human being like you and I, she wasn't God—I say to myself "What faith!" Have I got that kind of faith? I think I have faith, but then I look at her and say to myself, why don't I pray for more faith? Lord, I believe, help my unbelief.

People are beginning to go back to Our Lady. The essence is faith: that strange, incredible, unbelievable faith of a young girl. Faith that gave us God, God in the shape of man. Because all she would have had to say was "no".

Do I say *fiat*, "yes", to God? Think more on Mary.

When he was preaching in the Temple at 12 years of age, and Jesus said: "Don't you know? I am about my Father's business." She didn't understand that, but she said *fiat*.

After a while, her Son left her and became a preacher. Here he was going around barefooted, preaching what appeared to be a revolutionary doctrine. She said *fiat* to it all. When things happen to us that we do not quite understand, how many times do we say "Fiat"?

When she came to see him, in front of everybody he said, "Who is my Mother? ...Anyone who does the will of my Father in heaven, he is my brother and sister and mother." (Mt 12:48-50) Now, we who tremble when anybody rejects us, who seek the approval of our peers, we who are conformist to the last degree—how would we take this rejection from our son? With great faith? She did; she simply departed. Once more, she said yes, *fiat*.

Why is it that we are unable to say "Fiat" again and again? We go into our little cell and hide ourselves; we think, "God doesn't ask this of me." We need to remember that God is first, my neighbor is second, and I am third, and that we are called to be servants.

What is it that stops us from being who we are, Christians, followers of Christ? We're shy about our faith. Yet our faith is not something we "keep", it is something that we pass on to others.

We need to turn to Our Lady in humility and say to her, "Look, you are one of us. Teach us the heights to which we can rise. We can't bear Christ, but we can be "pregnant" with love of every human being, with a never-ceasing pregnancy, giving life to other people. Mother, teach us how to do it. Teach us how to love. Teach us how to hope. Teach us how to say yes to the impossible in faith."

A woman wrapped in silence, who lives in the Holy Spirit, in God the Father and God the Son. If you really don't know what to do or where to go, turn to her and she will tell you. In her awesome silence, she will solve your problem. She will, with a mother's love, a sister's love, show you the way, because she has walked it all her life—the way of her Son.

Like Mary, we should say "yes" to anything and everything that God gives us, even if it is painful. Such a small little word—*yes*—but when you say it, you become free.

Martyrdom and Death

Anyone who loses his life for my sake,
and for the sake of the Gospel,
will save it."

Mk 8:35

Do you realize that faith must be strong, stronger than death, strong as love? It stands immovable, battered by the winds of empires falling and empires rising, battered by the end of times and times to come. It makes no difference. Faith is there—strange, direct, lifting its eyes to God, unafraid.

You say that it's hard. I say, was the cross of Christ easy? Was it not made of green wood? Was the crucifixion easy? No, nothing of this was easy. Faith is possible only through love. Those who pass through pain in faith receive from God the keys of his kingdom: peace, joy, and love.

A group of Lithuanians were incarcerated in one of the gulags, the concentration camps in the Soviet Union, where many people died. One of the most beautiful things about those few Lithuanians was the rosary they made out of bread. Did you know that you can make bread into beads? Another one of the prisoners had a little Gospel. So in the night they were able to pray and recite the rosary. The faith of these people was unshakable. Then one day the guards came, took them away and shot them. Later someone found the rosary and the little Gospel and sent them to the Holy Father. They are some of his most treasured possessions.

Men cannot resist faith even when they deny it and laugh at it and jeer at it, and even kill the one who has faith. Killing those who believe is simply multiplying belief, for the blood of martyrs is the seed of faith.

Today the death of martyrs continues. Around the world women and children, young and old, are the innocent victims of bombs and bullets. In many countries priests, nuns, and lay people are still laying down their lives. They do not complain. Each one goes to their death as peacefully as a child dying in the arms of its mother. For when death is face to face with you and looks into your eyes, you reach the moment of triumph. It is probably a small moment. But it is certainly a joyous moment.

Have you ever stopped to think about death? What is it, exactly? It's a door, that's all! It is the door between this life and the next. It opens and closes, opens and closes. What does it open onto? It opens onto life, because death has been conquered long ago. This poor little moment which we call death is the door that lets us enter into life. It's nothing to be afraid of. It lets us go into the real life that we are expecting all through our earthly life. That's faith.

Other Books by Catherine Doherty

Available through Madonna House Publications

Apostolic Farming
Beginning Again
Bogoroditza: She Who Gave Birth to God
Dear Father
Dear Seminarian
Dearly Beloved: *Letters to the Children of My Spirit (3 Vol.)*
Donkey Bells: Advent and Christmas
Fragments of My Life
God in the Nitty-Gritty Life
Grace in Every Season
In the Footprints of Loneliness
In the Furnace of Doubts
Light in the Darkness
Living the Gospel Without Compromise
Molchanie: The Silence of God
Moments of Grace (perpetual calendar)
My Russian Yesterdays
Not Without Parables: *Stories of Yesterday, Today and Eternity*
On the Cross of Rejection
Our Lady's Unknown Mysteries
People of the Towel and Water, The
Poustinia: *Encountering God in Silence, Solitude and Prayer*
Season of Mercy: Lent and Easter
Sobornost: *Unity of Mind, Heart and Soul*
Soul of My Soul: Coming to the Heart of Prayer
Stations of the Cross
Strannik: The Call to the Pilgrimage of the Heart
Uródivoi: Holy Fools

Some books available in electronic format at

www.madonnahouse.org/publications